Praise for Jack Whyte

"Of the scores of novels based on Arthurian legend, Whyte's Camulod series is distinctive, particularly in the rendering of its leading players and the residual Roman influences that survived in Britain during the Dark Ages."
                                                    —*The Washington Post*

"From the building blocks of history and the mortar of reality, he's built Arthur's world and showed us the bone beneath the flesh of legend."
                                                    —Diana Gabaldon

"As Whyte waves off the fog of fantasy and legend surrounding the Arthurian story, he renders characters and events real and plausible."
                                                    —*Booklist* on *Uther*

"A top-notch Arthurian tale forged to a sharp edge in the fires of historical realism . . . with a nuts-and-bolts, nitty-gritty, dirt-beneath-the-nails version of the rise of Arthurian Camulod, this series is more realistic and believable than nearly any other Arthurian epic."
                       —*Publishers Weekly* (starred review) on *The Singing Sword*

"It's taken 1,500 years to work through, but now we have the Arthurian legend the way the noncoms saw it: tough and gritty and compelling."
                       —Tom Shippey, former professor of English language and
                                    medieval English literature, University of Leeds

Also by Jack Whyte from Tom Doherty Associates

THE CAMULOD CHRONICLES

The Eagle

The Lance Thrower

Uther

The Sorcerer: Metamorphosis

The Fort at River's Bend

The Saxon Shore

The Eagles' Brood

The Singing Sword

The Skystone

The Forest Laird

A TALE OF WILLIAM WALLACE

JACK WHYTE

A TOM DOHERTY ASSOCIATES BOOK

NEW YORK

THE FOREST LAIRD

Copyright © 2010 by Jack Whyte

Originally published in Canada by Viking Canada, an imprint of the Penguin Group.

A Forge Book
Published by Tom Doherty Associates, LLC
175 Fifth Avenue
New York, NY 10010

www.tor-forge.com

Forge® is a registered trademark of Tom Doherty Associates, LLC.

The Library of Congress has cataloged the hardcover edition as follows:

Whyte, Jack.
    The forest laird / Jack Whyte. — 1st U.S. ed.
        p. cm.
    "A Tom Doherty Associates book."
    ISBN 978-0-7653-3156-4
    1. Wallace, William, Sir, d. 1305—Fiction. 2. Scotland—History—Wallace's Rising,
1297–1304—Fiction. I. Title.
PR9199.3.W4589F56 2012
813'.54—dc23

2011024971

ISBN 978-0-7653-3159-5 (trade paperback)

First U.S. Edition: February 2012
First Forge Trade Paperback Edition: November 2012

Printed in the United States of America

0 9 8 7 6 5 4 3 2 1

This book is dedicated, like all the others, to my wife,
Beverley, because I couldn't have found a better or more
suitable companion on this journey...

AUTHOR'S NOTE

The prospect of writing about Sir William Wallace, post-*Braveheart*, was a disconcerting one from the outset because the screenplay reflected, to a very solid extent, what I had been taught about the great man during my childhood and school days. Arguably, there were inaccuracies and omissions in screenwriter Randall Wallace's treatment of his subject, but by and large it was remarkably faithful to the essence of its source, which was the epic poem "The Wallace," written by Blind Hary more than a hundred years after the events with which it dealt. That hundred-odd years' gap poses serious problems for anyone looking to make, let alone prove, assertions about the hero's life. Add to that the fact that we can't even be sure if the poet was blind or if his name really was Hary, and the "iffiness" of making any authoritative declaration about Wallace becomes even more pronounced. All we can say with certainty today is that Sir William Wallace definitely lived, he was one of the most important and influential men of his time, and that his influence is still a potent force in Scotland.

I was born in a town called Johnstone, in Renfrewshire, near the city of Paisley and a few minutes' walk from the Wallace Monument in the neighbouring village of Elderslie—the communities were separated by an imaginary line across the main street. The monument was a common but significant presence in my boyhood, as was an awareness of Wallace himself. Now, after more than four decades living in North America, with everything from historical perspectives to social realities changing radically and rapidly in form and texture from month to month, it seems strange to look back and remember how genuinely and ungrudgingly we revered him as boys. In a time when our fathers and uncles were still returning home from World War II and when the only electronic medium in general use was the vacuum-tube radio, Wallace was a real and almost living presence in our lives.

Embarking on the task of writing a novel about William Wallace, then, especially after *Braveheart*, was a daunting prospect, if for no other reason than running the risk of being accused of cribbing from the movie. In approaching this book and considering what I would need and how I might go about acquiring it, I was forced to accept, very reluctantly, that after forty-odd years of living in Canada, I had forgotten (or at least had difficulty remembering) much of the authenticity of the land in which I had grown up. Once I acknowledged that, however, I had no difficulty at all in accepting the inevitable corollary, which was that I was long overdue for a fact-finding mission to Wallace's Scotland. The question I then had to answer was *Where is Wallace's Scotland, and how does one find it?* I didn't know the answer at the time, but I *thought* I knew, so I planned my itinerary carefully, estimating that I would need five weeks to do everything and see all the places I wanted to see. And that last consideration is where the entire structure of my plan began to fall apart.

The plain truth is that the Scotland Wallace knew no longer exists, except in the loneliest, most inaccessible spots, places where the Guardian himself seldom ventured. Seven hundred years of increasing population, with spreading settlement and agriculture, deforestation, road building, and democratic civilization have transformed the country beyond recognition. There are towns, cities, villages, and hamlets everywhere, all linked by a sophisticated, intricate network of roads. Where there is any semblance of open country remaining, it is dotted with farms and cottages and divided by stone walls and fences. And there is no such thing as silence. No matter where you go in Scotland today, even in the most remote spots such as Glencoe or the Moor of Rannoch, you will hear human presence in the roar of a jet overhead, the whistle of a distant train, or the in the sound of traffic on a nearby road.

Wallace would not recognize his own country. No trace at all remains of the original wooden bridge at Stirling, the site of his major victory over the English. The area known as the Carse of Stirling, along with the treacherous bogs that lined it on both sides and made crossing the River Forth so hazardous for invading armies throughout Scotland's history, has been tamed for hundreds of years, broken to the plough and cultivated into rich farmland, criss-crossed with good roads and sturdy bridges. The enormous forest that once covered almost the entire southeastern and southern quadrants of Scotland, known variously as Ettrick Forest and Selkirk Forest, has vanished almost completely, with only tiny remnants remaining, carefully planted and ordered, nurtured, and meticulously tended under the auspices of the Scottish Forestry Department. Even the few major historic buildings that Wallace would have known are skeletal today—St. Andrews Cathedral and Sweetheart Abbey are beautiful and imposing, often breathtaking in certain light and circumstances, but they are ancient ruins with no vitality, and it is almost impossible for modern people to imagine them full of bustling life.

Places such as Stirling Castle and Edinburgh Castle appear to us to be timeless and unchanging, but the truth is that the fortified and wooden palisaded "castles" shown in *Braveheart* give a far more accurate idea of what they would have been like seven centuries ago because the great, imposing stone edifices we see today had not yet been built when Wallace was alive. Paisley Abbey was there in the early fourteenth century, but even it has changed beyond recognition. Edward of England burned it down in 1306–7, two years after Wallace's death, and left only two arches standing, and when the abbey was rebuilt, those arches were incorporated into a new, very different building. They are still easily visible today, if you know where to look, but the building itself is a relatively modern edifice.

This book, then, is my attempt to accommodate and interpret some of the new ideas that have recently emerged regarding William Wallace, and it incorporates several intriguing ideas and suggestions proposed by people far more qualified to judge them than I am. In one very narrow and particular respect, and with no disrespect in mind, his life can be compared to that of Jesus, in that both emerged from obscurity at a late age—between twenty-seven and thirty—and each had a short, brilliant, meteoric public career that ended in execution. No one really knows what either man did in the years before he stepped into public scrutiny, and this tale speculates what might have been in the case of Scotland's greatest Guardian.

Jack Whyte
Kelowna, British Columbia
July 2010

PROLOGUE

It pains me to hear people say nowadays that William Wallace died defiant, a heroic patriot, with a shout of "Freedom!" on his lips, because it is a lie. William Wallace died slowly and brutally in silence, to my sure knowledge, for I was there in London's Smithfield Square that morning of August 24th in 1305, and all I heard of defiance was the final, demented scream of a broken, tortured man driven beyond endurance long before he died.

I was the last of our race to see him alive and to speak with him, the sole Scot among the crowd that watched his end and the only one there to mark and mourn his passing. I did not really see him die, though, because my eyes were screwed shut against the tears that blinded me. When I was able to breathe again and wiped my eyes to look, they were already quartering his corpse, the chief executioner proclaiming his death and holding aloft the severed head of the Scotch Ogre who had terrified all England.

Sir William Wallace, Guardian of Scotland, my friend, my blood cousin, and my lifelong nemesis, would never terrify another soul.

But, by the living God, he had terrified enough within his lifetime for his name to live on, in Scotland at least, long after his death, a grim reminder of the punishment for disloyalty, treachery, and disobedience.

As I watched the executioners dismember his remains, I accepted the reality of his death as I had accepted its inevitability two weeks earlier, when word reached me that he had been taken by Sir John Menteith and handed over to the justice of the English King. I had known that was coming—not that Menteith would arrest him, but that someone would, and soon, for William Wallace's time had passed and he had fallen from grace in the eyes of the people he had led and inspired just a few years earlier. He had become an embarrassment; a source of discomfort to all of them; a thorny, disapproving, uncompromising reminder of all that they had fought for and then abandoned. For they had come to terms, nobles, clerics, and commoners, with England's Edward Plantagenet, and the English King was being regally lenient, exercising forbearance towards all Scots rebels who would join his Peace, save only the outlawed traitor, Wallace. The price of that forbearance was the surrender of the brigand Wallace to Edward's justice. Every noble, sheriff, and justiciar in the realm of Scotland was charged with the duty of apprehending the former Guardian on sight and dispatching him to London as a common criminal.

I was in England when I heard the news, bearing documents from my superior, Walter the Abbot of Paisley, to the Bishop of York and the Bishop of London. I had stopped to rest at the Priory of Reading, and there found the sole topic of conversation among the brethren to be the recent capture of Wallace. Everyone knew he would be tried summarily and executed out of hand, but the manner of his death was a matter for debate and conjecture among the jaded monks, who seldom had open cause to speculate upon such worldly things. I listened to their prattling, and thought about how different was the man I knew from the monster they were all decrying.

I resolved then and there to see him, somehow, while I was in London. I had powerful friends there among the clergy, and I promised myself that I would use them to find him wherever he was being held and, if it were possible, to visit him and offer whatever small comfort I could in his final, friendless hours among an alien people who loathed and feared him.

In the event, I had no trouble finding where he was imprisoned, for the whole city of London was agog with the news, and with the help of a trusted friend, Father Antony Latreque, Sub-abbot of Westminster, I was admitted to the prisoner's cell on his last night, to hear his last confession.

The tears I would later shed in Smithfield Square, blinding me to his final moments, would have nothing to do with the barbarity that I was witnessing that bright, late-August morning. They would surge instead from a sudden memory of Wallace's own tears earlier, long before dawn and before they came to lead him out to death. The sight of those tears had shaken me, for I had never seen Will Wallace weep since the day our childhood ended, and the anguish in his eyes there in his darkened cell had been as keen and unbearable as the pain he and I had endured together on that long-ago, far-off day.

He did not recognize me when I entered, for it had been four full years since he and I had last seen each other. He saw only a cowled priest accompanying a portly, mitred Abbot. The jailer had seen the same thing, ignoring the priest while he whined to the Abbot about his orders to permit the prisoner no visitors.

"We are not *visitors*," Abbot Antony replied disdainfully. "We are of Holy Mother Church and our presence marks a last attempt to make this felon repent the error of his ways and confess himself before God. Now provide us with some light and open up this door."

The fellow slouched away to bring each of us a freshly lit torch, then unlocked the heavy door, set his shoulder to it, and pushed it open. My first glance showed me a broad, flagstoned floor, dimly lit by one flickering flambeau in an iron sconce on the left wall. I saw no sign of the prisoner, but he spoke before we had crossed the threshold, his words accompanied by a single brief clash of chains.

"I need none of your English mouthings, Priest, so get you gone and take your acolyte with you." He spoke in Latin, and the Abbot turned to me, brows raised in surprise. I merely gestured with a cupped hand, bidding him continue as we had rehearsed. The Latin was no surprise to me, although I had not thought to speak of it to my companion earlier. Wallace and I had learned the tongue together as students at the same Paisley Abbey that was now my home.

Abbot Antony spoke to the prisoner as we had agreed, but now in Latin.

"I have heard of your hatred for all things English, William Wallace, but although I deplore both that and your wilful intransigence, I find myself constrained, through simple Christian charity, to offer you the benefit of God's sacraments in the hope that, in the end, His clemency will absolve you of your many sins."

"Seek your own people, then, Priest, beginning with your King, and absolve them, for their sins are greater than mine have ever been." The voice was flinty with scorn. "Shrive you the slaughterers who slew my family and friends. Pray with the drunken animals who raped me and savaged my people. Mumble a Mass with your grasping earls and barons, who despoiled my home and sought to rip it asunder to sate their own lusts for land and power. But leave me to my God. He knows my sins and what drove me to commit them. I need no English translator to poison my words before they reach God's ears."

They were not the exact words I had expected, but I had estimated precisely the tone and content. Abbot Antony was mortified, and it showed clearly on his face. To hear such venom in a single voice, directed not merely at him but at his entire Church and his people, left the poor man speechless, but not addled. I had warned him that he might hear appalling things when he confronted this prisoner, and so he pulled himself together quickly and returned to the script we had prepared against the risk that others might hear us.

"I had heard," Antony said, "that you were obdurate in your hatred of my kind, but it is my Christian obligation as a man of God to do all in my power to help you towards salvation. And so …" He hesitated. "And so I have taken pains to bring you an intermediary, twixt you and God, to whom you may speak in your own tongue. Father James is of your folk. I will leave him to commune with you and hear your confession."

Now the prisoner turned his eyes towards me for the first time, and though he was merely a shape stirring among blackness, I could tell that he was squinting to see me better.

"What is a Scots priest doing here?"

"His duty," Antony answered, "comforting the afflicted. Will you speak with him? If so, I will leave the two of you alone."

Wallace shrugged, the movement easily visible now that my eyes were adjusting to the darkness. "I'll talk with him, if only to hear my own tongue. Who are you, Priest? Where are you from?"

"Thank you, Father Abbott," I said quietly, and Antony turned away towards the still-open door. I heard him speak to the jailer outside, and then the man hauled at the massive door until it scraped shut, leaving me alone with the prisoner. "Where am I from? I am from Paisley, from the Abbey. Do you not know me, Will?"

The shadowy figure straightened up as though he had been struck. "*Jamie?* Jamie Wallace? What in God's name are you doing here? Your very name could hoist you to the gallows alongside me."

I pushed my cowl back off my head and let him see my smile. "Plain Father James? I doubt that, Will. The Wallace part of me is unknown here in England."

"Then pray you to God it stays that way. This is madness, Jamie. But, man, it's good to see your face."

"And to see yours, Cousin, though God Himself knows I had never thought to see you in such straits." I stepped forward to embrace him, but as the light from my torch fell upon him I stopped short. "What kind of barbarism is this?"

He grinned at me and drew himself up to his full, imposing height. "D'ye no' ken," he said in our own tongue, "I'm a dangerous chiel? They ca' me the Scotch Ogre and they a' believe I eat bairns whene'er I get the chance."

His hair and beard were matted and unshorn, and he wore only a ragged shirt, one arm of which had been torn from his shoulder, exposing the massive knots of corded muscle there, but I paid little attention to those things. I was staring at the harness that bound him.

"Can you sit?"

His grin widened, but there was no humour in his eyes. "Sit? Sit on what? It takes me a' my time to stand wi'out cowpin' sideways. I ha'e to stand spread-legged and lean my back against the wa', else I'll fa', and these chains winna even let me dae that."

The chains that bound him, wrists and ankles, were thick and heavy, the manacles tautly fastened to a thick leather belt that circled his waist. The girdle was fastened right and left to short lengths of chain that were secured to a heavy iron ring mounted on the wall at his back. He could not fall, nor could he turn. All he could do was stand upright or allow his weight to sag into the harness around his waist, but there would be no comfort there, either, for now I saw that the chains from the belt were of different lengths, ensuring that he could only hang tilted to one side.

"How long have you been held like that?"

"Three days." He spoke still in Scots. "Ye'll pardon the stink, I hope, for they havena let me loose since they strapped me in here." He was unbelievably filthy, and at his mention of it the appalling stench of him hit me like a blow. I lowered my torch, looking down at his befouled legs beneath the tattered shirt he wore. They were crusted with feces, and the ground at his feet was a stinking puddle.

"Sweet Jesus," I said, my senses reeling. "Who is responsible for this? This is …" I stopped, unable to find words.

"This is Edward's vengeance, or the start o' it, for a' the grief I've caused him these past years. Tomorrow—no, today, he'll make an end o' it. But ere he's done, I think I'll be yearnin' for the comfort o' just standin' here, danglin' frae my chains. D'ye ken, he wouldna even come to look at me, Jamie? Ye'd think he'd want to look at least, would ye no'? To gloat a wee bit, wag a finger at me. But no. He left it a' to his judges …"

I opened my mouth to speak but nothing came out.

"It'll be a fine day, the jailers tell me. A grand summer's day to die on. But this London's a dirty, smelly place, Jamie, a sad and dirty place to die. I'd gi'e anything to hear the birds singin' to welcome the dawn in the Tor Wood one last time." He snorted. "But I *hae* nothin' now to gi'e, and we're a long way frae Ettrick Forest."

And at that moment, a miracle occurred.

Somewhere beyond the high, barred window above our heads, a bird began to sing, and the clarity and volume of the sound stunned both of us into silence. The song was liquid, brilliant in its welling beauty, the notes rising and falling with limpid perfection so that it seemed the creature producing them was here in the cell with us instead of outside in the pitch-blackness of the night. I watched Wallace's eyes widen and fill with a kind of superstitious fear.

"Mother of God," he whispered. "What kind o' sorcery is this? It lacks three full hours till dawn. What kind of creature makes such a sound in the blackness of the night?"

"It's only a bird, Will, nothing more. They call it a nightingale, because it sings at night. I think there are none in all Scotland, though I may be wrong. I've certainly never heard one there, and it's not the sort of thing you could easily forget. Is it not wonderful?"

He listened, and I could see the tension drain from him. Eventually he allowed his weight to settle slightly into his restraints. "Aye," he murmured. "It is that, a thing o' wonder."

I have no idea how long we stood there listening to it before the silence of the night returned.

"He's gone. Will he come back, think ye?"

"Your guess would be as good as mine. But he answered your wish. That was like a miracle."

"Aye …" He stood gazing into nothingness. "D'ye remember that day in Dalfinnon Woods, Jamie, before they caught us? Remember we hid from them, amang the brambles on our hands and knees? It was so quiet and we listened so hard for the sounds o' them comin' and then the only thing we could hear was a lintie singin' in a tree above our heids? God, yon bird could sing. Like a lintie, they say—he could sing like a lintie. But unless you kent what a lintie sounded like, you'd never be able to tell if that was true or no'. It was wee Jenny who tell't me that day that the bird was a lintie, for I didna ken. How was I to know? Poor wee Jenny …" He squeezed his eyes shut and flicked his head.

"Seven, she was, and yon big English whoreson killed her wi' a flick o' his wrist. Didna even look at what he'd done, didna even turn his heid to see. Just cut her wee, thin neck the way ye would a stoat. Jesus, Jamie, I saw that in my dreams for years, her head rollin' and bouncin' like a bairn's ba' kicked into the bushes, its mouth open and its eyes wide, as if she was wonderin' what had happened. What they did to you and me afterwards was cause enough to hate them a' and want to see them deid, but poor wee Jenny …"

He straightened up again, leaning his shoulders back against the wall, and reverted to Latin. "His name was Percy, did you know that? The man who killed Jenny? William Percy. Some base-born relative of the English Earl. I met him again, years later, after Stirling Bridge, when I recognized him among the prisoners. He didn't know me, but I had carried his face in my mind ever since that day. I hanged him by the heels and reminded him what he had done to us, and to my little sister. He denied everything, but he could not deny the scar that had marked his face that day and marked it still. I spilt his guts with my dirk and let them hang down over his face, and when he stopped screaming I cut off his head. Not as cleanly as he had cut off Jenny's, though, for it took me three blows, because of the way he was hanging."

I closed my eyes, trying to shut out the image he had conjured.

"England has had ample cause to rue that day's work in Dalfinnon Woods. And this new day will bring an end o' it, when they hang me up and draw my guts the way I cut out his.

"Some people—Archbishop Lamberton was one—have asked me why I hate the Englishry so much, but I have had so many reasons that I've never been able to answer any of them. Christ knows we Scots have never had far to look for reasons to despise these people's cruelty and arrogance, but that day in Dalfinnon Woods has much to do with all of it. Bad enough that they had already killed my mother and father that morning. But what they did to us in that wood, that earned them my true hatred—as strong today as it was then.

"But you forgave them, Jamie, where I never could and never wanted to." He shook his head in perplexity. "How could you do that, after what they did to you that day? You forgave them, and I never doubted your sincerity. But I never understood it either. We grew closer after that, we two, but then our ways parted. You took up the Cross and I took up the bow. And yet we remained friends, even while you disapproved of me and everything I did."

I held up my hand to stop him. "I seldom disapproved of what you stood for, Will, or what you wanted to achieve. It was the how of it, not the why, that caused me pain. I lauded your objectives, but I deplored the savagery in your achieving them."

"Savagery … Aye. But only a fool would turn the other cheek to enemies whom he knew would kill him dead for doing so. Or think you that the English are not savages?"

"What we saw in Dalfinnon Woods was depravity, Will, committed by a gang of drunken men. They might as easily have been Scots, but for the grace of God."

"They were English, Jamie."

"Aye, and they were drunk. No man improves with drink. But to hold their crimes, bad as they were, against all England and all Englishmen makes no kind of sense to me."

"Well, it's too late now to argue over it."

"Tell me about Cressingham."

"Cressingham?" My question plainly surprised him, for he cocked his head to one side and thought for a moment. "Cressingham was an idiot—a strutting, sneering fool. The most hated Englishman in Scotland."

"Aye, but he was also your prisoner, after Stirling Fight. Did you really skin him alive to have a sword belt made for yourself?"

He flinched. "No, as God is my judge! That is the talk of jealous enemies. I was nowhere near the place when he was killed."

"But he was killed. And flayed alive before that."

"Aye, he was. It's one of the reasons they're going to hang me as a felon. Retribution, they say. But I was not there, and I knew nothing of it until the murder was done. I had too much on my mind that day, after the battle and with Andrew Murray sorely wounded, to pay attention to what my malcontents were up to. But the responsibility was mine, as leader. That lies beyond argument and I accept it."

I turned away, thinking to lecture him about appearances and guilt by association, but when I swung back to face him I found his eyes awash with tears, and the sight turned my self-righteous words to ashes in my mouth. William Wallace had never been known to weep over anything. That was part of his legend among the wild, ungovernable men he had led for so long. But he was weeping now, unashamedly, the tears running down his cheeks and into the thicket of his matted beard.

"What is it, Will? What's wrong?" Silly, futile questions, I knew.

He raised up his head and looked directly at me. "Was I wrong, Jamie? Have I been a fool, all these years?"

I could only gape at him.

"I did but what my conscience told me, and I did it for our poor, sad land and for our folk. I knew I had no skill for it and no right to do it, and I set down the Guardian's flag after Falkirk, when that became plain to all. But the folk were crying with need, and they were never going to find support among Scotland's nobles. And so I stepped in and agreed to be Guardian, at Wishart's urging—Wishart and others, the Lords of Scotland's Church. They, at least, stood loyal to King and realm when the great lords were scrabbling solely for themselves. And so I led them, the Scots folk, against all those who would grind them down—Scots magnates and English parasites—led them to victory at Stirling with Andrew Murray, and then to slaughter at Falkirk. And after that, I walked away and left others to direct the path of the realm."

"There *were* no others to direct it, Will. You were God's anointed for the post, and the Falkirk defeat was not your doing. You should have stayed."

"Shite! It *was* my doing, Jamie. Andrew Murray would never have let what happened there take place. He would have found a way to make it work. His death after Stirling Bridge was Scotland's greatest loss, and mine. And what would I have done, had I stayed? Led another thousand men to death in some other slaughter? No, Jamie, no ..."

He cleared his throat and pressed his shoulders back against the wall in search of comfort. "I could not do that, not after what I'd learned, watching those whoreson horsemen run away, fleeing the field and leaving us behind like beasts for the slaughter. Scotland's pride! Faugh! That travesty at Falkirk taught me that Scotland will never be free until her own lords and magnates decide to turn themselves around, till they see that their own freedom, their personal honour—and few of them have any of that left, in the eyes of the folk—must be torn from England. As long as they sit on their arses arguing, giving more time and thought to the welfare of their lands in England than they do to matters at home, Scotland will be a wasteland, its folk slaughtered by the nobility on both sides while their magnates make bargains for their own enrichment."

"Come, Will, it's not that bleak. There are some among the nobility who show great loyalty to the realm."

"Aye, but damn few and nowhere near enough. The others are loyal to themselves alone. I saw it clear that day at Falkirk, and that's when I knew I could stand no more. I washed my hands clean of the whole mess, like Pontius Pilate, and it turns out they hated me for it. And so now I am to die when the sun rises and I ask myself— No, that's not true, Jamie. I ask *you*, was I mistaken in the path I chose?"

He stood up straight and rattled the chains on his arms, looking down at them before he raised his tormented eyes to me. "Did I wrong Scotland? God knows, I have committed sins aplenty in the eyes of men like yourself, and none of them have bothered me since I saw my duty clear ahead of me. But it would grieve me now to think I had been wrong for all these years, or that I had shirked my duty in the end." He lapsed from the churchly Latin back into Scots. "Ye've never lied to me, Jamie. Ye've confronted me, ye've shouted at me and defied me, but ye hae never lied to me. So tell me now. Have I been wrong?"

"I cannot answer that, Will. Only God can. Tell me, are you afraid of what they will do to you?"

He raised his eyebrows. "The executioners? Are ye daft? Of course I am. They're gaun to kill me, Jamie, to gut me and cut me into bits, and I'm no' like to enjoy any part o' it. God knows I'm no' feared to die, though. There were times, right after Falkirk, when I would ha'e welcomed death, frae any quarter, and every day God sent for years prior to that, I thought to die in one tulzie or another. It's no' the dyin' that worries me, it's the manner o' it, for I wouldna like to die badly, bawlin' like a bairn that's had his arse skelped. Will you be there?"

"You mean among the crowd? No, God forbid. Suffice that I'm here now."

"Would you come if I asked you to, Jamie? To be there as my witness? There'll be naebody else."

"To watch you die? That's something I have no desire to see, Will."

"Aye, but no' just to see it—to bear witness to it afterwards. An' forbye, your being there wad stop me frae girnin' an' makin' a fool o' mysel'."

It was easy to smile at that, I found.

"I think there's little chance o' that, Will. No Guardian of Scotland was ever any man's fool."

"Aye, but I failed as Guardian." He gazed at me soberly. "Will ye come, for me?"

I closed my eyes and then nodded. "I will, Sir William. I will be your witness, and I will honour your trust and be honoured by it. Will you confess yourself now? Are you prepared for that?"

His slow nod of agreement lifted a weight from my soul.

"Aye, Father James, I will. I'm ready … both to talk to God and to meet Him."

And so I stood in Smithfield Square and bore silent witness to the death of the man whom I believe to have been Scotland's greatest and most loyal son. He was thirty-five years old, two years my senior. I remember, because that day was my thirty-third birthday, and almost as many have gone by again since then.

Young Robert Bruce, the Earl of Carrick, seized the throne the following year, in 1306, and over the course of the next two decades ousted the English finally from Scottish soil and built a single, unified country out of a feudal chaos. He it was who brought our land the unity, peace, and prosperity of which my cousin William had dared to dream.

But it was not until recently, when these new rumours of "The Wallace's" heroic and defiant death began to circulate, that I recalled Will's insistence that I serve as his witness and speak out on his behalf. It had not entered his mind that he might be lionized; he was concerned about being defamed and demeaned in death. And now the opposite is happening, and that strikes me as being even more ominous than his dying fears. He is being recreated, and falsely, by people who seek to use his greatness for their own ends.

And so, the time has come for me to write of the William Wallace *I* knew, for the man these empty rumours would put in his place is painted in false and garish colours, portraying a hero of the ancients, without sin, without flaw, without remorse, and, worst of all, without the beguiling, infuriating mixture of lovable strength and deplorable faults that made my cousin Will the man he was.

The Forest Laird

CHAPTER ONE

I

Even now, when more than fifty years have passed, I find it difficult to imagine a less likely paladin. Yet paladin he was, to us, for he saved our lives, our sense of purpose, and our peace of mind, restoring our shattered dignity when we were at our lowest depth. Possibly the least attractive-looking man I ever saw, he quickly became one of the strongest anchors of my young life. But on that first evening when he startled us from an exhausted sleep, we saw only the monstrous, green-framed, and hairless face of a leering devil looming over us.

We were gibbering with terror, both of us, and our fear was real, because for two full days we had been running in terror, uphill and down, stumbling and falling and blinded with tears and grief, sobbing and incoherent most of the time and utterly convinced we would be caught and killed at any moment by the men pursuing us. We had no notion of the miles falling behind us or the distance we had covered. We knew only that we had to keep running. At times, rendered helpless by exhaustion, we had stopped to rest, huddling together in whatever place we had found that offered a hint of concealment, but we never dared stop for long, because the men hunting us had legs far longer than ours and they knew we could condemn them for the crimes we had seen them commit. And so, as soon as we could find the strength to run for our lives again, we ran. We drank whenever we found a stream, but we dared not stop to hunt or fish. We could not even steal food, because we fled through open country, avoiding people and places that might house our pursuers.

We had arrived at the top of a long moorland gradient and crouched there behind a tall clump of bracken ferns, looking back down the way we had come and astonished to discover that we could see for miles and that no one was chasing us. We strained our eyes for signs of movement on the sloping moor, but all we saw were hares and what might have been a wild boar, more than a mile below us. We finally accepted that no ravening murderers were hunting us.

Ahead of us, the hillside swept gently down for half a mile towards a grassy plain that was bounded on the right by the deep-cut, tree-filled gully of a mountain stream.

Will pointed towards the trees. "We'll go down there. No one will see us there and we can sleep."

As we set off, I felt myself reeling drunkenly, unable to think of anything except the fact that we would soon be able to sleep. It was late afternoon by then, and the sun was throwing our shadows far ahead of us. The grass beneath our feet was short and cropped here, and the going was easy. We soon reached the edge of the defile and jumped down into the first depression we found, a high-sided, grass-filled hollow enclosed by the tops of the trees that stretched up from below us in the steep, sheltered cleft. Within moments we were both asleep.

How long we slept I do not know. But something struck my foot, and I opened my eyes to see the most hideous face I had ever seen, glaring down at me, and I screamed, startling Will awake and sending us both scrambling to escape up the steep bank behind us, but the monster caught us easily, snatching me up to tuck me beneath one arm while pinning Will to the ground with a massive, booted foot. He silenced us with a mighty bellow of what I took to be raging blood lust, and then he thrust me down to huddle at his feet, after which he stepped back a pace and eyed both of us together. I reached out for Will and he squeezed my hand tightly, and we both prepared for the mutilation and death the apparition would surely visit upon us. But then the gargoyle turned its back on us, and we heard it speak.

"I thought you were thieves at first, bent upon robbing me. I was far away from you and thought you men."

It was a strange voice, unexpectedly gentle, and the words were carefully articulated. He spoke in Scots, but with an alien lilt. We knew not what to think, and, still gripped by terror, stared at each other wild-eyed. Now that the giant's back was to us, though, I was able to see that there was nothing supernatural about him. From behind, he was a man like any other, though enormous in his bulk. It was only when he faced you squarely that you saw him as hideous. He was dressed from head to foot in shades of green, his head concealed by a hooded cap that was a part of his tunic, and as I watched now, my heart beginning to slow down, he reached up and tugged, it appeared, at his forehead.

When he turned back to us, his face was covered by a mask of green cloth that he must have pulled down from his hooded cap. It was drawn tight beneath what chin he had, its only openings three ragged-edged holes, one for breathing and one for each eye. The right eye gleamed at me from its opening.

"There," he said. "That's better, no?"

"Better?" My voice was no more than a squeak.

"My face. It's one to frighten children. So I keep it hidden—most of the time." He tilted his head so he could look at Will. "So now that I can tell ye're no' here to rob me, I have some questions to ask you." He bent suddenly and grasped my ankle and I stiffened with fear, but all he did was twist it gently and pull it up so he could look at the back of my leg. "Your legs are covered wi' dried blood, caked with it. And so are yours," he added, nodding at Will. "Why just your legs, and why just the backs of them?"

"You know fine well." Will's voice was little louder than my own, but I could hear defiance in it. "You did it—you and your friends. Used us like women … like sheep."

"I did *what*?" The giant stood for a moment, opening and closing one massive, craggy fist, and then he quickly stooped and grasped Will's ankle as he had mine. "Lie still," he growled as Will started to kick. "I'll no' hurt you."

I had tensed, too, at his sudden move, ready to hurl myself to Will's defence, but then I remained still, sensing that there was no malice now in the man's intent. And so I watched as he flipped Will over to lie face down, then pinned him in place with a hand between his shoulders while he pulled up the hem of my cousin's single garment, exposing his lower back and buttocks and the ravages of what had been done to him. I had not seen what now lay exposed to me, for neither of us had spoken of what had happened, but I knew that what I was seeing was a mirror image of my own backside. I vomited painfully, hearing the giant say again, "Lie still, lad, lie still."

When I finished wiping my mouth they were both watching me, Will sitting up, ashen faced, and the giant leaning back, his shoulders against the steep bank at his back.

"Sweet Jesus," our captor said, in what we would come to know as his curious soft-edged and sometimes lisping voice. "Listen to me now, both of you. I know the sight of me frightened you. That happens often and I've grown used to it. But know this as well. I had no part in what was done to you, and no friend of mine would ever do such a thing. I know not who you are, nor where you came from, and I never saw you before you came across that ridge up there." He flicked a finger at Will. "When did this happen?"

"Yesterday." Will's voice was a whisper.

"When? Daytime or night?"

"Daytime. In the morning."

"Where?"

"At home, near Ellerslie."

"Near *Ellerslie*? That's in Kyle, is it no'?"

Will nodded. "Aye, near Ayr."

"Carrick land. Bruce country. But that's thirty miles and more from here. How did you get here?"

"We ran."

"You *ran*? Thirty miles in two days? Bairns?"

"Aye, we ran," Will snapped. "They were chasing us. Sometimes we hid, but mostly we ran."

"Who was chasing you?"

"The ones who— The ones who murdered my father, Alan Wallace of Ellerslie. And my mother. My wee sister Jenny, too." Now the tears were pouring down Will's cheeks, etching clean channels through the caked-on dirt.

"Christ!" The green mask swung back to face me. "And who are you? His brother?"

I shook my head, feeling the tears trembling in my own eyes. "No, I'm his cousin Jamie, from Auchincruive. I came to live with Will when my family all died of the fever, two years ago."

"Aha." He looked back at Will. "Your name's Will Wallace?"

"William."

"Ah. William Wallace, then. My name is Ewan Scrymgeour. Archer Ewan, men call me. You can call me Ewan. So tell me then, exactly, what happened yesterday to start all this."

It was a good thing he asked Will that and not me, for I had no idea what had happened. Everything had been too sudden and too violent, and all of it had fallen on me like a stone from a clear blue sky. Will, however, was two years older, and more than accustomed to being able to think for himself, since he had been taught for years, by both his parents, that knowledge and the ability to read and write are the greatest strengths a free man can possess. Will came from a clan of fighting men and women, as did I, but his father's branch of our family had a natural ability for clerical things, and two of his uncles, as well as several of his cousins, were monks.

"They were Englishmen," Will said, his voice still low, his brow furrowed as he sought to recall the events.

"*Englishmen?* They couldn't have been. There are no English soldiery in Scotland."

"I *saw* them! And I heard them talking. But I could tell from their armour even before I heard them growling at each other."

"Jesus, that makes no kind of sense at all. We have no war with England and they have no soldiers here. Unless they were deserters, come north in search of booty and safety. But if that's the case, they'd have been safer to stay in England. King Alec's men will hunt them down like wolves. How many were there?"

"Ten on foot and a mounted knight in command of them. He had a white thing on his surcoat. A turret or a tower. Some kind of castle."

"And what happened?"

"I don't know." Will wiped his eyes with the back of his wrist. "We were down by the old watchtower hunting squirrels, Jamie and me. We heard the noise and ran to see what was happening and we met my sister Jenny running away. She was witless, out o' her mind wi' terror. She couldna speak, didna even try. She just wailed, keenin' like an old wife at a death. I knew something terrible had happened. So I left her there wi' Jamie and ran to see." He fell silent, staring into emptiness, and a bleak look settled on his face.

"They were all dead," he said in a dulled voice I'd never heard before, "scattered in the gate yard. Jessie the cook, Angus the groom. Timothy and Charlie and Roddy and Daft Sammy. All dead … split open and covered in blood an' …" He sobbed then, a single, wrenching sound. "My da was sitting against the wall by the door with his head to one side and his eyes wide open, and I thought he was just lookin' at them, but then I saw the blood on him, too, all down his front … And then I saw that his head was almost off, hangin' to one side. My mother was beside him, lyin' on her face, wi' a big spear sticking up between her shoulders. I could see her bare legs, high up. I'd never seen them before." He hiccupped and shuddered. "The ones alive were a' strangers, what the English call men-at-arms, a' wearin' helmets and jerkins and mail, forbye a knight on a horse. The men were a' talkin' and laughin', but the knight was just sittin' on his horse, cleanin' his sword on something yellow. And then one o' them saw me watchin' and gave a shout and I ran as fast as I could back to where I'd left Jamie and Jenny."

When he stopped this time, I thought he would say no more.

"What happened then?" Archer Ewan prodded.

"What?"

"What happened after you ran back to Jamie and your sister?"

"Oh … We ran back the way we had come, but I had to carry Jenny and they caught us near the old watchtower. Five o' them. One o' them killed Jenny. Chopped off her head and didna even look at what he'd done. He was watchin' Jamie, wi' a terrible look on his face. And then they … they did what they did to us and then they tied us up and left us there, in some bushes against the tower wall. They said they'd be back."

"How did you escape? You did, didn't you?"

Will nodded. "Aye. I kept a wee knife for skinnin' squirrels under a stone by the tower door, close by where they left us. Jamie was closer to it than me, so I told him to get it for me. He rolled over and got it, then he crawled back, holdin' it behind his back, and I took it and managed to cut his wrists free. It took a long time. Then he cut the ropes on his legs and set me loose. And then we ran."

"And are you sure they chased you?"

Will looked up at the giant in surprise. "Oh, aye, they chased us, and they would ha'e caught us, too, except that there was a thunderstorm and you could hardly see through the rain and the dark. But we knew where we were going and they didna. So we gave them the slip and kept movin' into the woods, deeper and deeper until we didna even know where we were. We ran all day. Then when it got dark we slept for a wee while and then got up and ran again. But they found our tracks and we could hear them comin' after us, shoutin' to us to gi'e up, for a long time."

"Hmm." The big man sat mulling that for a time, studying each of us closely with his one good eye, and I began to fear that he doubted all that Will had said, even though he must surely see our terror and exhaustion were real. "Well," he said eventually, "all that matters is that you escaped and you're here now and well away from them. Who were they working for, do you know?"

Will frowned. "Who were they *workin'* for? They werena workin' for anybody. They were Englishmen! There's no Englishmen in Carrick. The men there are all Bruce men. My da's been the Countess o' Carrick's man all his life. He's fierce proud o' that."

"Aye, no doubt. Then if you're right, and they were Englishry, they must have been deserters, as I jaloused. Either that or your father must have crossed someone important. And powerful. Was he rich?"

"My da?" Will blinked. "No, he wasna rich. But he wasna poor, either. We've a fine herd o' cattle."

"That might have been what they were after. But whether yea or nay, those cattle winna be there now." He sighed loudly and then clapped his hands together. "Fine, then, here's what we're going to do. I have a camp close by, down at the bottom of the gully, by the stream. We'll go down there, where there's a fine, sheltered fire, and I'll make us a bite to eat, and then you two can wash yourselves in the burn and I'll show you how to make a bed of bracken ferns. In the morning we'll decide what you should do from here onwards. Away with you now."

2

The water was frigid, but the rushing coldness of it against my heated body was intense enough to dull the worst of the searing pain in my backside. I gritted my eight-year-old teeth and grimly set about washing away the evidence of my shame and the sin I had endured. I could hear Will splashing close by, and hear his muttered curses, for he ever had a blazing, blistering way with words. When I could feel that my legs and buttocks were clean again, I did a brave thing. I knelt in the stream, bending forward to splash water over my face and head and scrub at both until I felt they too must be clean.

"I'm finished," Will called to me as I was shaking the water from my hair, and we made our way together back towards the bank, stooped forward and fumbling with outstretched hands for river stones that could trip us.

Ewan's campfire was well concealed in a stone-lined pit, but we could see the glow of it reflected up into the branches overhead, and soon we were sitting beside it, each wrapped in one of the two old blankets he had tossed to us with a single rough cloth towel on our return.

"Eat," he said, and brought each of us a small tin pot of food. I have no idea what it contained, other than the whipped eggs that held it together, but there was delicious meat in there, in bite-sized pieces, and some kind of spicy root that might have been turnip. He had something else cooking, too, in a shallow pan, but it had nothing to do with what we ate that night. He had raised his mask and tucked it back into his hood, perhaps so that he could see better, and was carefully keeping his back to us as he worked. The stuff in the pan was a soggy, black mess of plants and herbs mixed with some kind of powder that he shook liberally into it from a bag he pulled out of a pocket in his tunic. He kept the mixture simmering over the coals in a tiny amount of water, stirring it with a stick and testing its heat with a finger from time to time—though I noticed he never tasted it—until he removed it from the heat and set it aside to cool. Still keeping his back to us while Will and I gorged ourselves on our stew, he then set about ripping up what I took to be a good shirt, tearing it into two large pieces and a number of long, thin strips. Will and I watched his every move, chewing avidly and wondering what he was about.

Will cleared his throat. "Can I ask you something?"

The big man glanced up, the ruined side of his face masked in shadow. "Aye, ask away."

"What kind of eggs are these? They're good."

"A mixture, but four of them were duck eggs. The rest were wild land fowl—grouse and moorhen."

"Are you not having any?"

"I had mine earlier, while you bathed."

Will nodded, then said, "You don't have to hide your face now. We're no' afraid any more."

Ewan's face creased into what I thought might be a smile. "Are you sure about that?"

"Aye, we're sure. Aren't we, Jamie?"

"Aye, we're sure, right enough." Then, emboldened by my youth and the sudden realization that I truly was not afraid of this strange man, I asked, "What happened to it? Your face."

The giant drew in a great breath. "How old are you, William Wallace?"

"Ten."

"Well, then, when I was a boy just two years older than you are now, I got hit in the face by a mace. You know what a mace is?"

"Aye, it's a club."

"It is. A metal-headed club. And it broke my whole face and knocked out my eye and all my teeth on the one side."

"Who did it?"

"I don't know. It was early in a battle, at a place called Lewes, in Sussex in the south of England." He went on to tell us about how he had gone, as an apprentice boy to a Welsh archer, to join the army of King Henry, the third of that name, in his war against his rebellious barons led by Simon de Montfort. The present King of England, Edward I, Ewan said, had been a prince then, and had commanded the cavalry and archers on the right of King Henry's battle line, on the high ground above Lewes town, but the enemy, under Simon de Montfort himself, had surprised them from the rear after a daring night march and won control of the heights after a short and vicious fight. In that early-morning skirmish before the battle proper, young Ewan's company of archers, running to take up new positions, had been caught in the open and ridden down by a squadron of de Montfort's horsemen, one of whom struck Ewan down in passing.

"So if you missed the battle," I said, "why do they call you Archer Ewan?"

"Because that's what I am. An archer, trained lifelong on the longbow. They left me for dead on that field, but I wouldna die. And when I recovered I went back to my apprenticeship. I had lost a year and more of training by then, but my apprentice master was my uncle, too. He took me back into his care and I learned well, despite having lost my eye. It changes your sight, you know, having but one eye." He made a grunting sound that might have been a self-deprecating laugh. "I adapted to it quickly, though, and learned very well, for I had little else left to divert me from my work. Where other lads went chasing after girls, I found my solace in my bow and in learning the craft of using it better than any other man I knew."

He picked up the pan that he'd set by the fireside earlier, testing its heat again with the back of a finger. "There, this is ready."

I watched closely as he folded each of the two large pieces of torn shirt into four and then carefully poured half of the mixture in the pan onto each of the pads he had made. I wrinkled my nose at the smell of it.

"What *is* that?"

"It's a nostrum."

"What's a nostrum?"

"A cure, made from natural things. This one is a poultice made of burdock leaves and herbs and a special mixture of dried things given me by my mother, who is a famous healer. Usually poultices have to be hot, but this one needn't be. It's for you." He glanced up to see how I reacted to that, but I merely stared at the nostrum. "There's one for each of you. What we'll do is put them into the crack of your arses, where the pain is worst, and bind them into place with those long strips. Then you'll sleep with them in place, and come morning, you should both be feeling better. You might not be completely without pain by then, but the worst of it will be bye. Now, let's get them on. They're cool now, so they'll not burn you."

Will and I eyed each other fearfully, acutely mindful of what had happened last time a man had come near our backsides, but the big archer was patient and unmistakably concerned for us, and so we suffered the indignity of allowing him to set the things in place and tie them securely. It felt revolting, but I imagined very soon afterwards that the pain of my ravaged backside was subsiding, and I sat still, enjoying the heat from the replenished fire and leaning against Will, who was looking around at the archer's camp.

I looked then, too, and noticed that what I had thought must be a purely temporary place had signs of permanence about it. The fire pit was well made, its stones blackened with age and soot, and there were several stoutly made wooden boxes, or chests, that looked too solid to be picked up and carried away by one man on a single journey. I peered more closely into the dimness and saw that they were fitted into recesses in the hand-cut bank that ringed the camp-fire and provided us with seats, and that their sides were hinged and could be closed by a latch.

"Do you live here all the time?" Will had voiced the question in my mind.

"No," Ewan said. "But I spend a lot of time here. My mother lives close by."

"Why don't you stay wi' her?"

"Because she lives in a cave." Then, seeing the astonishment on our faces, he added, "I stay away because I don't want to leave signs of my being there. I only go to see her when I think she'll need more food. To go too often would be dangerous."

"Why?"

The big archer gave a snort of indignation. "Because someone might see me coming or going, and if they did they might search and find my mother. And if they find her they'll kill her."

The enormity of that left us speechless, and Will, having seen his own mother killed mere days before, wiped at his eyes, suddenly brimming with tears. It was left to me to ask the obvious question.

"Why would anybody want to kill her?"

"Because she's my mother and I'm an outlaw. So is she."

"An outlaw?" I was stricken with awe. "How can somebody's *mother* be an outlaw?"

He reached out a long arm to tousle my hair. "Aye," he said quietly. "It's daft, isn't it? But she is, because I saved her life and was outlawed myself for doing it."

He looked into the fire, and I drew my blanket closer about me, sensing a story to come. And sure enough, he began to speak, slowly and clearly in that wonderful soft-edged voice. "D'you recall my saying she was a famous healer? Well, she was. She lived in a wee place east of here, about twelve miles from where we're sitting now.

It doesna even have a name—just a wee clump o' houses near a ford over a river. But she was known in a' the countryside, and whenever somebody got sick, they'd send for her. The land belonged to an auld laird called Sir Walter Ormiston, one o' the Dumfries Ormistons, but when he died it passed to his eldest son, a useless lump of dung called William, like your friend there. But he liked to call himself William, *Laird* of Ormiston. The old man had been plain Ormiston, but the son demanded to be called the *Laird* of Ormiston, by everybody. Anyway, this Laird William had a wife as silly as himself, and a wee son called Alasdair. The bairn took sick and the Laird had my mother brought to the big house to see to him. She was a great healer, my mother, but she couldna compete wi' God's will, and the bairn died. The father went mad, and his wife called my mother a witch, said she had put a curse on the bairn. They locked her up in a cellar in the big house.

"I heard all about it the next morning, and I went directly in search of her and got there just as they were going to hang her from a tree. I was too far away to stop them, too far away even to shout at them and be heard. I couldna believe what I was seein'. They put a rope around her neck and threw the other end over a high branch, and then three men gathered up the other end of the rope, meaning to run with it, hoisting her up into the air."

He stopped talking, and I had to bite my tongue to keep still and wait, but it was Will who spoke up.

"What did you do?"

"What *could* I do? I used my bow and shot them a' when they started to run, before they could hoist her off the ground. The rope burnt her neck, but they dropped her before she was even in the air. I was already running towards them. When I saw Laird William, I took a shot at him, but he was running to hide behind a tree and I took him in the shoulder. Sent him flying, but didna kill him. By the time I reached my mother there was just me and her and the three men I had killed. Everyone else had scattered."

He drew a deep breath and blew it out mightily. "That was two years ago, the end of my life as it had been. I took my mother up on my horse with me and we escaped, but we could not go home again, for they put a price on my head for murder, for the murder of the three men and the attempted murder of Laird William. I knew they would, but by the time the word got out we were far away, my mother and I. I took her into the forest and we stayed there for a few months, but then when the hullabaloo had died down I brought her back here, close enough to her own land to be familiar, but far enough away from everywhere to be out of harm's way.

"We hid in the woods here for a month or two longer, while I looked for a place for her to live that would be safe and comfortable, and one day I found the cave she lives in now. It's hard to find at the best o' times, and she's happy enough, but the ground below the hill-side at the entrance to her place is boggy, and it's too easy to leave tracks that might be followed. That's why I stay away most of the time."

"Except when you think she needs more food," I said.

"Aye, that's right. She has a few goats that run wild but come to her call, and that gives her milk and cheese. And she grows her own small crops in the clearings among the trees. I bring her oats and fresh meat from time to time, meat that I smoke out here so that it will keep."

"What kind of meat?"

"Deer meat. From Laird William's deer. I'm a poacher and a thief o' his deer. It's thanks to him that I'm an outlaw and so I show my gratitude by killing and eating his deer."

"What's it like to be an outlaw?" I asked him.

The big man smiled at me and I saw his face clearly, but saw nothing ugly there now. "It's like being sleepy. You learn to accept it and you hope it won't last." He nodded towards Will. "Your cousin's asleep already. Now let's get you both to bed. We can talk more tomorrow."

We awoke the next morning to the sight of Ewan standing beside the fire pit, gazing down at us with what passed for a smile.

"Will you sleep all day then, you two? I've done an entire day's work while you lay snoring there. Up, now, and down to the stream and wash the mess from your arses, quick. I need you to help me cut this up, and then we're going to visit my mother, so up with you and scamper about!"

If we were bleary eyed at all, that vanished at once, for the gutted carcass of a small deer was draped on a rough cloth spread across his shoulders, its pointed hooves held together at his chest in one massive fist. We sprang from our ferny beds as he lowered the dead beast to the ground and we ran the short distance to the burn with his hectoring voice in our ears all the way.

The stream was narrower and faster than I had thought the previous night, and it swept around us in a bow, the outer edge of which followed a steep, treed bank every bit as high and sheer as the one at our backs. The only way to see the sky was by looking straight up through a narrow, open strip between the overhead branches, and I saw at once that Ewan's camp was as safe as it could possibly be, for anyone finding it would have to do so by accident. Not even the smell of woodsmoke would betray it, for by the time the smoke reached anyone it would have been dissipated by the thick foliage on the slopes above.

The water didn't seem as cold as it had the night before, either, and we washed the remains of Ewan's poultice from our bodies quickly, remarking to each other that we could no longer feel the throbbing ache that had seemed interminable the day before.

Ewan had almost finished skinning the small deer when we got back to the banked fire pit, where heat still smouldered under a covering of crusted earth. We watched him sever the head and lower legs—I was amazed by the colour and the sharpness of the curved blade he used—and wrap them in the still-steaming hide. He then lifted the entire bundle into the centre of the cloth that had covered his shoulders.

"Here," he said, tying the corners together. "One of you take that shovel and the other the pickaxe, then go and bury this along the bank of the stream. But bring back the cloth. And mind you take it as far from here as you can carry it. Dinna think to bury it close by. Bury it deep and stamp down the ground and pile stones over it. We dinna want to be attracting scavengers, animal or otherwise. Then get back here as quick as you can."

It took us some time to follow his instructions, and we barely spoke a word to each other, so intent were we on doing exactly as he had said. As we made our way back, we walked into the delicious aroma of cooking. Ewan had rekindled the dormant fire, and a flat iron skillet filled with fresh meat and some kind of onion was sizzling on the coals.

We ate voraciously, as though we had not fed in weeks. Those two days of running had whetted our appetites to the point of insatiability. The deer liver was perfect, coated in flour and salt and lightly fried with the succulent wild onions, and when the last fragment was devoured we sat back happily.

"How's your bum?"

The question, addressed to both of us, was asked casually as Ewan wiped his knife carefully, removing any signs of food from its gleaming, bluish blade. We both assured him that we were much better.

"Good." He gestured with a thumb over his shoulder to where the deer carcass lay covered with fresh ferns. "I'll cut some of this up into bits that we can carry, and leave the rest here to smoke later. You can help me carry my mother's share to her."

"Does she live far from here?" Will asked.

The big outlaw shook his head. "Not far, a two-hour walk. Far enough away to be safe when anyone comes here hunting me. Laird William suspects I'm still around, so every now and then patrols come looking. But they haven't found me yet."

"Are you no' afeared they'll find your mother?" Will asked.

"She's to the north o' here, across the hills, on the far edge o' William's land. I leave signs to the south and southeast from time to time, to keep them hunting down there. Besides, she knows how to take care o' herself." Ewan took up his knife again and began to strop it against a much-used device that had been lying beside his foot. I looked closely at it, never having seen one quite like it before, a strip of leather, perhaps a foot long and a thumb's length in width, that he had fastened to a heavy strip of wood. The leather had a patina of long use, its colour darkened almost to blackness by the friction of a lightly oiled blade, and I watched him test the blade's edge with the ball of his thumb.

He had no beard. That was part of why he had frightened me so badly when I first looked at him. In a world where all men went unshaven, a beard would have done much to conceal the frightfulness of his visage, yet he had made no attempt to cover the deformity of his face by growing one. If he would wear a mask, why not a beard?

I had seen beardless men before, but very few, and my father had been the only one I knew personally. As a child, I had watched with fascination as he went to great pains, daily, to scrape his cheeks, chin, and upper lip free of hair, using a thin, short-bladed, and amazingly sharp knife that he kept for that purpose alone. It was hard work to shave a beard, I knew, a meticulous and time-consuming, seemingly pointless task, except that my father's commitment to it had a purpose that I discovered by accident one day, listening to my mother speaking to a friend. My father, she had said, had an affliction of the skin that he could hold at bay only by shaving daily. He might perhaps miss one day, but three successive days without the blade would bring his face out in boils and scaly patches. I never did discover what this malady sprang from, but from that time onward I accepted my father's daily regimen as necessary. Watching Ewan wield his strange bluish knife, I knew his blade was far sharper than my father's, and that he could use it to shave quite easily. Yet there was a smoothness to his skin that showed no sign at all of being scraped.

"Ewan, why have you no beard?"

He looked at me in surprise, then laughed. "For the same reason I have no eyebrows. I can't grow one."

I gaped at him in astonishment, noticing for the first time that it was as he said. He had brows, the undamaged one boldly pronounced, but they were hairless.

He laughed again. "I was born bald, young Jamie. And I have never grown a single hair anywhere on my body. Look."

He stretched out a hand towards me, exposing the skin on his forearm. It was perfectly smooth, tanned, and heavily corded with muscle but innocent of any trace of hair.

"No hair at all?" I asked.

"Not a single strand. That's another reason for the mask, and the hood. My bare head makes me too easy to notice. Folk will remember a hooded, masked outlaw, but they won't be able to describe him. But a bald and beardless man is another matter altogether."

My mind raced to absorb what he had said. "Did you not wear a hood, then, before you were an outlaw?"

"No, why would I? I didna need one. I had no reason to fear people knowing who I was. I had nothing to hide and nothing to protect. But that's all different now. And what about you two? Where will you go next?"

"I don't know," Will said quietly. He had been listening closely to our conversation. "I think we ought to go and see the Countess."

"The *Countess*? In Kyle? That's back where you came from, thirty miles away. How will you get there? And what will you do when you *are* there? Have you other kin close by?"

"No. There was only us, and Jamie's folk in Auchincruive, but they're all dead, too. I ha'e two brothers, but Malcolm's training to be knighted and John was knighted two years ago and they're both with the Bruce forces, somewhere in Annandale. I don't know how to find them, to let them know what's happened. But they'll ha'e to be told. But that leaves just Jamie and me."

"And ye've no other kin anywhere?"

Will shrugged. "Oh aye. There's my father's brother Malcolm. The one my brother's named for. He lives in Elderslie, near Paisley."

The big archer blinked. "Ellerslie and *Elderslie*? There's two places with the same name?"

"They're no' exactly the same," Will answered. "They just *sound* the same. I don't think there's any connection."

"Except they both ha'e knightly tenants called Wallace."

"My father wasna a knight, but my uncle Malcolm is. He has lands there, and a house."

"And how did he and your father get along? Are they friends?"

"I … think so. They're brothers, and I know they like each other. Or *liked* each other …" His voice faltered only slightly, but he ploughed ahead. "And I've another two uncles, or an uncle and a cousin, close by there. At least I think they're close by. Peter and Duncan Wallace. My mother talks—talked about them a' the time. They're both at Paisley Abbey, one a priest, the other a monk."

Ewan sat up straight. "Then you have a whole clan there, in this Elderslie, even if they be all men. Are there no women there?"

Will shrugged. "I think so. My uncle Malcolm has a wife called Margaret."

"That's where you should go, then, to your kinsmen there. There's nothing left for you where you came from. The Countess would not let you run your farm yourselves, two young boys, mere bairns. And besides, if the men who killed your family found out you were back, they'd finish what they started. I think the two o' you should go to Paisley, to your kin in the Abbey. They'll take you to this Elderslie place."

"But Paisley's miles away," I said, hearing the dismay in my own voice, and Ewan swung his big head to look at me.

"Miles away? God bless you, laddie, it's a lot closer than the place you came from. That's thirty miles and more back, but Paisley's less than twenty miles from here."

I looked to Will, but he just shook his head, as ignorant as I was, and big Ewan took that as a sign that he was right.

"That's what we'll do, then," he said, his voice filled with certainty. "My mother will find you something to wear, to cover your bare arses, and she'll wrap up some food for you. And then she'll tell you the best way to go and we'll set you on the road. You'll see, it will be easy, and you'll be in Elderslie in no time, chapping at your uncle's door."

3

From that day onwards, each time I have heard that kind of certainty in someone's voice, I have held my breath and braced myself for the worst that could happen, for the days that followed were far from being easy for any of us.

It began that afternoon as we reached the base of the low, forested range of hills that Ewan told us contained his mother's cave. The land there was heavily treed, but there were great stretches of open meadow too, dotted with dense copses in the low-lying lands in the approach to the hills, and they were home to herds of deer. We had been walking for almost three hours on a rambling route, skirting the open glades and keeping to the edges of the woodlands because Ewan had warned us that it was not only unsafe but foolish to risk crossing the open meadows, where we might be seen by anyone from any direction. The deer, which were plentiful and grazed in small herds of eight or ten, ignored us for the most part, aware of our presence as we passed but seeming to sense no danger from us.

But that changed in an instant when all movement among them froze and all their heads came up as one. Ewan froze, too, in mid-step, and held up a warning hand to us. A moment later the entire meadow on our left was transformed as all the deer broke into flight at once, bounding high in the air as they fled towards the nearest cover, and when they had all vanished Ewan still stood motionless, urgency in every line of him.

I started to ask him what was wrong but he silenced me with a slash of his hand.

"*Listen*," he whispered.

I strained my ears, aware that Will was doing the same, and then I heard what must have frightened the deer, a strange, ululating sound far in the distance, although in what direction I could not tell.

"What is it?"

Ewan dropped the parcel of meat and slid the great strung longbow over his head. "Hounds," he growled, already launching himself into a run. "Hunting hounds. You two stay here!"

His last words were shouted over his shoulder as he went, but Will and I had no intention of remaining where we were. We looked at each other with no need to speak, then dropped our own two cloth-bound packages and set off after him. We ran as fast as we could, but Ewan was moving like a man possessed, in great leaping bounds, paying no attention now to his own warnings about being seen. We saw very quickly that we could not catch up to him but we kept running, pushing ourselves to the limits, uphill and down, and watching hopelessly as he outstripped us with every frantic stride and finally disappeared among dense undergrowth on another rising slope far ahead.

Moments before we crested that slope, we heard a single, chilling howl somewhere ahead of us. It was human, and it was filled with anguish. We crashed through the last of the undergrowth and stopped abruptly. We were at the top of a steep, grassy hillside overlooking a narrow, tree-hemmed clearing that ran for half a mile to either side of us. I saw movement everywhere down there, but I was so winded by the effort of running that at first I could make no sense of what I was seeing, and I threw one arm over Will's shoulders and hung there gasping, trying to take in the scene below.

My first impression, still sharp in my mind today, was of two points of stillness among an eddy of distant, wheeling, far-flung, and fast-moving men, some of them mounted, others on foot. One of those points was Ewan Scrymgeour, poised at the foot of the slope below us and looking across the narrow valley to the other, hanging from a large, isolated tree on the opposite slope, a shapeless, brownish bundle. And then in the blink of an eye the horror broke over me. The giant archer screamed again and set off at a run, headed directly for the hanging bundle.

The eddying men had grouped at either end of the narrow valley, and now they turned back towards him, gaining speed as they came and shouting orders and instructions to one another. I became aware of Will's clawed fingers digging deep into my arm.

"We have to help him. They'll take him."

Even as I heard the words, I heard the futility in them, too. We had not a weapon between us, and there was nothing we could do. We both knew that. Knew, too, that exposed as we were on the open hillside, we were as good as dead. If we were taken here, obviously having come with big Ewan, we would not be hanged as outlaws. We would be chopped down by the first man to reach us, if we were not first used again as women.

The attackers were stringing out now, six mounted men spurring downslope hard from our right and two more charging more uphill from the left, the latter followed by six running men who had loosed four big dogs from their leashes, hunting hounds that bounded past the two horsemen leading their group and were now racing towards our friend.

In the space of the moments that I had been looking at his attackers, Ewan Scrymgeour had reached the tree, and I saw the flash of his blade as he cut the rope, then leapt to catch his mother before she fell to the ground. He barely succeeded, and he lowered her gently, stooping over her so that I could not see what he was doing. But then he knelt, his head bowed, and I clearly saw him cross himself before he rose to his feet and took up his longbow. His full quiver, with almost a score of arrows—I had admired them that morning—hung at his shoulders from the strap across his back, and now he reached behind him and drew one, nocking it to his bow and looking from side to side at the men approaching him.

I had never seen the like of what followed, nor have I witnessed the equal of it to this day. Ewan Scrymgeour dealt death in a woodland meadow that day as though he were the god of death himself. Standing alone beneath the tree on which his mother had been killed, he slew every man and dog who came against him, shooting them down indiscriminately as they attracted his attention, some within mere yards of him, like the first dog that died in the air as it sprang for his throat, and others from greater distances. None of the men attacking him had bows, and that was his sole advantage. To deal with him they had to come within spear-throwing distance, or within a sword's length of him, and he killed them one by one before they could.

His assailants soon recognized that he never missed, and they lost all desire to fight. But these men had murdered his mother, and Ewan shot them down mercilessly as they rode and ran away until only two of them remained alive—a man on foot, who had hung back beyond range of the archer's bow, and the leader of the mounted group. This man, who wore the mail and half armour of a knight, had held himself well clear of the fighting, sitting his horse below Will and me at the base of our slope and watching as the action swirled and eddied.

Ewan lowered his bow, still holding an arrow nocked, his eyes fixed on the man below us. But then the man on foot began to run away. I do not believe Ewan had been aware of the fellow until he began to run, but the archer spun towards him and raised his bow again. He stepped into his pull, drew the bowstring back to his ear, held it there for a moment, then released. The fleeing man had been close to three hundred paces distant when he broke into his run and he was running almost as fast as Ewan had run earlier when the arrow struck between his shoulders, its force, even from such a great distance, tumbling him forward, wide armed, into a sprawling, motionless lump.

Even at the age of eight and never having seen a longbow used before, I knew that the feat I had just witnessed was extraordinary. But the mounted knight had missed it, for he had swung his horse around as soon as he saw the other man divert Ewan's attention and was now driving hard up the slope towards us, his bared sword held high. I could not see his face, for he wore a visored helmet, but I knew that he meant to kill us.

Will pushed me down and away from him, shouting at me to *roll*, and as I threw myself to the ground I saw him run towards the oncoming man and then dive into a downhill roll, his head tucked into his knees. I heard a thunderous thumping of hooves above and beside me, then heard a violent hiss as the point of a hard-swung sword flashed past my face, and frightened out of my wits I rolled again, as the rider reined in his mount and turned, gathering himself to slash at me again, sure this time of his target. I saw his arm go up and heard myself whimper, and then came a sound like a dull, hard hammer blow. My would-be killer flew backward over his horse's rump and crashed to the ground.

I had not seen the arrow hit him, but when I scrambled to my knees to look it was there, transfixing him, buried almost to its feathered fletching in the very centre of his chest, sunk through the layers of armour meant to protect him. I could see Will's feet and legs beside me, and when I looked up at him his eyes were wider than I had ever seen them. Still dazed and hardly believing I had not been killed, I stood up to look for big Ewan, and there he was with his bow by his side, standing motionless where I had last seen him, beneath the tree, beside the body of his mother. It would be years before I learned to appreciate how difficult it is for a bowman to shoot accurately at a target that is far above or below him.

Will was still staring at the arrow buried in the dead knight's chest. He turned to me and blinked, then looked down the slope.

"Let's help Ewan bury his mother," he said.

As we stood silent over the grave Will had helped Ewan dig with the shovel his mother had used in cultivating her wild crops—I was judged to be too small for such heavy work—I found myself thinking of the carnage that had swept into our lives during the previous few days. Numbed by the grief in Ewan's face, I stared down at the mound of fresh dirt over the woman I had never known and saw the faces of my own recent dead—my uncle Alan and my aunt Martha, Will's parents; Timothy and Charlie, Sir Alan's oldest and most faithful retainers, bound to him and his family by a lifetime of service and dedication to the bloodlines of the healthy little herd of cattle they had bred and reared; Jessie, the plump, careworn household cook who had mothered me after my arrival in Ellerslie; Roddy and Daft Sammy, the slow-witted pair of labourers who had worked the cattle stalls and sometimes served in the stables with Angus, the dour old Highland groom; and sunny little Jenny, the laughing child whose severed head had bounced and rolled across the ground in Dalfinnon Woods before my eyes. Had that been only three days before? Ten dead, including the unknown woman we had buried here, and behind us, in the little valley, an additional eighteen, fourteen of them men, the others dogs. So much death. So much blood.

I have no recollection of leaving the graveside, no memory of entering the cave that had been Ewan's mother's home. I regained my awareness only after night had fallen, when I opened my eyes to find myself sitting against a wall close by a roaring fire. Ewan and Will were seated on the other side of the flames that filled the hollow space with leaping shadows. Ewan's legs were apart, stretched towards the fire, and he appeared to be asleep, his single eye closed and his slumped back supported by the sturdy frame of a short-legged chair of the kind my mother had used while nursing my younger siblings. Behind him, the mouth of the cave was outlined in light, its centre filled with blackness.

Will sat rapt, gazing at Ewan's massive bow as he ran his hands, first one and then the other, up and down the planed, polished surface of the unstrung stave. It was far taller than he was, and perfectly circular in section, too thick in the middle for his ten-year-old hand to grasp, but tapering gently towards either end, where it was less than a finger's width in diameter and carefully notched to hold the looped ends of the string of braided sinew that would transform it from a simple but beautiful staff into the deadly weapon that could hurl an arrow for hundreds of yards to pierce steel plate and heavy, linked-ring mail.

He somehow sensed me watching and hefted the weapon parallel to the floor so that I could see the flames reflecting along its polished length. "Have ye ever seen the like, Jamie?" His voice was filled with wonder. "Have ye ever seen *anything* like this? I want to learn to use one o' these, to use it like Ewan."

Our host had not been sleeping, for he spoke now without moving his head or opening his eye. "Then you have a long road ahead of you, Will Wallace, for it will take you years to grow big enough to grip it properly, and longer still to build the thews to pull it. That is from my mother's people's land of Wales. It is not meant for ordinary men, and ordinary men have neither the strength nor the skills to pull it, let alone use it."

"I'll learn," Will answered, "though it take me all my life from this day on. My name cames from the Welsh—Uallash. That's the Gaelic word for Welsh. Will you teach me?"

Ewan opened his single eye. "Teach you! How can I do that? I am an outlaw, and now a wanted murderer. I slew fourteen men today."

"You killed fourteen men who murdered your mother." Will looked directly back at him, his face strangely solemn, his words emotionless, and as he spoke it struck me that my carefree friend and cousin had changed greatly in the past few days. "Forbye four dogs that sought to kill you," he added in that same tone. "You didna *murder* anybody."

Ewan grunted something deep in his chest that might have been a sardonic laugh. "I doubt the folk who find Laird William and his men will see it that way."

"That was Laird William? The knight?" Again I noted the flatness in my cousin's voice.

"No knight, that one," Ewan replied. "Nobly born, but base in all things else. Aye, that was William, Laird of Ormiston, the craven who kept far off, then tried to kill you two when he thought himself safe from me. Who else did you think it might have been?"

Will still wore that expression that was new to me, a stillness marked by cold and angry-looking eyes.

"It matters not. He's dead, and so he should be. Where will you go now?"

"Back to the forest, to Ettrick. There's nothing to keep me here now. And if they hunted me before, they'll really hound me now."

Will stared into the fire, and what he said next came as a surprise to me as much as it did to Ewan.

"Come with us, then, to Elderslie. To our kinfolk there. No one there will ken you for an outlaw. They winna know you at all. We'll say you worked for my father and werena there when the farm was attacked. Afterwards you found us, then brought us to Elderslie. They will be grateful for that, and my uncle Malcolm will find a place for you. He's a good man, for I've heard my father say he set great store by him. And you, you're strong—worth your wage to any man that hires you. You'll be better off there, working for us, than hiding in the forest a' the time."

The big man produced what I now knew to be a smile. "Working for you, eh? How old did you say you are?"

"I'm ten. But I'll soon be eleven. And I didn't mean working for me. I was talking about my uncle Malcolm."

"And what about my face?"

"It's a good face … once you get over the fright of it. You can wear your mask at first, if you like, till folk get to know you."

"Hmm." Ewan's broad brow, the only unmarred surface on his face, furrowed. "How am I to know if I would like it there?"

"The same way we'll know. We've never been there either, so we'll find that out thegither. But you'll like it. And besides, I'll need you there to teach me to be an archer."

Ewan Scrymgeour placed one massive palm across his eyes and shook his head, then inhaled a great breath. "Well, William Wallace, that might be a good idea, and it might not. I'll ha'e to think on it. Now get you two to bed, the both of you. I'm going back outside to talk to my mother about it."

CHAPTER TWO

I

"**N**ow sit down, all of you, and tell me again. Will, you tell me. And this time, take your time. Tell me all of it and leave nothing out. Sit."

Sir Malcolm Wallace's voice was a deep, rumbling roll of sound, his mouth hidden beneath a bushy, greying beard. He was nowhere near as large as the archer Ewan, but he somehow conveyed the impression of being much larger than he was. I suspected that had more than a little to do with the fine quality of his clothing, which even I could see had been tailored to emphasize the width of his chest and shoulders. He had dropped into what was obviously his own chair by the unlit fireplace, one side of his head and upper body bathed in light from the window in the wall. Will, Ewan, and I stood in what felt to me like darkness in the middle of the large, wood-panelled room.

All three of us moved obediently to sit facing him on three straight-backed wooden chairs, and as Will cleared his throat nervously, I looked about me, noting the richness with which I was surrounded. Sir William's house was as big and solid as its owner, built of sandstone and far more grand than the house in Ellerslie where I had lived for the past two years with his brother's family. The room in which we now sat had two windows and housed a heavy table with eight plain wooden chairs. The room's only other furnishings were a massive sideboard against the rear wall and a slightly smaller armchair, padded with brightly coloured cushions, that sat across the fireplace from Sir Malcolm's. His wife, Lady Margaret, had gone to the kitchens to prepare food for us.

Will cleared his throat a second time, then launched into his tale—our tale—from the start of it on that already distant-seeming day in Ellerslie a week earlier. Sir Malcolm had already heard it once, a garbled, blurted version, but now he sat stock-still, his fingers in his beard, and listened closely. Will stumbled in his description of what the men had done to the two of us, unsure how much to say or how to phrase it, but Sir Malcolm asked no questions and sat stone-faced throughout the recitation. Only once did his eyes move from Will, and that was to gaze speculatively at Ewan Scrymgeour when Will spoke of how we had come to meet, and eventually his eyes returned to his nephew, who was already talking about the final stage of our journey, leading to our arrival here half an hour earlier. The knight waited until he was sure Will had no more to say, then turned to Ewan.

"You have my gratitude, Master Scrymgeour, but you'll forgive me if I ask a few questions." Ewan's nod of agreement was barely perceptible as Sir Malcolm continued. "Forbye the tragic matter of the murders committed here, which remains to be dealt with but canna be changed, it's clear you saved the boys from further harm and brought them safely here. But I have to ask myself why. Why would a grown man leave his life and walk away from everything he knows to help two lost and hapless stripling boys? Few men I know would do that."

Will had said nothing at all about Ewan's background and had left out the episode of the Ormiston slaughter, because we had decided, he and I, that we owed too much to the archer ever to name him outlaw. Ewan's plan, which we boys had decided to subvert so we could remain with him, had been to deliver us close by Sir Malcolm's house, then continue on his way to Selkirk Forest, where he hoped to join a band of others like himself, living in the green-wood. As it turned out, though, we had been discovered by a large group of Sir Malcolm's own workers, who had brought us to the home farm to meet their master face to face.

"Aye, yon's a fair question and I'll answer it fairly." There was no hint of subservience in Ewan's voice. He spoke as a free man addressing an equal. The big archer flexed his fingers and sat up straight in his chair. "I buried my mother the day before we left to come here, and there was nothing to hold me there any longer. No friends, no loyalties, nothing to bind me. The boys were alone and helpless, headed for Elderslie or Paisley. I have friends in Selkirk. So it made sense to me to see them safely here in passing."

A silence filled the room, broken only by the song of a blackbird beyond the windows. Finally Sir Malcolm nodded. "Friends in Selkirk, aye ... That would be in the forest there, I'm thinking?"

Ewan dipped his head again. "Aye, Sir Malcolm. In the forest."

Sir Malcolm rose from his chair and went to stand by the window, gazing out, his hands clasped loosely at his back. "It comes to me that I know no one in all these parts who has friends in Selkirk Forest," he said softly. "In the town, yes. I have two friends in the town. It is a small place. But in the forest? No. The men there are ... different. What did you do to earn their friendship, these men?"

"Nothing. I have never met a one of them. My home forest is Ettrick."

"Ettrick Forest covers all of south Scotland, with Selkirk Forest but a part of it. You are an archer."

"Aye, sir, I am. Trained in England and in Wales. I fought with Prince Edward."

Sir Malcolm turned back slowly, silhouetted now against the window's light. "Did you, now? I hear he is a doughty fighter. And what happened to make you change?"

For the first time, Ewan looked surprised. "He turned to invade Wales, to conquer my folk and make us part of England. I am but half Welsh, but I would have no part of that, and my father was newly dead, so I came to Scotland to care for my mother, who was Welsh."

"Scrymgeour. Your father was a Scot?"

"Aye, from Kyle. Bruce country."

"Archers are seldom farmers."

"True. Nor am I one."

"Your father did not own a farm?"

"Once, he did. But it was hard, sour ground. He fell sick and could not work. And then he died."

"So what entitles you to live in Ettrick Forest?"

I was having difficulty making sense of what was being said here because the two men were talking obliquely, their tones, although I could not see how, evidently conveying more than their mere words. I glanced at Will and saw from the frown between his brows that he was as perplexed as I was.

"*Entitles* me?" Ewan's voice was suddenly harder, and he moved his jaw in a way that emphasized the disfigurement of his mashed nose. "I might argue with you, Sir Malcolm, on your choice of words. But the entitlement, if such it was, sprang from the ill nature of a bullying, strutting fool who thought himself all-powerful."

Sir Malcolm's head tilted slightly.

"My mother, rest her soul, was a healer," Ewan continued. "Had been one all her life and was famed for it. A good woman with a good calling. A local lairdling had an infant son who fell sick, and so he sent his people to fetch her, to cure the boy. But the child was beyond help. He died of whatever ailed him and his mother named my mother witch and they tried to hang her. I saved her life, but in the doing of it blood was spilt and I was outlawed."

"What lordship was this?"

Ewan met the older man's eye. "Ormiston."

"Of Dumfries? Sir Thomas?"

"No, sir. Of Clewes, Sir Walter."

"Thomas's brother. I know him well. You call him fool, but he is not."

"Sir Walter is dead, sir, these three years. His son William is now Laird of Ormiston."

"Aha. And he seems not to be the man his father was. Is that what you are telling me?"

"I tell you nothing, Sir Malcolm. I was but answering your question."

"Aye, right." Sir Malcolm hesitated. "You said you saved your mother's life, yet buried her but recently. Were the two events connected?"

"Aye, sir. They found her again, in a place where I thought her safe."

"And?"

"They hanged her."

"I see. And this time you were not close enough to save her."

"No. But they were still close by when I arrived. They sought to hang me, too."

"And?"

"They will hang no more old folk. Nor young, for that matter."

"And so you head for Selkirk … How many did you kill?"

Ewan sniffed. "All of them. I am an archer. They had clubs and blades."

Sir Malcolm was frowning. "How many?"

"Fourteen men, all save one of them hirelings bought and brought to keep the local folk in terror. And four dogs."

"Sweet Jesus! And William of Ormiston?"

"He was the fourteenth man."

Sir Malcolm's frown deepened to a scowl, and suddenly Will spoke up, his voice taut with urgency. "He was trying to kill us, Uncle. The man Ormiston. Ewan had left him alive. We were watching from the slope above and he came at us, trying to ride us down. His horse almost trampled Jamie, but he rolled clear and the rider turned around again to kill him with his sword, and Ewan shot him from the valley bottom, two hundred yards below us."

The tense, dark brows smoothed slightly and the eyes beneath them turned to Ewan. "Is that true?"

The big man shrugged. "It was a touchy shot. I might easily have missed and had but one arrow left."

"From so far away?"

"It was a good distance. I made the shot."

"And my nephew and his cousin are here. Then we have much to thank you for, it seems. More than I thought."

"Not much. I was there, and I was fortunate not to miss. After that, the walking was simple, since we were all headed eastward."

"You could have travelled southeast and sent the boys on alone."

"Aye, but I enjoyed the company along the road and I was in no great haste."

"Hmm. And now what?"

Ewan smiled. "And now, if you will grant me your blessing, I'll move on south, to Selkirk."

I sensed Will look at me but I resisted the temptation to look back, knowing that his eyes would be filled with apprehension, for if Ewan left now, so too would Will's newborn dream of mastering the longbow.

Sir Malcolm looked from Will to me, his gaze lingering on each of us, before he turned back to Ewan. "You say you buried your mother. Will she be found?"

"Not easily, no. They found her alive, but they'll no' find her grave."

"And the others. Will they find them?"

"Aye, sooner rather than later. I left them where they fell, made no attempt to hide them. They were too many. But I cut my arrows out of them before I left."

"Because someone might have recognized them?"

"No. Because they were all I had, too valuable to leave behind."

"And think you anyone will believe a single man killed all of them? Fourteen, you said, and four dogs?"

The question surprised Ewan, for his eyes widened. "Aye, that's the number, but that thought had not occurred to me."

"Nor would it to most men. Whoever finds them will believe they were surprised by an armed band. No one will imagine a single man might be to blame. But will they think to name you as the leader?"

"No." Ewan's headshake was firm. "I had not been seen in those parts for more than two years until that day, and none expected to see me then."

"So you will not be accused. You are sure you left none alive?"

"I am."

Sir Malcolm nodded abruptly. "So be it, then. Blessings come in many guises. You can stay here with us, if you would like. No one knows you here, save the boys, and God knows I can find employment for a man of your size and strength."

"So be you mean that and are not jesting with me, I will stay gladly."

Sir Malcolm slapped his hands on his thighs and surged to his feet, unaware of the elation with which Will had beaten him to it. "It is done, then," he growled. "Welcome to Elderslie and to my household. Now I have much to do. I must send word of the boys' tale to Ayr, to the Countess of Carrick. My murdered family's blood cries out for justice and she will know what to do. I doubt the husband's there yet. Robert Bruce has troubles in his own lands of Annandale, and young Will's two brothers ride with him. The Countess will pass on the word to where it needs to go. Then I must summon my brother Peter and my cousin Duncan here, to meet these lads and help me decide what should be done with them. In the meantime, you three are hungry and road weary, so we will feed you and find you a place to sleep for a few hours, and after that you'll feel much better.

"Now, let's be about our business."

2

I thought at first that I would dislike my cousin Duncan the monk, for he looked cold and unfriendly the first time I set eyes upon him, but I was to learn that he was one of those men whose forbidding exterior conceals a vastly different reality. Of all men I have known, save only Ewan Scrymgeour, there has been none whom I loved more than my perpetually scowling cousin, for Brother Duncan Wallace's soul was a brilliant light shut up inside a leather bottle, its luminous purity glimpsed but occasionally through a dried seam. He was a transcriptor at Paisley Abbey, responsible for the translation, copying, illumination, maintenance, and welfare of the library's priceless manuscripts. Though at our first meeting I knew none of those words, and far less what they entailed, I quickly came to know them more than passing well, for they became my life as Duncan passed his great love of them on to me.

His cousin, Father Peter, was a priest at the Abbey, as open and friendly as Brother Duncan seemed aloof and distant, and Will and I both liked him immediately. He welcomed us with wide-stretched arms, and then, as though it were the most natural thing in the world, he invited us to walk with him around his brother's grounds, and there he spoke to us of Will's parents and the happy times he had shared with them. By the time we arrived back at the house, both of us felt we had known Father Peter all our lives.

The family gathering that followed was precisely that: a gathering of Sir Malcolm's family, with ourselves as the new additions. Lady Margaret was there—*presiding* was the word that occurred to me immediately upon seeing her matronly presence—as were her two younger sons, Henry and Malcolm, aged fourteen and twelve. The eldest son, Steven, was squire to a knight in Lanercost, we learned, and had not been home for a year. The family's two daughters were also in attendance, Isabelle, the younger at seven, being firmly kept in her place by her older sister Anne, who, even at eleven, showed signs of becoming a beauty. In addition to these, clustered around the table were Sir Malcolm, his brother Peter, his cousin Duncan, myself and Will. Ewan attended as Sir Malcolm's guest and stood at the rear of the room, close by the doors, leaning back against the wall with his hands clasped loosely in front of him as he watched.

This was only the second time I had ever seen Ewan without his longbow and quiver—even when they were not hanging from his body, they were usually within his reach. But this was also the first time I had ever seen him around children other than myself and Will. It was obvious that the children, especially the girls, had been severely warned about their behaviour, but children are children, and I had seen the fearful glances they cast in Ewan's direction. He had seen them too, of course, and carefully avoided making eye contact with either little girl and kept his face expressionless—insofar as that was possible—at all times.

The wide-eyed children often turned to stare at Will and me as Sir Malcolm told them, in a greatly simplified version, the story of what had befallen us in Ellerslie and later on the road. That we would join the family as adopted sons was not disputed, but there was more to be decided concerning our futures. Will and I could have happily blended into the family's life, working on the farm to earn our keep, but Father Peter and Brother Duncan were firm in their opinion that we should be educated as befitted our stations as the sons of a landowner and the adopted sons of a belted knight. Father Peter suggested that we be sent to Paisley Abbey as students, where he and Brother Duncan could oversee our studies. Sir Malcolm glanced at Lady Margaret, who nodded, and then he thumped his fist upon the table and declared it should be so.

I was excited at the prospect of going to school in the Abbey. Even in the far west, in Kyle, we had heard tell of the great Cluniac Priory of Paisley that had been famed for a hundred years before being raised to the exalted status of an Abbey. It was one of the wonders of the realm, as grand as the famed sanctuaries at St. Andrews, Glasgow, York, and London.

Will, though, was far from happy with what was transpiring. I could see both misery and panic in his eyes as he tried to come up with a sound reason for objecting to the elders' proposal. Paisley lay seven miles from Elderslie, a mere two-hour walk at a fast pace. But that time doubled if you had to return within the day, and we already knew that Will's scholastic life as a student in Paisley would be too full to permit any such effort. He would not have four clear hours and more in any day—and that fact eclipsed any possibility of his being able to work with Ewan on his archery. Both of us knew that Ewan had made no such commitment to Will, but Will ignored that truth. He was determined to become a longbow archer, and he was determined that Ewan Scrymgeour would be his tutor and trainer.

The entire dilemma was resolved within moments, however, when Sir Malcolm brought up the matter of our lodging. We could live at the Abbey, he said, as part of the establishment, but having endured and hated the same regimen himself as a boy, he believed that complete immersion in the Abbey's life might be unhealthy for us over the long term if we were not cut out by nature for the priesthood. Better, he suggested—ignoring the startled silence from the two clerics at the table—that we study at the Abbey school for the sake of our minds but remain lodged outside the precincts for the sake of our growth and independence.

Father Peter expressed his dismay at that, pointing out what he perceived to be obvious: the mere idea of our living unsupervised beyond the Abbey and its discipline was untenable, he said. We were too young to know our own minds, and that, to him, opened us and our immortal souls to great risk.

Sir Malcolm sat back in his chair and eyed his brother shrewdly. "It is not their souls I am concerned about, Peter, but their minds," he growled. "You and your brethren should be able to see to their souls. My thought is to ensure their minds are left free to grow without being influenced by too much … sanctity."

He raised a hand to forestall the other, whose eyes had gone wide with pious outrage. "I know, I know what you're thinking and I've heard it before. There canna be such a thing as too much sanctity. But I am here to tell you that there can. I, too, studied at the Abbey. The years I spent there taught me many things, among them the basic truth that while some men and stripling boys may thrive on being surrounded all the time with clouds of incense and constant choruses of prayer and hymns, others will not. I was one who did not, and I thank God I had the will and strength of mind to come through it unscathed. But I could name you others who did not fare so well, men who, as young lads, lacked the temperament that you call vocation, yet lacked the strength forbye to overcome the guilt of being seen by themselves and others as unfit to hear the calling. To this day many of those who survive are blighted by their failure, condemned to live as half-formed beings, neither men nor priests. Unable to enjoy the companionship of women yet incapable of renouncing them, they live between the two worlds of normal humanity and sanctity. I will not risk that happening to my wards, and if you seek to argue with me you will leave my house, so pay attention to me. I am not proposing anything unfitting, merely that the boys live outside the Abbey while they study within it. As to their ability to do so without supervision, I take your meaning and I am not entirely witless." He turned in his chair to look towards the rear of the room. "Master Scrymgeour, will you come forward?"

A quick frown came to Ewan's face, but he moved towards the table obediently and stood behind Brother Duncan at the lower end, directly opposite Sir Malcolm.

"We are all in your debt, Master Scrymgeour, and I told you on the day that you arrived that I could easily find work for you here in my household should you wish to stay. It comes to me now that I have a more important task for you than I originally thought."

Ewan was still frowning slightly.

"An uncle of ours died three years ago in Paisley, another Malcolm Wallace. He was my godfather and I was named for him. He was old and had outlived all his family, and so his farm and his lands passed down to me." I saw Father Peter's expression soften as he realized where this might be leading, and he sat back in his chair "It is a small farm," Sir Malcolm continued, "though larger than some around it, and it has pleasant lands attached to it—a large apple orchard, a fine paddock, and several arable fields of good size, forbye the house itself and surrounding byres and pigpens. I have done nothing with it these three years, despite my best intentions, and I fear it is falling into disrepair.

"Now, I know you have said you are not a farmer, but your father was, and this place I speak of is far richer and more fertile than your father's place that you described to me. If you have any feeling for the land at all, I think you might enjoy it. I wouldna set you to the plough, though, unless you chose to be a ploughman. You would be my overseer, your charge to see the farm well kept and well worked, without theft or shirking by the men I'd send you. The house is big enough to need a cook and a housekeeper, and large enough to accommodate you and my two new charges. By day you would be my factor. By night, you would tend and guard the boys, keeping them at their books and out of mischief. What say you?"

Ewan's eyes had grown wider as he listened, and now the big archer hesitated, looking from Will to me to Sir Malcolm. "You would entrust me with this?"

"I would, for I believe you worthy of trust. I decided that when first we spoke in this very room, you and I. As well, these boys have seen much evil this past week, but they appear to see no evil in you. Were it otherwise, I wouldna have mentioned it."

Ewan hesitated again, then nodded decisively. "Then I will do it. Gladly."

3

I loved the library at the Abbey from the moment I first saw it, despite the glowering look of displeasure from its warden, Brother Duncan, each time he thought I came too close to touching any of the treasures on display there. The occasion was our first day as students, and we were taken on a tour of the Abbey and its precincts by a visibly long-suffering monk called Brother James, who left us in no doubt of our menial status as newcomers and ignoramuses.

We had begun by visiting the Abbey church itself, primarily because it was empty of priests and worshippers at that time of day, after morning prayers and before nones, the afternoon prayer gathering that would fill the church again. And seeing it deserted, we experienced its humbling vastness, craning our necks as we peered up at the massively vaulted roof that was so far above us that its height defied belief. We stood abashed, side by side in front of the high altar, speechless with awe at the opulence of the shrine and the sheer scope of the sacred space surrounding us.

Brother James gave us little time to absorb its beauty, though. He hustled us away, impatiently identifying the various areas of the building, from nave to transept, sanctuary and choir, baptismal font to votive chapels to confessionals, telling us where we would be permitted to go and where we were forbidden to approach, let alone trespass, and he sneered at every turn, as though incredulous that anyone could be as ignorant as we were of such self-evident verities.

When we had finished in the church, he hurried us along the cloistered walkway outside to the corner of a vast quadrangle that lay beyond the Abbey proper, striding so quickly that we almost had to run to keep up with him. Meanwhile he spat out the names and functions of all the buildings that surrounded the quadrangle, all necessary to the maintenance of such a complex community: stables and dairy, cowsheds, pigsties and goat pens and sheep cotes and fowl yards and stone-built barns of fodder for all those creatures; wool manufactories with wheels for spinning yarn; charcoal pits; sawyers' pits; a shoemaker and cobbler's shop; a busy smithy filled with smoke and sparks and noise; a wheelwright's shop; a harness maker's barn for saddlery and trappings; pottery manufactories with potters' wheels and kilns for baking pots and bricks; bakeries and a brewery; tanneries and a cooperage where new-made barrels were stacked up to the roof; dyeing vats and felting ponds stinking of sheep's urine, and clothmakers' galleries with different-sized looms and what seemed like miles of shelving laden with bolts of woven fabric. There were also carpentry shops and stonemasons' yards; metal and glassmakers' foundries; roofed threshing floors surrounded with bales of straw and mountains of hay; a stream-fed mill for grinding grain; storage houses for lumber, fine woods, grains, oats, barley, flour, hides, beer, and a hundred other things, and a long, low building in a far corner of the complex where the sole occupation of the brothers assigned there was the manufacture and preparation of fine vellum sheets for use in the scriptorium, the writing room attached to the library. And, of course, there were men everywhere, swarming like ants wherever I looked, and so I asked Brother James how many monks were in the community.

He stopped in mid-word, plainly astonished that I would dare to interrupt him, and an angry surge of red suffused his narrow face. "That is none of your affair," he said venomously. "Suffice you should know there are enough to live and work together to keep the likes of you in more comfort than you merit." And then he strode away, not waiting for us to follow. I looked at Will and saw the broad grin on his face, and I knew two things with certainty: I had made an enemy on my first day here, and Brother James had never had any idea of, nor interest in, the size of the community to which he belonged.

Hurrying to fall into place behind him again, I wondered how that could be so, and suddenly, even at that young age, I understood that such oblivion, for many men, must spring from a monkish and unchallenging existence. Brother James's place within the Abbey's ranks was finite, his duties clearly defined. He had no need for curiosity, no reason to explore his surroundings. By asking him a question that he could not answer, I had, in his mind, attempted to belittle him. I resolved to say not another word that day.

My resolution vanished as soon as we entered the library. I still remember the awe, verging upon sanctity, that swept over me as soon as I crossed the threshold. Though I often thought, afterwards, that *sanctity* should have been a strange descriptive after having so recently seen the majestic interior of the Abbey church, I never sought to change it, because the reverence I felt in those first few moments never faded, and it remains with me to this day. This, I knew instinctively, was a place of wonders and incalculable value, of power and mysticism, of great learning and knowledge, and of immense worth, inestimable beauty, and abiding peace and tranquility—grand words, I know, for a small boy, who knew none of them at that time and nothing at all about libraries.

I know I stood gape-mouthed, because Brother James hissed angrily and pushed me sharply forward into the soaring space that was filled with light, brilliant with stark-edged sunbeams and dancing dust motes. I knew the floor beneath my feet was of flagged stone like all the other floors, but somehow it felt softer, cushioning my soles from making any noise that would disturb the peace. Scattered throughout the central space were tables, some large, some small, some flat, and others sloped like pitched roofs, and all of them covered with books and parchments.

I saw three men in there at first, then four and then five, all of them hard at work. Two of them glided silently along the walls beneath high, pointed windows filled with thousands of tiny, diamond-shaped panes of clear, green-tinged glass, each man stooping to peer into deep, box-like shelves filled with rolled parchments and big leather-bound books. The other three sat hunched, with pens in their hands, each focused on the parchment sheet in front of him. Brother James cleared his throat loudly and all five men turned to us. One of the three writers rose from his seat and came swiftly towards us.

I heard Will quietly gasp, and then I recognized the sombre, scowling face of Brother Duncan.

"Brother Armarius," our guide greeted him. "These two are new boys. Father Abbott instructed me to show them the Abbey and to bring them here last." He did not attempt to name us, and I knew he could not have done so. To him, we were nameless nuisances, inflicted upon him as a penance for some unremembered sin.

Brother Duncan, or Brother Armarius, ignored us, looking without expression at our guide.

"And so you have completed your duty?"

"After this, aye, Brother."

I turned to whisper something to Will, but before I could open my mouth, a stinging blow to my ribs made me catch my breath in pain.

"Silence!" Brother James hissed. "Keep your mouth shut in the presence of Brother Armarius."

Will stepped in front of me, raising clenched fists and glaring at Brother James. "Keep your hands to yourself," he snarled.

Brother James swung his hand hard at Will's face, but before the blow could land it was caught firmly by Brother Duncan.

"That will be all, Brother James," Duncan said quietly, releasing the other's wrist slowly. "You may return to your duties. I will see to these two."

Brother James glared, his pinched face flushed again, but then he dropped his eyes and nodded. "As you wish, Brother Armarius. I pass them to your care." He threw one last, venomous glance at us, and then he stalked away, his sandals scraping on the stone floor until the solid thud of the door closing at his back left us in silence again.

Our cousin looked down at both of us, his face disapproving. "This is the library," he said. "I am its custodian. I believe it to be the most sacred place in all the Abbey, save for the sanctuary itself. I am not without prejudice, admittedly, but there is nothing within these walls, within this library, that any single person could afford to purchase, even were that possible. Nothing in here is for sale, and nothing has an assigned value. Everything you see here, and much that you will never see, is beyond price, for there are no duplicates, other than those we make ourselves here in this room. So you may look but you must never touch anything. Is that clear?"

When we had both nodded in acknowledgment, he walked to the closest table, where he waved a hand over the single sheet of parchment that lay there, its colours, gold, crimson, blue, and bright green, coruscating in the bright sunlight that shone down on it. "This piece was made more than seven hundred years ago." He stopped, giving us time to react appropriately to this unimaginable span of time, then picked the document up reverently, and set it down carefully out of the direct light. "Sunlight can harm it, leach the colours. This came from Ireland, from a monastery at a place called Kells, and the name of the man who made it is forever lost. Think of that. A faceless, nameless monk, working alone, in close to darkness for countless years, created it to the glory of God. It is unique. Our very finest artists cannot duplicate it. Copy it, yes, but poorly, inadequately, for we have lost the secret of the pigments and cannot replicate the colours. Do you begin to see why I permit none but myself and a few others to touch it?"

We nodded, and he dipped his head in return. "Good. Come, then, and meet those others."

With that, we were introduced to the other monks in the room, Brothers Anselm, Joseph, Bernard, and Bede. Brother Joseph was the eldest and most frail, his bald, mottled pate fringed with wispy, pure white hair. Brother Anselm and Brother Bernard were next in age, and Brother Bede was the youngest, with a full beard and a head of dense, curly black hair surrounding the shaved square of his tonsure. Brother Duncan introduced us by name, although he made no mention of our relationship to him, and all of them welcomed us warmly, the first members of the community at large to do so. Bede and Bernard were librarians, tasked with the care of the library's contents, while the other three were transcriptors, who spent their entire time copying the collection's most valuable texts.

Brother Duncan then led us on a journey around the library, explaining what it held and how it functioned. It was easy to tell that he loved his library, and yet his grim face never relaxed from its scowling watchfulness, which led me to think he did not really want us there. When we had completed a full circuit of the room, he asked us if we had any questions.

"If you please, Brother, I heard—" My voice had emerged as a squeak, and I coughed and tried again, relieved to hear it come out normally this time. "Brother James called you Brother Armarius, but I thought your name was Brother Duncan. Which is correct?"

A sudden change came over his face and his eyes gleamed, so that I thought, for the merest instant, that he was about to smile. But then his face resumed its normal expression.

"Both are correct. I am Brother Duncan and Brother Armarius, but the first is the mere man, while the other is a title. The word *armarius* means provisioner, and it describes my duties. I am the director of the scriptorium, this room in which my colleagues and I work. One of my responsibilities is to provide the material that we need—inks and pens and parchment and fine brushes. Another is to supervise the work being done. Thus the armarius is a form of supervisor. Do you know that word? Excellent. Then I am the supervisor here. I have other duties within the Abbey as armarius, but you will learn of those later. For the time being, supervisor will suffice, and

my brethren address me as Brother Armarius. Do you understand
now?"

"Yes, Brother," I said.

He looked from one to the other of us then. "And what think you
of our library? Be frank."

Will shrugged vaguely, but I had no qualms about what was in
my mind. I told Brother Duncan that his library was the most
wondrous place I had ever seen, and I meant every word I said.

He studied me for a few moments, his lips pursed. "Then you
may see it again someday," he said. "But now we must return you to
the Abbey. Father Peter is waiting for you and will tell you all about
your tasks, your daily duties, your tutors, and your classes. Off with
you, then. Brother Bede will see you safely to where you must be."

4

Our first year as pupils at the Abbey school quickly defined
the differences that would circumscribe our lives from that
point on, although neither Will nor I was aware of
anything unusual occurring at the time. Our bright new life in
Paisley was *too* new, too different, and too exciting for either one
of us to have concern for subtleties or self-examination. We were
healthy boys, full of enthusiasm and engrossed by the challenges
thrown at us daily, and we were too involved in conquering the
ever-changing aspects of our diverging pathways even to be aware
of the divergence.

We shared a single room at night, in truckle beds that we stowed
upright against the wall each morning, and we were up and astir
every day before dawn, grateful for the few extra hours of sleep we
would have lost to prayer had we been lodged at the Abbey. Ewan
was frequently up and about before we awoke, but Aggie the cook
served breakfast to us every day—oatmeal and bannock invariably,
with goat's milk to wash it down, and, very infrequently, a slice of

salted pork or venison that was delicious to eat but always made us thirst long before the noon break in our lessons.

I was the scholar, Will the earnest, plodding student. Latin, Greek, French, and mathematics came so easily to me that I barely thought of them as tasks; they were simple pleasures that I soaked up like sunshine. For Will, though, they were chronic tribulations that he tackled grimly every day, jaws clenched, eyes squinting in ferocious concentration. Latin and French he mastered eventually with much help from me, but Greek remained Greek to him— incomprehensible. Simple arithmetic he grasped easily, but the more arcane elements of mathematics, the recently discovered algebraic calculations from Arabia, failed to capture his interest. It was the same with the more classical elements of what the monks tried to teach him: the theories of logic and polemic were lost on Will, and yet he would debate some point of philosophy for hours, principally because some assertion of Augustine of Hippo, or Plato or Aristotle, had struck a chord in him, challenging or confirming something he believed intuitively.

Now that I think about it, it may have been at that time, towards the end of our first scholastic year, that I first began to suspect my cousin lacked imagination. I was very young at the time, of course, but I had been soaking up knowledge like a sponge for close to a twelvemonth by then and I can remember being puzzled about what I sometimes saw as a startlingly obvious inability in Will to connect salient points of a debate; to make intuitive leaps from one abstract notion to another. God Himself knows William Wallace had no diffi- culties with logical thought or decisive action, but something occa- sionally troubled me about the way he would seem to hamper his own progress in a manner that struck me as obtuse. I remember, hazily, one of our teachers saying something about Will being unable to assimilate shades of grey in striving for a goal. I know that Will saw life, particularly in later years, in black and white: bad and good, darkness and light, perfidy and honour.

Or perhaps I never did think of him as lacking in imagination, if I am truthful here. The gulf between ten years of age and seventy is vast, and memory can make fools of us, so my opinion on these things might be misguided, formed unwittingly in retrospect while mulling over all that William Wallace did and might have done.

Be that as it may, a different rule applied at eveningtide. Released from our scholastic studies each afternoon just before vespers, we would hurry home to eat, and then our daily studies with Ewan would begin, and in those our roles were completely reversed. This was the arena within which Will Wallace soared while I stumbled behind him; here he was the gifted and intuitive disciple offering advice and assistance to me while I laboured in his wake, flailing and floundering as I tried to absorb the lessons and the disciplines that to him were the basic elements of life.

We had no bows at first. Instead, every day after school in the first week after our move to Paisley, Ewan took us deep into the surrounding greenwood, where we spent the hours until dusk, each evening for six days, finding and then painstakingly selecting eight straight, heavy lengths of sapling ash and elm, the thinnest no less than a full thumb's length wide and the thickest half that width again. Our search was for whole young trees that contained a straight length greater by a hand's span than the length of each of our bodies and did so without tapering, which meant we had to gauge each selection with great care before we cut it, and then trim it so that when we held it close it rose perfectly straight from the ground at our feet to where we could hold its upper end with the base of our hands resting on the top of our foreheads. It was not a simple task, and the time taken to complete it reflected that: six whole evenings to find and cut eight poles. But then, these were not mere poles: each of them was an axis around which our training, our entire lives as Ewan's students, would revolve for the next two years, until we outgrew them and had to make new ones.

The next stage of our instruction started immediately after Mass the following day, which was a Sunday, our only day of rest from school. As soon as we arrived home from the Abbey after morning Mass, Ewan set us to work. Each of us began with a staff of green elm, solid and heavy with sap. We stripped it of bark and then rubbed it with a compound of alum that Ewan provided, which soaked up the natural slippery outer juice of the wood, leaving it smooth and dry to the touch. We set these two aside for what Ewan called daily use, although we had no idea at the time what that meant, and turned our attention to the other six, stripping those as we had the first pair, while Ewan cut long, finger-wide strips of leather from a cured hide. He had a big iron pot of water boiling over the fire, and he immersed the strips in the boiling pot until they were supple again. Then he pulled them out one by one with a pair of tongs and laid them to cool on the stone floor. We stopped for a meal at noon, and as soon as we were finished, Ewan tested each of the stripped poles for straightness, holding each one up to his eye to peer along its length. He then separated them into groups of three, one elm and two ash in each, and had Will and me hold each bundle securely while he bound it tightly with the wet strips of hide.

That was slow work, and clamping the poles together for so long taxed our hands and arms sorely. Ewan worked patiently and methodically, knotting the strips together end to end until he had several individual strips each five or six paces long. Then he knotted six long lengths together at one end and wove them tightly around the rods in careful, overlapping spirals from top to bottom. When the bundles were fully bound, he gathered the overlapping ends at the bottom of each, clamped them between the jaws of an iron clamp, and twisted them tightly until Will and I could no longer hold the bundle steady against the torque. He then bade Will hold the bundle securely while I took hold of the clamp, and while we strained against each other, fighting to keep the tension he had gained, he bound the twisted ends together with another tool, a long, bent iron needle into which he fed the end of yet another wet strip and knitted it tightly crosswise through the clamped bindings. When he had finished, he straightened up, tossing the first bound package into the air and catching it again.

"There," he said. "That should do the job. Now all they have to do is dry properly, which will keep them from warping."

Will's head jerked up. "What's warp?"

"Twisting out of true. By the time they warp, they'll be dry, and when they're dry we can fix the warp. It's tedious, but it can be done."

"How do you do it?"

Ewan rubbed his hairless pate. "You take the warped stave, soak it with hot steam, and bend it until it's straight again. All it takes is time and a measure of care."

"Will these warp, d'you think?"

"Not if we watch them and tend them carefully. The leather straps will dry as hard as iron. We'll set them on the rafters here above the fireplace and turn them every day so that they never get too much heat on any side for too long. That way, they should dry evenly."

Will studied the bundles. "You haven't told us what they're for."

Ewan raised his hairless eyebrows. "What do you think they're for?"

"To make bows."

"No, they are not, so you're wrong. That must be a new feeling for you, eh?" His toothless grin removed any sting from the words. "When they're done they'll be what the English call quarterstaffs. And before you ask, a quarterstaff is a fighting stick for men who can't afford a sword. They've been around for hundreds of years. The ancient Romans used them. They're twice the weight of a sword and you'll learn to fight with them as swords. Then, if you ever have to use a real blade, it will seem featherlight in your hands."

"I don't *want* to use a sword," Will said. "I want to learn to use a bow."

"I know that, boy, but look at yourself. And look at Jamie here. And then look at me." He quickly shrugged his tunic over his head, baring his upper body, and as we gaped at him he crossed his arms on his chest and grasped his enormous shoulder muscles, then tensed himself and raised his elbows forward stiffly to display the corded strength of his forearms, the bull-like thickness of his massive torso, and the pillar of his neck. Beneath the taut arch of his ribs, his belly bulged with twin columns of muscled plates.

"Here's what you're lacking, lads," he said, making his belly muscles twist and writhe from side to side like some thick snake. "Thews. Archers' muscles." He dropped his arms and reached for his tunic. "You'll never pull a bow until you have them, and the quarterstaff's the only thing that will give them to you. You'll use it every day, hour after hour until you can't lift your arms and the staff falls from your fingers, and then you'll rest until the blood returns and start all over again."

He faced Will. "You want to be an archer, William Wallace? Well, I'll teach you to be one and you'll hate me while I'm doing it. But I promise you, within this year you'll see the benefits of the quarterstaff. You'll see muscles growing where you don't have places yet. And once you've seen the first of them, you'll never want to stop. Believe me on that." He pointed at the two lengths of stripped elm that we had set aside at the start. "Those are your first ones, and they're green with sap—wet and heavy and cumbersome. They'll introduce you to the pains of becoming a warrior. Tomorrow, after school, I'll teach you how to hold one."

He spoke the truth, and we spent the whole of the next evening learning how to hold a quarterstaff. Anyone with hands can grasp a stick, we thought at first, so whence was the promised difficulty to come? The answer, of course, lay in what we had not yet considered: a quarterstaff is not a mere stick of wood but a potent weapon, and there are many ways to hold one but only a very few in which to hold one effectively. And so began three months of torment as we sought in vain to please our tutor, whose amiable nature had vanished when we first laid hold of those elm staves. He made us work so hard, so endlessly, that by day I found myself falling asleep at my lessons and often incapable of closing my bruised fingers on my pen, a situation that too often drew my tutors' disapproval.

But then came a day when I survived my entire schedule of lessons without lapse or mishap and began to realize that the agonies that had plagued me for so long were no longer noticeable. I went directly to Will with the news, and he told me that his, too, had died away, and we marvelled together over the difference, wondering what had caused it. The regimen so grimly imposed on us each evening by Ewan was no less brutal or demanding; he still badgered us relentlessly for hours each day, driving us harder and faster every time, but the pains had receded and the effort we expended on our drills no longer sapped us to exhaustion.

Three months had elapsed by then. A month later, Ewan had been summoned to Elderslie by Sir Malcolm, leaving us with an unaccustomed gap in our after-school training. It was late summer, and so Will and I had gone swimming in the river that flowed near our house.

"Wait," Will cried out as I prepared to dive back into the pool from which I had just emerged. He was standing neck-deep in water, fanning his arms to hold himself in place against the sluggish current. "Wait you. Stay there."

"What?" I said hastily, looking down at my loins. "Is there a leech on me?"

He launched himself forward and swam until he was directly below me, then stood again and peered up at me, flicking the wet hair out of his eyes. I still could see no leech, though the thought of one unnerved me. I loathed the things.

"Where is it, the leech?"

"There's no leech," he said. "I see muscles. Your belly's hard and your shoulders have grown out. And look at your arms."

I looked, but could see no difference there from the last time I had looked. And then I realized what he was talking about, even before he went on to say, "Ewan was right. You're growing muscles where you had none before. What about me, am I?"

He pulled himself up onto the bank, and as I looked at him this time I saw it, the change that had been so gradual that I had not noticed it before. Naked, Will was now far bigger than he had been when we first arrived in Paisley. His shoulders were wider, his chest broader and deeper, and his arms and legs were sculpted with muscles that I had never seen before. So impressed were we, so enthused by what we had discovered, that we raced home to work at our drills without Ewan's supervision for the first time.

Neither one of us had yet raised his staff against the other. All our drills were carried out against an immovable, unconquerable enemy: a thick length of elmwood that neither of us could encircle with our arms. We had found it close by the firewood pile at the bottom of the garden and had helped Ewan to dig a posthole and entrench the thing. Now it reared high above us, impervious to the worst assaults we could inflict on it. For months now, all we had done was hit it with our staves. But four months had brought great change in how we hit it. In the earliest days, our blows had been clumsy—heavy, sullen, and repetitive, aimed at areas that Ewan had marked clearly—and we had tired rapidly without being permitted to rest. Now we could hammer out tattoos on the different marks, using both ends of our staves to attack several simultaneously. The sound of our hammering blows was as fast and clear as the rapping of a woodpecker.

The staves now felt natural to us, extensions of our arms and hands, and our minds and eyes directed our assaults without conscious thought. Little wonder our bodies were now responding visibly to what we had demanded of them. As we had grown inured to the monotony of the drills, we had devised another use for them; the regular, rhythmic staccato of our drumming blows turned out to be the perfect accompaniment for the daily exercise of learning our Latin and French vocabulary, so that each evening we would hammer through declensions and conjugations as we belaboured the unyielding post.

When summer turned to autumn that year, Ewan presented each of us with bows that he had made for us, and that occasion was the first time I had ever stopped to wonder what he did all day while we two were at school. The bows were beautiful, made of elmwood and a finger-width flat in section, less than half the size of Ewan's own giant weapon of rounded yew. Each came with a dozen arrows fletched in different colours, blue for me and red for Will, and iron points that sleeved the ends and had no barbs. These were not hunting bows, Ewan told us. They were practice instruments through which we would learn accuracy and rhythm, the two most vital elements of archery.

The following year, he made two more for us, larger this time to fit our growing size, these fashioned of ash and round in section, which gave them greater tension and demanded far more strength in pulling. I worked hard with both bows for the space of those two years, practising diligently until I became adequately skilled, but Will, from the outset, was a prodigy. By the time I was thirteen and he fifteen, from sixty paces I could plant five arrows out of six within the central ring of the straw targets Ewan had built for us. Will could do the same with all six arrows from a hundred paces and group them so closely that they often touched one another in the very centre of the ring. Even Ewan doffed his hood to Will the first time he achieved that feat, but having done it once, Will then proceeded to do it almost every time, steadily increasing the distance of his casts until he could hit the ring from one hundred and sixty-three paces, the extreme range of his ash bow. No matter how he tried, he simply could not hurl a projectile any farther than that distance. But then, he was fifteen years old, and not a single man we knew, other than Ewan, could match him with the same bow. He had already begun supplying fresh game and venison to the Abbey kitchens.

Watching ruefully as Will outstripped me yet again in matters physical, I was facing a difficult decision of my own, one that I knew would lead us apart from each other. Brother Duncan had invited me to work in the library, where I would take over the duties of Brother Bernard, who would in turn replace the aged and increasingly blind Brother Joseph. I knew that to have been invited to replace Brother Bernard was an unprecedented honour for a boy my age. It was also a dream come true for me.

Brother Duncan told me that he believed I had a natural talent for the kind of work to which he had dedicated his life—the study and care of books—and had been watching me closely since my first visit to his library. He had taken note for several years now not only of the frequency of my visits but of the care and attention with which I treated the texts and documents to which I was permitted access. He also enumerated the reasons why I could be forgiven for refusing the position, explaining that the work itself could be injurious to one's health. "Few people recognize how arduous is the writer's path," he said. "It dims the eyes, makes the back ache, and knits the chest and belly together. It is, in short, a terrible ordeal for the whole body."

His warning had no effect. I wanted that librarian's position more than I had ever wanted anything, and no mere threat of physical affliction would deter me from taking it. The single obstacle was my life with Will.

We two had never been apart for any length of time since coming to the Abbey, and everything we had experienced had been shared. I now faced a choice that would alter our relationship forever. I would have to abandon my archery and the sheer enjoyment of all the time spent with Will daily at the butts, and making that break frightened me. Though he knew something was troubling me, I put off telling Will until I had no other choice and no time left.

After five full years of tuition, we spoke to each other all the time in fluent Latin, the primary language of our studies, and he listened carefully to what I had to say, his head cocked in the way I still associate most closely with him. When I had stammered my way through my tale and asked him what I should do, he narrowed his eyes at me. But then, instead of saying anything, he unslung his ashwood bow from across his shoulders and held it up in front of him.

"D'you know what this is?"

I blinked at him. "Of course I do. It's your bow."

"No, Jamie, it's far more than that. This is my life. I know it makes no sense to you, but I live only to master this weapon and I can't say why or how; I only know I have to learn everything there is to know about it and about the craft of it. I have to learn to wring every ounce of power out of it, to cast my arrows farther and more truly than any other man I will ever meet. I have no choice in any part of that and no understanding of why it should be so. It's like being bewitched. It is simply something that consumes me, all the time, and I will never have my fill of it."

He pulled an arrow from his quiver, nocked it, and sent it, almost absent-mindedly, flying into the centre of the target that stood more than a hundred paces away.

"I am an archer. That is what I do, what I am, and it's all I want to be." He slung the bow across his chest again and pulled the bowstring snugly against his back. "You feel the same way about books, Jamie. I know that. Your need to learn about the library is just as strong as my need to learn the bow. So why waste time in wondering if you should? Go and do what you want to do, and do it to the full. You already know all you need to know about archery, but you know almost nothing yet about what you truly love most—your library. I'll miss you in the evenings, but it's not as if we'll never see each other again, is it? You'll still live with me and Ewan, and you can bore me with your talk of inks and parchment just as I'll bore you with mine of bowcraft. But you're not gone yet, so we had better be about our drill, or Ewan will have our heads. Come on."

He hooked an arm around my neck, and I came close to weeping with gratitude.

CHAPTER THREE

I

One Friday morning in February 1286, we were released from our lessons at mid-morning and informed that there would be no more classes that day. This was a rare enough occurrence to be welcomed boisterously by the Abbey's small student body, and there followed a frantic exodus as almost two score of boys sought to escape the premises before some joyless monk could come along and set them all to work at other tasks.

Will and I had been forewarned by Brother Duncan, who had heard from Father Peter what was happening that day, and so we knew that we had no need to run and hide. On those rare occasions when the Abbey was visited by distinguished guests, the entire complement of the brotherhood turned out to honour them and to participate in the ceremonies attending the visits. Today's visitors had come to the Abbey as representatives of the King of Scots, Alexander III. We knew little more than that the Bishop of Glasgow headed the religious element of the deputation.

It was a bright, beautiful day for the time of the year, the third one in succession and a harbinger, everyone hoped, of an early, welcome spring. We made our way contentedly to one of our favourite spots, far enough away from the Abbey buildings to be secure from interruption and yet close enough for us to be able to return quickly in the unlikely event of an alarum being sounded on the iron triangle that hung by the main entrance. Our destination was an oxbow loop in the small river that ran through the heavily wooded area to the north of the Abbey, a place of dappled shadows on a sunny day but one that could be cold, boggy, and treacherous in inclement weather. The loop of the river there was wide and placid, the dry land within the oxbow covered with lush grass. Below an outcrop of rock was a long, chest-deep swimming hole for our personal enjoyment. There were fish in there, speckled trout that hovered, barely visible, at the edge of the current below the falls, and the soft earth of the banks showed the cloven hoof marks of the deer that came there daily to drink.

The main attraction of the place for us was a recent modification, the result of a violent windstorm that had brought down an enormous ash tree athwart the stream the previous spring. At first we had been dismayed, thinking our favourite place ruined. It had taken us several days to become aware that the collapse of the giant had resulted in a double bridge over the deepest part of our swimming hole, the main trunk splitting in such a way as to lay two major limbs side by side and less than three feet apart. We lopped off all the trailing branches, leaving only the two bare poles of the main limbs in place, the thinner of the two resting slightly less than a foot below the level of the other. It was perfect for our purposes, and we had put it to good use throughout the summer and autumn months that followed.

That February day was the first time we had returned to the spot that year, and we wasted no time. Will ran lithely out into the middle of the lower limb and leaned against his staff, propping it on the upper pole and looking down into the water as I sprang up and across the narrow gap to the upper log.

"Sunshine or no," he said, "that water's cold enough to kill the first man in." He leered up at me. "And guess what? It's not going to be me."

"Then we'll both go home dry, for it won't be me, either," I said, grinning back at him.

I remember I felt strong and confident that day, highly aware of my own physique and conditioning. It was true that I was a librarian now and spent much of my time cooped up indoors and out of the sun, but I was far fitter than any of my contemporaries and most of the brotherhood's younger members. Five years and more of constant drill and exercise with the heavy quarterstaves had made a man of me, in physical size at least. I was broad and strong, nimble and sure-footed and filled with energy and stamina. I can see, looking back now, that I was quite proud of myself, but I had good reason. I also had a constant reminder that I should never crow too much, for Will dwarfed me. He towered a full head over me, and his shoulders seemed twice the width of mine. He had legs like tree trunks and arms to match, and his chest was almost as broad and deep as Ewan's though he was not yet seventeen.

It was that difference in our sizes that made the twin bridges perfect for our needs, because the extra height I gained by standing on the upper log fairly cancelled out Will's advantage, and the few extra inches of girth in the log beneath my feet accorded me an added measure of stability and foot room, so that when we faced each other across the narrow gap we were as close as we could come to being evenly matched.

We began slowly—not cautiously, for we knew what we were doing, but we had not stood on the logs for months and they had become coated with a thin film of moss, so our opening moves were tentative, each of us gauging his own balance and ease of mobility rather than paying attention to the other. Finally Will straightened his back.

"Are you ready?"

In reply I hefted my staff in both hands and snapped my arm straight in front of me, rapping one end against the centre of his weapon, but even as I made contact he was whipping his staff away to the side, raising it high and bringing it straight down in a tightly controlled, two-handed slash that would have cracked my skull had I been there to receive it. But I had already swayed back on my heels and raised my own staff in a horizontal block that stopped his attack but left both my hands stinging. He grinned at me and dropped one end of his staff to rest against the log by his feet.

"I almost had you there, Cuz," he said, in that quiet voice I had long since come to recognize as signalling a coming attack, and I took two quick steps to my left, placing myself to the right of his natural swing, fully prepared to take revenge if he lunged at me and missed. He grinned again and shifted his staff to a two-handed grip, and for several moments we manoeuvred opposite each other in watchful silence, each waiting for the other to make an error and invite destruction. When neither of us did, though, and it became plain that neither would, Will straightened up again.

"Basics, then," he murmured, and we went into the fundamentals of our daily drill, our early movements stiff and formal, exactly as we had learned them in the beginning, each move and countermove precise and cleanly executed. As we progressed through the familiar exercises our ease and speed increased, until our staves rang loudly and rhythmically against each other, the intervals between the strikes growing shorter and shorter until the noise was an incessant rattle and the sweat began to roll down our bodies.

And then I saw something from the corner of my eye, and in the instant my concentration broke, Will smashed the staff from my hands, sending it flying to the grassy bank.

"Hold!" I shouted, and he hesitated, his staff already drawn back to push me off my log.

"What?"

"There." I pointed to a cloaked and hooded figure watching us from the trees along the riverbank.

Will glanced over his shoulder and spun immediately to face the silent presence, twirling the heavy quarterstaff in one hand so that it spun in his fingers. "Get your staff," he said to me over his shoulder, and I ran to obey him, not looking at the figure on the other bank again until I had rearmed myself and returned to stand by Will's side. The watcher had not moved, and the shadows of the trees in which he stood obscured him sufficiently that we were unable to tell whether we knew him or not.

"Come out, then, and let us look at you."

Will's voice was quiet yet pitched clearly enough for his words to carry to the fellow, who straightened up from the tree he had been leaning against and stepped into the light. He was a stranger, and as he came into full view he reached up and slipped the hood from his head, exposing a full head of thick, golden, shoulder-length hair that caught the sunlight. The face was young and beardless, barely older than Will's own, and unsmiling as it gazed at us. But it was the size of the fellow, the immense width of the shoulders beneath the cloak, that made me catch my breath. He was almost of a height with Will, I thought, though I could not be sure from the distance that separated us, but he was slimmer somehow. The legs beneath his kilted tunic were long and well formed, bare above the knees and swathed in fur-lined leggings below, the latter secured by criss-crossed leather straps attached to heavily soled, ankle-high boots. His tunic was richly made, some thick, green fabric that marked him as well born; Will and I had never owned, and seldom seen, anything so fine. A heavy, supple leather belt that held a long, sheathed dagger cinched in his narrow waist.

"Have you no manners, then?" Will said in Scots. "Or are you a thief, creeping up on folk to steal whatever takes your fancy?"

I stiffened at the calculated insult of the jibe, but the yellow-haired stranger merely smiled, flashing brilliantly white teeth, and came to stand at the edge of the bank, beside the bridge. He moved like a cat, lithe and flowing, his arms hanging loosely by his sides.

"You have nothing worth stealing," he answered easily, the lilt of his voice proclaiming him a Highlander from the North. "I saw that at first glance." He was still smiling. "I merely wished to cross this bridge and decided to wait until you had thrown the poor wee fellow off before I bothered you for passage."

I drew myself up, stung, but before I could say a word Will waved me to silence. "The poor wee fellow, as you've seen, is no' so easily budged," he replied, his voice dangerously quiet to my ears.

"Aye, I know that now. He is stronger than he looks beside your bulk and he fights well. Well enough to withstand the flailings of an oaf twice his size." His eyes moved to me and I saw that they were startlingly bright blue. "Well done, lad," he said, and then looked back at Will. "Now, if I ask you civilly, will you move off and let me cross?"

I saw the wolfish grin light up Will's face and my stomach churned. I sensed that nothing good could come of this.

"Let him cross, Will."

Will bared his teeth in what I thought of as his mad grin. "Let him cross? I'll do that, Jamie. I'll let him cross. But he'll have to climb over me first." He turned back to the stranger. "Well, Saxon, d'ye think you can do that?"

The stranger pointed at the staff in Will's hand.

"What?" Will asked, all innocence, hefting his staff. "Does this bother you? Think naught o' it. I'll throw it on the bank there and we'll settle this bare-handed, just you and me."

"No, you misunderstand me," the stranger said quietly. "And misjudge me. Mine is Norse blood, not Saxon. My folk were Vikings, on a time. And you may keep your stick, so be it I can borrow your friend's."

"Borrow it?" Will's grin seemed to grow even wider. "Aye, I think you could borrow it. Jamie, hand the man your staff and show him how to hold it."

"No need," said the Viking, as I had already named him. "Throw it to me. I'll manage."

"Will …"

"Just throw it, Jamie. You heard the man."

I bit my lip, knowing this was wrong, and lobbed my quarterstaff across the gap. The stranger caught it easily in one hand, and as I left the bridge he hopped up effortlessly to stand on the upper log, facing Will, who was suddenly frowning, his mad grin vanished. He was now aware, I realized with relief, of the grossly excessive advantage he would have over his unsuspecting opponent.

"Do you know how to use one of these things?" Will's voice was rough now with concern, and I began to feel better, but the Viking merely flicked the hair off his forehead with a toss of his head and took the staff in both hands, holding it as though it were a felling axe.

"I'll manage," he said again, flexing his knees. "Don't worry about me. Look to yourself."

With that he launched a swift attack that left me open-mouthed with shock, a spear-like thrust so fast and well executed that Will had to spring back to avoid it, whipping his staff up in a defensive block that the stranger immediately used against him, dropping to one knee and hooking a vicious crosswise blow under Will's horizontal guard, aiming for his knees and almost connecting as Will leapt back again, giving ground for the second time.

From that point on, their battle was hard and heavy, each of them giving the other the respect due to an opponent who was his match and neither of them taking foolish risks, ever conscious of their footwork on the curved, moss-coated surface of the log beneath their feet.

The tempo increased suddenly as Will's foot caught on a slight bump on the log, throwing him off balance just long enough for his opponent to seize the advantage. As Will swayed, the Viking swung a short-handed, chopping blow that caught him high on his right shoulder. I thought it was all over as soon as I heard the solid thump of the hit, for I knew Will's arm must be deadened, but he surprised me by dropping to one knee, still clutching the right end of his staff with now lifeless fingers, and brought the other end sweeping inward for a crashing blow as powerful as a swung axe, hammering towards the Viking's knees and pivoting through chest and shoulders for added impetus.

It was a prodigious effort, but the Viking's response to it was miraculous to me. Like a threatened cat, he sprang into the air with both feet, drawing his knees clear up to his shoulders as Will's staff whistled through the air where his legs had been a moment earlier, and the blow that would have shattered his knee almost missed him completely. But the tip of the scything staff struck the edge of the thick sole on the Viking's left boot and smashed it sideways, tumbling him violently while he was still close to the top of his mighty leap. He fell headfirst in a sidewise somersault and his skull struck solidly on the log before he slipped into the deep water of our swimming hole. He sank instantly, his eyes closed and blood streaming from his yellow hair.

"Will!" I threw myself forward in a running jump, but even before my feet had left the ground I saw the arc of my cousin's body as he dove ahead of me, and we landed together, one on either side of the sprawling body.

"I have him!" Will shouted, surfacing with his hands beneath the floating shoulders. "Take his legs."

We hauled the inert body onto the bank and knelt beside it, staring in horror at the blood that oozed through the sodden yellow hair. But then the Viking snorted and coughed and writhed away from us, spewing up water, and I thought I had never seen or heard anything so beautiful. He pushed himself up shakily on straight arms, spitting the sour taste of vomit from his mouth, and then sat hunched, clutching his head, his elbows supported on his raised knees.

He groaned after a moment and cocked his head to squint painfully at Will. "You hit me?"

"Aye, but not on the head. Christ, man, I thought I'd killed you. I caught the sole o' your boot and cowped ye sideways and your head hit the log. Are you all right?"

"Sweet Jesus, no, how could I be? My head's broken. Let me be for a minute." We did as he wished and he sat silent for a spell, groaning quietly from time to time and cradling his head in his hands, rocking it tentatively from side to side. But then he took his hands away, still grimacing, and gazed at the blood on the fingers of one while he probed gently at his scalp with the other.

"Ye've got a bump there like a goose egg," Will told him, "but it doesna seem like a deep cut. Just a dunt."

"Aye, the bone stopped it frae bein' deeper." He looked down at himself. "Was I in the water?"

"Aye, for a bit. We pulled ye out."

"I'm freezing!"

"Aye, well, so are we. It's February." All three of us were shivering, and Will stood up. "I'll light a fire, 'gin my tinderbox is still dry."

"Ah, Jesus!" Another hiss of pain and a gentle dab at the swelling on his head. "Mine will be, if yours isna. It's in my scrip, sealed wi' wax. Let's do it quick then, for I'm turnin' blue."

Half an hour later the three of us sat naked by a roaring fire, and the pale warmth of the sunlight felt cold on those parts of us the flames could not reach. Will and I had cut willow sticks and stuck them in the soft earth to support our wet clothes, and the garments were steaming steadily, closer to the fire than we could sit.

Will reached out and took the Viking's chin in his hand, tilting it to where he could see the large swelling beneath the still-wet mat of yellow hair. "Can you see right?"

The Viking twisted his head away and glared at Will. "Of course I can see. My eyes are open, are they not?"

Will held up his first two fingers. "How many fingers?"

"Two. D'ye think I'm daft?" The Viking shut his eyes and rolled his head carefully on his neck. "My head aches hellishly, but I'm fine otherwise. So … who *are* you two, and what are you doing here?"

"We live here. Or close by. We're students at the Abbey." Will introduced the two of us, naming us the nephews of Sir Malcolm Wallace of Elderslie. "And you?"

"Andrew Murray. That's our family name today, but it was once de Moray, and before that de Moravia."

The name was familiar to me. "There's a Sir Andrew Murray who is the King's justiciar in the North, is there not?"

"Aye, Sir Andrew Murray of Petty, on the Moray Firth. My father."

"You have a firth named for you?" Will was impressed, but the other shook his head, smiling.

"No. It was we who took our name from the firth, back in the days of King David, when first we came from Normandy."

Will whistled. "How come you here, then?"

"I came with my master, Lord John Balliol. He is now in conference with your Abbot, on the business of the King."

"Your *master*?" Will contrived to sound amused. "Are you a servant, then?"

Murray shrugged. "Of a kind, I am. I am squire to Lord John. His senior squire. I am to be knighted come my eighteenth birthday, in three months."

"You are to be a knight?"

The other looked surprised. "Aye. Aren't you?"

Will laughed then, but did not pursue the topic. Instead, he reached sideways to pick up one of the quarterstaves we had rescued from the river. "Where did you learn to use this?"

"Lord John. He spent much time in England when he was a boy and learned the skills of it there. He has used one ever since, and watching him and Siward training with them when first I joined his service, I asked to be taught it, too."

"Who's Siward?"

"Lord John's Master-at-Arms. An Englishman. He's also my instructor."

"He taught you well. You almost had me off the bridge."

Murray sniffed. "I hate 'almost.' It never wins. I was the one who went down." He glanced then at me and smiled. "Are you two brothers, then?"

From that point on the day passed quickly, with Andrew feeling better all the time and soon losing the ache in his head. We discussed a surprising number of things, sitting there waiting for our clothes to dry sufficiently to be worn again.

It was obvious to me early on that Will and Andrew would be firm friends, and it pains me, looking back, to admit that my first reaction was one of intense jealousy. The logical part of my mind told me at once that this new friendship must surely be a transient thing, since Andrew Murray would move on within days, returning with his master to his home in the far north. But the wrench of recognition that I would no longer be Will's single boyhood friend came hard and brought with it a bitter resentment of the newcomer.

But then, thank God, my sourness vanished as quickly as it had arisen, for I saw that their attraction to each other was as natural as sunlight. They were almost equally sized, and only a year separated them in age, and they both thought similarly about many things, including physical prowess, of which the quarterstaff was merely the first symbol. Of course these two would be friends, I thought, for they were equals, in athletic prowess at least, and Will could no more resist Murray's natural grace and charm than I myself could.

I was spared from thinking too deeply about it that day, however, when the talk turned to archery.

We were all dressed again by that time, our clothing dried but stinking of woodsmoke, and Will had surged to his feet, making a point of some kind. I had been sitting cross-legged, and I stood as soon as he did, pushing myself up using only my legs. Andrew tried to do the same, but as he tensed to make the effort his eyes flew wide and he blanched. He groaned and brought both hands to his temples, squeezing his forehead between them. Will and I froze, watching him with alarm, but his face cleared quickly and he took his hands away from his brow cautiously.

"My head started to spin," he said, a little shamefacedly. "I didn't expect that."

"Why not?" Will said. "You almost broke your skull but a short while ago, and that's the first time you've tried to stand up quickly since. Here." He held out a hand and Andrew grasped it, pulling himself up easily this time. I noticed that Will did not release his hand, but instead shifted his grip on it, an odd expression on his face, and then he raised his other hand to me, beckoning with his fingers. "Jamie, your hand."

I was mystified as he guided my hand to replace his own, my fingers curling beneath Andrew's.

"Feel that, and tell me if I'm wrong."

As soon as I felt Andrew Murray's fingers against my own, my confusion vanished. I turned our new friend's hand palm upward to see the ridges of callused skin that coated his first two fingers. I felt my eyebrows rise.

"You're a bowman?"

"What?" He pulled his hand away, clenching his fist and grinning again, uncertainly, I thought. "Aye, after a fashion. I am. It's not a knightly pastime, but I enjoy it from time to time."

"It's not a pastime at all." Will's voice was flat. "And you don't get finger pads like that by practising from time to time. That comes only from years of work with a taut bowstring, as these ones did." He held out his own right hand, his first two fingers extended and parted in a V.

Andrew's lips pursed in a soundless whistle as he gazed at the marked difference between Will's calluses and his own. "By Saint Stephen's martyred wounds, another bowman."

"No, not so." There was no speck of humour in Will's denial. "You are a bowman. So is Jamie. I am an archer."

The other's lip quirked. "Bowman, archer ... Is there a difference?"

"Aye—about two hundred paces."

Andrew blinked. "What? You can hit a mark at two hundred paces?"

"Sweet Jesus, aye. Nine times out of ten. And so can Jamie here, six of those times. But I meant I could hit a mark two hundred paces *beyond* any you can reach."

"I think not," Andrew said, his tone reflecting disappointment that his new friend would lie so blatantly.

"Think what you like, my friend, but I will prove it to you once you tell me what kind of bow you use."

"Elmwood. Five feet long."

"Go, then, and fetch it. I will get mine and meet you here again in a half-hour."

Murray's face tightened. "Sweet Jesus! What hour is it?"

I glanced at the sun and shadows. "About the fourth after noon."

"I lost track of the day! Now I must get back. Lord John might be looking for me." He bent down to gather up his cloak, then looked at Will again as he straightened. "You have a yew bow, don't you? A longbow."

"I do."

"A round one."

"Yes."

"Aye, I see it now ... those calluses. So be it, then, I believe your claim. But where in the name of God did you find it? Yon's an English weapon, and English archers don't part with their bows. There are not many big yew trees in Scotland."

Will smiled. "I didn't need many—just the one. But in truth my teacher found it near our home in Elderslie. He cut the stave, cured and dried it, and taught me how to make the bow from that point on."

"A full longbow of your own! Can you be here tomorrow? I would like to test it."

Will grinned. He had been using his huge yew bow for more than two months by then and knew its power, and I knew the anticipation of demonstrating it to his new friend must be more than he could bear. "Aye, if you're still here and your master keeps the Abbot and his brethren in conference."

"We will be here. The same time?"

"I'll be waiting," Will answered.

2

The following morning I went directly to Brother Duncan and asked to be relieved of my tasks that day. He gave me a stern look, though I had learned long since that his air of disapproval was but a sham. I had never asked for such a dispensation before, though, and he asked me what I was about. I told him of our meeting the day before with the visiting Andrew Murray, and he merely nodded and granted me leave. I ran to find Will, and we had time to collect our targets and set them up in the glade by the river bridge well in advance of Andrew's arrival.

He could not stay long, he told us when he came, for Lord John had need of him that afternoon, but there was ample time for Will to demonstrate his new bow's power and for Andrew to try it for himself. Try as he would, though, the lad from Moray was incapable of pulling the powerful weapon to its full stretch, and he finally surrendered it to Will and watched ruefully as my cousin sank six arrows into the centre of the farthest target, two hundred paces away.

"How far will it reach fully flexed?" Andrew asked as we went to fetch the arrows.

"Three hundred, probably more," Will said. "But at full stretch you can lose too many arrows, so I keep my distance to around two hundred. These are target arrows, bear in mind. Barbed warheads and hunting tips make a big difference in flight. The weight of those heads alters everything."

"You have warheads?" Andrew sounded impressed.

Will shook his head. "Nah, but even hunting barbs make a big difference. Man-killers would be heavier yet, but I have no need of those."

"Aye … Well, Will Wallace, I have never seen the like of it. I wouldn't like to have you aiming at me. Not even Siward is that good. But then, Siward is a swordsman above all else. He has a bow, but seldom uses it as you do." He snorted a laugh. "I wondered yesterday at the shoulders on you, the bulk of you. Now I know it's from pulling that thing. But what about a sword? Do you use one?"

"Nah!" Will was retrieving his arrows by then, examining each of them for damage before replacing them in his quiver. "Swords are for knights and I'll never need one. I ha'e my quarterstaff and a good knife. If e'er I'm in a spot where I'm threatened, the knife should be enough to finish anyone who gets by my arrows and my staff." He grinned. "I'm no' that violent, ye know."

I knew that what he had said was true. For all his size and fearsome strength, I had never seen Will lose his temper or provoke a fight with anyone. I had seen him fight savagely, but rarely and never with a weapon, and only in response to the kind of provocation that most people, seeing the sheer size of him, were loath to offer. Yet I find myself examining those words of his years later, wondering whether I might have had any presentiment of what the years ahead would hold for him. But of course I did not. We were innocents in those days, incapable of foreseeing the pain and chaos that lay ahead for all of us.

The remainder of that morning flew by pleasantly, and when the time came for Andrew to return to the Abbey to attend his master, we went with him, all three of us aware that his departure the following day would leave a gap in each of our lives. We walked slowly, our bows slung over our shoulders, as he answered our questions about his life as a knightly squire, and any thoughts Will and I might have had about his lot being one of privileged sloth and luxury were quickly banished. His day-to-day training to become a knight was far more demanding than anything expected of us in the Abbey school.

We had reached the main entrance to the Abbey proper, and it was plain to see that Lord John and his associates were still in conference, for there was little sign of life other than the routine activities of the resident brothers, and so we stood talking quietly in the forecourt, about fifty paces from the main entrance. I have no memory of what we were discussing, for it was Will and Andrew who were speaking while I was merely looking around, but I saw a figure emerge from a side door and start towards us, then stop suddenly and take careful note of us. The man appeared to be both tall and elderly, stooped with age but walking youthfully enough and wearing a long habit of brown wool trimmed with green edging. I might have paid him no more attention had he not stopped so obviously, and the manner in which he stood there peering at us struck me as peculiar.

"Who's that?" I asked, and both of the others looked to see who I was talking about. I heard Murray inhale sharply.

"Shit!" he said, from the side of his mouth. "It's Wishart. The Bishop." He bowed towards the distant figure, and Will and I awkwardly followed his example. The Bishop nodded in acknowledgment, then came sweeping towards us.

"Master de Moray," he said as he approached, emphasizing the French pronunciation and then continuing in the same language. "I am pleased to see you have been able to find friends with whom to amuse yourself while you are here." The words were addressed to Andrew, but the Bishop's eyes were scanning Will and me, taking note of everything about us, including our quarterstaffs and the bows strung from our shoulders. Andrew drew himself up and responded in the same language, gesturing courteously with one hand.

"I have, my lord. I met them yesterday, by accident. They are local lads, as you can see, but I have enjoyed their company during what might otherwise have been a tedious time." His French was fluent and polished, and it was clear that neither he nor the Bishop expected Will or me to understand it.

I was about to speak up, but decided suddenly to hold my peace and give no indication that I understood them. Will, I knew, would barely have registered a word of what they said, for he lacked my facility with languages. I looked at him and found him gazing back at me, his face blank. Wishart, in the meantime, had turned to look more openly at Will, taking in the size of him and looking up and down the thick length of the quarterstaff in his hand and the heavy bow that dangled from his shoulder. I in turn took the opportunity to look more closely at the Bishop himself.

I could not even guess at his age, for he was one of those rare men whose appearance changes little with the passing of years. I could see he was not young, but whether he was forty or seventy I could not say with any confidence. His face was gaunt and weathered, swarthy and deeply lined beneath the sparse covering of a wispy, square-cut beard, and he had a high, broad forehead, emphasized by a close-cropped widow's peak of dark brown hair that he wore short and cut bluntly at the back, well above his shoulders. Dark, intelligent eyes gleamed keenly beneath his bushy brows, and a large, bony beak of a nose made his entire appearance fierce and hawk-like. His lips appeared to be smiling, but I could see no humour in his eyes.

"Unless I miss my guess," he said in Latin, "and judging merely by the size of you and the bow you carry, you must be Sir Malcolm Wallace's nephew, William. Am I correct?" The Bishop's smile grew wider, and this time the warmth of it reached his eyes. "I am no mind reader," he continued, his voice deep and level. "Nor, I fear, has fame yet marked you as being worthy of compelling notice. I come directly from a meeting with your uncle Father Peter, and he spoke to me about you, describing you and your longbow and telling me of how you keep the brotherhood supplied with the best of meat. My sole surprise was in finding you in the company of Master Murray." His eyes came back to me. "And you must be James Wallace, the cousin who is such an asset to Brother Duncan in the library."

It was a flattering moment but an awkward one, for neither Will nor I knew how to respond properly to such an informal approach from the man who was the senior prelate of Scotland and personal confessor to King Alexander himself, but somehow we found ourselves strangely at ease in speaking casually with one of the most powerful men in the realm. I noticed, nonetheless, that Andrew Murray stood wide-eyed, his eyes darting from one to the other of us as Bishop Wishart catechized us closely for the next quarter of an hour about our lives in the Abbey, our feelings for our Elderslie kin, my own deceased family, and the slaughter of Will's family. He even asked us about our tutor, Ewan, and our studies with the bow. He included me graciously in everything he said, but it was plain to me that his consuming interest lay with Will and that he was not showing such interest out of simple courtesy.

And then suddenly he nodded, grunted deep in his chest, and bade all three of us farewell, informing Andrew at the last that Lord John was still deep in his discussions with the Father Abbot and was unlikely to require his services for at least another hour and perhaps even longer. With that, he walked away, already deep in thoughts of something else, leaving us staring after him.

"What was all that about, I wonder?" Murray sounded troubled, and Will cocked his head.

"What d'you mean?"

"That friendliness. I have never seen the old man behave so ... so *amicably*. The revered Bishop Wishart is not a friendly man. Not like that, with utter strangers."

"Should I beware, then?" Will drew the backs of his fingers along the soft down on his jawbone, smiling. "Does he like boys?"

"What? Oh, no, I meant nothing like that. Sweet Jesus, no! But he is …" Murray searched for words. "This is the fifth time I have travelled in the company of Bishop Wishart, as part of Lord John's train. It's also the briefest. I rode with him for three months last year and I know him to be a notedly silent man, solitary and self-guarded. He has few friends. He is no man's puppet and I'm told he was once a fearsome warrior. But he is dour and largely without humour, close-mouthed and famed for being niggardly with words."

"Mayhap he likes me, sees me for what I truly am. Had you thought of that? Just because it took you an hour and more to grow to love me, that doesna mean that more gifted folk shouldna see the gold in me sooner."

Murray nodded judiciously. Then he gently took the quarterstaff from Will and removed the long yew bow from where it hung on his shoulder. He handed both to me along with his own weapons. Then he hooked his arm about Will's neck and tripped him with one leg, dropping him to the ground and leaping on top of him to rub a handful of dirt into Will's hair. Will, with a roar of mock rage, heaved valiantly against the weight pinning him and managed to turn on his side while keeping Murray's arms away from his throat and the chokehold the other was trying to assert. I cannot say how long the struggle might have gone on had not Brother Brian, one of the brawniest of the Abbey brethren, emerged from the main door of the church and caught all three of us in sacrilegious ignominy. He dragged the two wrestlers apart and preached us a stern warning on the evils of fighting, then growled that we should get ourselves well out of sight.

We contrived somehow to suffer straight-faced through the dressing-down, but by then the fight had gone out of both contestants, and so we collected our bows and staves and for the following hour we merely walked and talked about whatever came into our minds. Andrew mentioned his lady love, a beautiful young woman from his own lands called Siobhan. He pronounced it *Shivonn*, and from the moment I heard it I was enamoured by the name's beautiful sound. Her full name was Siobhan MacDiormid—I heard it as Shivonn Macdermid—and she was the niece of Alexander Comyn, the Earl of Buchan, from whom Andrew's father held the lordship of Petty. It was plain that our new friend saw in her the sun and moon of his existence, and from the self-same moment both Will and I were captivated by what we heard.

There was nothing prurient or even mildly provocative in anything Andrew had to say of the young woman; on the contrary, he spoke of her in terms that rendered her almost superhuman in her virtues and ethereal in her beauty, his voice ringing with that ardour and conviction that is the shining characteristic of young men in the flush of first love. And Will and I listened, entranced because we had never heard the like of it. To us, girls were alien creatures, seldom if ever seen within the Abbey precincts. The mere sight of a woman, it was feared, might induce sinful thoughts among the brethren, and therefore women were forbidden entry to the community, save to attend services in the Abbey church, at which times they were heavily swathed, their faces, heads, and bodies covered, and they were accompanied by their God-fearing menfolk. Femininity was anathema within the Abbey precincts, even when the women concerned were old or middle-aged, shapeless and unattractive. Girls and young women inhabited the outside world, and they were matter for endless conjecture among the body of students at the Abbey school.

I knew beyond a doubt that, at almost sixteen, William Wallace had never known, nor spoken more than a few words to, any young woman who was not related to him by blood. Nor had I. But neither of us had ever suffered by that. Our lives were governed in every aspect by the rule of the Abbey community and the activities that filled our daily life, in school by day and away from it by night, and it never occurred to either one of us that we might ever fall into the company of young, attractive women. The key word, of course, was *attractive*. The two elderly women who ran our household on the farm were simply *there*, shapeless, sexless creatures whose sole purpose was to cater to our comfort and whom we scarcely noticed. Similarly, the young women who sometimes came to visit them, their daughters, nieces, and neighbours, were all but invisible to us. Plain, largely unwashed and sour smelling, ill dressed and unkempt, coarse spoken and generally repellent, they possessed none of the attributes that might have attracted our eyes or our thoughts.

This girl whom our new friend now depicted so eloquently came to us therefore as a revelation. We were enraptured, hanging dewy eyed on Andrew's every word as we strove to picture the radiant beauty he described. Small wonder, then, that our reaction was less than courteous when a voice from behind us interrupted our fantasies, speaking Andrew's name.

Will and I both spun around peevishly, prepared to send this interloper packing, but our first sight of the newcomer struck us mute.

To say that he was splendid is simply inadequate. The man was magnificent, dressed entirely in white and red, from knee-high, red-dyed boots and matching leather breeches, to a lustrous, blindingly white tunic surmounted by a white, open-fronted surcoat with a plain red shield, inset with a smaller outline of another, in white, on the left breast.

"Lord John!"

I had not needed to hear Andrew's shocked response to know at whom I was gaping. Sir John Balliol, King Alexander's personal envoy and an heir to the kingdom in his own right, was unmistakably a man of power, with wealth and privilege stamped into his every feature. He had come to a sudden halt, looking at us with one fine dark eyebrow raised high in surprise, occasioned, I had no doubt, by the ferocity with which Will and I had spun to face him.

"Forgive me, my lords," he said in a voice that matched his smile. "I had no wish to impose myself, merely to speak a moment with Master Murray. But since he is clearly occupied, I will return later." And with that he turned on his heel as though to walk away.

Will and I were speechless, appalled by our own ill manners, but fortunately that was not the case with Andrew. "My lord," he said quickly, his voice tinged with desperation. "My lord, forgive me. We were deep in talk and did not see you coming."

Lord John swung back towards us, still smiling. "That much was obvious," he said. "But I find myself wondering about what you found so engrossing. When I was your age, the only topic that could inspire such dedication and reverence was consideration of the beauties of young women."

None of us was capable of responding to that, but from the corner of my eye I could see the wave of colour that engulfed Andrew's face as his mouth opened and closed. Balliol, however, was merciful and allowed his squire to slip easily off the gaff.

"I am new come from a meeting with the Abbott and his staff, which means I have spent the entire day talking about affairs of state and bruising my backside through a too-thin cushion, and so I thought to take some fresh air." He reached behind him and kneaded his buttocks. "I had been thinking about you, young Andrew— guiltily, I suppose—imagining you waiting and fretting somewhere and no doubt cursing me, and so when I saw you here I thought to bid you good day and tender my regrets for having summoned you only to leave you waiting, since even a squire has the right to a little freedom." He glanced sideways at Will, who had finally managed to close his open mouth. "You have made friends, I see."

"Yes, my lord, I have." Close to stammering, Andrew made us known to his master, who extended his hand to each of us in turn, nodding and smiling and making us feel at ease, a feat I would not have thought possible mere moments earlier. He was neither as tall nor as broad as Will, but such was the impression of confidence that radiated from the man that he seemed to occupy no less an amount of space, and I noticed now that he was eyeing Will's staff.

"That looks like a quarterstaff," he said. "Or is it simply a big walking stick?"

Will actually smiled. "My tutor tells me it is a quarterstaff, my lord."

"And who is your tutor?"

"A man called Ewan Scrymgeour."

"Scrymgeour ... A Scots name."

"Aye, sir, but his mother's family is Welsh. He was an archer with King Edward, until the Welsh wars."

"Hmm." Lord John glanced at Murray, then looked quickly over his shoulder, his eyes scanning the deserted forecourt behind him. "Good. Then walk with me, if you will, to where the air is even fresher."

The three of us fell in behind him as he walked steadily towards the fringe of mature elms and oaks that began some hundred paces from where we had been standing. He seemed to float ahead of us, moving easily and gracefully with long, confident strides, the red and nested white shields of the great House of Balliol emblazoned across his wide shoulders and the wind of his passage making the long skirts of his surcoat billow at his heels. None of us spoke, though all three of us boys exchanged curious looks as we followed him. He led us into the trees until we were concealed from any eyes that might be watching from the Abbey behind, then stopped in a clear space between the boles of two enormous elms. There he shrugged out of his beautiful white surcoat, allowing it to fall from his shoulders. He caught it in one hand and threw it aside, all the while smiling at Will.

"This will suit, no?" he said. "A fine spot to test your skills and permit me some exercise." He extended his hand. "Andrew, your staff, if you will."

Murray looked mystified, but he held out his staff, and his master took it, spun it easily in one hand, then moved gracefully into the opening stance for combat.

"You want to fight me?" Will asked, wide-eyed.

"Not fight—to try you. So come."

A sharp shake of his head indicated Will's bewilderment. "I can't fight you. You are—"

"I am a student of this weapon, which I use for sport, trained in its use but rusty from long lack of practice." The easy smile was back on Balliol's face, and he flipped the staff until he held it cross-handed. "You start."

"You are the King's envoy, my lord. It would be death to strike you."

"Pah! What makes you even think you could strike me, a stripling youth like you? I've been training with this thing since I was half your age and now I'm twice as old as you. If you *can* hit me, though, then hit me hard, for I intend to drub you." He straightened up again quickly and took a step back, his smile now a wide grin. "Besides, would you deny me in my pleasure and my need? The King's envoy? I need the exercise and you're the only one here to supply it. I can hardly fight my own squire, can I? Imagine, were he to beat me! You, on other hand, might beat me soundly with no ill effect, if God's asleep. So come, let's be about it, shall we?"

Clearly Will had no option other than to appear the buffoon here. He raised his staff reluctantly and shuffled forward.

Lord John Balliol sprang into action, attacking immediately and compelling Will to defend himself. Will responded half-heartedly at first, until the first few solid blows that rattled his defences told him he was facing an expert who was bold and dangerous and determined to thrash him soundly. I saw Will's face suddenly harden, and from then on the fight was waged between two well-matched rivals. Back and forth they fought grimly, neither seeking nor giving quarter, sometimes standing toe to toe, belabouring each other's defences without either one scoring, sometimes ranging widely around the small clearing between the trees, scanning each other for signs of weakness or an unguarded opening and prepared to leap and strike.

I recall two solid hits, the first to Will's left thigh and the other to Lord John's right shoulder when his foot slipped and he reeled for a moment. By that time, sweat was pouring from both of them, soaking their clothing, and the grass of the clearing was trampled flat, scuffed deeply with the marks of their grinding feet. And then came a flurry of hard, rapping blows too fast to follow with the eye, and Balliol reeled and fell back against one of the two trees. Will swept up his staff to finish it, then hesitated.

Lord John threw down his staff and raised his hands, waving them and labouring for breath. "Enough," he cried. "I'm done. You have me, by God's holy beard."

Will opened his hands and let his own staff fall, then doubled over, his hands on his knees, gasping for breath as hungrily as his opponent. Andrew Murray and I simply stared at each other, wide-eyed with awe, fully aware that we had just witnessed our friend defeat one of the most noble men in Scotland.

"Sweet Christ, yon was a tulzie." Balliol spoke in Scots, straightening up to his full height and wiping his streaming brow with the back of his wrist. "I havena fought that hard in years, and never against a beardless laddie. Andrew, my coat, if ye will."

Andrew had picked up the discarded garment long since and now he stepped forward, holding it open for his master to shrug into. Lord John flexed his shoulders to adjust the coat until it hung properly, then turned again to Will, who had also straightened up by then, though he was still breathing heavily.

"You flinched," he said, "at the end there, stopped because of who I was, forgetting what I was: your enemy. That kind of hesitation could kill you in a real fight. You need to learn a truth, William Wallace, so learn it now. When fighting man to man there can be no rank or titles involved. If ever you cross blades with any man in earnest, no matter who, there can be only one outcome. Either you kill him or he will kill you. Never forget that." He held up his palm to silence Will before he could respond. "*Never* forget that. Had it been I who had you off balance there, I would have felled you like a tree, and so would any other opponent worthy of his salt. Do you hear me?"

Will Wallace nodded. "Aye, my lord. I do."

"I pray you'll heed me then, in future. Mercy can be fatal in a tulzie, so when you have the chance to end things, end them. Never hesitate. Clear?"

"Clear, my lord."

"So be it, then." Balliol drew the open edges of his surcoat together and glanced around the clearing. "And now I must go. It was a good bout and I thank you, all of you."

Then he said a strange thing.

"King Alexander, may God bless him, is hale and strong, newly wed and eager to breed sons to replace the heirs whom God saw fit to take from him these past few years. He will have need of men like you when you are come to manhood. See you hold yourselves in readiness to serve him when he calls on you. This realm—any realm—depends upon the loyalty and strength of good, true men, of any rank, to stand behind their King."

The edges of a grin flickered about his lips and he nodded, this time in dismissal. "So be it. Fare ye well, William and James Wallace. Andrew, follow me, and seek me in half an hour in the Abbot's chambers."

I knew that what Lord John had said would not apply to me, since I would be a priest when I was grown to manhood, a warrior of God, perhaps, but not a fighting man in the world of Will and Andrew. But if God spared me to serve Him and my King, I knew that I could do so as loyally and strongly and perhaps even better in the priesthood than I ever could have in the army.

King Alexander, who had ruled Scotland by then for thirty-six years, had married for the second time, mere months earlier, at the age of forty-four. His first wife, Margaret, had been the daughter of Edward of England, and she had borne Alexander two sons and a daughter. The Queen had died ten years before, and was swiftly and tragically followed by all three of her children, leaving Alexander with one sole, distant heir, an infant girl born to his now dead daughter, who had been married to the King of Norway. Determined to breed other sons, Alexander had wed a high-born, beautiful, and nubile young French woman called Yolande of Dreux. The King was young and in good health; the country was at peace and prosperous; and God seemed content to smile upon the realm of Scotland.

CHAPTER FOUR

I

The unthinkable happened less than a month after our meeting with Andrew Murray. Alexander III, King of Scots, died in his prime, killed by a lightning strike while travelling to reach his new wife in Fife. He left his country and its people leaderless, the King's authority invalid without an heir.

His body was found the day after, sprawled on the rocks that lined the shore beneath a high cliff, and no one could say what had happened to him. Determined to rejoin his new Queen that night in defiance of the tempestuous weather and of the widespread rumours that the day in question, March 18th, was to be a Day of Judgment, he had crossed the storm-racked Firth of Forth from Edinburgh Castle in a small ferry boat. From there, refusing shelter offered him, he had ridden northeastward with two guides, against their advice and that of others who thought him mad to brave the storm. In the tumultuous darkness some time later, the three men, king and guides, had been separated.

The word spread slowly at first, for that part of the kingdom was wild and isolated, but once the tidings reached Edinburgh, the news flew from there as though on the wings of birds, so that soon all of Scotland knew of its sudden deprivation. Few of the common folk who heard the news were capable of thinking beyond the moment, and far fewer yet could begin to imagine an outcome to what they had heard. But there were others, men of power accustomed to thinking for and of themselves, who perceived everything that was involved in Alexander's death, and those men moved quickly. They understood that Scotland, within the space of a single night, had been thrown headlong into a turmoil they might use to their advantage.

I was in the Abbey library, transcribing a document, when the tidings reached us, having taken eight days to speed from Edinburgh to Glasgow and thence to us in Paisley. I recall Brother Duncan rising from his table and moving across the room in answer to a hissed summons from someone who had entered at my back. I remember that he looked angry at being thus interrupted, but Duncan always looked forbidding and so, having my own work to occupy me, I paid no more attention as he swept by me. After a deal of whispering between him and whoever had come looking for him, I heard the door close, and he came back into the room, but moving slowly now. Sensing something amiss, I set down my pen, looking at him idly to see what might be afoot. But as soon as I saw the stricken look on his face, a rash of gooseflesh swept up my nape, and even as my mind formed the thought that something was far wrong, the great bell in the Abbey tower began to toll. In all my time there as a student, I had heard it toll but once, announcing the death of one of the senior brethren.

The Abbot's dead was the first thought that came to me, and I would to God that had been all it was, for now I know what chaos would endure for twenty years before the next strong king would wrest back control of the realm.

Brother Duncan paid no attention to the measured sound. He stood wringing his hands like a penitent, and I became aware that everyone else was staring at him as intently and as fearfully as I was. Eventually he blinked and looked around at us all, his assistants, then summoned us to him with a wave of both hands. He waited until we had surrounded him and then he made as if to speak, raising his hands before letting them fall to his sides.

"In God's name, Duncan, what is it?" The voice was Brother Anselm's. "Someone has died, that much is plain, but who?"

"The King." Duncan's voice was so faint that I thought I had misheard him. So, clearly, did the others, for they all broke into a spate of questioning. But when he responded only by repeating the same words in the same shaken voice, the horror of it silenced all of us.

We all *knew* the King could not be dead. He was God's own anointed, crowned King of Scots at Scone and beloved by all; a champion in the prime of life, healthy and hale and lusty, newly wed to a young and lovely wife. His representatives had been here in our own Abbey mere weeks earlier, conducting his royal affairs and expounding his wishes for both Church and realm. It was impossible that he should now be gone so suddenly, after ruling the kingdom so well and wisely for so many years. The sound of my own heartbeat filled my ears with a dull, leaden throbbing, and the air outside the green-tinted windows seemed to darken.

2

The Abbey routine was shattered. All the brethren who were not summoned into conference of one kind or another were sent to pray for the soul of the departed King, and soon the sound of massed chanting swelled from the Abbey church as the brotherhood immersed itself in ritual prayers for the dead. The resident students, unexpectedly left at liberty, found themselves free to do as they wished and quickly disappeared as boys will, eager to be about their own pleasures. My sole wish was to carry the news home to Will and Ewan before they could hear it from anyone else, for I wanted to see the look on their faces when they first heard of it.

The farm we tended for Sir Malcolm lay a mile beyond the Abbey precincts, on the far edge of Paisley town, and I ran the entire way, bursting with the import of my message. Will had stayed home that day, too enthralled by the new project that Ewan had set him even to consider going to school, and I ran directly to the stone cottage that he and Ewan had converted into a bowyer's workshop.

They were huddled together, almost head to head in the dim little room, their attention focused tightly on the object that lay before them on the table, and so great was their concentration that they barely looked up when I burst through the door.

"The King's been killed," I blurted. "King Alexander's dead, fallen from a cliff."

Ewan had been in the act of picking up the object on the table in front of him when I charged into the room and had scarce accorded me a glance, so I knew that they had seen me from the open window, running across the yard. Now he raised the long, regular block of wood to his good eye and held it towards the shaft of pale sunlight from the window, squinting along the perfectly squared length of it and turning it until he had compared all four edges. Will had half turned to look at me, but he said nothing, merely turning back to watch Ewan with the length of wood. It was, I knew, the single most precious item—in the eyes of Ewan and Will at least—in the entire household, but at that moment it meant nothing to me, and I found it incredible that Ewan and Will had both ignored my announcement.

"Didn't you hear me? King Alexander's dead."

"Is that why you're home so early?" Ewan lowered his arms and turned to me, holding the heavy wooden batten easily.

"Aye. Word came from the Bishop in Glasgow not an hour ago."

"Ah, then it must be true." He laid his burden carefully back on the table and ran a finger across the tiny guide marks that had been inscribed into the piece at varying distances, then glanced at Will. "And what would you have us do, Jamie, now that we know?"

"What?" I felt utterly deflated, having run so far and so fast to shock them, only to find them indifferent. "What did you say?"

Ewan shrugged. "I asked what you would have us do, about the King."

My mouth opened and closed. There was nothing any of us could do, but I felt a great lump swelling in my throat and fought to speak through it.

"We could pray for his soul and wish him well on his way."

"We could, and we will, later, once I have finished this." His fingers stroked the length of wood on the table, and he spoke down towards it, splaying his fingers to span several of the incised lines on its surface. "We'll pray for him together, all of us, tonight, for I have a thought that every monk in the Abbey will be praying for him at this moment. If that's true, God will not miss us if we are tardy by an hour or two. In the meantime, though, Will and I have been working on these measurements all morning and we need to finish them ere we forget what we're about and have to start again at the beginning." And then he swung towards me with a great smile on his face and reached out to tousle my hair. "So away you go now and leave us to it. Aggie has some fine stew in the kitchens, fresh made, and Will and I are stuffed with it. Fresh bread, too, with the smell of it rich enough to draw the moisture from your very soul. We'll finish here within the hour, God willing, and we'll come and find you."

Crestfallen, I made my way to the farmhouse kitchen, where I told my news to Aggie the cook and Maggie the housekeeper, only to have them show even less interest than Will and Ewan.

"Oh, aye? Poor man," Aggie said, then looked at Maggie, who laughed and responded, "We'll ha'e a new King, then."

"Aye, nae doubt we will. And soon."

Maggie added, "Aye, I wonder will he ask us up to Scone to see him crowned?"

I closed my mind to their callousness and consoled myself with the wonderful food that Aggie laid in front of me. And as I ate, instead of dwelling upon things I could neither influence nor change, I thought about the new project that had kept Will away from school that day. It was a bow, of course, or it would be eventually, but for the time being and for some time to come it would remain as it was now, a straight length of plain, ordinary-looking timber.

Yet I knew well that the yew stave that fascinated both my friends was neither plain nor ordinary. It was one of four identical pieces that Ewan had brought back several years earlier from his visit to his uncle Daffyd ap Gryffyth, in the English town of York. Daffyd was a master bowyer, transformed by his skills, within the space of two decades, from an extraordinary Welsh archer into one of the most powerful and respected bow makers in all England. Ewan had been his apprentice at the battle of Lewes, where the boy had almost been killed by the mace blow that disfigured him permanently, and his uncle had developed a great pride in the single-minded determination with which his badly injured nephew had pursued his goal of becoming an archer thereafter. The two then lost touch for years, after Ewan had left Edward of Caernarvon's army and returned to Scotland.

Ewan had gone in search of his uncle, of whose success he had heard from time to time, with the underlying intention of purchasing some decent bow staves, but Daffyd ap Gryffyth had refused to sell to him. Instead, the old man took him into the massive warehouse where he kept his finest and most precious materials, supplies of yew imported from Tuscany and the forests southeast of Salerno, and led him straight to four of the finest staves among the thousands stockpiled there, all four lying side by side in their own ventilated space. These, he insisted, were beyond price and would be his personal gift to Ewan, the sole inheritance within his power to bestow, since his sons, now full partners in the enterprise, must take precedence. All four staves had been taken from the same tree, he explained, stroking the fine wood as he spoke of them; a tall, straight tree of Iberian yew. Iberian yew was unobtainable now in its native form, since most of Iberia had fallen to the Moors in the eighth century, but prudent merchants had salvaged a few thousand seedlings and saplings from the largely unoccupied but still contested areas of Galicia and Asturias during the tenth century, and plantations had been established in Italia and had flourished there, precious and close guarded.

The bole of this particular tree, Daffyd said, had been recognized early for its excellence and tended throughout its life by careful foresters who knew its value. It had grown perfectly straight and virtually free of imperfections until it was almost twenty inches in diameter, and from it the Tuscan sawyers had obtained four magnificent, perfectly straight, and knotless staves, a thing almost unheard of. Each of the four was square in section, four inches to a side and seven feet long, and each appeared to be made of twin laminated strips of reddish-brown colours. But the striations were natural. The darker strip, which would become the inner belly of the bow, was the iron-strong heartwood of the yew, capable of sustaining great compression; the outer, paler side was the sapwood, more pliable than the denser heartwood; it would form the outer "back" of the bow, and its tension, combined with the compression of the heart-wood belly, would make the war bow that sprang from it the most powerful weapon of its kind for a single man in all the world.

Ewan had brought the four staves home to Scotland with great care, for they were truly priceless and irreplaceable, but he had brought others with him, too, staves of lesser quality, perhaps, yet cleaner, finer, and less knotty than any native yew remaining today in England.

Will had been practising the bowyer's craft for years, working until all hours of the night under Ewan's tutelage, the size of each ash or elm bow he made increasing as his body and strength grew. He had graduated, with great but private ceremony, to fashion his current bow from one of these lesser staves of yew, slowly and patiently perfecting the art of using the bowyer's razor-sharp, double-handed drawknives to pare down the wood and taper the bow's length under the proud but watchful eye of Ewan Scrymgeour.

Now, however, Will was close to outgrowing his own bow, and the time had come for him to make another, a longer, thicker, stronger bow that he would be hard set to pull. I knew that, but I knew, too, that his massive muscles would grow larger yet to master its challenge. And I knew that the pride both my friends would take—had already begun to take—in making Will's new bow from one of Daffyd ap Gryffyth's finest staves would be fully justified. But I wondered how it could justify their lack of concern over the death of their King.

Ewan and Will came into the kitchen while I was still sitting there mulling. The aroma of fresh-baked bread and of the spicy stew in the pot was still strong in the room, and they helped themselves hungrily to more food while Aggie poured them each a pot of ale from the large, covered wooden jug she kept beneath the stone sink in the corner farthest from the fire. It was still light outside, but the winter-weak March sun was lost in heavy cloud and sinking swiftly, and Aggie left us to our own devices as she bustled away to the quarters she shared with Maggie.

The two talked incessantly about the scale and measurements they had been applying to the stave, and I sat watching and listening until Ewan shovelled the last of his broth-soaked bread into his mouth, chewed and swallowed it, then lounged back in his chair with a contented sigh and took a big gulp of ale. I waited for the inevitable belch that always followed such a draught, and when it had subsided I asked him, "Will you really pray for the King tonight?"

He pulled his bowstring-callused fingers pensively down along the ruined bowl of his cheek, tracing the concave curve of its tooth-less emptiness.

"I will," he said in his soft, lisping voice. "I said I would. But, Jamie, what do you suppose this means, this death of a King? What do you think will happen now?"

I did not have to think about my response. "I know what will happen. There is an heir, the King's grand-daughter Margaret, born to his daughter the Queen of Norway. Brother Duncan says she is an infant, and she will need guidance, but they will bring her home and crown her Queen."

"Guidance?" Ewan's face crumpled in what I knew to be a rueful grin. "And who will do this guiding that you speak of? How old is this princess?"

"Three, Brother Duncan said."

"Three … A child of three, and a lass at that, forbye a foreigner. They won't like that."

"Who won't?" This was Will, speaking for the first time.

"The magnates, lad. The men who think they themselves have the right to rule this land."

The Scots magnates were the men of power in the realm. They were of varying ranks, from earls to barons and chiefs, and of different bloods, some of them Gaels, a few of Danish and Norwegian stock, and others Norman French. Collectively they called themselves the magnates and individually they each looked after their own interests.

"The magnates," Will said with a sneer. "Ravens, you mean. They're carrion eaters, all of them. Only the lawful King has the right to rule this land."

"Aye, and each o' your magnates will seek to claim that right. You wait and see." Ewan's voice had quieted. "They willna settle for a wee lass Norwegian-born. It has been but twenty and three years since the fight at Largs, when Alexander himself threw the last of the Norwegians out of the Isles. There are men alive today who fought there and still mind that well. They'll not take the risk of courting that again."

"And who stands foremost among these magnates?" Will asked. "They can't *all* expect to become the next King, surely? Some of them must have stronger claims than others."

"Some have," Ewan said mildly. "You spoke with one o' them yourself, less than a month ago—Lord John Balliol. He'll claim direct descent from David I, King of Scots, whose grandson, Balliol's own grandsire, was David, Earl of Huntingdon. He has the lineage, no doubt of that. And besides, his mother, Devorguilla, rules all of Galloway in her own ancient Gaelic right."

Will looked at me wide-eyed, and I stared back at him, astonished that we two had met, and Will had bested, this man who was now named a potential King of Scots.

"And then there's Bruce of Annandale," Ewan continued. "He is an old man now, but his claim is near as strong as Balliol's. And there are the Comyns of Buchan and Badenoch, though they're related to the Balliols. Aye, I'm thinking there will be no shortage of claimants. Mark my words, lads, this Scotland will be shaken by wild storms before that matter's settled."

He took another long swallow of his ale. "But I doubt any of it will be o' great concern to us. We'll get on with our lives and leave the affairs o' state to them that deal in them."

3

For several months it seemed that Ewan would be right in his assessment of how little we would be affected by the affairs of kings and magnates. Life continued as it always had, and after no more than a few weeks had passed, people began to forget about the death of King Alexander. Will and I did not forget, but that was solely because of our kinsmen Father Peter and Brother Duncan, both of whom used us as a conduit to pass on tidings and information from the Abbey to Sir Malcolm in Elderslie. Thus as couriers we knew that there were grave and deep-set stirrings beneath the fabric of the country's daily life.

It began most noticeably with a sudden increase in the number of religious colloquies and hurried assemblies all across the land, several of which were held in Paisley and all of which involved senior churchmen. Several of these took place at our own Abbey, and I remember one in particular that threw all of us into disarray because it was hastily summoned and included the Abbots of Holyrood, Dunfermline, Melrose, and Kelso as well as Bishop Wishart of Glasgow and William Fraser, the powerful Bishop of St. Andrews. Such men did not travel alone. They progressed like the lords they were, lords of Mother Church, and each had his retinue of followers, including secretaries, scribes, acolytes, servants, bodyguards, and camp followers, so that we were hard put to accommodate all of them within the precincts.

As unofficial messengers, we soon came to see that the churchmen had valid concerns, not always solely for the welfare of the Church. The word had come out, within a month of the King's death, that Queen Yolande had been pregnant before he died. As such rumours often do, it spread like windblown fire and captured the attention of the entire land. If it were true, though, and the Queen bore Scotland a new heir, be it boy or girl, there could be repercussions, for the accepted word in those early days, also unconfirmed, was that the magnates had closed ranks surprisingly quickly at the

King's funeral, despite Ewan's pessimism that first night, and had accepted the young Norwegian Princess Margaret. Some people even said they had acknowledged her as the official heir, but that, too, was merely hearsay. Nothing, according to our sources, had yet been formally declared. If this latest rumour proved true, however, the magnates would have no choice but to declare in favour of the new child.

Rumour, of course, led to counter-rumour, and many whispered that the Queen, a Frenchwoman closely related to France's young and ambitious King Philip Capet IV, was not pregnant at all and intended to present some base-born upstart as her own in order to maintain her position as Queen of Scots and to bring the Scots realm under the influence of the Crown of France.

In the last week of April, barely forty days after Alexander's death, our Abbot left for a great gathering at Scone Abbey, in the course of which the realm's most powerful and important men—the earls, barons, bishops, abbots, and priors—intended to deal with the situation of the interregnum. When he returned, less than two weeks later, Will and I were sent by Father Peter to inform Sir Malcolm that the matter had been settled. In the course of the Scone parliament, as men were calling it, it was revealed that no heir was yet forthcoming, and the magnates had formally sworn their loyalty to the young Norwegian Princess as the official heir, taking a solemn oath, on penalty of excommunication, to guard the realm for her and to keep the peace of her land.

In support of that oath and in earnest of their open goodwill, the parliament had also dispatched three emissaries to find the King of England, who was campaigning in Gascony against the French, to seek his advice and protection on the rights of the young heir. That done, and for the interim governance of the land, the parliament had appointed a council of six custodians, called Guardians, chosen from what they termed the community of the realm. Two of these six, Alexander Comyn of Buchan and Duncan MacDuff of Fife, were earls; two were barons, John Comyn the Red, Lord of Badenoch, and James, the hereditary Steward or Stewart; and the final two were bishops, William Fraser of St. Andrews and Robert Wishart of Glasgow.

Sir Malcolm listened carefully to me and Will as we reported all of this, and then he nodded in satisfaction. "Three from north of Forth and three from south," he rumbled. "Two o' the ancient earldoms. The senior bishops, north and south. And two Comyns representing the barons, one in the north and the other in the south. Aye, cunningly done."

Until that moment I had not given a single moment's thought to the composition of the Council of Guardians, but now I saw what my uncle had perceived immediately: the new council was an inspired piece of political juggling, masterminded by I knew not whom, but aimed unequivocally at unifying and protecting the integrity of the Scots realm by emphasizing its differences north and south of the River Forth and ensuring that both halves were equal in voice and influence. The Forth had great significance in the eyes of all Scots. It was the river that partitioned the land into its two halves, the mountainous northern Celtic portion known as Scotia and the southern, more English- and Norman-speaking half. Along its short length from the North Sea to Edinburgh and Stirling it provided the only access routes for heavy traffic travelling between north and south.

"What's wrong, lad?" The question startled me, but it was not directed at me. Uncle Malcolm's eyes were on Will, who sat frowning into the fire. We were in the main room of the house, just the three of us, and Lady Margaret, who was about her needlework and seemingly paying no attention to what we had been saying. Will jerked upright and flushed.

"Nothing, sir. There's nothing wrong. I was but ..." His voice tailed away.

"But what, lad? Speak up. Is there something that troubles you?"

"No, sir. Not *troubles* me. Not exactly." He was still red faced. "But it seems senseless."

Sir Malcolm raised an eyebrow. "Senseless? Yon's a word that could provoke an argument. What seems senseless?"

Will jutted his jaw and charged ahead. "It insults the Bruce," he said. "Makes no recognition of his rank or status. The Lord of Annandale will take that ill, from what I've heard of him."

Sir Malcolm scratched idly at his beard. "Aye, he might," he said. "You make a good point, young Will. One worth considering." He bent forward and struck a small bronze bell on the table by his chair, and when a servant responded he sent the man to fetch a jug of ale.

"What think you, Jamie?" he said then. "Will the Bruce be vexed?"

I could only shake my head, for the possibility had not occurred to me. Lady Margaret came to my rescue.

"How could the boy know that?" she asked her husband amiably, looking up from her work. "He spends most of his life shut up in that great library. How could he possibly know what Robert Bruce is like to do?"

"He is as like to know as I am, my dear," her husband replied mildly. "Jamie has a long head on him, and not all his life is spent among his books." He looked back to me. "So, lad, what think you?"

I shook my head again. "I have never met or seen Sir Robert Bruce, Uncle. But Will's father, Uncle Alan, was his man, and though I only heard him speak of his master once, he said he pitied any fool who dared to offend Annandale. That said, I agree with Will."

The manservant came in bearing a heavy jug of the household's weak, home-brewed ale, known as small beer. He crossed to a table in the corner that held a pile of earthen mugs, and we watched in silence as he poured four measures and then served each of us, beginning with Lady Margaret and Sir Malcolm.

"Good," the knight said once the door had closed again at the man's back. "Your support of your cousin's opinion pleases me. It shows loyalty, as well as reason, though I confess I hoped you might point out that Lord John Balliol and his House have also been neglected here. So let us look at this senselessness, as Will calls it, for what it truly is." He glanced at each of us in turn. "Are you ready?"

We both nodded.

"Let us suppose, though God forbid it should, that everything goes wrong from this day forth. The Queen fails to produce an heir and, even worse, some tragedy befalls young Princess Margaret. What would happen then?" He did not wait for an answer. "There would be dire competition for the throne among the magnates. And among those, who would have the paramount claim?"

"Balliol and Bruce," Will said immediately, for he and I had discussed this very matter the previous week.

"Exactly. Balliol and Bruce. And which would take precedence?" When neither of us responded, he nodded. "Wise lads," he said. "For no one knows the answer to that question. Both men have valid claims and both are descendants of David II, though one claims through the female side and the other through a male but arguably less direct descent. The settlement of their dispute would require abler and more subtle minds than ours to arbitrate. And seen from that viewpoint, it would clearly be madness to appoint either of them to serve as a Guardian.

"But take it one step further and consider this supposedly senseless Council of Guardians. Of the six, three are close bound to Balliol by family ties and loyalties—Fraser of St. Andrews, the Comyn Earl of Buchan, and Lord John Comyn of Badenoch, who is wed to Balliol's sister. The other three align themselves with Bruce—Wishart of Glasgow, MacDuff the Earl of Fife, and James the Stewart. A balance of power, lads. Three Guardians in support of each claimant, and equal representation from north and south. Ask yourselves now, does it truly seem so senseless?"

4

On an afternoon towards the end of autumn in the following year, our sixth year as students, William Wallace turned on the churlish monk called Brother James, picked him up, and flung him headlong to the ground. I was there, and it was in my defence that Will had acted, but in doing so he broke the greatest of the Abbey's unwritten laws: anyone who laid angry hands on one of the brotherhood was guilty, *ipso facto*, of a crime against the fraternity that the Abbey represented. Certainly no Abbey student had ever done such a thing before that moment.

Appalled at what had happened, I knew we would both suffer for it, regardless of the provocation that had spurred it. Stunned as I was by the sight of the monk sprawled at my feet, I was amazed that my cousin had restrained himself as much as he had. Mere moments earlier his face had been wild, his huge fist upraised, ready to smash the older man's face into a pulp. Now, the downed man squirmed in terror, the skirts of his robe soaked by an involuntary voiding of his bladder, while above him Will struggled with himself, his face suffused with blood and his hands clenching and unclenching as he swayed back and forth with the power of his emotions.

Will looked around for the object that had precipitated this disaster. It lay almost beneath his feet—the solid walking staff that Brother James had smashed across my shoulders without warning, driving me to my knees. Will bent slowly and picked it up, hefting it in one hand. It was a heavy, sound staff of hazel wood about five feet in length and worn smooth from long use. The monk had risen to one elbow and now remained motionless, staring up, aghast, at the fury he had provoked. Without looking at him, Will took the hazel staff in both his hands and snapped it in half across his knee, then held both halves together and did the same again, a prodigious feat of strength. He then extended his arm, allowing the pieces to drop one by one onto the man on the ground.

"You spineless, Godless lump of excrement," he growled in his newly acquired adult voice. "If you ever dare bring your foul presence close to my cousin again I will cripple you so badly that you will never leave your cell thereafter. Do you understand me?" His voice was profoundly deep, rolling and sonorous, yet also calm, but its pitch left no doubt that he was waiting for an answer.

"Yes, yes, I understand. I do." The monk was bobbing his head rapidly, no trace of arrogance or dislike discernible in him now.

"Then take your skinny, piss-wet arse out of my sight. *Now!*"

The roar of rage galvanized the wretched monk, and he scrambled to all fours and scurried away, lurching towards the Abbey.

I turned to Will. "You know he's running straight to Father Abbot, don't you?"

"Aye, and I don't care. This day has been coming for years and now it's done with." Suddenly he switched to Scots. "And ye ken? I dinna gi'e a damn what they dae to me. Yon was worth it. Did ye see how quick he pished hissel', the watter rinnin' doon his robe? I could hear the gush o' it. He didna think we'd daur face up to him."

"They'll expel you, Will. Me, too."

"No, Jamie, not you." He reverted to Latin seamlessly. "He attacked you with a weapon, unprovoked. And that reminds me." He stooped and gathered up the four broken pieces. "We might need this for proof. Pull up your shift."

I struggled to do as he said, suddenly aware of the band of pain across my shoulders, and when my back was bare he pressed his thumb against the welt that was evidently visible.

"Aye," he murmured. "That'll bruise beautifully, too clear to be denied. Don't lose it." I looked at him in disbelief, amazed to see him grinning.

"How can you laugh, Will? We are deep in trouble."

He shook his head. "No, Jamie, no. I might be, but you're not. I told you."

"They'll throw you out. What will you do then? You'll be disgraced."

"Aye." He barked a laugh, which astounded me. "And *they'll* go hungry for fresh meat forever after." He reached out to dig his fingers into my shoulder. "I'm finished here anyway, Jamie. Nothing more here that I want to learn. I've only stayed this past half year to keep you company, but nowadays you're so lost in your books that I spend most of my time alone. So if they throw me out, and I hope they will, I'll go back to Elderslie and be a forester. That's all I want to do anyway."

"A *forester*!" I was sure he was jesting. "You can't be a forester, you speak Latin and French! Foresters know only trees and animals, poachers and hunters."

"And bows, Jamie. Some of us know bows. But I might be the first monk-taught forester. Think of that. And never fear, Uncle Malcolm will welcome me because he can always use good foresters, and he'll accept my leaving here once he knows what caused it. You, on the other hand, will stay here and take up your calling and we'll see each other often."

I knew he spoke the truth about being welcomed back in Elderslie, for he was right about the need for a good forester on the Wallace lands, and I knew too that the old knight would forgive him, for Will and Sir Malcolm had grown close, and the older man had scant respect for clerics. Some, he would concede if pressed, were well enough, honest in their endeavours and their calling like his own two kinsmen, but he had found too many far less suited to his taste. Parasites, he called those who used the privileges and seclusion of the clerical life to keep themselves well fed in relative comfort and free of the responsibilities that encumbered other men.

Brother James, I had long known, was one such specimen. He had never overcome the dislike he had conceived for us when he had been charged with showing us the precincts on our first day there. He had not known who we were that day, and when he discovered later that we were Wallaces, close kin to Father Peter and Brother Duncan, his resentment and dislike had festered and grown deep, although he was usually at pains to mask it. But even that masking bred more resentment.

Will and I tried several times to placate him in the months that followed that first encounter, but it was a thankless task, and we soon resigned ourselves to his dislike and avoided him as much as possible. Yet, inevitably in such a small community, there were times when our paths crossed, and those occasions were generally unpleasant. That became increasingly true as the years passed and we continued to disappoint Brother James by failing to disgrace ourselves as he expected, rising instead to positions of relative prominence within the community, myself as the youngest librarian ever and Will as supplier to the pantry.

I discovered later that our final encounter that September day had been caused by jealousy, and it was inconceivable to me that any full-grown man should be jealous of me. But I learned that James had once worked in the library and had been banished for negligence after several valuable manuscripts were damaged through his carelessness. He had also applied to study for the priesthood, but had been found deficient in several areas and was rejected. The word of my acceptance as a seminarian had been brought to me by Father Peter on the morning of the day Joseph attacked me, and clearly the unfortunate man had heard of it, as he attacked me soon afterwards.

And so our shared days as students ended. Will admitted to assaulting Brother James, but he was merciless in asserting the details of how and why he had done so, offering the broken weapon in evidence and bidding the monks bare my back to show the mark James had inflicted upon me. He went out of his way, too, to describe the antipathy James had held for us since our arrival at the Abbey and offered detailed accounts of several encounters we had had with the man, to our cost each time.

Being a student and one of the transgressors by association, I was forbidden to witness Will's arraignment, confined under the guard of two senior brethren outside the tribunal chamber until I was hauled in briefly to show my injuries. But Brother Duncan was there in his capacity of armarius, and it was he who described the proceedings to me later. The judging panel, headed by Father Abbot himself, believed Will's tale unanimously, and Brother James was confined to his cell on bread and water for three months, an unheard-of punishment. On the matter of Will's infraction, however, there was no recourse. He had struck down one of the community in blatant contravention of the law, unwritten though it was, and had created a precedent. Moreover, he had openly admitted during the hearing that, similarly provoked, he would do the same again, though more thoroughly and effectively next time.

But then, in acknowledgment of the troubled faces of the men who must unwillingly condemn him, William Wallace did something that confounded me when I heard about it, something so noble and so honourable in one so young that it strengthened me years afterwards when I began to hear, and to disbelieve, tales of the alleged atrocities being tallied against his name and fame: he took pity on his judges and absolved them of any guilt they might be feeling, assuring them all that he had long since decided that his time of usefulness to the Abbey community had reached an end. His dearest wish now was to become a forester on his uncle Malcolm's estates, he told them, because that was what he truly believed God had intended for him and he was impatient to begin. He thanked them for the opportunities they had given him to learn to read and write and converse in Latin and French, as well as for the training they had offered him, perhaps unwittingly, in the paths that he would follow thenceforth, by according him the freedom of the Abbey's lands in which to hunt and learn the lore of his future craft. And then he requested their permission to quit his formal studies immediately and to return to Elderslie.

The tribunal heard him out in silence—gratefully, I like to think—and then they permitted him to withdraw from his studies and return home with no disgrace attached to his name.

Listening to Brother Duncan's recital of the events, I was moved to tears by the way he summed the matter up: "Your cousin Will is a fine young man," he said, with no trace of harshness on his normally forbidding face. "And I believe God has moulded him to be what he is with some great purpose in His mind. We may never know that purpose, but I have no fears that William Wallace will ever let anything stand in his way to achieving it."

S

Ewan accompanied Will back to Elderslie, his own tasks in Paisley completed. He left the farm, which had flourished under his stewardship for years now, functioning smoothly under the guidance of a tenant called Murdoch, who had done the actual farming and supervised the labourers over those years, quickly earning the ungrudging trust of both Ewan and Sir Malcolm. The abrupt departure of my two friends, however, meant that everything familiar in my life had changed; they had taken the entire contents of the workshop with them, leaving only an empty stone shell. They had left me my bow and a supply of arrows, and even a brace of targets, but I knew, even as I collected those to take them with me back to the Abbey, that I would probably never use them again. The Abbey cloisters would be my permanent home from then on, and although I had enjoyed my archery greatly, I knew that without Will and Ewan to keep me interested and active, I would soon abandon it. Librarians and priests have no need of weapons, even for recreation.

Somewhat to my surprise, I adapted effortlessly to life as a full-time member of the close-knit Abbey community. My work in the library continued to absorb me, as it had since the beginning, and the time I now had to myself in the evening hours was soon taken up by my studies for the priesthood. It came as a welcome discovery, too, that Brother Duncan and Father Peter intended to continue using me as their go-between with Sir Malcolm, for it meant that for at least one day out of every fourteen I was dispatched to Elderslie to deliver information to my uncle and to bring back his reports to them. Thus I was able to keep myself informed of Will's activities, even if I did not see him on every visit.

He had, as he had wished, become one of my uncle's foresters, and the faithful Ewan Scrymgeour had chosen to join him. Both of them were carefree now, busily involved in a brief but intense apprenticeship under old Erik Strongarm, my uncle's senior forester. By the year's end they would be responsible for the care

and maintenance of the surrounding woodlands. They would cull
dead and dying trees, keep the forest free from the buildup of flam-
mable undergrowth, and from time to time they would inspect the
activities of the charcoal burners, whose vast smouldering turf-
covered pits produced the charred, hard-burning fuel essential to
the estate's smithies. They would also be charged with the welfare
of the wildlife on Sir Malcolm's lands—the deer, wild swine, and
other game, including fowl, that thrived in the woods and in the
open glades and pastures among the trees—and with the safety of
the cattle and domestic swine in the various pastures and paddocks
close by the main farm, protecting all of them from theft and
depredation.

Ewan had worn the green garments of a forest dweller when first
I met him years before, and now he wore them again. But so, I
discovered, did Will. The first time I saw him thus, garbed from
head to foot in close-fitting, hooded green tunic and trews, I gaped,
for he was bigger than ever. His arms and shoulders were enormous,
larger, I thought, than those of any other man I had ever seen, and
his thighs and legs were as solid and substantial as healthily growing
oaks. At seventeen, he was now a man in all respects, save one that
I knew nothing of, and I had never seen him happier.

He had grown quickly to accommodate the demands of his newly
fashioned bow, itself a thing of beauty that glowed richly with love
and care, coats of laboriously applied wax and tallow enhancing the
different colours of its wood. It was tapered to perfection for his
height and capped on both thumb-thick ends with ram horn tips, the
horn boiled to the melting point and then moulded and slotted to
anchor the loops of his bowstring. One glance at the thickness of its
massive grip was all it took for me to know I could never begin to
pull it. He carried it unstrung most of the time, in a protective case
of bull's hide, thickly waxed and waterproof, that hung from his
shoulder opposite the bag of yard-long arrows, but he could free it,
bend it and string it with hemp, nock an arrow, and be ready to shoot
in mere moments when he needed it. It was the pride of his life, I
could see. He told me he kept it unstrung and cased in the English

fashion, to avoid any danger of the bow's shaft shaping itself permanently to the arc of the string's pull and thereby losing some of its power. All in all, my cousin had turned into an imposing man, and the dark growth now fuzzing his cheeks and chin would complete the transformation very soon.

I was not quite correct in that respect, though. Will's transformation to manhood was effected by another element altogether, one which had little or nothing to do with the density of his beard. But my error was understandable: I was a cloistered boy, barely sixteen, and studying for the priesthood. I had no idea of the natural forces that can transform the merest boy into a man.

Her name was Mirren Braidfoot, and on a brilliant summer day in 1288 she came to Elderslie in a light, horse-drawn cart, accompanied by four other young women and a group of eager young men, all of those afoot. She was there to visit a cousin, a plump, plain girl called Jessie Brunton, whom both Will and I knew by sight. I witnessed the first meeting between him and Mirren, but apart from smirking to myself over his tongue-tied awkwardness, I missed the fateful significance of it, too grateful that it was Will, not I, who had to deal face to face with such a fetching stranger. Will was abashed, I knew, and that was unusual, for he had learned much about young women since leaving the Abbey, but I myself would have been struck mute by her smiling confidence had it been I who had to speak to her.

Standing beside Will, barely reaching the middle of his swelling upper arm and looking for all the world like a slight and tiny child—though she was anything but either one—the girl Mirren stood gazing up at him, watching his face with a deeply thoughtful look on her own. As I approached, the young woman stepped away from him to make room for me. I was aware of her bright blue eyes scanning me from head to foot, her lips smiling gently. But being me, I ignored her look and turned instead to Will, blissfully unaware that in the short time I had been watching elsewhere, William Wallace's life, and all of Scotland's destiny, had been changed forever.

CHAPTER FIVE

I

"Where first we find love, there also we encounter grief."

I cannot remember who said that, but it springs into my mind unbidden whenever I think of Mirren Braidfoot and my cousin Will, and it never fails to grip me like a fist clenching around my heart. I am a priest, and although that in itself is no guarantee of chastity or lack of prurience, I have never known the love of a woman, either physical or emotional. I have known temptation, certainly, for that is the common burden of mankind, but I have always managed, somehow, through no strength of my own and most often by the power of fervent and sustained prayer, to avoid yielding to it.

That said, however, I have been fascinated all my life by the overwhelming strength of the love one sometimes finds between certain men and women, and I have always found the power of it, for both good and ill, to be close to frightening. Had King Alexander not yearned for the welcoming warmth of his young wife, for example, he would not have died as he did on his way to join her. And had William Wallace never met Mirren Braidfoot, he would not have died as he did in London's Smithfield Square.

I do not mean this to be taken as a condemnation of Mirren. In all the years that passed after that first meeting in Elderslie, neither Will nor she did any wilful thing to harm the other. As a courting pair, two young people discovering each other, they were the very essence of God's intent for His beloved children; as a married couple, they knew bliss together; and as supporters of each other's dreams, even when apart, they were unshakable. There was no weakness in their love, no inborn flaw, no fault; merely perfect love and fidelity. But as these attributes buttressed their love, they also left them open to their enemies.

It had already begun that day of their initial meeting, though none of us would learn of that for months to come.

Will told me many times about being swept away by love that day, about what he saw and how he felt when he was smitten by the woman who would quickly come to mean all the world to him, and as I listened to him over the first few months of such outpourings— for by then Mirren had returned to her home in Lanark—I was struck by the resemblance between the way he spoke of her and the ardour with which Andrew Murray had described his own love, the young woman with the liquidly beautiful name Siobhan. Both young men burned with the same ardent passion, and from the lambent purity of Will's enthusiasm I came to see, through his eyes, what my own eyes had missed that afternoon.

I had arrived in Elderslie at mid-morning, mere hours before they met, and as soon as I had delivered the letter that had brought me there to Sir Malcolm, I set out to where he had told me I would find Will, a good half-hour's walk from the main house. I found him near the westernmost edge of Sir Malcolm's lands, close to the village of Elderslie itself and hard by the wagon road that led to it from Paisley. He was crouched over a narrow track through the long grass that lined the roadway, pawing at the grass with spread fingers, his head moving from side to side as he inched forward. He heard me coming, glanced up, then returned his attention to the ground ahead of him.

"Good day, idle Forester," I greeted him. "Have you lost something?"

He swept his open hands through long grass, then looked at his palms and shrugged to his feet. "Not lost, nor found," he said. "I'm looking for blood. But there doesna seem to be any." It had been two weeks since last we met, but he spoke as if we had parted no more than an hour earlier; no greeting, no acknowledgment, no surprise.

"And should there be?"

He stooped then to pick up the strung bow in the long grass and then unstrung it, bracing the stave with his foot as he pulled it down to free the loop from its end.

"Aye, there should. I shot at a doe here … Throw me my case, there." He caught the case easily and flipped off its cap, then turned completely around, his eyes scanning the surrounding grass as he slid the long stave into its tube. He replaced the cap and slung the case over his shoulder, shaking his head. "She should be lying here dead, but my eyes tell me I missed her from sixty paces."

I made no reply to that, not knowing what to say, for I had never known him to miss any target from that range. He was still looking about him, his eyes now checking the line of flight from the base of an ash tree sixty paces away and passing his right side, right over the road and into a dense thicket of brambles.

"Anyway, she ran, and I thought I'd gut-shot her and would have to hunt her down, but there's no blood. And no sign of my arrow. Mind you, I felt it flutter as it left the string. I must have torn the fletching without noticing and it flew off course. But God be my witness, I hate losing arrows."

"What was wrong with the doe?"

Will sniffed and pulled several broadhead hunting arrows from the bag at his side, peering closely at the fletching on each one. "Old age and a lame leg. She'll no' last the winter and might no' even reach it. I thought it would be kinder to kill her now and end her pains … But she's well away from here by now." He dropped the arrows back into his bag. "What brings *you* here this fine morning, then? You're like to shrivel up and blow away in the brightness out here if you're no' careful, after being cooped up in your old, dark library."

"Came to see you, and to deliver a letter to Sir Malcolm."

"In that order, eh?" His thickening beard almost concealed the quirk of his grin. "Well, you see me now, and you seem to be in fine fettle. Though you look more like a damn priest each time I see you."

It was true. Since taking up residence at the Abbey I had worn the grey habit of the resident monks. "I am a damn priest—or I soon will be."

He grunted, then took hold of my right wrist and held my hand up to examine my fingers. "Ink … Are you still practising wi' your bow? I don't see any calluses."

I freed my hand and wiggled my fingers, looking at them almost ruefully. "No, I never seem to find the time nowadays. And besides, it's no fun if you're not there. I've lost nearly all my calluses this past year." I glanced across the road to the bramble thickets. "Are you not going to look for that arrow?"

"Nah, we'd never find it. It was moving flat across the ground. It could have passed right through that whole thicket without hitting anything. Did you bring anything to eat?" I shook my head and he grimaced. "Damn. Neither did I. Ran out and forgot all about eating this morning, wanting an early start. Looked for this wee doe for hours before I found her, and then missed her completely from close enough to touch her. Not a good morning's work … Ach well. Let's go into the village and find something to eat. It's no' far, and I'm famished."

We talked about trivial things as we walked the half mile into the village and made our way directly to the sign of the Boar's Head by the side of the common, where a few of the loiterers sitting by the entrance nodded to us as we entered. The dim interior reeked of stale beer, bad food, and smoky, guttering lamps even at noon. Supposedly a hostelry, as announced by the crudely painted sign of the mightily tusked boar's head that hung above the front door, the place was in reality what the local folk called a howff—a drinking hole that could not even claim the respectability of a tavern. It was a den where men came at night to whore and gamble, drink and blaspheme, but it was also the only place in the village that sold food for instant consumption during the day, and as such it attracted a wider variety of customers in daylight than it did by night.

There were few customers inside, and we seated ourselves in a dark corner at the end of the plank table that served as a crude counter and sipped at flagons of thin, sour ale while we waited for the slatternly wife of Big Rab, the owner, to slop two platters of the day's meat pie in front of us. Neither of us made any remark on the food or its delivery; we had been there many times before and were familiar with the way things were done. To my surprise, though, the pie that day was the best I had ever tasted there, hot and savoury and well stuffed with chunks of onion, turnip, and meat, and topped with a well-made crust. We ate without comment, neither of us daring to wonder aloud what kind of meat was in the pie, or where it came from, although I fancied that I could detect both venison and wild hare in the well-spiced mixture. We both knew that if it were venison, it had been taken illegally, so I kept silent and merely enjoyed it while Will, the forester and keeper, ate it without expressing either curiosity or enjoyment.

I could see he was far from happy with the situation, and at the same time I was aware of Big Rab loitering anxiously in the background, glancing worriedly at us from time to time and plainly expecting Will to say something. As we drained our flagons and stood up to leave, Rab's wife came bustling towards us, the look on her face holding sufficient guilt to condemn both her and her man. Will muttered a gruff word of thanks and threw a coin on the table. I followed him wordlessly out of the place, noting the look of relief on Big Rab's face as he scuttled away into the rear of the establishment.

As soon as we were outside I noticed that the loiterers had all gone. "Good pie," I said. "I wonder who cooked it."

"I don't want to know," he growled. "No more than I want to know where the deer came from."

As he spoke, someone called his name in the distance, and we both turned to see one of Sir Malcolm's tenants, a man called James Laithey, waving to us from the butts on the common. Here, as in any town or village, anyone who owned cattle had the right to graze them on the common, but in Elderslie, a strip of ground along the longest side was set aside in the summer months for archery. It was barely wide enough for three men to stand side by side and shoot towards the far end, some two hundred paces distant, but it was sufficient for the needs of the archers who used it, none of whom owned a longbow. The normal bow of Scots huntsmen and archers was broad and flat in section, sometimes laminated with layers of horn or sinew, and made from local ash or elm or even beech, and their average length was a yard and a half. One sometimes saw a five-foot bow being used, but those were usually in the hands of visiting bowmen, travellers who roamed the countryside matching their skills against the local marksmen and usually prospering. Will's bow was an entirely different weapon from all of those, and he was generally reluctant to demonstrate its power in competition, a delicacy that was accepted gracefully by others once they had seen its power, and Will's accuracy, for themselves.

I noticed strangers among the usual gathering of villagers, including a noisy group of about ten young people of both sexes and an unknown bowman who stood apart from the crowd and seemed to be the centre of attention. It was obvious from the height and width of both him and his long, broad bow that he was a wandering archer, looking to win money from the local marksmen.

"Shit," Will muttered. "I suppose I'd better see what James wants. I could do without knowing, though, for I'm guessing at it already and I don't like it."

We waited for the other man to reach us.

"What is it, James? I have to get back to work."

Laithey wasted no time in telling us. The stranger's reputation had preceded him, for he had been making the rounds of the neighbouring villages and was far more proficient at his art than he professed to be. He would compete, appear to falter, lose several bouts, and then, on the point of paying his losses, would ask for one more match at double the stakes, at which point he would rally, and finish up with deadly precision, winning everything.

Will shrugged. "What do you want of me, James? You know I don't shoot for money. This fellow will take one look at my bow and walk away."

Laithey nodded. "He might. But he's awfu' cocksure and pleased wi' himsel'. He likely thinks he can beat you."

"How does he even know me? I've never seen him before."

"Some of the fellows saw ye goin' into the howff. They were talkin' about ye, and the fellow was listenin'. And besides, if he walks away now, he'll take every coin in the village wi' him, for they're a' in his pocket already."

Will sighed and looked sideways at me, rolling his eyes. "Who are those other folk, the young ones?"

"Just visitors, frae Paisley," Laithey told him. "They're here to visit young Jessie Brunton—her sisters and their friends."

Will sighed. "Well," he said at length, "I'll offer him a match, but I doubt he'll take it. If he's won everything already I'm surprised he's still here."

"Don't be. He was interested in what the lads had to say about ye. That's why he's waitin'."

"Then he's wasting his time. I've no money other than a groat or two."

Laithey, who was known for both sobriety and thrift, grinned, for he had admired Will's skill for years. "I'll put up the coin," he said. "Just this once, to see you beat this thief. And when you win, I'll gi'e back the winnings to the fools who lost them."

"You will? I'll hold you to that. But what if I lose?"

The other man shrugged, still smiling. "You willna. But 'gin you do, I'll take it as God's judgment on me for gambling."

Will dipped his head. "So be it. Let's try him, then. But I doubt he'll take the wager."

The stranger, who introduced himself as plain Robertson, agreed to Will's challenge with apparent reluctance, eyeing the long leather case that hung from his shoulder. But as the one being challenged, he had the setting of the terms, and it was immediately obvious he knew what he was doing. The most effective range of the yew longbow was between two hundred and two hundred and twenty paces, shooting at a six-inch target centre or a similarly thick fence post; beyond that distance, the yew archer tended to lose accuracy, and at lesser ranges the arrow flight was constrained by the bow's huge strength, and the inaccuracy became even greater.

"Targets," Robertson said. "Split posts, three inches thick, two feet high." He watched narrow-eyed as Will considered that before nodding slowly, but then he could not hold back a wolfish grin as he continued. "At a hundred."

It was an outrageous proposition, the short distance and half-width targets putting Will at an enormous disadvantage with his great yew bow. Will pursed his lips, appearing to think long and hard and be on the point of refusal, but then he sniffed and nodded. "Agreed. Even bets?"

"What? D'ye take me for a fool? Against that thing?" Robertson nodded at the longbow's case as though he were not convinced that he had already crippled Will's chances of winning. "Two to one. On your side."

Will gazed for a long time at Robertson's own bow, a flat, layered weapon of wood and sinew that flared to a hand's breadth wide above and below the grip before tapering to the ends. Five feet long, I estimated. Will nodded, stone faced. "Accepted," he said. "Set them up."

Laithey shouted the terms to the waiting crowd, and a cluster of men quickly set about making the targets from the pile of six-inch posts at the edge of the butts, some of them splitting the lengths of wood into quarters and others hammering the stakes firmly into the ground until they were of uniform height, their freshly split wedged faces towards the archers. The crowd along the edges of the range grew denser as others were attracted by the activity. To my eyes the target stakes, barely projecting above the ungrazed pasture of the narrow strip, were barely visible from a hundred paces, and for the first time I could remember, I found myself doubting Will's ability to hit them, recalling his missed shot at the sick doe earlier.

Will was by now stringing his bow and pulling target arrows from among the broadheads in his bag. The target arrowheads were long and heavy, solid and round and tapered like armour-piercing bodkins, shorter but no less sharply pointed; hollowed out, they fitted tightly over the arrows' shafts, and were fletched with grey goose feathers. When he was satisfied with his six selections, he stepped forward to the firing line and thrust the arrows point first into the ground in a row by his right side.

Robertson had defined the range and the targets; Will's was the choice to shoot first or last, and the right to determine the number of casts.

"One flight," he said to his adversary. "Six shots only. You first, then me."

Robertson nodded, plainly having expected this. "Six each, then. All at once, or shot by shot?"

"All at once. Straight count. Your six first, then mine. The winner the man who leaves most arrows in the marks. No repeats. I ha'e to get back to work."

"Right. Let's be about it."

The crowd had separated in anticipation of the contest, a few of them flanking the firing line to watch the bowmen, but the majority crowding near the targets at the end of the narrow firing lane. I could see they had no fear of being killed by a stray shot. They were accustomed to such contests and they knew the skill of the contestants.

Robertson stepped forward to his side of the aiming line, nocking his first arrow to his string, and Laithey raised his arms and shouted for silence, bringing a hush to the crowd. Will's eyes were narrowed, taking stock of his opponent's stance and missing no single element of the man's preparation.

The targets were small and the distance to them was short, but no one there, man or woman, would have thought to criticize. Every one of them knew how difficult the contest was, precisely because of those constraints.

Robertson stood stock-still, his eyes narrowed to slits as he stared at the first mark, its bottom half obscured by waving fronds of seeding grass. He held the bow loosely, resting horizontally across his left thigh, the fingers of his right hand gripping the string above and below the nocked end of the arrow. Then, still slit-eyed, he spread his feet, taking a half-step back with his right, and brought the bow up smoothly, leaning into it and drawing the taut string to his cheek as though it was weightless. He released quickly. The sound of the arrow's flight was lost in the snap of the bowstring against the shaped guard of bull horn that protected his forearm, and the crowd hissed as his shaft struck solidly, within a palm's width of the top of the distant mark. The peg was deeply buried, almost two-thirds of its length firmly seated in the earth, but the force of the arrow's impact moved it visibly and split it; the arrow was gripped there, pointing sideways and down.

Without pausing, Robertson drew and loosed again, nocking a fresh arrow within seconds of each shot until he had fired all six within the span of a single minute. As the sixth hit home, some of the distant watchers clapped and whistled. Only his third shot had missed its mark. Another, his fourth, caught the very top of its stake, where the wood was flattened and frayed by the maul that had hammered it into the ground; the point lodged in the damaged wood, but the arrow hung precariously in place. The other four missiles were firmly lodged in the target stakes. He turned to Will with a tiny smirk.

"Five, you agree?"

"Aye, five hits. A fine try. Not bad at all. I've seen far worse."

"Not bad?" The smirk widened. "Let's see you do better, then."

Will's six arrows were still where he had set them in the ground, about a pace behind the firing line, and now he moved to stand beside them, plucking up the first of them and laying it across his horizontal bow stave, holding it in place with his left index finger while he nocked the end slot securely onto the taut string. His arrows were longer than Robertson's by a full finger's length, thicker and therefore heavier than the other man's. He flexed his fingers on the bow's grip, then froze, concentrating.

For long seconds he stood there, looking at the first slender target. Robertson harrumphed and muttered something. It was surely intended as a distraction, but Will ignored it. He drew a deep breath and went to work.

He stepped forward, leaning into his pull as his left foot went forward to the line, his straight left arm pushing the arcing bow stave forward while his massive chest, back, and shoulder muscles pulled the thick string of densely braided hemp back smoothly to his ear. The release was immensely powerful, and the line of flight was low, the arrow sinking so swiftly that I thought, for an instant, that it had fallen short. But then the target stake whipped violently and the arrow in its cleft sprang free and spun to the ground, its fall accompanied by a great shout from the crowd.

Will had already nocked another arrow by then, and before the shout could die away he stepped into his second shot. His movements were a joy to watch, a sacred dance to a rhythm known only to himself, and he loosed all six of his arrows in less time than Robertson had taken for his. But Will struck five marks close above the ground, within a hand's breadth of their bases, and two of them dislodged arrows that Robertson had already placed. The sixth arrow had struck the ground at the base of the mark the other man had missed, but on closer examination it was found to have pierced the stake beneath the surface. Even without it, though, Will's tally stood at five to Robertson's remaining three.

To his credit, the other archer said nothing. He walked the hundred measured paces to the line of target posts, where he stood looking down at Will's handiwork. He shook his head in disbelief, for Will's grouping truly was astounding. Of the five shafts that had struck above the ground, the highest was less than an inch above the lowest. Robertson reached into the pouch at his waist and brought out a small leather purse; he hefted it in his hand, then lobbed it underhand to Will.

"I've never seen the like," he said. "And I've never been so outmatched. I'll stay out of your way, 'gin we ever meet again, Will Wallace."

The two nodded to each other, in mutual respect, then bent to gather up their spent arrows as the crowd surged forward, and there was pandemonium as every man there wanted to shake the hand of each of the contestants. Will turned his back on the well-wishers and caught my eye. He threw the purse to me. "Take that to James while I finish up here."

I took the money to Laithey, and as I turned away I saw the group of young people who had come to visit Jessie Brunton now thronging around Will. Jessie, I knew, had been recently married to a friendly young fellow called Tam Brunton, a miller who worked on Sir Malcolm's estate. I had known her by her unmarried name, Jessie Waddie. She was the eldest daughter of Ian Waddie, a prosperous Paisley wool merchant. Waddie, it now turned out, was married to Margaret Braidfoot of Lamington, near Lanark, whose brother Hugh, a successful sheep farmer and therefore a valued associate of Ian Waddie, had a daughter called Mirren, whose presence was the underlying reason for today's visit from all these young people. Mirren, aged seventeen, had come to Paisley on what had become an annual visit, to spend the summer with her beloved Auntie Meg and her daughters.

Jessie herself was standing close by, a slightly bemused smile on her face as though at a loss to explain her sudden popularity even to herself, and I went and spoke to her for a few moments, asking about her visitors. When I turned away from her again, I saw the tallest youth in the party struggling to pull Will's bow, and I was amazed that Will would permit such a thing. It was only later—much later—that Will gave me his own slightly dazed account of what happened while my back was turned.

2

"**W**ho was the fellow trying to pull your bow? The big fellow the girls were all admiring?"

"Who? I don't know. He's one of Mirren's friends."

"He was dressed as a forester. Had you ever seen him before?"

"No, but he's a Bruce man. He's a woodsman, though, not a forester."

"Is there a difference?"

That earned me a stare from beneath slightly raised eyebrows. "Aye, there's a big difference, and fine you know it. A woodsman patrols the woods, looking for poachers, but that's all he does. He has a forester to tell him what to do and where to go and when. He wears the green and he works in the woods, but he knows nothing of forestry, beyond being able to move quietly in the thickets."

"Which Bruce does he work for, Annandale or Carrick?"

"The old man, Annandale. He owns the land alongside ours, to the south and west."

We were sitting together by the fire in Sir Malcolm's main room, late that same night. Sir Malcolm and Lady Margaret were long since abed, and we would have been, too, save that I was enjoying my time away from the Abbey too much to want to sleep, and Will was too tightly wound over the events of the afternoon. If he had mentioned Mirren Braidfoot once since we came home that day he had mentioned her a score of times; her name was rarely absent from his conversation, what little there was of that. I was perplexed, for I could hardly remember him ever mentioning any girl by name twice in the same day. But there he was, sitting across from me yet barely there, his gaze focused on whatever vision he was seeing in the leaping flames in the grate.

"So you don't know this fellow's name, the one who had your bow?"

"No."

"Why did you let him take it?"

"What? Oh, because he wanted to."

"He *wanted* to. And you just *let* him? Will, you won't even let me *carry* that bow. Why would you give it to someone you didn't know, and let him play with it?"

"Mirren wanted me to."

"Mirren wanted … I think you'd better tell me— Will? Are you listening? Tell me what happened when you met this Mirren. How did you meet her?"

He frowned, blinking. "I don't know." He shook his head. "I don't remember. She was just there, suddenly, yellow and blue …"

It was enough for me to see her clearly. She had been wearing a yellow kirtle over a blue gown, and Will's eyes were wide again with the recollection of it.

"I'd seen them there," he continued, "the folk from Paisley, but I hadn't noticed her before they all came flocking around me, and then there she was. Sweet Jesu, Jamie, but she's bonnie. She was looking right at me, her eyes on mine, and I swear I near fell into them, they were so big. And so blue, like her gown. They were all talking to me, shouting at me, but I could hardly hear them and she never said a word. She just stared at me, and then she smiled. I thought she was going to laugh at me and my heart nearly stopped for shame, but she didn't. She just looked and smiled. And God help me, I couldna smile back at her. I tried, I wanted to, but my face felt as though it was made of wood. I couldna make it work. And I just stood there, gawking at her like some daft wee laddie ...

"And then that fellow tried to take my bow, wanted to try it. She saw me start to turn on him and stopped me ... with her eyes. She didn't speak. Her eyes ... they flashed at me, warning me, I thought, though I didn't know against what. Then she looked at him, and at the bow, and back at me, and nodded. And I let him take it, along with an arrow from my bag, a broadhead. Then he walked away and all the others followed him to see how he would do. And we were left alone, the two of us." He looked at me, and his eyes were wide with wonder.

"What did she say to you?"

"That her name was Mirren. She knew mine already. Someone must have told her. She asked me where I lived, and when I told her, she said that I should come and look for her within the week, at her uncle's house in Paisley, in the evening when my work was done ... It was the strangest thing, Jamie. She told me how to find her, and when to come, and yet she never looked at me. She kept her eyes on the young fool with the bow the whole time, as though watching him and leaving me ignored, like a log on the ground. And then she said I should take my bow back, so I did. The poor gowk hadn't even drawn it to half pull. I took off the string, put the stave back in its case, and when I turned around again he was helping her up onto the wagon, and they left. She never looked at me again. Just left me standing there like a witless stirk."

"But she told you when and where to find her, Will. And did it privily, with no one being the wiser. Plainly she wanted none of them to know. Women do that sometimes."

He looked at me as though I had crowed like a cockerel. "Do what?"

I shrugged, aware of my own witlessness. "Behave strangely."

"How would *you* know that? Who told you such a thing?"

"Nobody *told* me … I must have heard it somewhere."

"Hmm. Then did you happen to hear what I should do now?"

"No, but I know … You should do as she bade you. Look for her in Paisley at her uncle's house the next time you are free of an evening."

3

The woodsman's name was Graham, and he came from a village called Kilbarchan, some twelve miles from Elderslie, though he now lived in a bothy on the Bruce lands south of us. Will learned his name quickly, for Graham of Kilbarchan was forever underfoot—like dung on a new boot was how Will put it—whenever he went to Paisley to see Mirren, and he soon grew to loathe the sight of the man. A week elapsed before he could wind up the courage to go and look for her at the home of her uncle, Waddie the wool merchant. He found her without difficulty, for she had been expecting him and was watching for him, but there his true difficulties began.

Mirren's uncle took his responsibilities seriously, and the safety and moral welfare of his sister's only daughter while she was in his care was one of his main concerns that summer. The girl was beautiful, and wealthy by Paisley standards, so she attracted admirers and suitors as a blooming bank of flowers draws bees, and Ian Waddie had to deal with all of them.

Unfortunately for Will, he dealt equally with all of them save one, treating them uniformly with hostile disapproval. The sole exception was the young woodsman from Kilbarchan, who was the only son of Alexander Graham of Kilbarchan, another of Master Waddie's prime suppliers of fine wool. This Graham had amassed sufficient wealth and property in a lifetime of hard work and sharp dealings to make his son appear as a supremely qualified suitor, despite the young man's general fecklessness, and that impression was greatly enhanced by the father's advanced age and rapidly failing health. Young Sandy would inherit everything, and for that reason alone, according to Mirren, Ian Waddie would have encouraged his suit even had the young man been a drunkard and a leper.

We spoke about this, Will and I, when next we met, about three weeks after his first encounter with Mirren, and I asked him, naively I suppose, why he put up with the fellow instead of sending him packing. He glanced at me sidelong, and I immediately saw how his involvement with Mirren had already changed him. The Will I had known all my life would have purged the young woodsman from his life as soon as Graham began to be a nuisance. The Will eyeing me now, though, was another person; he flushed slowly, and admitted, sheepishly, that it was Mirren's idea to keep young Graham close by. The woodsman had her uncle's goodwill and his full approval to spend time with her, and Mirren was clever enough to know that she could benefit thereby, simply by including Will in their excursions whenever he could arrange to visit Paisley. And when Will could not be there, to keep up the appearance of both consistency and propriety, she invariably invited another from her coterie of admirers to join her and Graham on their evening walks. It worked, of course.

By being unfailingly pleasant and congenial with Graham, yet keeping support and moral guidance close to hand at all times in the form of a third, amorously interested presence, Mirren managed to avoid awkwardness or entanglement with any of the young men, and by the time her stay in Paisley was half over she had overcome all her uncle's suspicions and won grudging acknowledgment from him that she was more than capable of protecting herself against the blandishments of the local swains. Waddie came to accept that there was nothing he could do to overcome his niece's refusal to encourage Sandy Graham's attentions, since it was obvious she did nothing to discourage them, either. Much as he was attracted to the idea of bringing Graham's wealth into his own family, and by association into his own purview, he was realistic enough to accept that he was not the girl's father and that the best way to promote his plans must be to gain her father's support in favour of a union between his daughter and the young woodsman.

I discovered that by merest happenstance, for Master Waddie came to the Abbey one day in search of assistance in composing and writing an important letter, and I was the one assigned to the task by Brother Duncan, since I had performed similar clerical services in the past for several of the town's merchants. By the time Master Waddie's letter began to take shape and I began to discern what was involved, I could hardly stop the work in progress. Besides, I judged the content harmless, apart from the sole consideration that its effect might have a bearing on the affairs of my closest friend. And so, in the spirit of the confessional, I resigned myself to keeping its content to myself. Will would never know of its existence, and I would use my knowledge of it only if such knowledge should ever be of benefit.

The letter was, of course, to Master Waddie's goodbrother Hugh Braidfoot, and it extolled the shining virtues of a potential husband he had found for young Mirren, namely Master Alexander Graham. The letter was duly signed and sealed and sent off to Mirren's home in Lamington, a few miles outside Lanark town. I no longer wondered about Will's tolerance of the woodsman Graham.

In the meantime, to Will's appalled disbelief, the summer weeks sped by and Mirren returned home to her family, leaving him close to despair at the thought of the empty year that yawned ahead of him before she would return to Paisley. He could talk for hours on end, and often did, about the wonders and the exploding complexities of their burgeoning love. Many times I listened to his outpourings almost in disbelief, confounded by the intensity and the passion in what he was telling me and by the mysterious changes the experience had provoked in him. He had kissed her once, he confessed to me in breathless bliss; just once, and fleetingly, seizing a moment when they were alone, and he swore that the taste and textures of it lingered on his lips and in his very vitals weeks later. Floundering with what that could mean, I found myself regretting, almost painfully, that I would never experience such strange and tempestuous sensations.

But then, as time swept onwards, a degree of sanity returned to my cousin's world, and he became engrossed again in the work that he loved. I became his *ex officio* liaison with Mirren then, serving as postmaster for the bulky letters he inscribed to her almost daily and ensuring that they were forwarded to Lanark in the custody of the regular procession of brothers travelling on the Church's affairs. Mirren, on her own behalf, had arranged to have her responses returned to me by the same route, though she was far less regular in her correspondence.

Beyond our little world of church and greenwood, much was happening, and none of it, it seemed at first, had anything to do with Will and Mirren. At the Abbey we learned that the magnates of the realm had been successful in their approach to England's King and had enlisted his aid in assuring the succession to the Scots throne of the child heir Margaret, whom people were already calling the Maid of Norway. A treaty to that effect had been signed at Salisbury in January of the new year, 1289, and a conclusive part of the same agreement was to be added the following year. Under the terms of these twin treaties, which would become known collectively as the Treaty of Birgham, Margaret's succession was guaranteed by her betrothal to Edward of Caernarvon, the English Prince of Wales. Wondrous news for all who cared, but Will Wallace was much more concerned with his own betrothal, a secret pact about which I had learned only very recently, when his frustration with the slowness of time boiled over.

Royal betrothals were, of course, affairs of state, and ordinary people knew little or nothing about them. We of the Abbey fraternity learned a little more as the proceedings developed, since the treaties

were drafted by our religious and clerical brethren in various loca-
tions, and the word, privileged and close held as it was, spread
quickly through our communities. In those early days everyone was
happy with what was happening because it served multiple
purposes, not the least of which was a settlement of the increasingly
rancorous rivalry between the two noble Houses of Bruce and
Balliol—including by extension the House of Comyn, inextricably
linked with Balliol through blood and marriage—over their
competing claims to the succession. Fostered by those feelings of
goodwill, and unbelievable though it seems now from more than
fifty years' distance, no one in Scotland objected strongly to Edward
Plantagenet's claim to acknowledgment as feudal overlord of
Scotland in return for his services as arbiter. That was perceived to
be a matter of semantics rather than literal interpretation, for the
feudal laws of the time attested to the *spirit* of that convention of
overlordship—most of the Scots magnates had held lands in
England for generations under feudal grants from English
monarchs—and the Treaty of Birgham clearly stated that the realm
of Scotland would remain "separate and divided from England
according to its rightful boundaries, free in itself and without
subjection." No man in Scotland could even have imagined that
Edward of England might soon insist upon the *letter* of that
unwritten accord and claim the throne of Scotland for himself.

In the eyes of the Scots populace, the single noticeable thing to
grow out of those preliminary agreements was an increasing presence of English soldiery and men-at-arms within the realm. It began
quietly and with all the appearances of legitimacy; England's King
had declared his goodwill in the matter of the Scots succession and
was involved with the magnates of the noble houses in ensuring
their commitment to the Birgham agreement. To that end, and on his
regal behalf, detachments of English soldiery soon began to move
freely throughout the land, tending to King Edward's affairs and
safeguarding his interests, and in the beginning no one, including
our little circle of family and friends, paid much attention to their
comings and goings.

But within a half year of the Birgham agreement, disquieting stories of English misbehaviour began to circulate, and although many of those were discounted at the outset, the reports became more frequent. All of them described English abuses and transgressions against the common law and the Scots folk, quickly forming a pattern that could not be denied.

Will showed no interest as these reports came to us. I tried more than once to coax out his opinions on the matter, but only once did he respond, on a night after dinner, when Peter and Duncan had been in Elderslie with me. He had refused to be drawn into their debate around the table. Afterwards, though, when only he and I were left in front of the fire, he spoke eloquently, and the quiet fury underlying his words shook me to my core.

"What d'you want me to tell you, Jamie?" He spoke in Scots, not in Latin, and that alone told me something of the depth of his emotions. "That these stories are no' true? That folk are just makin' them up to cause trouble? That the English wouldna do such things? For the love o' Christ, these are the people who cut off wee Jenny's head and used two wee boys as women. And now they're doing things folk dinna like … What did anybody expect, can ye tell me that? The only thing that surprises me about it is that it's ta'en so long for folk to see it. The English treat the common folk like slaves, here for their pleasure, and they've done it frae the outset. They don't think we're human. What was it Peter said? They lord it over us because they believe, deep down in their bones, that we're … what in the hell was it? A subservient people. Aye, that's what he said. They see us as a secondary race inferior to anything that's English. Shite. Don't get me started on it, Jamie."

"I thought you were already started."

He flexed his shoulders. "Well, what did *you* expect? Are you surprised? You've been asking me for weeks what I think of all this, and I've been trying not to get involved because I know there's nothing I can do about it." He had switched back to Latin.

"So why are you talking about it now?"

"Because I can't believe how blind people are."

"Explain."

"I don't know if I can, but I shouldn't need to. Like this nonsense about the Englishry only doing what they do because their local commanders are too lenient. Everybody's tripping over themselves to make excuses for the poor soldiers, blaming it all on the attitudes of the officers. In God's name, Jamie, are they all mad? They sound like it, whenever I listen to them. There's not a single knight, not one petty commander among all the English forces in Scotland, who would dare attempt any of this rubbish unless he knew beyond a doubt that his masters, the barons and earls of England, up to and including their King, would approve of it. And there's the nub of it. Whatever is happening here, from general disregard for the common law to the organized arrogance with which they swagger through our land, has the support of the English lords and barons. Nobody seems to believe it yet, but you mark my words, Jamie, they will, and by then it could be too late to change it."

"Then why don't you speak up?"

'Me, speak up? Who would listen to me? I'm a forester, Jamie, a verderer. I have no voice that anyone would hear, let alone listen to."

"Uncle Malcolm would listen."

"Aye, he might, because I'm family and he likes me, but would he change his mind? That would mean thinking about doing something to change things … and that's a daunting thought."

"More people than you think are starting to grow angry, Will. There's a great swell of discontent spreading everywhere in Scotland nowadays, I'm told."

"Told by whom?" His eyes were suddenly wide with interest.

I shrugged. "Travellers, visiting priests."

"Aye, well you know what I think of most priests. They're great talkers, but they don't often do much more that that. I put more faith in my opinion of visiting soldiery, and it's plain to me what that opinion is. The English are here apurpose, and they won't leave until they have achieved whatever is in their minds, and that means in the mind of their King, this Edward Plantagenet."

"He is a noble and most Christian monarch, Will. A Crusader."

He looked at me for long moments and then he hawked and spat into the dying fire. "He's an Englishman, Jamie, so I mistrust him. If he's so hotly bound on the welfare of our realm, why has he sent so many of his people here? What's his intent? And what does he want of us? Today he claims the title overlord of Scotland. What will he claim tomorrow, when his troops are everywhere from Berwick to Elgin?"

4

Will's love for Mirren, and hers for him, had seemed invincible by the time she left Paisley that first summer, and neither of them had doubted that they would soon be man and wife. Since then, however, it seemed to both of them that Fate itself was conspiring to keep them apart.

Will spent the winter making arrows, not only yard-long shafts for his own enormous weapon but hundreds of shorter missiles for the smaller, flat bows in common use among the Scots, and he had planned to sell them in Glasgow or Edinburgh that autumn, once they were fully cured and fletched, adding the proceeds to his marriage fund. He bore the news stoically when Mirren's letter arrived, telling him she would not be coming to Paisley that summer because of her mother's failing health, but I could see that he was devastated, faced with another yawning year before he would see her again. But then, being William Wallace, who thrived in adversity, he resolved to go to her instead. He sought a month-long leave from Sir Malcolm, who granted it without hesitation since his estates had never been in better condition, and Will set off for Lanark.

He stopped to visit me on his way though Paisley, riding one of Sir Malcolm's finest horses, and I could tell he was apprehensive about what he might find upon his arrival in Lanark, for he had not had time to write and tell Mirren he was coming. But he was almost too impatient to sit still as he spoke of his love for her and his determination to ride all the way there without stopping, scoffing at the mere scores of forested miles that separated them.

I laughed with him, and wished him God speed, and then I walked with him to the Abbey gates to see him on his way with my prayers to accompany him. But as he swung around to mount his horse, we heard his name being called and turned back to see the distinctively green-cassocked Bishop Wishart of Glasgow trotting across the grassy forecourt towards us, waving his arms to attract our attention. Will waved back, still holding his reins, then turned to me.

"Did you know he was here?"

"Not at all. He wasn't expected. He must have arrived this morning, while I was in the library."

The aging Bishop was slightly breathless by the time he reached us.

"William," he gasped, eyeing the reins in Will's hand. "I'm glad I caught you. Are you leaving?"

"Aye, my lord, I'm on my way to Lanark. I stopped by to say goodbye to Jamie."

His lordship acknowledged me with a smile and a nod, but turned directly to Will again. "I had been thinking of you as I walked, enjoying the day, and then I turned to retrace my steps and there you were. It was most fortunate."

Will cocked his head. "You were thinking of *me*, my lord? You'll pardon me, but you and I have not set eyes upon each other these two years. Why should you think of me today?"

"I shouldn't have. I had other things to ponder, of great import to this realm, but something that caught my eye reminded me of the occasion when I met you and young Andrew Murray near here, and then I found myself daydreaming." He glanced at Will's horse. "Must you leave this minute, or can you grant me a little time?"

"I should be on my way, my lord, for it's a long ride to Lanark and I am … expected. But another few minutes will make little difference if you think it important."

"I do, and I thank you. I saw Murray but ten days ago, and when he found I was returning here to Paisley he asked to be remembered to you." His eyes moved to acknowledge me. "To both of you. He has pleasant memories of his visit here, brief though it was. He is well, though not yet a full knight, for several reasons, and in service to his father as sheriff of his territories." His mouth quirked into a tiny smile. "You made a strong impression on him, Master Wallace. He asked me—instructed me, in fact—to inform you that should you ever find yourself in need of employment, in any capacity, he will make a place for you at your request. That impressed *me*, in turn, I must admit. I can assure you, Master Wallace, there are very few men in this land to whom Andrew Murray would make such an offer."

Will nodded, somewhat stiffly I thought. "I am honoured that you should mention it to me, my lord, and that Andrew should even think of it, but I have a place of my own here now and am content with it."

"And that is as it should be." Wishart hesitated, then glanced at me again and changed his tone. "How long will you remain in Lanark?"

"I have a month's leave. I doubt I'll return before that. Why do you ask, my lord?"

"Because I have matters I should like to discuss with you— within the month, or as close as may be. Would it be possible, think you, for you to come by Glasgow on your way home? It would take you a day or two out of your way to take the north road, but you will benefit from it if you make the effort, I promise you. I will be there by the end of this coming month and would welcome you."

Will shook his head. "I can't promise that, my lord Bishop, for I have already promised Sir Malcolm to come back directly from Lanark at the end of the month. But I will be in Glasgow in September. I have a cartload of fine arrows to sell, and I've heard that Glasgow is a better place than Edinburgh for such things—more markets and more archers. I could visit you then. It would be a few weeks later than you asked, but no more than two."

Wishart nodded. "Done. Come to me as early as you can. And if you come to me first, before going to market your wares, I'll see to it that your arrows are quickly sold at better than fair prices. Is that acceptable? If so, I'll leave you two to your interrupted farewells."

"What was that all about, do you suppose?" Will asked once the Bishop had retreated.

"I have no idea. But he seems to have some kind of liking for you. Hard to understand why anyone would feel that way, let alone a saintly bishop, but there you are. God works in mysterious ways."

I ducked as he swung a hand at my head, but it was true. Wishart had always shown a keen interest in Will, ever since their first meeting that day with Andrew Murray. For the remainder of his time as a student in Paisley, Will had been summoned to undertake long and intense tutorial sessions with the Bishop each time Wishart visited the Abbey, listening in fascination after his initial reluctance, and absorbing as much as he could of the older man's thoughts on such arcane matters as patriotism, loyalty, duty, integrity, and honour. Will and I always talked about these encounters afterwards, of course. He called them penances for a while because they seemed much like unwarranted punishments, taking him away from his beloved archery for hours on end, but it did not take long for us to learn to appreciate their true value, although we remained mystified as to the reasons underlying them. Their content, we soon saw, was not nearly as abstract as it first appeared. The Bishop tied everything he spoke of to the reality of the times, expounding upon the manly and patriotic virtues he so admired and relating them to the condition of the realm and the duties of a man to his king and kingdom, He put particular emphasis on the politics and family loyalties of the various magnates and the affiliations of their various fiefdoms within the realm.

It is plain to me now in my old age that even then, when Will was a mere boy, the good Bishop, who was perhaps the greatest and most selfless patriot in all the realm of Scotland at that time, had discerned in him that special quality that would propel him into greatness. That alone, I am convinced, could have induced in Wishart such painstaking efforts to shape William Wallace's mind to his own way of thinking. He moulded the future Guardian of Scotland, though none of us then knew it, and Will was malleable.

We said no more on the matter after the Bishop had left us, and after bidding each other God speed again, I stood and watched as Will rode away to the east in search of his beloved Mirren.

S

When he returned home a month later, my cousin was a very different person. He had somehow reached full manhood in the interim, and he came back with evidence of a new maturity stamped into his every aspect. He did not tell me that he and Mirren had become lovers or that he had taken her to wife. There was no need. Even I, callow and unworldly as I was, could see the new strength in him, reflected in the way he spoke and acted. The carefree exuberance of love-stricken youth that had marked him before his departure had been replaced by a sober deliberation, and his former preoccupation with the distant, unattainable Mirren had been replaced by a quiet determination to bring her to Elderslie as his wife.

Those changes were clear as day both to me and to his family, for his aunt and uncle were nothing if not astute. But there were other, even more profound changes afoot by then, as well. Will's entire life had begun to change in ways that neither he nor I could ever have anticipated, and even though I have been a Christian priest now for half a hundred years, I still tend to think of those changes in terms of intervention by the pagan Fates of whom the ancients spoke in fear and dread. Although these changes did not at first appear to be radical, each one, with hindsight, brought about the end of my plain, hard-working friend and cousin Will and the simultaneous emergence of his alter ego, the implacable, the terrifying William Wallace.

It began during that visit to Lamington, where he arrived to find Mirren under siege from the love-smitten woodsman Graham of

Kilbarchan. Mirren had not expected Will's arrival, and her whole-hearted delight at seeing him was witnessed by the hapless Graham, who saw in it the death of his own hopes of winning her. Graham of Kilbarchan vanished that same night, not to be seen again.

It was the suddenness of that disappearance that finally brought both Mirren and Will back to thinking of him again. Days had gone by since either of them had seen him, and that began to alarm Mirren because there had not been a single day in the previous five weeks when she had not seen him everywhere she went. Will, typically, had not given the fellow a single thought, relieved to be rid of the man's irksome presence. But Mirren knew that Graham of Kilbarchan would not simply fade graciously away; she came to expect he would seek redress for the humiliation he would believe she had thrust on him.

She waited anxiously to be summoned into her father's presence to explain what Hugh Braidfoot would construe as her disgraceful conduct towards a well-qualified suitor. But the days passed and no summons came. Her father's treatment of her remained as it had always been, benevolent and even doting; his attitude remained unchanged, at once loving and slightly bemused by her flourishing beauty. And still they saw no sign of Graham.

Days later, filled with guilt, she spoke to Will about how badly she regretted her treatment of the woodsman, though she had intended no harm. Will kissed away her misgivings, assuring her that there was nothing she could have done to alter any of what had happened, and finally she came to believe him and allowed herself to believe that the sorry affair was over.

But it was far from being over.

Will went looking for me in the library on the day he returned through Paisley, and Brother Duncan sent him to find me among the cloisters, where I was studying my breviary, pacing back and forth in the familiar space with my eyes closed much of the time, memorizing the texts set for me that day. I was so engrossed that I did not see him arrive, and I have no idea how long he had been sitting watching me by the time I finally noticed him perched on a stone bench, one foot flat on the seat with his back against an archway and his right knee raised against his chin, enfolded by his arms. The sight of him startled me, and he grinned, his white, even teeth flashing amid the dark curls of his suddenly rich beard.

"Priest," he said, his eyes flickering with mischief. "When do you start to shave your head?"

"When I'm ordained," I told him, feeling the glad rush of well-being that always hit me at the sight of him. "When did you get back?"

"Today, this minute, and I came to see you first. They'll be expecting me at home, though."

"They've been expecting you this past week. And Lamington?"

"It's there, where I'd been told it was. A wee place, like Elderslie. But I enjoyed it."

"And yet—? It could have been better?"

"It could. I had to leave Mirren there."

"Ah. And when will she come here?"

"As soon as I can arrange it."

I detected a hint of uncertainty in his response.

"*Can* you arrange it?"

"I think I can. I have to. Otherwise life will not be livable."

"Did you meet her father, speak with him?"

He glanced away from my eyes. "No. Mirren thought it best not to."

"Because he would disapprove."

"Aye. Her mother is very ill, near death in fact, and with that on his mind, he had already decided in favour of Alexander Graham."

"The forester? He was in Lamington?"

"*Woodsman*, Jamie. But aye, he was there when I arrived. But then he left, the same day."

He told me everything that had happened during his visit, but when he had finished and I asked him what he thought the Graham fellow might be up to, he merely shrugged. He had decided that Graham was an indolent ne'er-do-well, unworthy of further attention.

"So what will you do next?"

He stood up, facing me and smiling again as he collected his bow case and the quiver of arrows that leaned against the wall. "I'm for Glasgow, as soon as I've made sure all's well at home and the forest's still as I left it. I have a cartload of arrows for sale and I need the money now more than I thought I might."

"Why is that?"

"Because I have a wife to see to now, Jamie. A man needs money even to contemplate such a thing. I won't bring a new wife to an empty, bare-floored hut."

It took me several moments to absorb what I had just heard.

"You *married* her? Mirren?"

"I did." He looked at me with an expression of utter seriousness. "It seemed like the right thing to do, while I was there ..."

"But how—? I thought her father didn't like you."

"He didn't, when he thought I was just another tomcat circling around his daughter. But he changed his mind once he discovered I was a tomcat with influential friends and could support a wife. Bishop Wishart knows the man and he vouched for me." He paused, then asked, "Is that all right?"

"Of course it is." I realized how stupid that sounded and raised my hands. "Forgive me, Will. That took me by surprise and it should not have. I hope you will be very happy together. Will you take her with you to Glasgow?"

"I will. 'Whither thou goest ...' I know I have no need to tell you where that comes from."

"No, you don't. But it was Ruth who said it to her mother-in-law, not to her spouse. But I know what you mean ... You'll see the Bishop while you're there?"

"Aye, as soon as I get there, as I promised him. And he said he would see to it that my arrows were sold for the best price. Besides, Murray once said he keeps a fine table, and I enjoy good food while I'm listening to anything profound ... Speaking of which, I'm starved. I've been on the road since before dawn and it's close to noon. Have you eaten this morning? Can we go by the kitchens while we talk?"

Time passed as quickly as it always did in his company, and when the bell for nones summoned me to noonday prayer we parted, me to my duties and him to Elderslie and Sir Malcolm. I had not the slightest doubt that I would see him again very soon, but in those days I had not yet learned the folly of expecting anything in life to turn out as we expect.

CHAPTER SIX

I

They came for him in Elderslie the following Saturday at first light. Sir Malcolm himself heard the hammering at his doors and roused himself from his bed to cross to the window, where he could look down into the grey dawn from his upstairs room. The yard was full of soldiers wearing the red saltire on gold of Bruce of Annandale. Ordering his startled wife to stay where she was, the knight charged out of his bedroom and made his way downstairs, shrugging hastily into a thick robe to cover his nakedness. He shouldered his way past his steward, who was holding the door open while attempting to bar entry to the men outside, and found himself face to face with a large, glowering man clad all in black.

"Who in Hades are you, and what madness brings you here like this to Wallace's door? D'you come seeking criminals in my house, or are you merely looking to provoke my wrath?"

The stranger raised a gauntleted hand, holding out a rolled parchment stamped and sealed with a broad wafer of heavy, red wax. Sir Malcolm frowned suddenly, recognizing the elaborate seal.

"What is this?"

"A warrant for the arrest of one William Wallace. Are you him?"

Sir Malcolm's fury had vanished and he drew himself up and answered mildly, his voice pitched low. "No, I am not. And I think you know that. I am Malcolm Wallace, knight of the realm and lord of this estate. Who are you?"

"Walter Armstrong, bailiff to Robert Bruce, Lord of—"

"I know who Robert Bruce is, man. He has held my oath and my loyalty all my life, as he held my father's before me. I have already asked you what nonsense brings you hammering so damnably at my door at this hour, for I cannot believe Bruce himself would send you thus. Did he?"

"I hold a warrant for the arrest of one William—"

"*Did Bruce send you here?*" Sir Malcolm's roar cut the words from the bailiff's mouth and brought up the heads of the soldiers at the fellow's back.

A sullen flush crept slowly over the man's cheeks and he looked as though he wanted to spit in the knight's eye, but both of them knew it would mean his death to do so. "No," he said. "But I am here on his authority."

"No, *what*? Are you insolent to every knight you meet?"

The bailiff's eyes grew angrier, but when he spoke again his words were subdued. "No, Sir Malcolm. Lord Robert is in Glasgow, on the business of the realm. But I was sent on—"

"Be damned to you, you oaf. You were sent here by someone who hopes to see you dead for it, knowing your surly tongue." Sir Walter looked down in silence at the warrant until he had recovered himself, and then he spoke again in a calm voice. "William Wallace is my nephew. What does this warrant concern?"

"Poaching. The slaughter and theft of deer belonging to the Lord Bruce, from his lands adjoining your own."

Sir Walter reared up again. "That is arrant nonsense. My nephew is a verderer, my senior forester, and a justiciary officer of this estate. Such a crime is beyond his nature. When did this atrocity take place?"

The bailiff smirked. "Four days ago, Sir Malcolm. And as for it being beyond your *nephew's* nature, that may be your opinion, but it needna be the case, not if the man wields a long yew bow and shoots white-fletched, white-banded arrows. Your nephew does both, I'm told."

Sir Malcolm felt a sour sickness roiling in his gut. He had watched his nephew paint the broad white band around the midpoint of each of his arrows. That, plus their distinctive white snow goose fletching, made them, Will had explained, easier to find in feature-less clumps of undergrowth. He nodded his head slowly.

"As you say, he does. And so he must plainly answer to you, on whatever grounds he may stand accused. I will bring him to you, but he is not here now. Not on my lands or anywhere within reach this day. You have my word on that, on both counts. Tell me about this supposed crime."

When the bailiff spoke next his voice lacked much of the truculence that had marked it earlier.

"There's no supposing involved, sir. We ha'e sworn testimony frae an eyewitness who saw the accused William Wallace slaughter a small herd of deer and leave them where they fell, a wanton atrocity. He cut out all the arrows afterwards, save one that he could not dislodge, and he cut the end off that, to hide the fletching, but he mistook an' left one broken bit o' flightin' behind him."

"And you have that piece of feather."

"We do, sir. Forbye the cut shaft. It bears white paint. No' much, but enough to mark it plain enough."

"I see. So my nephew is not merely a felon, he is a careless fool, to boot. I must say that surprises me. I had not thought him foolish. Why would he do such a thing? It seems senseless. Wanton, as you said."

The bailiff nodded, seeming more sympathetic now that the knight's anger had died down.

Sir Malcolm looked beyond the bailiff, out into the yard. A full score of soldiers stood there, all of them armed and watching the group at the open door, and the knight's gaze took in the two half-armoured sergeants-at-arms who stood vigilantly at the bailiff's back, missing nothing. He sighed.

"These are ill tidings, Bailiff. A sore start to any day. But you have my attention and my belief, and I fear I do you a disservice, keeping you here like this on the doorstep." He stepped back from the door. "Come you inside and bring your sergeants with you, and we'll decide what's best to do. Come."

The bailiff hesitated, glancing back over his shoulder.

"Commendable distrust, I suppose," Sir Malcolm said. "You fear I ha'e lied to you and my nephew might escape while I detain you.

Well, I'll ignore the slur upon my honour because of the circumstance, and you may have your men search the grounds and buildings while we talk. But mind you see they do no harm. There has been damage aplenty done to me and mine already this morning. Make your arrangements, then my man here will bring you to me when you're done. I'll be back down as soon as I have calmed my goodwife and put on some clothes."

Neither man required much time to do what he must do, and Sir Malcolm heard the sounds of shuffling, mailed feet on the flagstones of the hallway as he reached the head of the stairs, having left Lady Margaret waiting anxiously in their bedchamber.

"Sit ye down, gentlemen," he said, entering the large family room where they awaited him. He took his own big chair while they seated themselves, the two sergeants-at-arms removing their steel bonnets. Fergus the steward was already pouring mugs of the household's ale, and the men drank in silence, until the knight set his cup down on the small table by his chair.

"So," he began. "A sorry tale, and one I had no need to hear, this day or any other. A herd, you say? How many?"

"Seven, sir. A buck and six does."

"And left there? To rot?"

"Aye, Sir Malcolm, just so."

"And it was done out of sheer malice? Are you sure of that?"

"As sure as any man who wasna there can be. Assured on oath, as witnessed."

"Is your witness trustworthy?"

"He is, sir. One of our own. A verderer himself. He saw it all."

"And made no move to stop it?"

For the first time, a flicker of uncertainty disturbed the bailiff's gaze. "He was alone, Sir Malcolm, and feared for his life."

Sir Malcolm's eyebrows rose in disbelief. "His life? Are you telling me now my nephew is a would-be murderer as well as a poacher of deer?"

"Our witness thought so, sir, being there alone. And I canna say I blame him. Who can say what any man will do, caught in a crime?

There's no' a man among us who doesna have the power to do murder, 'gin he's provoked enough."

Sir Malcolm growled deep in his throat. "Aye. Provocation makes the difference. Who is this timid verderer of yours?"

"His name is Francis Tidwell, sir."

"That sounds English."

"It is—he is English born and bred. He came to Lord Robert's employ as a verderer ten years ago."

"So when did this happen? The crime was discovered four days ago, you say?"

"Aye, sir, on Wednesday. Six days after the accused man, William Wallace, was observed returning here from—" He stopped short.

Sir Malcolm's eyes narrowed. "He was *observed*? How and by whom?" He did not wait for an answer. "Does it not strike you as strange, Master Bailiff, that my nephew should be *observed* days before he supposedly commits a crime? And even stranger that the observer should know he was *returning* from somewhere?"

"Aye … Well … I canna answer that. I ken only that Tidwell mentioned it, but I canna tell you how he knew it."

"I'm sure you can't, but there's one thing you can't deny, since it came from your own mouth. Someone was watching my nephew long before he was accused of anything." Sir Malcolm leaned back in his chair. "So, who sent you here to arrest our William, Master Bailiff? You said Lord Robert is in Glasgow."

The other man stirred and his boots scraped on the floor as he shifted his weight. "I was sent by Master Bellow, Lord Robert's factor."

"Ah, Master Bellow. I should have known. Master Bellow has harboured little fondness for me or my kin since he and I fell out, nigh on twelve years ago. He is a dour man. A fine factor, no doubt, but an unlikeable man … Would you know where Lord Robert is, in Glasgow? Exactly? You said he was on the business of the realm, did you not? "

The bailiff blinked. "Aye, I did, but how would I know where his lordship bides? I'm his bailiff, no' his friend. He wouldna even know my face, was I to meet him."

"Then I might be able to help you. In all probability he is in residence at the Bishop's Palace. That is where most of the realm's business is conducted nowadays, at least in these southern parts. And that, if my guess is sound, makes this entire affair very interesting …"

"What d'ye mean?" The man was frowning now.

"I mean, Master Bailiff, that if Lord Robert Bruce is in Glasgow, and at the Bishop's Palace, he would likely be aware that my nephew, this same slaughterous William Wallace, has been there, too, for this past week and more, conferring with Bishop Wishart. He came home ten days ago from a journey, that much is true. But he left again the very next day, bound for Glasgow, to meet with Bishop Wishart at his lordship's invitation. He left at daybreak, to be in Glasgow by nightfall, so I have little doubt that his going was *un*observed, and your story proves that it was. So unless my nephew has seduced the Bishop of Glasgow himself into returning with him to these parts to poach and slaughter Lord Robert's deer, I would suggest you question your witness more closely as to the truth surrounding the events he was so eager to swear to under solemn oath. The man is plainly a liar, and if I have to bring Bishop Wishart and Robert Bruce himself here together to confront the knave and judge him of the attempted murder of my nephew through false testimony, then by God's beard I will do so. Have you heard me, Master Bailiff?"

As soon as the bailiff had led his men away to arrest their false witness, Sir Malcolm dispatched two men to summon a family gathering. That done, he called in his wife, whose judgment he trusted above any man's, and the two of them set to planning what must be done.

2

The adults of the family met in session late that afternoon, before the sun began to set, and Sir Malcolm wasted no time in telling us that he had already discussed the matter with

Lady Margaret and with Ewan, and they were all in agreement that much had to be done in a short space of time. I did not have the chance to wonder why Ewan should be involved as Sir Malcolm launched into a word-for-word description of what had transpired that morning. He was a natural storyteller and he held all of us enthralled as he brought the morning's events to life.

"Where is Will now?" Father Peter asked when he had finished. "Do we know?"

Sir Malcolm shrugged. "Your guess would be as good as mine. Somewhere 'twixt here and Glasgow, unless he bides there yet."

"Who bides where yet?"

None of us had heard or seen his arrival, but suddenly there he was, his arms filled with bolts of brightly coloured cloth that he carried straight towards his aunt Margaret, weaving his way between tables and chairs. He lowered the bundles into her lap and then bussed her soundly while she reached up from her seat to embrace his neck and ruffle his hair in welcome. He winked at me in greeting, and then glanced around at the rest, and his face and voice became grave.

"The Wallaces in conclave. Have I missed something important?"

"Aye, you have," his uncle replied. "Armed men—Bruce's men—come to take you away for hanging."

Will looked sideways at his uncle, a laugh forming on his lips. "For hanging? What, they'll hang a man now for swearing his allegiance?"

"No, for killing his lord's deer." There was no doubting his uncle's seriousness, and Will straightened abruptly, all signs of humour fading from his face.

"What are you saying, Uncle?"

"I said it clearly and it is true. But it is already dealt with. What did *you* mean by 'swearing allegiance'? Did you meet the Elder Bruce?"

"Aye, in Glasgow. Bishop Wishart named me to him."

Sir Malcolm frowned. "To what end? Why would he make you known to Robert Bruce, and you a mere verderer?"

Will's eyebrows rose. "In courtesy, Uncle. Lord Robert arrived while the Bishop and I were talking, and he asked me who I was. Bishop Wishart introduced us and then left us together for a time while he attended to something else. We talked, the old man and I, and I ended up offering him my allegiance. He remembered my father, vaguely, through the Countess of Carrick, and he knows you, of course, as his own man, but he even knew that my brother Malcolm is another of his knights, riding with his son, the Earl of Carrick. I liked him. He is an impressive old man, if somewhat stiff—distant and old-fashioned."

"Aye," said Sir Malcolm. "He has lived long enough to be old-fashioned with legitimacy. And he has the right to be aloof. He is next in line to the throne, should anything befall the Maid. Where is he now, do you know?"

Will shook his head. "In Glasgow yet, I suppose. It was quite the noble gathering there. The greatest men in the realm. He was deep in conference with them, magnates and clerics both, when I left." He checked himself. "But how … How could his men come hunting me for poaching when I was with Lord Robert himself at the time?"

"That's what has been dealt with, Will," Father Peter answered. "You were falsely accused of poaching and mayhem. Malcolm defended you stoutly and proved your innocence, so that danger is behind us. But that's why we're all here. Malcolm and Margaret summoned us to discuss what's best to be done for you now."

Will frowned. "What's best to be done for me? I have no idea what you're all talking about."

"This fellow Graham, from Kilbarchan." Sir Malcolm's voice was peremptory. "Ewan told me about him, that he was there when you went to visit that young woman. You had not expected that, had you?"

Will glanced at Ewan before responding. "No, I had not. But it was of little import."

Brother Duncan spoke for the first time. "What did you do to him, Will?"

"Do to him?" Will's eyes were wide with incomprehension. "I did nothing to him, save ignore him. The man's a fool. A popinjay. Jamie? What is going on here?"

Sir Malcolm intervened before I could say anything. "Then you underestimate him, Nephew. Popinjay he may be, but he's a dangerous popinjay, and treacherous. Tell us what happened between you two when last you met."

"Right, then." I saw a flash of the anger that too often lurked beneath his calm exterior, but then he caught himself. "The last time we met," he said quietly, "Graham was in Lamington, where I had gone to visit Mirren—"

"The Braidfoot girl, you mean."

"Aye. We nodded to each other and I greeted him by name— coldly, I suppose, for he did not answer me. I was not friendly, but I had not expected to see him there, so far from home and hunting my quarry. I expect he was no more pleased to see me. But Mirren was glad to see me come, so he and I glowered at each other for a spell, and then he walked away. I have not seen him since."

"He was angry, then, when he left?"

"Spitting, I would say, had I spared a moment to think of it. But why did you call him treacherous?"

"Think. Did you lose any arrows while you were there?"

Will's headshake was immediate. "No, sir, I did not."

"Are you sure?"

I saw Will's eyes narrow. "I am always sure about my arrows, Uncle. I carry few of them, and when I travel I cannot replace them easily, and so I am aware of every one. I took twelve broadheads with me and eight bodkin target shafts. I brought them all back and have them with me now."

"An arrow belonging to you—white fletched and painted with a central band—was found in a slaughtered deer—one of a slaughtered herd—on the Annandale lands. It was the only shaft left behind, and it was cut short, but it was one of yours beyond a doubt. Can you think of any way in which an enemy might have stolen one without your knowing?"

Will shrugged. "Aye, easily, if he broke into my hut in the woods. I keep a supply there. Anyone could steal some. But unless they had a longbow, there would be no point to such a thing. Those arrows are too big and heavy for flat bows."

"There was a point. Do not deceive yourself. Someone used one of them to entrap you." Sir Malcolm then retold the tale of the morning's events, and Will sank into a chair and sat open-mouthed.

"This verderer, Tidwell," he said when his uncle was done. "I've never met him. Why would he do such a thing?"

"He was suborned, clearly."

"By whom, in God's name?"

Ewan spoke up for the first time. "Clear your head, Will, and think. The man worked the Bruce lands next to our own. Who else do you know who works those woods?"

Recognition flashed across Will's face. "Graham."

"But Tidwell has been arrested," I said, "so he will confess and name the man who suborned him."

Sir Malcolm flicked a hand at me impatiently. "We don't know that, Jamie. The bailiff went in search of him, but he may not have found him."

"Why would he not, Uncle? If the fellow thought his plan had worked he would have no reason to hide and they would have found him easily."

Sir Malcolm was shaking his head. "Not so, Jamie, not so at all. That is your priest's mind speaking. This man Tidwell is corrupt. He was paid to lie under oath and therefore he is far more dangerous to the man who hired him than he can ever be to us. I doubt he'll be seen again."

"You mean he'll run?"

"No, Jamie. I mean he's like to die and disappear. Once he is silenced, no one can question him." Sir Malcolm looked around the table, engaging each one of us. "This man Graham is clever. Let no one here doubt that. The sole flaw in this foul scheme of his was that he knew nothing of your plans to visit Glasgow, William. Had you remained here at home, you would now be in jail under sentence of death, and safely hanged and out of his way when next he goes wooing your young woman. This man hates hard and harbours great malice. Having met his kind before, I think it likely that he followed the bailiff and his men here to watch you be taken. And when he saw them leave without you, he might have been moved to protect himself by covering his tracks."

"By killing Tidwell, you mean?" Will said. "But what could he gain by that? We know what he did. We know where he lives. He would be risking everything."

"He would be risking nothing. Without Tidwell, we have no proof of his involvement in any of this. He would run free and probably return home to Kilbarchan, to dream up some other means of killing you."

"Killing me?" Will's laugh was a harsh bark. "That popinjay? He would never find guts enough to face me."

"He would not *need* to face you!" Sir Malcolm's shout startled us all. "Nor need he dirty his own hands. This *popinjay*, as you call him, is *rich*, William. He can hire others to do what he could not. Think you this Tidwell killed all those beasts alone? You're a forester, so use your brain. Do you think for a moment that seven deer would stand calmly and let him kill them, one at a time? Besides, Ewan assured me Tidwell uses a flat bow, a short bow. He has never owned a long one. I'll warrant he was nowhere near the place when those deer were killed. He went there later, knowing what he would find and what he had to say. Which means that others did the killing, using nets to pen and hold the beasts until they were done. It would take three men at least, possibly more."

"So you mean—?"

"I mean that any man well enough paid to take part in a plot like this would take more money without thought to kill an ongoing threat to his paymaster. And Tidwell, through no fault of his own, has become such a threat."

"No more than the others, surely?" My question earned me a pitying look from my uncle.

"Infinitely more, Jamie. We *know* Tidwell. That's why he's dangerous to Graham. The others are unknown. They could be anyone, anywhere."

"So what must we do?" Will asked, addressing all of us.

"*We* must find a way to deal with this disgusting Graham fellow." Lady Margaret's contribution took everyone's attention, and I am sure no one missed the emphasis she placed on her opening word. "*You*, on the other hand, dear nephew, must leave here until we have done so." She whipped up a warning hand to cut off Will's protest before it could be formed. "Do not argue, William. Your life is in danger, and we have no hint of the identity of the possible assassins, any one of whom could kill you from concealment at any time. And so you will leave here, for a time at least, and let us deal with this serpent Graham. We will put an end to him through his employer, as soon as his lordship returns. The Bruce will not tolerate such treachery among his people. Until then this Graham will no doubt think himself safe, with Tidwell gone, since he dare not ask questions that might point to his involvement and he knows nothing of what transpired while you were in Glasgow. And thinking himself safe, he will come after you again. But by then you will be far from here, in the south with Ewan, who has always wanted to visit Selkirk Forest. That was Ewan's idea, and your uncle believes it to be a good one. I am not so sure, but I am prepared to accept my husband's judgment."

Will, from being unwilling to budge, was seduced instantly by the prospect of losing himself in the forest with Ewan, subsisting there on their own merits and unbeholden to anyone. Of course, it did not escape my attention—nor perhaps anyone else's—that the route to Selkirk and the great southern forest led directly past Lanark, and Mirren's home in Lamington was less than a good spit away from there.

Dinner that night was remarkably sombre, and although I was itching to know what Bishop Wishart had wanted to talk to Will about, I hesitated to bring the matter up when no one else did. Immediately after dinner, however, Sir Malcolm took Will away to talk to him alone, and I suspected that he, too, had the same curiosity but had not wished to air the subject openly at table. I stayed awake for a long time that night, waiting for Will to return to the room we shared, but at length I fell asleep, and he did not waken me when he sought his own bed.

3

"Are you ever going to tell me what the Bishop wanted you for?"

It was early the next morning, and I was in the stable yard, helping Will brush down his horse, brushing the right side of the sturdy animal while he worked on the other. This was not the fine animal he had ridden on his previous journey, for this time he would be travelling through the lawless territory of the Selkirk Forest, where a fine horse would have been too much of a temptation to flaunt. So his mount this time, like Ewan's, was a stocky Scots garron, the hardy, shaggy, sure-footed breed native to the North.

Will's face appeared over the garron's back, gazing at me with troubled eyes. "He's in love wi' me, Jamie," he said in a deep, sombre voice. "He wanted me to do terrible, unnatural things, and my immortal soul's in peril. I'd tell you what he said, but I'm feared to scandalize your priestly ears."

I felt horror rise up in me, but then I saw the leering grin flash out.

"Whoreson," I spat, and threw my horse brush at him. "You could burn in Hell for saying things like that."

"The Devil isna ready for me yet, Jamie," he said, bobbing back up, his grin wider. But then, within a heartbeat, he sobered. "He wanted to talk. To me," he said in the scholarly Latin he had grown to love as a student. "Don't ask me why, because I can't tell you, any more than I could before. Not even Uncle Mal could tell me why. But that's what he wanted."

"To talk … Well, he's wanted that before, for the same reasons, whatever they may be. And what did he want to talk about this time?"

"About this English business—the growing numbers of them and their reasons for being here. He's worried that there's more to what we're seeing than what we're seeing, if you know what I mean."

"And? Did you tell him you agreed with him? That you think the same thing?"

He shook his head. "I didn't tell him anything. I listened, and he talked, the way he always does." And then his frown faded and his whole face lightened as though the sun had shone on it. "But d'you know what? I think I know now why he did it, why he's always done it. It just came to me this minute." He stood staring into the distance, smiling strangely.

"Well come on, then," I said. "Or are you going to keep me standing here all day?"

"Oh … He wanted to talk because he *needed* to, Jamie. I still don't see why he'd pick me, but I'm probably one of the few people he can speak his mind to without fear of criticism or of being influenced by how I reply. A memory of him talking just came into my mind and I saw him sitting in front of his fire, talking to me very seriously, his brow creased, and it came to me that he was talking *at* me, not *to* me."

"Cousin, I don't know what you're talking about."

His grin flickered back. "I'm not sure *I* even know, but I think the Bishop has come to trust me over the years. He's a powerful man, with much influence, and everyone in his world appears to want something from him. That's why he's so tight mouthed and self-contained all the time. But somehow he learned that he could talk to me, test his ideas and opinions and even voice his private thoughts and suspicions straightforwardly, without fear of being used or betrayed. Does that sound sensible to you?"

"Perfectly," I said. "So what did he talk about this time? You mentioned the English situation. Does he really see that as grounds for concern?"

"Aye, he does. He worries about Edward of England, about what's in his mind, for though the man himself has done nothing wrong, and everything he does appears to be straightforward and to a noble end, aspects of his behaviour have Wishart worried: his attitude, above all. Why is Edward allowing his men to behave as they do on foreign soil, flouting the laws of our land in defiance of all the rules of protocol and hospitality? He is encouraging them by his silence, there's no doubt of that. But no one dares call him to task on it, because his goodwill is deemed too important to the realm in this matter of the young Queen's succession."

"So what does Wishart want of you?"

"Of me? Nothing. He spoke much of Andrew Murray, though, and ventured the hope that, should anything go wrong, which God forbid, he would like me to offer my services to Murray on the realm's behalf."

"And what did you say to that?"

"What do you think? I told him I would, if Murray would have me." His smile widened. "But that's not going to happen. The Maid is still a child and the Guardians of the realm are all at their posts. One of these days, we'll have a young, new Queen to bend our knees to, and Edward Plantagenet will be settling back to dream of a grandson who will inherit Scotland's throne. You wait and see."

We finished our preparations for departure, then went into the house, where we broke our fast with the family, said our farewells, and were on the road by mid-morning as planned, arriving at the Abbey shortly after noon. The brother on duty at the gate was watching for us and informed us that Father Peter, who had set out from Elderslie with Brother Duncan before dawn, was waiting for us in the common room. Surprised, because the community was at noon prayers, we left Ewan with the horses and went directly to where our priestly uncle waited for us, standing with his hand on one of two chest-high bales of fine, recently shorn wool that filled the common room with their distinctive oily smell. He barely nodded to us before slapping the one beneath his hand.

"I thought you should see this, Will, before you go anywhere. Mirren's uncle brought it in this morning."

"Two bales of wool?" Will glanced at me, his face blank. "In return for what?"

"Not simply wool, Will. Rich, prime wool. His best. An offering, in return for Masses for the soul of Alexander Graham. The old man died last night."

Will was slow to respond, but eventually he asked, "Why did you think it important for me to see this now, Uncle Peter?"

"Because it changes everything we talked about last night. Now young Graham can legitimately quit his employment with Lord Bruce. He'll return to Kilbarchan to claim his inheritance, free of obligation."

"And free of any penalty for what he did to me. Is that what you are saying?"

Father Peter shook his head. "No, not quite. Lord Bruce will still have jurisdiction over what was done while Graham was his man. No doubt of that. But that will yet have to wait upon Bruce's eventual return, so nothing has changed there save that Father Abbot informed me earlier that he does not expect to see his lordship any time soon. Apparently the Bruce has ridden north, beyond the Forth, and may be gone for some time. What has changed, though, with the old man's death, is that Graham will now be free to do whatever he wishes, at least until he is brought to justice. He is now a man of property and substantial wealth. If he chooses, he could move against you immediately, so you should waste no time in losing yourself. Prior to this"—he nodded towards the woollen bales—"you had at least a few days of grace. Now it is conceivable that you have none at all."

"Is he likely to send his people sniffing around Sir Malcolm's place, think you?"

Father Peter shrugged. "He might, but it will do him no good. You won't be there and Mal is ready for him. Should he trespass too far, he will rue it. My brother is no man's fool, and more than a match for any shiftless ne'er-do-well, rich or no. In the meantime, though, you must be on your way. Do you have everything you need?"

Will was eyeing the bales of wool. "Aye, Uncle, everything. Food for a week, ample clothing, and a good supply of arrows and bowstrings. We require nothing else. But I'm curious. How much would those bales be worth?"

Uncle Peter's eyes narrowed at the unexpected question. "They have great value—sufficient to purchase daily Masses for a year, I would guess. Why do you ask?"

"Merchant Waddie is not known for his generosity. I'm surprised he would put up so much to pray for the soul of a man who was not related to him."

Father Peter smiled. "I'm sure he hopes the old man's wealthy son will be related to him soon. And besides, he'll doubtless retrieve two more in recompense from the old man's storehouses."

Will reached out to touch one of the bales. "Aye, I suppose he will, now that you mention it." He straightened. "I should be going now, Father."

"Aye, you should. I wish you God speed and hope to see your frowning face again within a month or two. Kneel down now, and I'll bless you."

I walked back with my cousin to where Ewan waited with the horses, and as we went Will draped a long arm over my shoulders, pulling me close to him. "Work hard at your priestery, Jamie," he said quietly. "You'll be a good one someday."

I grinned and pulled away from him. "Priestery, is it? That's a word I've never heard before. Well, I intend to be good at it and I promise you, I'm working hard at it. How long d'you think it will take you to reach Selkirk?"

"Oh, I don't know … D'you mean the forest or the town?" Then, before I could respond, he said, "I'm going to need to write to Mirren soon, Jamie, to warn her about Graham and let her know where I'm going. I'll send the letter to you within the next few days. Waste no time getting it to her, will you?"

"You know I won't. I'll look out for it. Now get out of here and be safe, and I'll see you again soon."

Had anyone asked me when we might meet next, it would have been inconceivable to me that two years would go by before I saw either one again.

CHAPTER SEVEN

I

When I bade farewell to Will and Ewan at the Abbey gates that day in 1290, I had no notion that Will had already changed his mind about where they would go and what they would do as soon as they were out of my sight. He told me nothing, in order to protect me from the need to lie later, and for the next two years I remained unaware of the truth, immersed in my studies.

It was some time before the matter of Alexander Graham's perfidy was settled. For many months, Robert Bruce's affairs took him far into the northeast, and he returned to the south only in early August. He stopped in Glasgow to confer with Bishop Wishart before continuing south to Lochmaben, his home castle near the English border. It was during that meeting that Wishart told the patriarch about the slaughtered herd of Bruce deer and the attempt to foist the blame upon Sir Malcolm Wallace's nephew, reminding Bruce that he himself had met Will in the Bishop's own palace precisely at the time the deadly charges of poaching were being brought against him. Shortly thereafter, Bruce arrived in Elderslie to speak with Sir Malcolm, and within hours, officers were dispatched to arrest Alexander Graham of Kilbarchan and bring him to the Wallace house for trial.

Graham protested his innocence, claiming that the case against him was untenable, but Robert Bruce's certainty about Will's innocence was absolute. The suspicions surrounding the events, including the one-sided rivalry over Mirren, attested to by herself in writing and witnessed by her local priest, combined with the mysterious disappearance of the perjured Tidwell, the sole witness against

Will but far more likely a potential witness against Graham, proved overwhelming. Bruce's judgment was Draconian. Graham of Kilbarchan was hanged on August 25th, his entire estate forfeited to Robert Bruce, in whose employ he had been and whose good name he therefore impugned when the crimes were committed. Bruce offered the estate to Sir Malcolm, as reparation for the harm done his family, but the knight refused any part of it.

Will Wallace was free to come home to Elderslie. But he did not do so.

I grew accustomed to his absence, although I often thought of him and wondered how he and Ewan were faring in their southern forest sojourn. We discovered in time that he was well, whatever he was doing, because twice that autumn, gifts arrived from him for Lady Margaret, brought by those itinerant traders who travel the length and breadth of the country, mending pots and pans and selling posies and herbal potions wherever they can find a purchaser. Both men had the same story: they had been stopped on a forest path by a stranger who had paid them well to deliver the packages however and whenever they could come to the Paisley district.

And then, as I rode along a woodland path on a bright summer afternoon the following year, I heard my name being called from a clump of brambles, and I almost fell from my old horse in fright. I spun around to see Ewan watching me from the thick foliage at the side of the path. I could not see him clearly, merely the bulk of his shape among the shadows, but I recognized him instantly by the green of his clothing and the mask that obscured his face, and I gasped his name in disbelief as I swung my leg over my beast's back.

"No! Stay!"

I froze where I was, half on and half off my mount, one foot in the stirrup, the other dangling behind me, and gaping towards where he stood with one hand raised, holding me there.

"Are you alone? Is anyone behind you?"

"No," I twisted in the stirrup nevertheless to look along the path at my back. "I'm alone. What are you doing in there? Are you hiding?"

There came a swell of movement as the big man pushed away the hanging fronds of bramble with his long staff and stepped towards me, the sound of thorns being ripped from his clothing clearly audible. I watched as he pulled his long cloak free of the last of them and then deftly tucked his mask up into his hood and stepped forward to look up at me, his ruined, beloved face creased into its old, lopsided grin.

"Aye, hiding—from you, until I knew there were no strangers with you. I saw you coming from a mile away, but you had others with you."

"I did, but they were on their way to visit old Friar Thomas. They turned off the path some time ago."

"Good. Now you can greet me properly."

I swung down and embraced him, inhaling the warm, well-remembered scent of him happily before he pushed me away to sweep me up and down with his eyes, taking note of my plain grey monk's habit.

"You're not a priest yet?"

"No, not yet, but soon now. My ordination—everybody's—was postponed after the Maid died, when we came close to war." Princess Margaret of Norway, the seven-year-old heir to Scotland's throne, had died in September 1290 of natural but unexplained causes. She had been living still in Orkney, where her father, King Eric II of Norway, had lodged her for safety.

"Where's Will?" I was looking around as I asked him.

"Not here," he said. "He couldn't come. Sent me instead, to tell you he is well. Content with married life and hoping you might visit us in the south. I was on my way to the Abbey, but from where I was it looked as though these other people were with you, or following you. What brings you to Elderslie in the middle of the week?"

"I'm on my way to visit Aunt Margaret. Isabelle is to be married in a few days, so between them they have conscripted me to help with the arrangements for the wedding. Aunt Margaret has been unwell since Uncle Malcolm died."

Ewan drew himself up as though I had slapped him. "Sir Malcolm's dead? God rest his soul." He crossed himself. "When did he die?"

"Six months ago, of dropsy, though he had been unwell for a year before that. But that is why young Isabelle's marriage has taken so long to arrange. She was supposed to have been wed soon after you left, you may recall, to a young fellow of good family from Paisley, James Morton. I know you've met him."

Ewan nodded. "Aye. His father holds extensive lands out there."

"He did, but he died, too, last year. Young James is master now."

Ewan whistled softly. "Master of his own lands! He must be what? Nineteen now? And he has waited two years for the girl?"

"He has, and I admire him for it, but Isabelle refused to wed while her father was sick, so he had little option, if he truly wanted her. Now that Sir Malcolm has been dead for half a year, Aunt Margaret has insisted that they go ahead and wed." I smiled. "She has three grandchildren, from Anne, but she is hungry for more."

Ewan's gaze was distant. "Will's going to be upset. We had no idea."

"I know. But no one knew where you were. The messengers we sent turned Selkirk Forest inside out looking for you. Where have you been?"

"Farther south this past year and more, near Jedburgh. Can I come with you to Elderslie?"

I nodded and began to walk with him, leading my horse and quizzing him as we went about what he and Will had been up to for the past two years, but in the mile or so that lay between us and our destination he parried all my questions patiently. He pleaded fatigue—he had been on the road all day and most of the previous night, he said—and asked my leave to put off his tale for a single telling, to my aunt and me together. I could see that he was determined to have his way and so I did not press him, though I doubted Lady Margaret would be capable of joining us in any lengthy session. Since Sir Malcolm's death she had been retiring earlier, it seemed, with each passing day and rising earlier each morning, hours before dawn, to prepare for the coming day. With Isabelle's nuptials less than a week away, I knew that all her energies would be tightly focused on women's things.

As it transpired, I was both right and wrong. The house, when we arrived, was full of young women, all of them busy either sewing or working on long lists of details that had to be attended to, and Aunt Margaret was delighted to see Ewan again after such a long absence. She banished all the young women to another part of the house with their fabrics and their endless lists and chatter, and then she settled down with us in the family room, voracious in her appetite for all the news she could possibly hear of Will and his doings, and about Mirren and the home she had set up for and with him.

It was only after listening to her questions for some time that I began to see that the information she was seeking had absolutely nothing to do with what I wanted to hear. Aunt Margaret was solely concerned with her beloved nephew and his new wife and the life they shared together, the details of their house and its furnishings, the likelihood of their having children, how Mirren spent her time while Will was away. I tried several times to intervene, seeking answers of my own, but Ewan turned my queries aside with ease and virtually ignored me, focusing all his attention solicitously upon my aunt while I sat silent. Not a word was said about the reasons for Will's departure two years earlier.

Eventually, though it was still daylight outside, her ladyship announced that she would soon retire to bed, but had no doubt that Ewan and I would have much we wanted to talk about without the constraints of an old woman's presence. We stood and bowed to her, and she went bustling off.

Fergus the steward fed us royally but simply on fresh-baked bread and the broiled, succulent meat of a months-old calf that had been fattened up for the wedding feast but had broken a leg two days earlier. The meat, though fresh and tender, was bland, but Fergus had prepared a mixture of berries and fruits into a sauce that transformed its plainness into something fitting for the palate of a god, and we devoured everything he placed in front of us, washing it down with the household's wonderful ale. Throughout the meal we talked of generalities, mutually consenting to discuss nothing of importance until the board had been cleared, Fergus had retired, and we were once more alone.

2

Ewan got up eventually from the table and threw two fresh logs on the big fire, then poured us both more ale and settled himself in Sir Malcolm's large, padded armchair by the fire. I moved to join him, sitting in my aunt's smaller chair. He was at ease, and it was clear he had decided it was time for me to know what he knew. I can hear his voice today in my mind as clearly as I did then.

"Right, lad. You've been very patient, and I thank you for it. What I have to tell you now is for your ears alone. So where do you want me to start?"

"Where do you think? Right at the outset, from the last time I saw you two, riding away on your trip south, two years ago."

"We didn't go south. Not that day." My surprise must have been obvious on my face. "That's right, you didn't know, did you? Will didn't tell you, and I couldn't."

"What d'you mean, you couldn't?"

"I couldn't tell you because I didn't know any more than you did. I thought we were heading southeast, too, until we reached the road and Will turned west. That's when he told me he had changed his mind. He'd decided to take the blood price."

"The blood price?"

"Aye. It's an ancient judgment, a penalty levied in return for blood shed or attempted."

"I know what a blood price *is*, Ewan. I want to know about *this* blood price. What's that about?"

"Ah, well. The one he was owed. Or decided he was owed."

"By Graham, you mean."

"Aye."

"How did he come to that, in God's name?"

He twisted his mouth into a wry expression that was not quite a grin. "He didn't. It came to *him*, that morning, while he was looking at the bales of wool used to buy Masses for old Graham's passing. Will looked at those two bales and saw a ransom paid to God to redeem the soul of an old thief who should have been beyond redemption. He saw that they had come out of the son's riches, though through someone else's impulse, and that they would never be missed among the wealth young Graham inherited. And that set him thinking about justice and retribution and, of course, blood prices." His voice became more reflective. "It had become clear to him, while he was standing there with you and Father Peter—and I could not fault his reasoning—that Graham's scheming had threatened his life. Not merely his livelihood but his life itself. Had the plot succeeded, Will would have hanged and Graham would have owed an unsuspected blood price to Sir Malcolm. But it had failed, through sheerest chance, and although Will had avoided the hangman, he and I were headed into exile while Graham was walking free." He hesitated. "Where is Graham now? And did they ever find the other fellow, the Englishman?"

"The verderer, Tidwell." I shook my head. "No, never. We believe he was murdered by Graham. But Graham's dead, too."

"He is? Since when?"

"Since the autumn of that year. Bruce had him hanged, for plotting murder and sedition. Uncle Malcolm sent word to you, but you were nowhere to be found."

"Aye, so you mentioned. Damnation. We've been skulking around for two years, not knowing that." He shook his head. "Ah well, even had we known, it would ha'e made but little difference. Will had his duties to see to, on several fronts. Still, it makes me feel better just to know he's dead. He was a nasty whoreson, that one, despite all his mild airs and seeming gentle ways. A murderous animal."

"So you knew nothing?"

"How could we? We didn't know anything after we left."

"Come, Ewan, that's a weak excuse. We didn't know where you had gone, but you knew where to find us. You could have sent home for word, failing all else. It's been two years."

"We couldn't contact you. Will didna dare. We didna know the threat had been removed. We knew only that Graham's treachery had left Will in danger of his life, under threat from assassins. And hand in glove wi' that went the threat of danger to his family from the same people. It was a risk Will didna want to take."

"All right. So instead of going east to Selkirk you went south to Jedburgh. Are you at the Abbey?"

"No. Close by, though, on Wishart's lands."

"The Bishop's?"

He nodded.

"And how did you come to be there?"

He arched an eyebrow at me. "Because that was the way things happened. We'll get to that. Right now let me tell you what Will was thinking when first we left here.

"He had been left with no choice but to quit his employment, his home, and his family, and to take me with him, which, as he saw it, deprived me of *my* livelihood as well. Nothing I could say would change his mind on that. And besides, in his eyes, he had lost his hopes of winning Mirren. He believed Hugh Braidfoot would never consent to having his daughter wed to a penniless forester who was under suspicion in a hanging crime—the selfsame man, mind, who had deprived her of a wealthy husband in the first place."

"But that is nonsense. Will was guilty of no crime."

"*Under suspicion*, I said. And he was. Think of it from Will's view. He couldna bear the thought of losing Mirren. And so he decided Graham should—what were the words he used? Something he learned in school … Graham should make reparations. That was it. And I agreed with him. Still do."

"I see. And what were these reparations?"

Ewan hooked one long leg over a padded arm and stretched his other foot towards the fire. "Restitution. And before you ask me, I'll tell you. Restitution for the threat to his life in the first place and the malice that bred it. Restitution, too, for lost opportunity—to woo, wed, and live a normal life as an honest man. Restitution for lost time in which to live up to obligations to employer and charges. Restitution for monies lost in recompense for filling those obligations. And restitution for losses other than those that can't easily be replaced—good name and reputation being first among them." He laid his head back against his chair, watching me levelly. "I'll tell you how we made the tally, too." He held up one hand, forefinger extended, preparing to count the points off on his fingers, but I interrupted him.

"We, you said. You were involved in this tallying?"

"Of course I was. Will had seen the two bales of prime wool proffered for a year of Masses to shorten the old man's years in Purgatory. That cleared his mind wondrously and set a value on his thoughts concerning how he had been wronged and how much he had lost thereby, in forfeiture. He would have made a canny merchant, our Will. And once I saw the way his mind was set, I helped him out. So …"

He began to count on his fingers. "For the two major offences against him, threat of death and loss of marriage prospects, two bales each. For the loss of work, wage, and good name, one bale apiece, making seven bales in all. But then, as any good merchant will, he included his costs. He added in the costs of transportation—two wagons with teams and drivers, he thought—and covered those with two more bales, making nine altogether."

"You *stole* nine bales of wool?"

"Nine bales of *prime* wool, Jamie. But we didna steal it and it wasna really nine, as things turned out. We just claimed nine as due to us. Or as owed to Will. The whole thing was"—he thought for a moment—"straightforward. Bar a few earlier arrangements."

I sat there immobile, my mind consumed with the thought that my cousin had become a thief and placed himself beyond the law. No wonder, then, that he had stayed away so long and that Ewan had been alert to the presence of others.

"Tell me exactly what took place," I said, "because all you've done to this point is confuse me. Start again at the beginning."

"It's a gospel you want, then." He sighed, then took a long swallow of ale. "Well, if I fall asleep in the telling, in God's name don't wake me.

"It started at the main road. I made to turn right and Will went left instead, as though towards Glasgow. When I asked him where he was going, he said Kilbarchan and pointed west. I kept my mouth shut and followed him for the next while until we reached the village.

"It's a strange wee place, a cluster of cottages, less than ten, I think, and all the folk are weavers. The houses all have looms in them, sometimes more than one, so there's hardly any room left for the folk to sleep. We stopped at one house and asked how we would find the Graham place, and the weaver pointed out the way to us. It was another mile distant. He said we couldn't miss it, and he was right, there it was.

"I said Kilbarchan was a strange wee place, but Graham's property was a strange *big* place. Four stone buildings in a walled enclosure. Prosperous, as you'd expect. One of the four was the main house and the other three were warehouses, we discovered. We sat on the crest, looking down at it, and counted the people moving about down there. There weren't many. I counted eight of them, and they were all around the main house. I thought we would leave then, but Will kicked his horse forward, and we rode down."

He pulled thoughtfully at his ale again. "Some self-important fellow met us at the front of the house, asking to know our business. He was the household steward, but with the old man dead, he thought himself in charge of everything. Your cousin amazed me by presenting himself as a well-bred man of affairs, addressing the fellow in Latin until it became clear that the man could not understand a word. From then on, he spoke plain Scots, saying he had been sent to make inquiries by his master, Lord Ormiston of Dumfries, regarding a contract that Sir Thomas had with Alexander Graham the wool merchant for the purchase of raw wool. Told the fellow that Sir Thomas had paid in advance months earlier but that upon reaching Paisley the previous day, with the intent of taking delivery, he had been informed of the merchant's untimely death and, not wishing to trespass upon the family's grief, had sent us two to ask when we might return to complete our business to everyone's satisfaction. That impressed even me—*to everyone's satisfaction.*"

"So what did this fellow say?"

"Nothing much. Will's manner had cowed him. He was the old man's steward, as I said, but a mere house servant. He had little knowledge of the working end of the old man's business, and he mumbled something about the workforce all having gone home to wait for what would happen next. And then he told us that another wool merchant, a Master Waddie, would be coming over from Paisley in two days' time to act in the interests of the son and heir, taking a detailed inventory of the materials in store and the contracts outstanding. He said word would not yet have had time to reach young Master Graham, who served the Lord Robert Bruce as a verderer and would most likely be somewhere on the Bruce lands in Annandale. It would take him, the man believed, at least two days to reach home, so he and the Waddie fellow might well arrive at the same time.

"Will said he would talk to Lord Ormiston, but that his lordship had been long away from home, about his affairs in Edinburgh, and was anxious to get back to his wife, who was infirm. He then asked if we might be permitted to pay our last respects to the old man before we left, on his lordship's behalf, and the fellow let us into the house and then left us alone. Old Graham was laid out on his bed in the main room. There was a priest there, and two monks, and a couple of others, men and women both, most of whom were peering about them as though they had never been there before."

"And then?"

"We knelt and prayed by the bedside. Well, we knelt anyway, while the priest prayed. And then, having established our right to be there, about our supposed master's business, we walked around the other buildings, the warehouses and barns and stables, and three big, stinking sheds where the wool was treated and combed before they baled it." A smile flickered at the corners of his mouth. "At that point I think you would have been right about the thievery. Will was looking, I believe, for an easy way to rob the place.

"One of the stone warehouses had a private room with a padlocked door, and it was obvious that the old man had worked in there on his affairs. But the padlock was unlocked, the door was open, and no one was nearby, so we went in. There were papers and parchments everywhere, strewn about all over the place, as though someone had been rooting around in there looking for something to steal. Will opened a small wooden chest that sat on the big writing table and pulled out a handful of scrolls—single sheets of parchment, all of them unsealed but rolled and tied, with ribbons and blank seals attached. He opened one, and then another, and then he began to smile. He flipped me the one that had made him smile. I looked at it closely, but it took me a while to realize its import ..." His voice faded and he smiled again at the memory.

"Well, what was it?" I prodded.

"A contract, a bill of sale. With spaces left blank for the details of the transaction. But it was signed by Alexander Graham. None of the others were, but for some reason the old man had signed his name and set his seal to this one. Will took it back from me and tucked it and three others into his scrip, and then we went off and continued our inspection. All three barns were stuffed to the roof with bales of wool, some of it prime, some poorer. But they were *stuffed*, Jamie. Hundreds and hundreds of bales. We found out later that they had been preparing to ship trains of wagons to Glasgow,

Dumfries, and Edinburgh the following week, for the Michaelmas Fairs in September, less than a month away.

"On our way back out to our horses, we met the steward again, and he was as friendly as could be. Will asked him if someone could tell us about wagons, and he directed us to one of the wooden barns outside the compound walls, where we found an old man getting ready to leave. He showed us an enormous wagon, the biggest I have ever seen, and told us it could carry ten full-sized bales with ease. Then he showed us the leather sheets they used to cover the bales for protection, and the long straps they used to secure the load. Will asked him how many horses, and he told us two. Two big whoresons was what he said."

In spite of my queasiness at the crime being described, I found myself fascinated. "So what happened then?"

"We came right back to Paisley, to find help for what Will had in mind. We needed some men we could trust, and so we went to Jamie Crawford's howff."

"Of course you did." I knew Crawford's howff well. It had been a favoured haunt of ours for a long time, a plain but well-run tavern frequented by archers and other interesting characters, where the food was simple but wholesome, the ale was dependable, and no one ever asked awkward questions.

"One of the sons, Alan, was there," Ewan said, "and he and Will went off into a corner. I could tell, watching them, that Alan liked what he was hearing, grinning and nodding his head and looking around the room."

Alan Crawford and Will had been friends since our first year at the Abbey. He was a big, bluff fellow, Will's age and almost as big. The only weaponry Alan ever carried was a long, single-edged dirk that hung at his side—I had never known him to bare the blade—and a heavy quarterstaff that Will had taught him to use. He was the only man I had ever seen who could best Will Wallace in a toe-to-toe bout. The respect that achievement garnered him was widespread.

"Did you know what Will was telling him?"

Ewan grinned. "That we had need of help and would pay well for two weeks' work. Four men, to help us take a heavy wagon north, then bring it back. Good men, willing to work hard and to fight if need be. A silver groat a day, each man."

I stifled the urge to whistle. A groat, our smallest silver coin, was worth fourpence, and the maximum going wage for a skilled labourer was twopence a day. A groat a day, for two weeks' worth of easy work, was a deal of money.

"So," I said instead. "Did you find your four?"

"Five," Ewan answered, his grin still in place. "Alan was the first, but there was a man there we had not expected to find. You remember Robertson, the archer Will bested the day he first met Mirren? Well, he was there, and Alan vouched for him. He remembered Will and was glad to see him—no hard feelings at all—so he was our second. Then there was Big Andrew Miller, who's always ready for anything that smells of a fight, and Long John of the Knives was the fourth."

The faces of the last two men flashed into my mind, although I had not seen either one in years. Big Andrew's name was a jest, for he was one of the smallest men in Paisley, but he was lean and wiry and as strong as a braided sinew bowstring, and he carried a crossbow wherever he went. Long John of the Knives, on the other hand, towered several inches over Will, and there was never any doubt of where his name came from. He wore a heavy belt around his waist, and from it hung a dozen sheathed knives, all of different sizes. Long John could sink any one of them into any surface, with astonishing speed, from twenty paces. He was a peaceful man, though, and threw only at targets, perhaps because no one ever gave him cause to take offence. Will, I thought, had chosen well.

"Who was the fifth, then?"

"An outlander, a Gael from the northwest, from an island called Skye. He had been in Paisley for a month or so, and Alan and Robertson had both befriended him. No one knew much about him, but both men vouched for him as being tight lipped, trustworthy, and a dour man in a fight. They called him Shoomy, but his real name is

Seumas, Gaelic for James. Will had been watching him since we arrived, and I could tell he was taken by the man, though it might just have been the sword. Shoomy carries a sword that's much like Will's bow—bigger and longer and more dangerous looking than any other to be seen. He's a big lad, tall and lean, but well muscled and quick, and that sword gives him twice the reach of any man around."

He scratched gently at the side of his nose. "So, there we were within the hour, seven of us in all, and a bargain struck. Will borrowed ink and pens from Jamie Crawford and went away to make his own arrangements for the following day, while I rented some nags for the five lads.

"We slept in the stable at the howff that night and were on the road by dawn. By mid-morning we were back at the Graham place. There was hardly anyone there—a few labourers lazing about and a huddle of women carding wool was all we saw. Will presented the steward with a completed contract for the delivery of nine bales of prime wool and the rental of a heavy wagon and team to transport them. It bore the name of Lord Thomas Ormiston of Dumfries—we discovered later that he had been dead for six years by then," he added, flashing me a grin, "and the signature and seal of Alexander Graham himself, indicating the full amount had been paid months earlier, delivery to wait upon Lord Ormiston's return from the north. We received a written bill of sale in return, left one of the nine bales as surety for the return of the wagon, then loaded the remaining eight and headed, everyone supposed, for Dumfries."

"It *was* theft, then. So where did you go?"

"To Glasgow, to Bishop Wishart. He heard Will's confession and granted him absolution once he'd heard the entire tale. Restitution received for harm done, he said—all right and proper. And then he sent us north with the wool, to Sir Andrew Murray."

"In *Moray*? Why would he send you all the way up there?"

Ewan rearranged his long legs, crossing one over the other. "Because he is a bishop and God works in mysterious ways. You should know that, and you almost a priest."

"I'm serious, Ewan. Why?"

Ewan looked at me directly then, no trace of humour in his eyes. "Because he is the senior Bishop of Scotland at this time and he believed, for reasons he didna see fit to explain to us, that sending Will up there would be for the good of this realm. There were fell things happening at that time. Edward of England had named Bishop Bek of Durham his deputy in Scotland, for one thing. Bek is a dour and humourless man devoted to his King before his Church. Wishart had no love for Bek then and has even less now.

"He required Will to make contact with the younger Murray and renew their acquaintance while delivering certain … matters— several documents of what he termed 'some delicacy'—directly to Sir Andrew's attention. He left us in no doubt of the importance of what he required of us."

"Wait. Are you saying Wishart included *you* in his designs?"

"Aye, but only because I was already there with Will and Will vouched for me. But in return for Will's services, and very much to the point at the time, Wishart offered rich payment. He would speak personally, he said, with Mirren's father, whom he knew well, on Will's behalf. And the blood-price wool would be of use to Murray, he said, for there had been a blight of some kind among the sheep in the north, and we would be well paid for it. The money gained from that would enable Will to offer Master Braidfoot a suitable bridal price for his only daughter, and the Bishop would then grant Will a position as a verderer, with a good, strong house, on the Wishart family lands near Jedburgh." He looked at me from beneath his arched right eyebrow. "Ye'll see, I think, it wasna an offer Will could refuse."

I felt slightly abashed. "Yes, I can see that. Especially in his frame of mind at the time. And so you travelled north. I'm guessing it went well there, for you've said Will is married and living and working in the south now."

He nodded. "Aye. It took us eight days to reach Murray's lands, and it was an interesting journey. Scotland is a wild place nowadays, much changed since King Alexander died, and there were times when we were glad there were seven of us, for had we been fewer in number we would have been plucked like fowl along the road and left wi' nothing."

"What d'you mean? You would have been robbed?"

"Robbed and killed, lad. None of us doubted that, once we saw how it was out there. There's no law beyond the burghs today. Once out of the towns and into the countryside, it's every man for himself and God help the unprepared. The whole world is out of balance. Without a king to hold them in check, the nobles—or so they like to call themselves—are all become savages, every petty rogue of them looking out for himself alone. Each one of them treats his holdings as his own wee kingdom, to be ruled as he sees fit, using whatever private army he can afford to hire. Which means that there's no order anywhere—no discipline, no loyalty, no honour—and a traveller moving through the land runs a gamut of risks at every turn, like to lose everything he possesses each time he meets a stranger. They are all bandits, Jamie, soldiery as well as outlaws, and common, decent folk live in terror of their lives.

"Three times we encountered what might have been serious trouble on the road. Three times in eight days. And on one of them, north of Stirling, we had no other choice than to fight. We left eight dead men behind us, eight out o' nigh on twenty who attacked us, but thank God none of them were ours. We took down five o' those early, with our bows—me and Robertson and Will—and Big Andrew's crossbow. By that time, though, the others had come too close for bow work, but Long John and Shoomy killed three more of them before they could blink, and the rest ran away."

I could only shake my head, unable to believe that the situation could be as bad as Ewan was saying.

"Anyway, we found Sir Andrew where he was supposed to be, and young Andrew was with him. Between the pair o' them, they gave us a chieftain's welcome. I couldna believe how happy your friend Andrew was to see Will, and it seemed to be mutual—Will was brighter than I had seen him since before he fell foul o' the

Graham fellow." He lapsed into silence, staring into the fire, and I saw his eyelids starting to droop.

"Don't nod off now, Ewan," I said, afraid of losing him and the story both. "They were still friends, then?"

He blinked owlishly. "Oh aye! It was one of the strangest things I've ever seen. You know Will, he seldom mixes well wi' strangers, and there they were, after five or six years, embracing each other and laughing together like brothers who had been apart for no more than an hour. Brotherly, though God knows there's little resemblance between them apart from size. And yet there's something each of them has that's reflected in the other. Don't ask me what it is, for I can't say. The closest I can come to it is that they share a common ... *light*." He winced. "That sounds daft, I know, but each of them has this *glow* about him that seems to spill out whenever they're excited, and those two get each other stirred up all the time. You can almost see it—their excitement, I mean—everyone around them feels it."

He raised his hands in surrender. "That's it, lad. I barely know what I'm saying, but I know I have to sleep. I've been on the road since before dawn, and now that I'm old, I need my rest." He looked across at me. "An hour or two wouldna hurt you, either."

"But I want to ask you about—"

"Ask me tomorrow. I'll be in better fettle for talking once I've slept."

There was no point in arguing, and so we went to find our beds. Whereas I have no doubt that Ewan was asleep before he even lay flat, I lay awake for a long time, thinking about all that he had told me. And then, just as I was drifting to sleep at last, I tensed, my mind suddenly crystal clear again.

Ewan had been hiding as he waited for me to reach him that day. Ewan, masked and unexpectedly returned after two full years away from Elderslie, should have had no reason to hide himself in a clump of brambles. Reason to be cautious, yes, but to hide from the whole world?

3

People had already started arriving from neighbouring houses and hamlets by the time I rolled out of bed soon after daybreak, and more kept coming throughout the morning, turning the entire household and the grounds into a frenzy of preparations. Cousin Anne arrived before mid-morning with her husband and her three children, and Aunt Margaret conscripted me to take the children for a walk in the grounds, to keep them out of the way of the work ongoing everywhere, so I did not even set eyes on Ewan until after the midday meal had been served. Trays and platters of cold meats, pickled roots and onions, and slabs of fresh bread with jugs of cold spring water from the well were carried out from the kitchens and set on tables for people to help themselves however and whenever they wished.

I had already eaten by the time Ewan appeared, and when I saw the long tube of the bow case hanging from his shoulder I guessed he had been practising in the nearby woods. He winked at me as he approached the serving tables, then unslung the bow case and set it down beside his quarterstaff before beginning to load a wooden platter for himself. I went to fetch us a couple of mugs of ale from the kitchens, then crossed to where he had found a seat at an unoccupied table under a tree, against the wall of one of the outbuildings. He nodded his thanks as he took the ale, and I sat sipping at my own as he wolfed down his food. When he had swallowed the last mouthful, he leaned back and quaffed off what seemed like half of his ale. Then, typically, he belched.

"That was good," he said. "But you don't look happy. What's on your mind?"

"Questions," I murmured. "More questions."

He looked around us casually "Ask, then. We're alone. What do you want to know?"

"I want to know why you were hiding yesterday when we met, because I don't believe it had anything to do with your being cautious about Graham of Kilbarchan." He didn't stir and his expression betrayed nothing of what he was thinking. "Whatever you were hiding from, whatever it was about, it's much more recent than the trouble that sent you away from here two years ago. Is it not?"

He tilted his head slightly to one side, and then he nodded. "Aye, it is. I was going to tell you about it." He glanced around again. "Will wants to come home. Sent me to see if it was safe."

"He wants to—? What's stopping him? Let him come! Go back and tell him we're waiting for him, then bring him back, wife and all."

The big archer ducked his head. "Not quite that simple, Jamie. That's why he sent me up alone. To check out the possibilities, see what's to be seen."

"In what sense? What are you looking for?"

"Englishry."

"In *Elderslie*?" I made no attempt to hide my scorn.

"Why not? They're everywhere else."

"Not here, they're not. Not yet."

"Are they in Paisley?"

I shrugged. "At the Abbey, aye, sometimes. There's always bishops coming and going, and the English ones have taken to riding with escorts ever since Pope Gregory gave Edward the right to appoint Scottish bishops last year."

Ewan grunted. "Aye, Bishop Wishart wasna pleased about that at all. Said—and he was right—it undermined the entire authority of the Church in Scotland. A foreign pope granting a foreign king authority over the Scots clergy. 'Gin I were an English bishop in Scotland today, I'd travel wi' an escort, too, lest my holy arse got booted back into England."

"Then … has Will crossed the English?"

Ewan hesitated. "Aye, you might say that."

"What did he do?"

His huge shoulders flexed beneath his clothing. "Nothing you wouldna ha'e expected him to do, knowing Will."

"Tell me, then."

"He hit an English soldier."

"He *hit* an English soldier. In a brawl, you mean."

Ewan sighed. "No," he said, in a strange, tight voice. "It was no brawl. But there's background to it that you need to know in order to understand it. Last year was bad, Jamie, all upheavals, as I'm sure you know from living at the Abbey, filled wi' politics and posturing and praying and positioning by folk of every stripe, and all of it shaped to suit the dreams and schemes of the men who would call themselves great. And it culminated last May and June, we're told, with Edward Plantagenet being named overlord of Scotland. That was his price for agreeing to serve as judge in the matter of the king-ship, overseeing Balliol and Bruce, and none of the magnates seemed inclined to argue with him at the time." He shrugged. "Mind you, how could they, really? As Bishop Wishart made clear to us at the time, they all hold great and prosperous lands in England, through Edward's goodwill and at his royal pleasure. Lord John Balliol himself owns fifteen vast estates in England, many of them in the richest, southern areas, did you know that? And Bruce holds almost as many—at least ten that Wishart knows of—and both men openly pay homage to Edward as their feudal lord and benefactor in England. Their *feudal lord*."

Ewan unclenched his fist, flexing his fingers slowly, and continued in a quieter voice. "And so Edward was named feudal overlord of Scotland in May last year—and within days there was an English army at Norham and all the Scots royal castles were surren-dered to the English." He turned his head to look directly into my eyes. "According to the lawyers on both sides, they were handed over temporarily, to be returned later, of course, once a new King of Scots has been crowned. But in the meantime, Edward holds them and we lack them, and their strength looms over us, manned by English garrisons.

"And then in June, less than a month after that, all the Guardians resigned and were reappointed by Edward the same day, and two days after that they all swore fealty to Edward—but not as feudal overlord, as was agreed at Norham. Oh, no. This time they swore their allegiance and fealty to Edward Plantagenet, Lord Paramount of Scotland. God help us all!"

"Ewan," I said, "I know all that, knew it while it was happening. But you. You were never this political before."

"No, I was not." He leaned forward. "You're right. Not even when Edward was doing to my homeland of Wales what he is now preparing to do to Scotland."

"Oh come, Ewan," I said, close to scoffing. "That was war, and Wales was his enemy. I would hardly say it's as bad as that here."

"Oh, would you not?" He raised his chin until he was almost looking down his boneless nose at me. "Then you will have to pardon me, Master James. How old are you now?"

I hesitated, dismayed by the hostility in his tone. "Twenty, as you know."

"Aye, twenty …" He managed to make it sound like an infantile age.

"It's clear you have a point to make and I am missing it. Explain it again, if you will."

"It's nothing you would know, Jamie," he said in a kinder tone. "You're a priest, or as near as can be, living in an Abbey. Everything you hear is filtered for the Church's ears. It's those of us who live outside who know what's really going on. The south is full of English soldiery nowadays. They're everywhere around us, like a coating of slimy, foul-smelling moss, and there's no way to stay clear of them. They lord it over everyone, and there seems to be no one to whom they are accountable. At the lowest level, the common men-at-arms are ruled by knights and sergeants. Those in turn are commanded by bailiffs and petty officers, who are appointed to various duties by sheriffs and justiciars, who hold *their* power through the various barons Edward has brought with him to Scotland. And the barons serve the earls—"

"The English earls, you mean."

"Aye, in most instances, but when the Scots Earl of Carrick's men, many of whom are Englishmen, are mixed with those of the English Earl of Hereford, who is to tell which is which in the heat of an argument? The earls are all Edward's deputies, of course, Scots and English—that goes without saying—but collectively their retainers act as though they are a law unto themselves. They lean heavily on the Scots folk and treat them like serfs."

"Like serfs? How is that possible?"

"How is it *possible*? Jamie, it's *commonplace*. Certainly where we are, in the south, but I'll be surprised if it is different anywhere else. There are too many English here nowadays, and too few of *us*, and there is no war between us—only arrogance on their part and long-suffering acceptance on ours. But they treat us like a conquered folk and make no effort to disguise their contempt for us."

"Can you give me an example?"

"Aye, I can. It's the reason Will needs to come home. He's a wanted man because of it, but he did nothing wrong. He committed no crime, broke no laws. He simply crossed the English. But now there's a price on his head and he's in hiding and dare not come home."

"A price on his head … How much?"

"Five silver marks."

"And for what is he being sought?"

"For assaulting an English soldier who was doing his duty."

"And is that true?"

"I'll tell you what happened, and you can judge for yourself." He wedged his back against the wall behind him and launched immediately into his story.

"About three months ago, perhaps three and a half, Will and I travelled to Glasgow to meet with Bishop Wishart and report on our stewardship, and on our way home again we stopped at Lanark, to pick up some yarn and thread and the like for Mirren at the Lanark Fair. The town was full of soldiery, most of them English, though some of them were Scots, but we had grown accustomed to that, because we had noticed, on the way north, that there were more English everywhere than we'd ever seen before. But we had kept to ourselves, avoided contact with anyone and encountered no difficulty, and behaved the same way on our return journey—until we came to Lanark.

"Something was different there," he continued, "something was amiss, and we didn't know what at first. And then we turned a corner into the marketplace and it was all but empty, save for a half-dozen people who immediately stopped what they were doing—they were huddled together over something we couldn't see—and turned to look at us. They looked frightened, and guilty, and that's when Will recognized what was wrong. They were afraid of us, though we couldna tell right then what was frightening them. But they werena talking, and they certainly werena laughing. It was scarce mid-morning, and the stalls were all quiet and the only other people there at all were soldiers.

"'These folk think we're English,' Will said to me, watching them. 'They're afraid of us. It's our bows. They've taken us for English archers, and no wonder. Look over there—half the men on the other side of the square are archers, dressed just like us.' He was right, and I hadn't noticed it until that moment. He held up a hand and stood watching the group of folk in front of us, and when they were all looking at him, waiting for him to do or say something else, he raised his hand a little higher. 'We're not Englishmen,' he says, just loud enough for them to hear. 'No matter how you think we look, we are Scots like you. We carry English bows, but that means nothing. We are merely passing through on our way south to Jedburgh. What has been happening here?'"

"I thought for a while that no one was going to answer him, but then one of them, he looked like the oldest man among them, looked from one to the other of us. 'Come forward,' he says, 'and see for yourselves what's happening.' So we did. There was a young fellow among them, lying on a stall table and covered in blood, and they were trying to stop him bleeding. I was able to help them with that, and once we had the bleeding stopped it didna take us long to find out what had happened.

"The old man—his name was Nichol—told us the English had discovered a new game with quarterstaves and were having a grand time with it. It had started earlier, in another town, but word of it had spread quickly so that everyone now knew what was involved. Gangs of English soldiery would swagger through a town, driving the local men ahead of them the way beaters drive game, until they thought they had gathered enough victims for their sport. Then they would round in their prey and the games would begin. The rules were very simple. Two English soldiers would compete in a bout of staves, watched by an audience of mixed Scots and English. When the bout was over, the quarterstaff being an English weapon, the Scots were invited to try them out. Any Scot who dared was encouraged to knock down a braced English soldier by hitting him across the shoulders. Should he fail, there was no penalty other than the recognition of the fact that the Scots were no match for Englishmen in the use of an English weapon. Should he succeed, on the other hand, he would be rewarded with a silver groat for his accomplishment."

"That sounds fair enough," I said.

He raised a hand to silence me. "But the Scots could not win, because the weapons they used were flawed."

I frowned. "How can a quarterstaff be flawed? It's essentially a club."

"True, but even a club can be weakened. When they finally found someone who was willing to try for the groat—and believe me, they made a grand business of provoking people, challenging their manhood, insulting them, and questioning their bravery—the contenders were offered their choice of any of the staffs carried by the soldiery. The weapons were laid out on the ground and their owners stepped away from them. The locals were unsuspicious. They had just watched the English soldiers laying about each other with the same weapons.

"Yet two groups of Englishry were mingled there, one carrying sound, solid weapons that they used to fight each other, and the others carrying weakened staves that were used to gull the locals. So some young fellow, like the one we found bleeding in the market-place, would eventually take up a staff and smash it across the armoured shoulders of the Englishman who stood there waiting for the blow. But every weapon laid out for the young man's choice had been cut diagonally, and the damage skilfully disguised. So when the hapless dupe, encouraged by everyone, swung the wretched thing at full strength against the armoured man's back, the staff shattered, the jagged, broken end rebounding viciously to strike the unarmoured Scot, drawing blood most times and frequently inflicting brutal damage, to the great amusement of the watching English …"

A shadow fell across the table between us, and I looked up to see a pretty young woman gazing down at us, her body tilted sideways against the weight of the great wooden jug she balanced against her hip. "You two are deeply into something," she said, flashing us both a merry grin. "It must be thirsty work, talking so much. Will I pour you some more ale?"

We sat happily and watched her as she filled our mugs and meandered away in search of other drinkers, and as she went, Ewan turned to me, waggling a finger at her departing form.

"I know you're not a priest yet, but does that—?"

"Not even slightly," I said, smiling at the tone in his voice as I waved his question aside. "Now tell me what Will did when he found out about this game the English were playing."

Ewan grinned wolfishly, the girl already forgotten. "Why would you even think he might do something, a quiet lad like our Will?"

"Because that's the way he is—quiet and shy and bashful and loath to speak his mind. Tell me, what did he do?"

"Will stripped off his green tunic and cloak and pulled on a plain homespun shirt that he borrowed from one of the men in the marketplace. Then he laid his bow case down, and I set aside my quarterstaff and picked up his instead. We left the weapons and the rest of our belongings with Nichol and his people—we'd told them what we were going to do—and we went looking for English bully boys."

"And found them, no doubt."

"Oh yes. On the far side of the town, away from the main road. The forest grows right to the edge of the town there—one minute you're among buildings, the next you're in the deep forest. Anyway, it was the right kind of place for what the English wanted. There were men-at-arms aplenty there, but most of them were archers, which surprised us at first. We found out later that they were attached to a force brought up from the Welsh borders by the English baron John de Vescy, a crony of Bishop Bek. Anyway, by the time we caught up with them, they had herded a group of locals into a clearing in the woods and were taunting them, defying them to pick up the cudgels and try their luck against an unarmed Englishman. I simply marched Will up to them, holding him by the arm as though I had taken him by force, and pushed him into the middle of the clearing."

"Just like that? And no one challenged you?"

Ewan looked all innocence. "Why would anyone challenge me? They took me for one of themselves, dressed as they were and carrying a quarterstaff, a cased longbow, and a quiver of arrows. The only two who spoke to me did so in Welsh, and I answered them in Welsh, telling them I was a newcomer, arrived that day. Who was to doubt me? Besides, I had brought them a victim for their amuse-ment. He stood there mute, glaring around him like an angry bull. Everyone was impressed by the size of him at first, but then they saw that he was weaponless, and none too clean, and ill dressed in a tattered old tunic, with bare, dirt-crusted legs and ruined sandals. So they dismissed him and began again as though he wasn't there.

"But as they talked and harangued their prisoners and explained what they were proposing, he appeared to take an interest, and his interest grew until he began to nod his head and shamble about—not saying a word, mind—and gesturing with his hands to indicate that he wanted to try one of the staffs."

"And eventually they gave in and let him," I said.

"They did. When it was plain that no one else wanted to take up the challenge, he was their only chance for amusement. And so the party with the doctored staves came forward and dropped them on the ground, so that he could pick one. No one noticed that I stepped forward with them and dropped mine at the same time. But of course, it was not mine at all. It was Will's, and he picked it out of the pile, peering at it as though he had never seen such a thing before, and swinging it awkwardly as though that, too, was new to him. I backed away quietly and made my way to where I could take up a covering position to guard his escape, for I knew he would soon be heading towards me, and moving quickly.

"Sure enough, I saw the biggest man among them take up his stance and prepare for Will's blow. He was armoured heavily enough, with a metal cuirass over a quilted leather jerkin, and his arms were well guarded against injury, and it was plain from the way he swaggered up that he was prepared for what was to follow.

"Well, he was not prepared at all. Who could prepare against a hard-swung staff from Will Wallace? The blow landed like a falling tree and knocked the fool right off his feet, flying arse over end until he smashed into the nearest tree and fell unconscious. And then, before anyone could react, Will took out the two men standing next to him, with two hard chops, side to side, his staff barely moving a foot in either direction, dropping them both where they stood. The first man hit was lucky, though the blow probably cost him a few broken ribs, even with the armour. But Will broke heads that day, and three of the men he struck down stayed down for good. In all, he disabled seven men—and I mean he *disabled* them—before anyone could even begin to rally against him. And by the time anyone did, he was already racing towards me, the other locals scattering in all directions.

"I'd had an arrow nocked to my string since before Will swung his first strike, and now I brought it up and pulled. There were three runners close to catching Will. I felled the first of them, shattering his left shoulder and throwing him backward with the force of my arrow. By the time I had another arrow set, the second man had recognized me and knew what was coming. Still running flat out, he threw himself sideways into the brush by the side of the path and lay there, making no attempt to come out. The third man had pulled a sword from his sheath and was swinging it up to hack at Will when my arrow took him low, just above the left knee, knocking the legs from under him. I nocked a third arrow, but no one moved now among the small group of Englishmen remaining in the clearing.

"I counted five men left there, each of them staring intently at either Will or me, and I knew our descriptions would be spread and they would hunt us down for this, or try to. I waited until Will ran past me and then I spun and followed him, neither of us slacking our pace until we reached the market square and reclaimed our clothing and weapons from Nichol and his companions. We told them to scatter and deny they had ever seen us, and then we made our way to where we had left our horses, and we were quickly out of Lanark."

I sat silent for some time, absorbing all that he had told me. "So that was three months ago?" I asked eventually.

He shrugged. "Don't know for certain. Where are we now?"

"September. Today is the sixteenth."

"Then it would have been four months ago. Late May."

"And where have you been since then?"

"In the forest, near Selkirk village."

"Did Mirren go with you?"

"Aye, she had to. Too many people knew who we were. It would no' have been safe for her to stay. Besides, she wouldna leave Will."

"A rough life for a woman, that, living in the forest, under open skies."

"Not at all. They live in a cave, those two, and it's better than many a house I've seen. It's dry, warm, spacious, and well lit, comfortably furnished, and well hidden. It even has separate bedchambers and a clean pool."

"A pool? You mean for bathing?"

"Aye, though it's chilly, even in high summer. It's spring fed. Pure, crystal water."

"Do they live alone there?"

"Aye, except for me and half a hundred others. We have an entire community there."

"Hmm. So why does Will want to leave?"

Ewan shrugged. "Who can say? He doesna talk about it much, but I think he's had enough of the outlaw life, and I think he would like to bring Mirren home to meet her new family here in Elderslie and visit her aunt and cousins in Paisley."

"Then he should do so," I said, "as soon as he can."

CHAPTER EIGHT

I

I have not had to resort to writing a commentary for many years, perhaps not since the day I left my beloved Abbey library in Paisley; real commentary requires time and leisure to reflect upon abstractions, and everyday life leaves ordinary men and priests little time for such luxuries. But commentary is a natural outgrowth of the translator's art, and I learned to use it soon after I gained full membership in Brother Duncan's library fraternity. In those days, left to my solitary work and encouraged to trust my instincts, I would add a notation whenever I encountered some anomaly in an ancient text on which I had been set to work. Sometimes I would merely note the oddity of a word or character, but once I grew more confident in my own judgment, I would write down my observations, and less frequently the opinions I drew from those observations, on whatever I had found anomalous in the document. Compiling such commentaries was, I found, enjoyable, and they were certainly invaluable later, when I would return to a document that I had not, perhaps, examined in months, to find my own notations carefully attached to the manuscript, usually by a tiny blob of wax at one edge.

This passage, then, is a commentary, an observation set aside from, but necessary to the understanding of, this chronicle of my cousin's life. And yet it troubles me that I should find it necessary to add it at all. My studies for the priesthood intensified during those same months, spurred by a mystifying display of interest in me and my progress by the revered and powerful Bishop of Glasgow, and my superiors decided that I would be ready for ordination by Christmas that year. The time flew by, and almost without our noticing, the trees fell bare and winter's onset grew steadily more threatening from day to day.

The death of the Maid of Norway, which had dealt the trivial blow of delaying my ordination, turned out to have far more important repercussions. It took eleven days for word to reach the mainland, and it came first to the attention of Bishop Fraser of St. Andrews on the eastern coast. A week after that, Robert Bruce was on the march to claim what he perceived to be his indisputable right to Scotland's Crown, headed for Perth by way of Stirling and summoning all his supporters to join him, once again beating John Balliol to the initiative. The Earls of Mar and Athol called out the men of their earldoms in support of Bruce, and for a time it looked yet again as though the entire country might be plunged into civil war, for the full might of the House of Comyn, the most powerful family in Scotland, under the Lords of Badenoch and Buchan, stood aligned with Balliol's claim and would not stand idly by while Bruce usurped the throne.

Bishop Fraser, though, had anticipated what would happen when the evil tidings of the Maid's death became public knowledge, and he reacted even more quickly than Robert Bruce. Within days, he sent messengers riding south at the utmost speed with a letter, composed by him and his cousin Sir John Comyn, Lord of Badenoch, appealing directly to Edward Plantagenet, advising the monarch of the death of his great-niece and voicing the writers' own fears of unrest in the aftermath. In order to avoid civil war and to protect the welfare of the realm of Scotland, the Bishop entreated the English King to use his good offices to ensure the legal settlement of the Scots Crown upon the brows of the best qualified of the various claimants. And thus began the events now known as the Grand Cause—the search for Scotland's true king.

I cannot think of a single soul among my acquaintances of my own age—and few of those remain alive today—who is not familiar with the events of the Cause. It dominated all our lives for two decades, and thus it seems inconceivable to me that I should now have to set down the details of it here when my main intent is to chronicle the life of my cousin Will. Yet I know I live already in a land full of people who have never known the fear and uncertainty, the daily terrors and hopelessness, that haunted their parents and their grandparents in those now far-off times. The Scots folk today remember nothing of the Grand Cause, apart from dreary, scarce believable old tales told by their elders, who were already forgetful in the telling, insulated from their own memories of horror by the peace and order that had finally come to them through the efforts of King Robert.

From that general and, I fear, irreversible ignorance has sprung the widespread disregard for truth that first spurred me to these writings: the invention, through whispered innuendo and defiantly blatant lies, of a flawless and endlessly admirable, patriotic champion; a hero, near mythical within a few brief years of his spurious creation, called William Wallace—*The* Wallace.

Thus I am forced, if some future reader is to understand my tale, to deal to some extent, at least, with recent history, if for no other reason than to identify the people and events that were to shape my unfortunate cousin's destiny.

Edward, of course, agreed to Bishop Fraser's request immediately, and sent an English army up to Scotland's border to oversee the peace while his deputies, Antony Bek and John de Vescy, sought out both Bruce and Balliol to inform them that, at the request of the Guardians, the English King had undertaken to adjudicate in the matter of the succession to the Scots Crown.

The hostilities ceased at once. Neither Bruce nor Balliol could claim legitimacy in contesting such a development, for the Guardians had acted authoritatively in accordance with their duty, and Edward of England, who had already successfully negotiated similar disputes in Sicily and Gascony, brought to the proceedings a reputation for probity and integrity. Assuming correctly that neither of the disputing nobles would defy him, Edward convened a great court at Norham, one of his border castles, and for the next two years a cumbersome diplomatic dance ensued.

In the years since then, in view of the revealed monstrosity of Edward's ambition, Bishop Fraser and John of Badenoch have been reviled for making that first approach to Edward, but as a man of God and only incidentally a man of Bruce during the ensuing conflicts, I believe that they have been unjustly maligned. Both men were Balliol adherents, and unashamedly anti-Bruce, but that has little bearing upon what happened later. When Fraser and Badenoch wrote to Edward in the last days of September 1290, they did so out of genuine concern for the good of Scotland's realm. No one, in those days, had the slightest suspicion of the canker that was already growing within the English King's breast.

That was soon to change. Eleanor of Castile, the Queen of England, fell sick in mid-November and was dead before month's end. Edward was devastated, cut adrift from the solid anchorage she had always provided for him. He was fifty-two years old and he had been married to Eleanor since he was sixteen, and in all of their thirty-six years as man and wife, they had been virtually inseparable, she his strongest bulwark and his most able adviser.

Edward vanished from public life that winter, leaving the affairs of his kingdom inert in the hands of deputies and caretakers. All important matters of state were set aside while the King remained in solitude for months. And by the time he emerged from his self-imposed exile, Edward Plantagenet had become a different man—bitter, less tolerant, and more demanding of everyone around him. He had always been capable and ambitious, but now, lacking his beloved wife to constrain him, he was intransigent and implacable and he evinced a ruthless obstinacy that would brook no interference to his royal will; he had become the man who would soon abandon all the finer achievements of his earlier life and arrogantly proclaim himself *Malleus Scottorum*, the Hammer of the Scots.

He began, in the spring of 1291, by formalizing his status as feudal overlord of Scotland. The matter had arisen before, and without great objection from the Scots magnates, most of whom owned lands and estates in England by Edward's permission, but now Edward made it the *sine qua non* of his intercession in the matter of the Scots kingship. The Guardians and the magnates debated it half-heartedly but soon yielded in the face of Edward's argument, which was that Scotland needed a judge and not an arbitrator. Edward had had extensive experience of both and he could demonstrate, with utter credibility, that arbitration was useless without the strength of authority to support it. By according Edward the full rights of feudal overlord, the Scots nobility would give him the full power to judge the Cause and to pronounce a victor. The solution appeared to be both logical and sensible, as, it must be said, did Edward himself at the time. And so the compromise—the tipping point—was reached.

No doubt sensing that decades of strife and bloodshed lay ahead, Robert Bruce the Competitor, who was over eighty at that time, resigned his claim to the throne in favour of his son, Robert Bruce VI. His son's wife, Lady Marjorie, Countess of Carrick, had died mere weeks before at the age of thirty-six—far too young to have died so suddenly. The earldom that she held, Carrick, was one of the oldest in the realm, and she had inherited it in her own right, as her father's sole heir. She had been married young and widowed childless during the Crusade of 1270, and soon after that she had wed Robert Bruce VI, presenting him with an astonishing ten living, healthy children. Bruce had carried the honorary title of Earl of Carrick, purely as Marjorie's consort. Upon her death, however, in accordance with Lady Marjorie's wish, he became Earl of Carrick in fact.

Only two days after his father passed to him the claim to the throne, the younger Bruce resigned his newly acquired earldom and invested the title and all its lands and holdings in his own son, Robert Bruce VII, who was then eighteen and living in England, in the household of King Edward. That development, with its realignment of claims and responsibilities, set all of southern Scotland abuzz.

Before anything could come of it, however, the court of auditors declared the following week that John Balliol, Lord of Galloway, had best rights to the kingdom of Scots. And so, Edward chose the weakest of the contenders for the Scots throne as the man who would be King.

No one quibbled at the verdict, for the auditors—a hundred of them in all, appointed from the nobility of Scotland and England— had been debating the question for two years. There were murmurs that the elder Bruce had resigned in favour of his son precisely because his own advanced age was being bruited as an impediment to his success; others said that the emplacement of the younger Bruce would ensure that if Balliol was chosen and then failed—and it was already being rumoured that he would—then the younger Bruce would be ready to step quickly into his place.

By and large, though, the Scots were generally glad to have the matter resolved at last, and to have the realm's affairs safely back in the hands of a legitimate king. In my own mind I believe that Balliol's claim was probably stronger than Bruce's, based as it was upon the law of primogeniture and the inheritance of the firstborn child, a system in which I believe. Balliol, as I knew from my own admittedly brief experience of him, was a forthright and likable man. He had few overt enemies and he was blessed with a pleasant, agree-able personality, combined with great charm and a marked ability to listen to others and actually hear what they were saying. Of course, he had detractors even then, mainly dour old warriors, all of them Bruce supporters, who muttered about his being incapable of dealing decisively enough with Edward of England. They shook their heads over what they saw as Balliol's lack of backbone and his too-eager willingness to placate the English King, and they warned that he would never find, or show, the kind of courage that would be required to keep the ambitious Edward in his place. Bruce, the proud and unyieldingly arrogant old Competitor, would never have bent the knee to Edward or any other Englishman, they maintained, and said Balliol had been selected purely because Edward believed he could control him.

Indeed, Edward used him from the outset as he would never have dared use the old and autocratic Robert Bruce. He manipulated the new King shamelessly and mercilessly to achieve his own ends, which proved to be the complete subjugation and absorption into England of the Scottish realm. Balliol, poor weak vessel that he was, never succeeded in asserting himself as anything other than Edward's catspaw.

He was crowned and enthroned at Scone on November 30th, and he took the title John, King of Scotland, thereby claiming kingship of the land rather than of the people and setting himself apart himself from every other monarch, all of whom had ruled the realm as Kings of Scots. The next day, he paid homage to King Edward of England as his feudal superior. His years in Purgatory had begun.

Balliol, as all men ought to know, was deposed and forced to abdicate eventually by his own nobles, his name disgraced forever in the eyes of his countrymen. But one man, one defiant rebel, continued to name him King and to champion his cause, to the great grief of Edward, England, and the majority of the Scots magnates.

That man was William Wallace.

CHAPTER NINE

I

Will spent his own years in Purgatory, a period that began on Wednesday, November 19th. I have never forgotten that date, partly because, as a librarian, I had become obsessive about such things. More than that, though, the date became memorable because of a concatenation of unforeseeable events.

Word of the auditors' decision arrived from the south in the dead of night, in the middle of a torrential rainstorm that lasted through the dawn and threatened to flood the countryside for miles around, but the entire Abbey community awoke in darkness to the joyous tidings of the new King and happily ignored the foulness of the weather as they threw themselves into preparing for a solemn Mass to celebrate such a triumphal occasion. Mass was celebrated every morning in the Abbey, of course, but on certain occasions, such as liturgical feasts and festivals, holy days of obligation, and days of general rejoicing like this one, special efforts were expended to make the experience of the Mass more memorable. The Sacrifice was concelebrated by the senior members of the clergy in residence; the regalia worn by the celebrants was the finest that the Abbey possessed; and the instruments and vessels used in the ceremonials, from thuribles for the burning of incense, to candle holders, Crosses, and ciboria and chalices for holding the Communion bread and wine, were the most magnificent in our treasury. Even the congregation, the Abbey brethren themselves, dressed in their finest habits, and the sound of their massed voices in the incense-laden air always seemed to take on a new dignity on those occasions. And so Mass that morning, filled with the promise of an early coronation and a return to righteousness and order throughout the reunited land, was a wondrous affair.

Those feelings of goodwill and renewed hope, unfortunately, barely survived the ending of the ceremony.

I had left the Abbey church directly after Mass and run through the pouring rain to the library, where I was helping Brother Duncan with a study of several water-damaged documents from the oldest monastery on the island of Iona. They had been drenched during a catastrophic storm, when one wall of the ancient building collapsed and many priceless and irreplaceable documents were soaked almost beyond redemption. We had not been back at work for long, I know, but we were already sufficiently engrossed in what we were doing that the clamour of excitement from outside took a long time to register. When it did, though, we knew that something unusual was unfolding nearby, and so we carefully set aside our work and made our way outside to the cloisters, where we found ourselves in a scene out of Chaos. I could make no sense of what was happening, for though there were people moving everywhere I looked, none of them appeared to be going anywhere, and all of them looked stunned or appalled and were chittering like frightened squirrels.

Brother Duncan roared for silence, and within moments everyone was gazing wide-eyed at him. He looked around at the watching faces and spoke into the hushed stillness.

"My thanks for your silence. Now, will someone please explain to me what is happening here? The reason for this uproar, so soon after Mass on a peaceful morning?"

"Murder."

The single word, spoken in a dull, lifeless voice, provoked a concerted hiss of indrawn breath. The speaker was Brother Callum, one of the principal assistants in the Abbey kitchens. Duncan swung to face him.

"Murder, Callum? Are you sure of that? Who was murdered?"

Callum swallowed hard. "Women, on their way here to attend Mass this morning."

"Who told you this?"

"I heard someone shouting it to somebody else, when I came out of the kitchens."

Duncan and I exchanged glances and then he raised his voice again. "Is there anyone here who can tell us more about this? Anything at all?"

The faces staring back at him all remained blank and slightly panic stricken.

"Very well," Brother Duncan said. "Something is clearly afoot, but since no one here knows what, it might be safe to presume that we are granting too much significance to something that might not be as serious as it appears. I want all of you, therefore, to return to what you were doing. Those of you with tasks to perform, return to them. Those of you with none, retire to your cells and pray that what we have heard is no more than speculation and misunderstanding. God grant it be so."

As the monks dispersed, Duncan waved me to his side. "You and I will go and find out what's going on. Let's hope it's not as bad as Callum reported."

It was as bad, and worse. We had to search diligently to find someone who could tell us anything, and even then the significance of what we heard was slow to sink home to us. The monk on duty at the main gate told us that a messenger had run up, staggering, a short time earlier, shouting his tidings to the winds in a voice filled with panic and outrage. Fortunately, Father Dominic, our Sub-abbot, had been present, doing penance by praying in the pouring rain, and he had spirited the man directly into the Abbey proper before he could upset any of the brethren.

Duncan grasped my arm and pushed me firmly towards the Abbot's quarters, where Dominic and the Father Abbot himself told us what little they knew.

It seemed that a party of women from the town really had been attacked on their way to the Abbey early that morning. There had been five women in the group, Dominic told us. All of them had been sexually violated, two of them killed in the process; the three survivors had been badly beaten and were all unconscious. They had been taken to the nunnery just outside the Abbey precincts, where they had been placed under the care of a visiting Hospitaller knight from Rome, and no one was sure if any of them would live out the day. If any did regain consciousness, it remained to be seen whether they would be able—or willing—to identify their assailants. It was a stupefying crime, the like of which had never been known in Paisley, and no one was yet equipped to deal with it.

Duncan, ever the pragmatist, immediately asked the question foremost in my own mind: Who were these women? No one, it seemed, knew at this point, though Dominic had already sent his deputy out to discover all he could. What was known was that they appeared to have been attacked on a public pathway, within shouting distance of the nearest houses, and subdued quickly before being herded off the road and into a copse. They had been found by a local blacksmith, who had gone for a pre-dawn walk in the rain to clear his ale-clogged head before going to work and stumbled upon the scene. He had not recognized any of the women, presumably because they had all been in bloodied disarray and he himself had been too badly shaken to look closely at them.

The Abbot and Sub-abbot, being who they were, wanted to start prayers for the victims immediately, but my cousin Duncan was far more concerned with the how and why of this event than he was with anything else. He kept interrupting Father Abbot with questions. Who could have done such a thing? That was the primary question, and even as he asked it, I sensed the overwhelming implications, for it was instantly clear to me that no one in Paisley town would have dared to contemplate such a sin. The worst ne'er-do-wells in the community were, at worst, opportunistic thieves and pickpockets, and thus it followed that the attackers were unlikely to be local men. The surprise, abduction, and violation of five women suggested a large and organized group of men.

Duncan sucked air between his front teeth as he turned to me. "Soldiery," he said, making no attempt to hide his disgust. There were soldiers everywhere that autumn, Scots and English both. "But whose? And how and where do we start to look for them?"

I didn't even have to think about it. "Where the attack took place. It will be a quagmire, so there should be tracks."

"Aye, there will be," Duncan answered, "but half the town of Paisley has likely traipsed through there by now, so it will be impossible to tell one set of tracks from another."

"Not if we follow them away far enough from wherever this thing happened. None of the townsfolk would go running after that many men alone, especially in weather like this, and especially not murderers. I think we'll be able to follow the tracks far enough to isolate them, sooner or later, and see if perhaps there's something identifiable about them."

He eyed me skeptically. "You don't believe they would have scattered afterwards? That's what I would have told them to do, had I been there."

"Nah," I said. "I don't think so. Not if they're strangers, and not in this weather. Too much danger of someone getting lost and caught. They would have stuck together, made their way out as a group, avoiding being seen. That tells me we'll find a trail, though only God Himself knows where it may lead us."

Duncan was gnawing at his lower lip, but then he jerked his head in agreement. "You could be right. Better fetch your foul-weather cloak, then. It's nasty out there."

2

The day was grey and leaden, almost dark, though it was not yet noon. The rain had grown heavier, and now the noise of it filled the air, drowning out everything else. I pulled the hood of my woollen foul-weather cloak down over my face and wrapped the rest of the garment as tightly about me as I could, fully aware that the carefully brushed-on coating of wax that covered its thickly felted surface would not stand up for long against this strong a downpour. Water puddled beneath our feet at every step, and none of it seemed to be draining away. Standing on the hard gravel of the

Abbey's forecourt, we were relatively safe from discomfort, but Duncan and I both knew that the moment we stepped off the gravel and into the grass, we would sink to the ankles. Not for the first time in my life, I wished for a solid pair of heavy boots, but monks and undistinguished priests wore simple sandals in all weather and all seasons, and so I was somewhat inured to painfully chilled feet.

"Ready?" Duncan asked, and when I nodded he stepped out in front of me, his stride purposeful. I followed him closely, trying to ignore the icy wetness of the ankle-high grass.

It took us less than ten minutes to reach the place where the attack had occurred, and as we had expected, it was a seething hive of people, most of whom had no reason to be there, other than simple curiosity and the human need to gawk. The ground had been churned to mud, as we had expected, and there was no hope of being able to make sense of what had happened there after the events of the early morning. We merely looked about us briefly and moved on, ignoring the throng and focusing instead on finding the tracks of the people who had passed this way earlier in the day.

It was not difficult to find the route they had taken, but it was surprisingly difficult to escape from the depredations of the gawkers who had since added their own tracks to those left behind by the attackers. Many of them had struck out boldly to follow the original tracks and had stayed with them for a surprisingly long time, so that Duncan and I, following in turn, had no way of knowing whether we were following the footprints of the attackers or the amateur hunters who had preceded us. Small groups occasionally came straggling back towards us after giving up the hunt, and it was all I could do to maintain a semblance of civility towards them, but the last of them revealed that there was only one more group ahead of us, three men, none of whom they had recognized.

We had emerged from behind a screen of head-high bushes to find ourselves in a small, open glade surrounded by waist-high undergrowth. I was walking with my head down, studying the ground at my feet, and I sensed rather than saw a flicker of movement very close to me. I raised my head in time to see a long, broad sword blade come hissing towards me and stop within a hand's breadth of my face. I froze. Duncan, half a pace to my left, stopped, too, his hands flung up involuntarily against the threat, his eyes flaring.

The man wielding the sword was tall and lean, his body solid beneath his sodden clothing. But my attention had already been caught by a second man, behind him.

"Hold, Shoomy!" he shouted, and I recognized him instantly. As the man lowered his blade and stepped back, the other continued, "What are you two doing here?"

"Will?" I asked, hearing the bleating disbelief in my voice. "Is that you?"

The image of a hugely bedraggled rat came to me immediately, suggested by the sodden sleekness of his clothes, literally aflow with running water as they clung to his enormous frame. I was seeing him clean shaven for the first time, and the water streamed down his cheeks. I could see that he was bristling with fury, too, but my powers of perception were addled at that moment and so I understood nothing.

"Aye, Jamie, it's me, right enough. You didn't answer. What are you two doing out here?"

As he spoke, a third man, short and slight as the first was tall, stepped out of the bushes, lowering his crossbow. I recognized him as Big Andrew Miller, though I had not seen him for years.

"We're looking for signs of who might have … have done this … this …" I began again. "Some women were attacked this morning, in Paisley, on their way to Mass. We set out to find some sign of who had done it, but we've had to come this far searching for clear tracks."

"Aye, and good luck. There are no clear tracks. Muck-filled holes, but no tracks that can be used, even were this accursed rain to stop this minute."

"You know about the women? But … Where have you come from, Will? What are you doing here?"

The look he threw at me was one that I had never seen before, a mixture of scorn and intolerance. But he answered me civilly enough. "I was on my way home, bringing my wife to Elderslie to pay you all a visit. But when we came to Paisley early this morning, we found the place in an uproar."

"Aye, those women."

He glared at me. "What d'you mean, *those women*? D'you not know who they were?"

He could not have asked me anything more mystifying, and I shook my head.

"They were *my* women, Jamie! *Mine!*" His voice, the outrage in it, hit me almost palpably in the chest. "Mirren's aunt and her four cousins. *That's* who those women were."

"Holy Mother of God!"

My lips continued to move, but nothing more emerged, and Will paid no attention anyway. He spoke almost to himself.

"They were taken unawares on their way to worship God, and they were ravaged by devils. Even the old wife, Mirren's aunt. Two of them were killed on the spot, the others left for dead."

"Which of them were killed?"

He looked at me almost absently. "The mother, Meg Waddie, Mirren's aunt. And her eldest daughter, Christine. I think the old woman might have died of fright. But the daughter was clubbed to death. When I find the man who did it, he will regret that his bitch mother ever whelped him. I will feed him his own balls, I swear, fresh cut from their sac. And I will find him, Jamie. Believe you me."

I did. I believed him implicitly, appalled and fascinated by the look in his eyes.

"But work like this is no fit matter for priests, Jamie. You would please me more were you to look to the women, see to their comfort." He jerked his head, flinging his soaked forelock away from his eyes. "I heard someone say they were taken to the nuns. Mirren is with them, wherever they are, and I left Ewan with her. He can help her with whatever needs to be done, and it will be good for everyone to have a priest to hand. I came out here to try to find out who did this, but there's nothing here."

"Oh yes, there is." Now that my mind was functioning again, I was looking about me and seeing what was really there to be seen. "See those marks there?" I pointed to a series of three footprints that had clearly been made by three different feet, slightly to my left and leading to a rain-swollen streamlet. It was plain that the three men had each jumped across the water, planted a foot on the far bank, and used it to push off in a scramble to the top of the gently rising slope.

I crouched beside the footprints and touched the rows of small, deeply indented holes with my fingertips. "Look," I said. "Hobnails. Who wears hobnailed boots?"

"Men at arms." Will's voice was strangely quiet. "Regulars. Supplied by a quartermaster."

"And what does that tell us?"

"The whoresons were English. Almost certainly. As far as I know, none of the Scots magnates has the kind of wealth that pays for hobnails for their men ... Which means that when we find which English baron has troops in the vicinity, we'll know where to look for the culprits in this day's madness."

Duncan spoke for the first time. "Might not be a baron. I've heard of no baronial forces near here, not recently."

Will growled in his throat. "Baron, earl, or plain damned knight, I care not. If there's an English force within walking distance of Paisley, I want to talk to its commander, though it be Edward Plantagenet himself." He looked at me. "How can we best find out?"

I glanced at Duncan. "At the Abbey, wouldn't you say?"

3

ithin half an hour of returning to the Abbey, we knew that an armed force of some two hundred men belonging to Antony Bek, Bishop of Durham, had bypassed Paisley two days earlier and made camp less than six miles farther on, towards Glasgow, to await the arrival of Bek himself from Norham, where he had been in attendance upon King Edward. Bek had served as King Edward's lieutenant in Scotland for two years, since the commencement of the prenuptial arrangements between the Maid and Edward of Caernarvon. Renowned for his fierce piety, his single-minded dedication to his master's affairs, and his intolerance of anything that threatened either of those, he nevertheless had a reputation for even-handedness, and no one had yet accused him of anything dishonourable in his treatment of the Scots.

Will was sitting across the table from me, and I found him staring at me and nibbling at the inside of his cheek in what I knew to be an indication of deep thought. I knew, too, that he was not watching me but staring through me, his eyes and his thoughts focused on matters far beyond the room in which we sat.

"What think you, Will?" I asked. "What should we do?"

I watched his eyes readjust to where he was, and as they shifted and grew more intense, his face darkened into the scowl I had become too familiar with in the past hour, so that I thought: *This isn't my cousin Will. This is Wallace, the wild one.*

He scratched at the stubble on his chin as he answered me. "What we *should* do and what we *will* do are two different things, Jamie. We *will* go and talk to Bishop Bek, but what we *should* do is follow those tracks to wherever they lead us and then spill the blood of every shifty-eyed whoreson we find at the end of the trail." His voice emerged flat and emotionless, but I had known this man all my life and I knew the effort he was expending to keep his quivering fury concealed.

"What if Bek won't talk to us?"

He raised his eyebrows in surprise. "Why would he not? I'll go to him as my uncle's messenger. He'll listen to Sir Malcolm Wallace of Elderslie, if not to plain Will Wallace."

I didn't doubt what he said, though I saw no benefit in pointing out to him that Bek might well know that Sir Malcolm was dead. "When will you go?"

"This minute."

"No point in that, Cuz. He's not there, remember? He was in Norham yesterday, for the auditors' decision, so even supposing he left immediately after that, he would barely have had time to get here."

"The messengers got here last night."

"Aye, but they were messengers, Will. They rode non-stop, in relays. Bek is a Bishop. He will travel at leisure and in dignity, so it will be at least tomorrow before he shows up."

"Do we know where his army is encamped?"

Duncan shook his head. "Not precisely, though we can easily find out."

"Find out, then, as quickly as you can," Will growled. "I want to be there by dawn."

I looked at him. "Why so early? Bek won't be there at that hour."

"No, but I'll be waiting when he gets there." He stood up. "In the meantime, I'm going to find Mirren, if only to wrap my arms around her and dry her tears. I'll see you all later."

"Wait." I pushed away from the table. "I'll walk with you, at least part of the way."

Neither of us spoke again until we were beyond the Abbey gates, on our way into the town. I knew he was thinking about Mirren and I had no wish to interrupt him. The tragedy of what had happened to her aunt and her cousins would no doubt have appalled her, but from all I'd heard she was a strong young woman and would take no permanent ill of it. The violation of women, though everyone deplored it, was far from being unknown, after all, and most particularly so when the land was disputed by opposing armies. At such times, the unspoken right to plunder and to violate enemy women was regarded as a victorious soldier's privilege, and everyone, women included, understood that to be so.

This particular act, however, had not been committed in war. God could not allow it to go unpunished, and I knew my cousin was determined that it would not.

"So, Cousin, what was it you wanted to say to me?" He spoke in Latin, a sure sign that he knew his question, and my answer to it, to be important.

A hundred thoughts sprang to my mind at once, but I forced myself to ignore all of them and respond quietly, also in Latin. "That you should proceed cautiously in this."

"I should? And why is that?" Will spoke with his head down, his eyes on the pathway ahead of him. "What need have I of caution here, Jamie? Five good women have been attacked and ravaged without provocation. Two of them are dead, with more, perhaps, to follow, who can tell?"

It had stopped raining sometime in the past hour, and the early darkness of full winter obscured everything, save glints of moonlight reflected haphazardly from the puddles all around us, where beams had managed to penetrate the broken mass of clouds overhead. Will sidestepped towards me to avoid a large puddle. "Why should it be *I* who needs to be cautious? The evidence we have found indicates that the women's attackers wore hobnailed boots, which indicates soldiers, clearly in the employ of some lord wealthy enough to equip his hirelings with such footwear, which means that in all likelihood these murderous animals are English. The only force of English soldiery in the district is commanded by Master Antony Bek, whose pride in his men and their accoutrements is sufficiently well known for him to be called the Warrior Bishop. And *I* have need of caution?

"Now I know I don't have to tell you, Cousin, that as King Edward's own lieutenant in Scotland, and as a prince of Christ's Church, Bishop Bek should decry even the possibility of any man of his being involved in such a crime, and therefore I intend to go and speak with him, to bring the affair to his attention in person. Of course I see a need for respect in how I approach him, taking care to recognize his rank and to offend none of his dignity. That need I can see clearly, and I will attend to it. But you are warning me of a need for caution, and I see no such need."

As I listened to him, marking the bitterness in his words, it occurred to me that this was the longest speech I had heard Will Wallace make in years. What did *not* occur to me, though—in fact I only thought of it long afterwards—was that he had spoken with authority, with the assuredness and conviction that comes only after months and years of performance. I completely missed the evident fact that my closest friend and dearest relative had become a leader in his own right, accustomed to speaking with conviction to men who listened to him closely.

And so, in my ignorance of what had happened to him in the previous two years, I continued talking to him as though he were still the lad I had known before.

"I'm not talking about—" But I fell silent, suddenly aware that he had already responded to what I *was* talking about, even before I had mentioned it.

He cocked his head in a well-remembered gesture and grinned at me. "Come on, then, spit it out. What's your mind?"

I sucked in my breath "Caution … the need for it, despite what you say. I want to come with you tomorrow. When you meet the Bishop."

"There's no need for that. Or do you think I'll need your protection?"

"No, but I think it might not hurt to have a cleric there prepared to swear an oath to bear witness on your behalf. Even such a poor half-cleric as I am."

He grunted in what might have been a laugh. "You are something of a neither-nor, aren't you? Ewan told me that your ordination was postponed when the Maid died. But that was a long time ago. Will you ever see ordination?"

"Aye, within the month, in fact, in time for Christmas. And nothing will stop it this time."

Will stopped in his tracks and grasped me by the upper arms, tilting his head to catch my face in the light of the moon. "You will be priested then? Truly? Then by the living God, I will be there to stand witness to it, unless God Himself sees fit to blast me before the day. I'll be there, Jamie, as God is my judge."

"Good, then, and I'll be there with you, come morning, when you meet Bek, as God is my judge, too."

4

Sometime before noon, Bishop Antony Bek of Durham, or one of his close associates, committed what I have come to believe was the single most costly error of Edward Plantagenet's entire reign as King of England, casting the die for the ruination of his ambitious plans for Scotland.

To this day I cannot say with certainty who was truly to blame for what happened that morning. Not even Will could swear afterwards to the truth of who said what and to whom, and he was much closer to the events than I was. That single incident, a visit to a bishop, made in good faith by a man of honour seeking redress for an indefensible transgression against the laws of God and man, might have had incalculably beneficial consequences for King Edward's designs had it been handled otherwise. But it was not, and the injustice that took place instead became the catalyst that aroused William Wallace to anger and thereafter focused all of Scotland's rage against the would-be usurpers. Bek's unconscionable treatment of William Wallace that day threw the English into a struggle that would last for twenty-two years and end with their being driven from Scotland completely.

The day began badly and deteriorated steadily. Will and I presented ourselves at the Bishop's encampment as planned, unarmed and alone—Will had ordered the others to remain at Paisley—soon after first light, after a two-hour walk through a black, wind-racked darkness that paled gradually into a grey and cloudy dawn. We spoke quietly with the acting sergeant of the guard, at what passed for the main entrance but was really nothing more than an opening in the high hedge that bordered the extensive pastureland Bek had chosen for his campsite.

The guard sergeant, a surly, slovenly looking type, was more interested in impressing his own four-man detachment than he was in listening to what Will had to say. He barely listened, preening for his men all the while, rocking back on his heels with his hands clasped around the buckle of the heavy sword belt at his waist and his face twisted in a sneer. As soon as Will had finished speaking, the lout waved us away with a curse. The Bishop was not yet in camp, he said, and not expected soon, so he wished a pestilence on us and told us to get out of his gateway, out of his sight.

Will showed no reaction to the man's ill manners; he merely stepped a little closer as the sergeant turned away and requested, respectfully, that we be permitted to await the Bishop's arrival off to one side, out of the way of the people coming and going to and from the camp. The guardsman swung around, starting to raise his fist, but then he stopped, doubtless noting the width of my cousin's shoulders and the depth of his chest. His fist opened up and he flicked his hand, indicating a nearby log that had obviously been used as a seat by many people over many years. Will nodded his thanks mildly, and together we crossed to the log and sat down.

As I passed the gateway in the hedge, I took a look through it, and was surprised by how empty the place looked. There was nothing to indicate, at first glance, that this was a military encampment, other than the presence of the guards themselves. The space I could see directly beyond the gates, an empty stretch of sodden turf, perhaps thirty to forty paces deep, must have been used as a parade ground or marshalling area. Beyond the grass, though, almost invisible in the half light, I detected the distant tops of uniform rows of tents rising up from the morning mist behind a row of skeletal trees, and as the light grew stronger we began to hear shouted orders and the sounds of organized military activities back there.

Sometime around mid-morning, we heard the sounds of hooves and marching men approaching from behind us, and we turned to watch the Bishop and his mounted escort arriving from the south.

There were about thirty men in the party, all of them well mounted and armed from head to foot, except for the group surrounding Bishop Bek, all of whom were clerics and rode the smaller, gentler horses known as palfreys.

I had never seen the Warrior Bishop, but I recognized him immediately as the only sword-carrying cleric in the central group. He sat very straight on his tall horse and carried his head high, his expression solemn and disdainful, his grip on the reins firm and confident. I saw him glance sidelong at us as he rode by. He ignored me in my plain robe after a single look, but he took all the time he needed to examine Will from head to foot, and I imagined him wondering who this tall, imposing, finely dressed, and clean-shaven fellow was and why he was waiting at the entrance to his camp. Then he turned back to resume his conversation with the man beside him and rode through the gates. Behind him, his men-at-arms rode in silence, one of them carrying a banner with the Bishop's escutcheon, three linked gold rings on an azure field, and none of them paid us the slightest attention.

At their rear, far less splendidly accoutred and travelling far more slowly, plodded a small detachment of weary-looking infantry, leading a ragtag, thoroughly cowed group of prisoners. Every man among the prisoners wore an iron collar, and they shuffled awkwardly along in single file and very close together, their arms tied behind their backs and their collars joined by a length of rope that was too short for the purpose it had to serve and so kept them off balance. Looking more closely at the armed squad as they approached, I decided that they were not, in fact, part of the Bishop's entourage but had simply been overtaken by the riders. Will looked from them to me with one eyebrow raised, and I was sure he was thinking the same thing I was. The prisoners, fourteen of them and all men, were Scots; they had that dour, inward-looking air about them. I wondered idly what they had done to warrant arrest, acknowledging wryly to myself that it would not have been too difficult to achieve.

They were halted by a stentorian curse from the sergeant of the guard. He was having no Scotch filth entering the camp under his watch, he swore, not until someone with authority came out and ordered him to let these animals inside. He ranted and raved, standing nose to nose with the corporal in charge of the prisoners, who argued back just as defiantly. All the corporal wanted to do was get rid of the ugly Scotch goblins—they'd been hanging around his neck for days, he said, weighing him down. He wanted to shed them like a wet coat and go about his own affairs and he didn't care what the gate sergeant thought. Eventually they reached an agreement, and the prisoners were herded into a circle around the trunk of the single large beech tree in the area, about twenty paces from where we sat, and their neck rope was retied securely to keep them there. And there they were to remain until someone inside the camp should decide what was to be done with them.

5

The gate sergeant had watched Will and me closely as the Bishop and his party approached, prepared to launch his guards at us should we attempt to interfere with the Bishop's progress. Now that they were safely inside the camp, though, he was more than content to pretend we were invisible.

We waited in silence for another half-hour before Will went up to the fellow and reminded him that we were waiting to speak with Bishop Bek, this time citing his uncle, Sir Malcolm Wallace, as the source of the request. I told myself this was not quite a lie, for I knew that had the knight been alive, he would most assuredly have used his name and influence to solve the matter of this heinous crime.

The sergeant was manifestly unhappy at the inconvenience of having to listen, but the knight's name and title were imposing enough that he sent one of his four scowling guards into the camp to carry Will's message to the Bishop. And once again we settled down to wait.

The messenger arrived back in no time, accompanied by a sergeant. There was no mistaking this sergeant's affiliation; he wore the livery depicted on Bek's banner, a bright blue surcoat with the three linked gold rings of the Bishop's crest emblazoned on the left breast, and he was flanked by two less brilliantly bedecked men-at-arms wearing simple quartered patches of blue and yellow squares on their plain leather jerkins. He marched directly to where we sat and stood looking down at us, like the guardsman sergeant making no attempt to disguise the sneer on his face.

"Right," he said after looking Will up and down and then shaking his head as if in wonder at the stupidity of the people he had to deal with. "Let's move it, then. Come on! On your feet. I haven't got time to be wasting, chasing after your idle Scotch arse, no matter what the Bishop thinks."

Will stood up, his meek and humble demeanour somehow de-emphasizing his great size, and the sergeant backed away from him instantly, signalling to the two spear carriers to flank Will on either side as though he were a prisoner. I stood up, too, assuming I was going with them, but as soon as I did the gate sergeant lunged angrily towards me, waving me back down to my seat on the log. He cursed me for a Scotch fool and made it abundantly clear that I was to stay where I was and *wait*, but the other sergeant, much to my surprise, ordered the fellow to shut his mouth. "They came together," he growled, "so they'll go in together. The priest might be an interpreter, who knows?"

Bek's pavilion-styled tent, fronted by a tall pole bearing his personal standard, was by far the largest of all, but there were many other, lesser pavilions similarly identified among the serried lines of troop tents laid out in neat formations. Men were everywhere, most of them either in organized drill groups or in work gangs being supervised by sergeants in the same white livery our guide wore. I saw few horses, but the strong aroma of dung told me large numbers were not too far away.

The sergeant stopped us when we were less than two paces from the entrance to the Bishop's tent. "Wait here," he said. "You'll be called in when the Bishop's ready for you."

He marched away then, leaving us unguarded, side by side beneath the Prince Bishop's banner.

"What d' you think?" Will muttered. "Should we run now, while we still can?"

It was the first flash of humour I had seen in him since the previous day, and it made me feel better immediately, but before I could reply, the flap of the main tent opened and a priest in green liturgical robes beckoned us with cupped fingers.

Antony Bek, Bishop of Durham, was at prayer, and the vaulted, shadowy spaces inside the pavilion provided the illusion that the tent itself was a church. *Mummery* was the word that sprang to my mind, along with an image from the previous year, when I had watched a travelling troupe of mummers present a drama in Glasgow about the Passion and Crucifixion of Jesus. The false sanctity and obvious insincerity of the spectacle had filled me with revulsion then, and I found the same feelings roiling in me now.

Bek knelt alone at a prie-dieu, before a small, portable altar that bore a covered tabernacle and a silver chalice. His back was arrow-straight, his chin tilted slightly upward as he gazed towards the tabernacle, his fingers caressing the beads of a large and ornate rosary. It seemed to me that he had positioned himself very care-fully, and for our benefit, before giving his acolyte the nod to admit us to his presence. He knelt for some time after our arrival, unmoving, ignoring us completely, but then he blessed himself with the sign of the cross and surged to his feet, removing the stole from his shoulders, folding it properly and kissing it before handing it to the priest who had admitted us. Only then did he glance at us quizzi-cally, and then indicated, with a wave of his hand, that we should walk with him to another part of the tent, where he took up a posi-tion beside a glowing brazier and close to a padded armchair that was almost large enough to be a couch.

He barely looked at me as he asked, "To which community are you attached?"

I was keenly aware of the cool impersonality of his tone and the lack of honorific he accorded me, and the awareness gratified me. In his eyes, I was clearly less than nothing, a nameless, faceless priest whose drone-like existence was to be taken for granted and not remarked upon, but I was not a priest at all, and his arrogance had blinded him to that. He had glanced at my grey robe and seen only the garb of a lowly Benedictine cleric, and his own hubris had elevated me to the status of priesthood, never deigning to imagine that anyone less significant would have the temerity to enter his presence. I had anticipated his question, though, and the lie fell from my lips with the ring of truth.

"Jedburgh, my lord. The Abbey there. But I am currently assigned to Selkirk parish." Were Bek to seek me in Jedburgh in future, I reasoned, he might or might not launch a search for me when he failed to find me, but had I named Glasgow, inviting him to seek me there afterwards at the cathedral, it might have caused a deal of needless embarrassment to others, among them Bishop Wishart.

He nodded absently and spoke to Will.

"You are the nephew of a knight, I am told, sent here on his behalf to question me. Is that correct?" He raised an interdicting hand. "If it is, then you must surely have an answer to my next question. If this matter has sufficient import in your uncle's eyes to merit intruding upon my privacy in order to bring it to my attention, why then would he offer me the discourtesy of not presenting it in person?"

Will dipped his head in acknowledgment. "He is unable, my lord. He is grown old in recent years and is now unfit to travel."

I held my breath. If Bek knew who Will was, and knew of Sir Malcolm's death, we were within moments of being arrested.

The Bishop nodded. "Go on, then. Voice your complaint. What does this concern?"

Will told him, delivering the only lie in his story right at the outset, when he claimed to be head verderer on his uncle's lands who had taken his wife into Paisley to visit her family there. From that point onwards, he related events exactly as they had occurred. Bek sat down in his big chair shortly after Will began talking, and rested his chin on his cupped hand, his face betraying nothing of his thoughts. When the tale was told, he sighed and sat up straighter, his gaze returning to Will.

"So ... Let me see if I understand what you are saying. Some women were molested in your town and you set out to find the miscreants. After weltering around in torrential rain for half a day and miles from anywhere, you found some muddy footprints—how many? three?—that may have been made by hobnailed boots. Am I correct? And based upon that ... that *startling* observation, you deduced that these footprints had been made by soldiers. English soldiers, *of course*. After that, it must have been the work of mere moments to arrive at the conviction that those soldiers must be mine, since I appear to be the only English commander with troopers in this area, and that, by association, the responsibility for the carnage in Paisley yesterday must be mine, too. Correct?" He made no pretense of waiting for an answer. "Excellently reasoned, though the logic involved is unmistakably Scots. So how may we proceed from here? Shall I assemble my entire force on the parade ground and have them flogged? And how many of them would you like me to hang afterwards? Will you have time to wait for us to build a gibbet?"

He stopped short, then added, "Who discovered these three foot-prints? To whom should I be expressing my gratitude for such a swift solution to these heinous crimes?"

Will turned to look at me, his eyebrows raised high in shock at what he was hearing.

"You?" Bek said, misinterpreting the look and gazing at me in disbelief. "You are responsible for this outrage? An ordained priest, accusing me of this atrocity? How dare you?" His voice remained level, but there was no mistaking the fury it contained. He turned to his acolyte, who had been standing in the background all this time. "Call de Vrecy and his guard. Now! Bring them here immediately."

The Bishop's glare returned to me, and when he spoke again his voice dripped disgust and loathing. "You will leave this camp at once and under guard. You"—he pointed a quivering finger at Will—"you will stay here. You and I have much to talk about concerning the responsibilities of leadership and governing men."

"Not so, Bishop. You have no power to hold me here. Father James came in with me, and I will leave with him."

"No, you will *not*. If you do, it will be as a rebel and an outlaw, and if I have to, I will have my men break your legs. I am King Edward's deputy in this accursed place, and you will be bound by what I tell you to do. I have words for you, and even as an upstart, contumacious Scot, you will be bound by them, so bide you there."

We had already heard the steady tramp of mailed feet approaching, and then someone held the flap of the great tent open while a dozen men marched in, accompanied by two sergeants and an armoured, surcoated knight. Bek pointed at me and spoke to the knight. "This one, the priest. Take two men and see him off the grounds—forcibly if he does not move quickly enough to please you. He will wait outside the gates for his friend. The rest of you, have an eye to the big one. I doubt he will have much to say, but attend us while he listens to what I have to say to him." Bek pointed at me again. "Do not think this affair is over, priest. I know your name and I promise you, wherever you may go from here, you and I will meet again and you will answer for this *in curia*, before a tribunal of your superiors." He flicked a finger at de Vrecy. "Out of my sight with him."

There was no point in resisting, and so I went quietly enough, with one burly guard's hand on each shoulder as they pushed me along between them. My escort marched me briskly through the outer gate and past the sergeant guardsman's post to the seat where Will and I had waited earlier. There they barked an order at me to halt, and one of them pushed me roughly down onto the bench, warning me that I should stay there unless I wanted to be flogged.

I sat and fumed and waited for what must have been an hour, and then I finally heard them coming from behind the hedge, shouting at each other, laughing and high spirited like any group of young men with idle time on their hands. But when they came into view in the gateway I could only stand and stare, stupefied. They carried Will out through the gates on his back, head down, feet raised behind them as they came. He was unconscious and dripping blood from his backward-hanging head, and six of them held him in a cradle of interlocked arms, like pallbearers, though it was clear from their expressions that they were neither mourning him nor enjoying the strain of carrying his weight. Four more men walked close behind them, men I knew immediately were archers, since all four were unarmoured and carried quarterstaves, and it was they who were shouting and laughing, though none of the hilarity appeared to be directed towards my unconscious cousin.

As I finally began to pull my wits together, one of the six bearers grunted something to the others and began to count aloud, and on three, they heaved in unison and sent their burden toppling heavily to the ground in front of the gate, where it sprawled in a puddle left from the previous day's rain. They drew away then, preparing to leave, and I heard what I knew was my own voice whining in wordless protest as I ran to Will and dropped to my knees beside him, but even as I landed, a booted foot struck me high on my right side and sent me reeling. One of the archers stood over me, looking down and grinning as he drew back his boot to kick me again.

But then an arm interposed itself, thrusting him back and away, and the largest of the four bowmen reached out one-handed, almost casually, and rapped me viciously on the knee with the heavier end of his quarterstaff. In that instant of flaring pain, I became a student with a quarterstaff once again, facing a drubbing from Ewan Scrymgeour.

I seized the end of the fellow's staff and jerked it towards me, using it, along with his surprised resistance, to support my weight as I surged to my feet, and then I twisted the weapon from his suddenly unresisting hand, switched my grip, and cracked the heavy butt above his ear before his mouth could even open in disbelief. As he fell sideways I spun towards the others, whirling the staff in my hands until it formed a blurred, semi-solid shield in front of me. I know not, honestly, who was the more surprised by the development, they or I. They certainly had not anticipated finding a scrawny Scots cleric who handled a quarterstaff with authority. I, on the other hand, had not thought to find myself suddenly facing nine armed and soon-to-be-vengeful enemies.

Even as I weighed the situation, though, it began to change. The man closest on my left began to sway towards me, raising his staff, and another swung away to circle around and come at me from behind. I dropped the first man with a straight-armed chop to the top of his skull, then flung myself sideways, spinning completely around and dropping into a crouch as I brought the full, accelerating weight of my weapon against the back of the other's knees, felling him like a tree.

By that time, though, my short-lived advantage had worn itself out, and I felt the weight of a smashing blow across my shoulders, driving me down and onto my face, and I knew as I fell that I would not be rising to my feet again unless someone helped me, which seemed highly unlikely at that point. I sprawled across the body of the man I had hit last, and he was already moving again, scrabbling and kicking in his efforts to stand up. I felt hands grasping me, pulling and heaving at me, and I ended up on my back, my shoulders flat on the ground, gazing up at the foul-tempered gate sergeant who had leapt to straddle me, roaring to everyone else to keep back as he swung a rusty, heavy-bladed sword high in both hands, aiming to cleave my skull. I saw his arms reach the top of their swing and pause there, and as he chopped the blade down towards my head, I remember thinking, "God never wanted me to be a priest," and I started to close my eyes.

Before I could, though, something extraordinary happened. The man above me went away. He went very swiftly and suddenly. There one moment, focused tightly on splitting my skull apart, and abruptly gone the next, his disappearance marked by a single flash of disbelief on my part as I saw the tail end of a squared steel rod sprout from his elbow.

It was a crossbow bolt. Fired by Big Andrew from close range, it had struck squarely and with immense force on the man's downward-sweeping left elbow, driving his upper arm bone straight back with sufficient violence to shatter the shoulder socket and throw its owner several paces backward in a spinning mass of whirling limbs and gouting blood. I blinked and saw another man go down, hurled backward by an arrow that struck him in the centre of his chest and pierced his iron cuirass and the linked-mail shirt beneath it as if they were made of cloth. *Bodkin*, I thought, recognizing the only kind of missile that could punch through armour, and then I became aware of the hiss and snap of arrows all around me, and the meaty thump they made when they hit human targets.

Someone leaned over me, and I heard Ewan Scrymgeour's voice close to my ear. "Lie still, and we'll ha'e ye out o' here in no time. Shoomy, ye have him? Right, then, let's away. Alan, bring they people wi' us, cut them loose. Come on, now, quick, afore they come lookin'."

I was not badly hurt at all, merely stunned by the blow I had taken across my back and shoulders, and as Ewan and another fellow dragged me hurriedly away, their arms hooked beneath my armpits, I realized that they had ignored Will's wishes and followed him anyway. And their instincts had been right. Had they not been there, Will Wallace and I would both have died there in front of the camp gates.

"Wait," I grunted, scrabbling with my feet. "I can walk. Let me up." The two men hauling me stopped and looked down at me skeptically. "Really, Ewan, I'm fine. I had the wind knocked out of me, but I'm fine now."

I looked back at the scene we were leaving and was unsurprised to see bodies everywhere: the six men-at-arms who had been carrying Will, the four loud-mouthed archers, the sergeant who had been so determined to kill me, the four guards of his detachment—none of them was moving. My gaze went then to the gate in the hedgerow, and I could not believe that no one had come to see what the commotion was about. There must have been at least two hundred men in that encampment.

Ewan removed his hooked arm from my armpit and helped me to my feet. I swayed there for a moment, collecting myself, then nodded towards Will, who was still being carried by the man Shoomy and three others. "How is he? I couldn't tell."

"No more could I," Ewan growled, "but he's breathing. Now come, we have to get away from here."

I fell in beside him, moving quickly, aware that we were less than thirty paces from the edge of the trees that would screen us from the camp gates, but knowing, too, that the pursuit that would follow was bound to be both grim and determined. We had killed English soldiers, and, irrespective of the provocation that had caused it, their companions would want our heads hoisted on poles, to show the world that English lives could not be taken lightly. We would not easily escape punishment for today's escapade, and that thought made me lengthen my stride.

The group of freed prisoners, still in their iron collars, scurried to keep up with us.

"What about them?" I asked Ewan.

He glanced over to see who I was talking about, then shrugged. "What about them? They're alive and they're free again. Outlawed, for a fact, but free."

"But what will happen to them?"

We had reached the edge of the trees, and Ewan turned, waving to the stragglers to hurry and get themselves out of sight. As soon as the last man had passed us, he braced his foot and pulled down the top of his bow stave, bending it until he could remove the bowstring. "Can't use a bow in the deep woods," he murmured. "What will happen to them? They'll continue as before, living in a Scotland that might soon be ruled by England."

"No," I said, "that will never happen. We have our own King now. Where's your bow case?"

"That way, about a hundred paces in." He pointed the way and I followed him. "Once we'd seen where we had to go, we went back in and left everything there."

We emerged into a small clearing, where Ewan's companions were snatching up their bow cases and the other weapons they had left. Knives or swords were distributed to some of the Scots prisoners. Everyone knew we had no time to waste if we were to get away safely, for the English would be hard on our heels, and their outriders would all be mounted.

We split up, with orders to reassemble in the woods behind Sir Malcolm's house as soon as could be after dark that night. I ran with Ewan's group, now numbering seven, and as we slipped away from the oak clearing, we heard the first distant shouts of discovery coming from Bek's camp.

CHAPTER TEN

I

We began to feel increasingly concerned about Will. We were about an hour along the road from Bek's encampment, and we had fully expected him to wake up cursing at us for our rough handling of him, but still he had not regained consciousness. Shoomy insisted that we set him down and examine him for fatal wounds that we might not have noticed in our rush to get him away, but we could see nothing that looked life-threatening. He had been badly beaten, evidently with clubs or quarterstaves, and there were other abrasions on his body where he had been kicked and trampled. He was still bleeding sluggishly in places, too, from a scalp wound and a deep puncture that looked like a stab wound in one thigh, but we found nothing to explain why he should remain unconscious for so long.

We had stopped right outside a farmyard, and when Shoomy declared that we could carry Will no farther, for fear of injuring him more gravely than he already was, the yard was the first place we looked for some other means of transporting him. A dog began barking as soon as we approached the gate, and moments later the farmer himself came out to investigate. He took one look at us in his gateway and turned to run, but one of Shoomy's men was already leaping to restrain him, and before he could shout to warn anyone else, the hapless man found himself with his back against a wall, a hand over his mouth, and a knife point at his throat.

Shoomy stepped up beside his man and pulled the knife wielder's arm down to his side. "You are in no danger from us, no matter what you think," he said quietly to the farmer. "We are Scots and freemen, but we had a tulzie wi' some English soldiery a few miles back along the road. They'll be following us, but they'll no' bother you, I think, so be it we're long gone by the time they get here. But we ha'e an injured man wi' us and we need some way of carryin' him. If ye can help us, we'll pay ye for your time and trouble and be on our way quickly. What say you?"

The farmer did not hesitate. "What d'ye need?"

"Something wi' wheels, but light, if you ha'e such a thing."

"Aye. I've a light cart I use for carrying poles. A handcart. There's room for a man to lie down on it. You can pull it atween ye. It's ower there." He pointed to a high-wheeled handcart leaning against the side of a shed, and a short time later he stood clutching a silver shilling—thrice the value of a new cart—as we strode away, having piled the cart with straw to make a bed for our passenger.

Ewan and I parted from Shoomy and his companions then, leaving them to go directly to the Wallace house in Elderslie while we took the long way round, passing through Paisley town to collect Mirren. That little task had been difficult for a few moments, because Mirren had come frowning to us after a nun summoned her, and as she grappled with the unexpectedness of seeing us there and then looked for Will, an entire range of expressions flickered over her face.

"Where is he? What happened?"

Ewan cleared his throat. "They took him … beat him … the English. He went into Bek's camp alone. You know what he's like. But we managed to get him away from them and he's fine, I think. Shoomy's ta'en him to Elderslie. We came to get you."

"You *think*? Am I supposed to take comfort from that? You *think* my man is fine? I don't care what you *think*, Ewan Scrymgeour. In God's name, tell me what you *know*. Is he wounded?"

"No, Mirren. Hurt, aye, but no' wounded. He was badly beaten— God alone knows how many men were involved in that, but there must have been a wheen o' them—and we knew nothing of it until they brought him out of their camp and threw him in the roadway."

She turned her wide eyes on me, and in spite of having done nothing wrong, I felt my face flush with shame.

"And you," she said. "You were there with him, were you no'? Did you just stand there and *watch*?"

I shook my head, but before I could speak she continued, "You were supposed to protect him, Jamie Wallace—to stand beside him with your pens and ink and bear witness for him, protecting him just by *being* there. That was why he took *you* instead of any of the others."

I was still shaking my head, though slowly now. "No," I heard myself say. "They forced me to leave. They kept me outside the camp gates while Will met with the Bishop."

She shook her head in a tiny gesture of disgust and looked back at Ewan, who started to tell her about how I had attacked the archers, but she cut him off. "Where is he now? Elderslie, you say?"

"Aye, he'll be there by now," Ewan said. "I told everyone to meet at his old hut in the forest behind the house as soon as it was dark enough for them to get there without being seen. Alan and Shoomy and John know where it is. They'll show the others."

"What others?" But before he could explain she was turning away. "We should hurry, then," she said. "It's near dark already. I'll have to see to Mairidh before I go. She'll fret if she doesna know where I am. You wait here. I won't be long."

As she began to move away, Ewan spoke again. "How ... how are your cousins?" He sounded more ill at ease than I had ever heard him, but at least he had been able to voice the question that had been stuck in my throat.

Mirren looked back at him, and her shoulders slumped noticeably. "My cousins? They are mostly dead, I fear." Her voice was low, her tone more sad than mourning. "Shelagh died this afternoon, and Morag has not opened her eyes since she was found this morning. Only Mairidh shows any awareness of who or where she is, and she is very ... weak." She straightened her shoulders then. "She'll be fine among the sisters here until I come back. But I need to see to Will. Wait you here, then. I'll no' be long."

2

Mirren stood looking down at Will's motionless form on the cot, her mouth compressed into a lipless line as her eyes flitted around the tiny, crowded room. "Just like Morag," she said, almost to herself, and then raised her eyes to where Shoomy stood at the foot of the cot. "When did he last say anything?"

Shoomy shook his head wordlessly, and a small frown ticked between Mirren's brows. "Moved, then—when did he last move?"

"He hasna moved, not since they brought him out o' that damned camp."

Mirren drew in her breath with a hiss and glanced towards the brazier on the stone slab in the corner of the hut. "Right, I want that fire built up and a pan of water on it to heat. And I'll want some clean rags to wash him with." She looked around at the crowd that hemmed her in. "How many of you are there, in God's name?"

Alan Crawford answered her. "There's a score of us, milady. Twenty."

"Twenty! And have you no other place to go? Am I to have all of you in here all night?"

"No, Mirren, you're not," Ewan said, and everyone turned to look at him. "Will and I have four big leather tents in the back store-room. They'll hold six men apiece, so there'll be room for everyone to sleep dry, and we'll be out of your hair once we've learned how to put them up in the dark. Forbye, there's plenty o' firewood in the stack out there, and a good, deep fire pit that canna be seen frae a distance, so some of you—you, Shoomy, and a couple o' others—can start building us a fire to cook on." He clapped his hands together loudly. "Right then, all o' ye, outside and gi'e Mistress Wallace room to think. Andrew and John, you come wi' me. You too, Alan, and we'll find those tents."

As the crowd began to file out of the hut, Ewan raised his hand to catch my eye. "Jamie," he said. "It might be a good idea for you to go up to the big house. Tell your auntie that we're here and explain what's going on, just in case she hears about it otherwise and grows afeared. I don't think there's much chance of Bek's people looking for us this far away, but we'd be fools to take risks when there's no need, so we'd better post some guards out by the road south. Tell your auntie we'll be away in the morning by first light, lest we endanger her."

"Aunt Margaret won't care about the danger," I said, and he looked me straight in the eye.

"Mayhap not. But would she thank us for being left homeless because we were careless? Bek would burn her place about her ears if he as much as suspected we might be here."

Abashed, but knowing he was right, I went outside and called Big Andrew to me, telling him to select six men, including the four who had armed themselves, from among our recent prisoners. I explained to Andrew what was needed and left it to him to set out his guards while I sought out my aunt.

When I returned to the hut about an hour later, I brought several of Lady Margaret's people with me, all of them bearing food and drink: cold fowl and mutton and half a haunch of venison, along with hard-boiled duck eggs, vegetables pickled in sour wine, a basket of recently picked pears, wedges of hard, sharp cheese, and heavy loaves of bread baked that same day. The men had been busy, and now there were four large leather tents erected in the clearing around the hut, and a leaping fire danced in the deep fire pit. Everyone was in good spirits, and I quickly learned the reason for that: Will was awake and alert and apparently none the worse for his long sleep, and Mirren was smiling again.

More thankful for both of those pieces of information than I would have believed possible a few hours earlier, I made my way directly to the hut and found Will propped up in his couch with his back against the wall, cradling Mirren in his arms. I stopped in surprise and, I admit, confusion, never having seen the two of them in anything resembling family intimacy, and I stood there in the doorway hovering on the point of leaving. Will laughed at my obvious dismay and called me inside to join them, where all I could think to do, after embracing him, was ask if he was hungry. Fortunately he was, and Mirren sprang up, and the business of feeding him quickly took care of my embarrassment.

When his hunger was satisfied, Will decided he wanted to join the crew around the fire pit, and he leaned on me as he hobbled painfully, bent forward, to the fire. Miraculously, I thought, his ribs appeared to be undamaged, for he could breathe deeply without a deal of pain, but his lip was split at one corner, both his eyes were blackened, and his left ear was swollen grotesquely, the result, he told me, of a kick that might have taken off his head had it landed properly. He lowered himself carefully to sit on one of the logs that ringed the fire pit.

Almost the first thing he did was ask to meet the former prisoners, and he greeted each one in person and asked him how he had come to be arrested by the English. All were equally confused at first about why they had been singled out for arrest and abduction, but it soon became evident, as one tale followed another, that there was a depressing sameness to their plaints. Each had come to understand that he had given offence to someone—not necessarily an Englishman and sometimes not even identified—or he had allegedly committed some transgression, usually unspecified, and had consequently been denounced for one petty crime or another, then arrested and removed from his home. Families had been dispossessed and homes confiscated.

When the last of them had finished his story, Will stood up carefully and spoke to all of them, pointing out that they would now be legally proscribed. They were twice guilty of outlawry, first by the fact of their arrest and removal from their dwelling places, and then by association with the fight and escape that had taken place that morning. None of them could return to their homes now, he told them, although he was quick to point out that they could not have gone home anyway once taken into custody by the English. In the eyes of the English they were now felons, no different from himself and his associates, and the fact that they had escaped from custody during, or as the result of, the murder of at least a dozen Englishmen compounded the seriousness of their plight.

Watching his listeners, I could see more than a few unhappy faces. Will was watching them too, though, and now he asked if any of them wished to speak. One fellow, who had been scowling ferociously since soon after Will began talking, thrust his hand in the air.

"Aye," he said, and there was no mistaking the truculence in his voice. "I want to say somethin'." He looked around him, and I thought that he seemed slightly surprised at his own temerity, as though afraid of having said too much already.

"Say away, then," Will said, smiling slowly at him before lowering himself back down on the log. "What's troubling you?"

"Troublin' me? You mean besides your telling me I'll never see my wife and bairns again?" He fixed his wide eyes on Will's. "Aye, well, there is one thing troublin' me … It's you, Maister Wallace. You're troublin' me. You're troublin' the shite out o' me."

He looked quickly around at the men flanking him and gulped a quick breath before turning back to Will again. "Who are you, maister? What makes you so special, and why should we pay you any heed? We're no' outlaws—at least we werena before now—but I think you're different frae us. You seem to be awfu' well set up here in the woods … for an honest man, that is."

He cast another nervous glance around the silent assembly. I could see the fear in his eyes, but he had plainly decided to speak out, even if he should die for it.

"I mean, I ken ye cut us free this mornin' and gave us the chance to run, and I ken ye've asked nothin' o' us since, and ye've fed us here and gi'en us tents for to sleep under, but what do ye *want* frae us? What ha'e we got that you need? What is it—?" He stopped abruptly and threw up his hands. "There. That's enough," he mumbled. "That's what I wanted to say. Ye asked us, and I tell't ye."

Will sat slightly hunched, his face unreadable as he looked at the speaker. "You're right," he said at last. "Right in your questions and right in your concerns, so let me try to answer each of them, for all of you." He looked around the fire pit at the faces staring back at him. "Because I think ye might all ha'e been thinking the same thoughts as our friend here … What was your name again? Rab, was it no'?"

"Aye, Rab Coulter."

"That was it. I'll no' forget it again. Well, Rab Coulter, as for who I am, I am plain William Wallace, from right here in Elderslie. I'm a forester, and I used to work these very woods, which were owned by my uncle Sir Malcolm Wallace. The hut there, and this clearing, were where I worked most of the time, as head forester. That's why I'm so familiar wi' them—so well set up, as you said. Ewan Scrymgeour, sitting over there, used to work with me, but we moved on a few years back. I got married and took Mirren here, my wife, to live down near Jedburgh, and then my uncle died last year. This was to have been the first time I brought my wife home, but when we reached Paisley yesterday morning, we discovered that her aunt and her cousins who lived there had been attacked and ravaged earlier that day, on their way to Mass, by a passing pack of soldiers. No local men would have dared attempt such a thing, and we found evidence—tracks of hobnailed boots—to back our claim that it was the English, and so I journeyed to meet with Bishop Bek of Durham, who leads the force you were being taken to join this morning."

"Bek. I ken that name. Is he no' the English King's lieutenant in Scotland?"

Will nodded to the man who had spoken. "Aye, that's his title. And he knows mine. Well, he knows my name. I ha'e nae title. But I met wi' the Bishop-lieutenant in his camp this morning to explain to him what had happened in Paisley and ask for his aid in dealin' wi' the crimes that had occurred, and I named mysel' to him openly, as nephew to Sir Malcolm Wallace o' Elderslie." He grimaced. "I'm beginnin' to think that might no' ha'e been the cleverest thing I ever did."

He waited for the outbreak of grim laughter to die down, then continued. "It's obvious to me now he didna like what I was sayin', because minutes after I left him I was jumped by some of his bully boys. They did a fine job o' stampin' on me, as ye can see. I dinna remember much about it, but when they had finished they threw me out into the roadway in front o' their camp. I ha'e no idea what they planned after that, but my cousin Jamie here swears that they would ha'e killed both him and me had the rest o' my friends here decided to pay no heed to what I'd told them and followed me anyway. The rest you ken—you were there and saw it for yourselves. But I didna cut you free and I didna bring you here. Nor did I feed you. I was unconscious the whole time that was going on. The decision to free you was made by Ewan, and you *are* free—free to join us, to stay here, or to go as you please. But ..."

He drew a long, deep breath as he looked deliberately around the gathering, meeting each man's eye. I saw, with a shock of recognition, that he was consciously moulding these people to his will for his own purposes, and I realized for the first time that my cousin, during his two-year absence from my life, had become an adept leader of men. I felt my skin ripple with a stirring of gooseflesh and I found myself looking at this man, whom I had thought I knew well, in an entirely different way.

"But ...," he said again. "I said you willna be able to return to your homes, but I didna say you would never see your families again. I canna tell you that. How could I? That all depends on you— on who you are, each and every man o' you. You can go home tomorrow, those o' ye who want to run the risk, and find your wives and bairns and tak' them wi' you when you leave, 'gin they'll go wi' ye. But then ye'll be faced wi' the matter o' *where* to take them. For ye are all outlaws now, like it or no'. It's the truth, and it has already changed your whole life, frae the minute they marched you away. So where will ye go? Now that you canna show your face where folk might recognize it? And how will ye keep yourselves alive, if ye find a place that's safe enough to stay in?"

He paused again, and they hung on his words, waiting for him to tell them what they needed to hear.

"Look at yourselves," he told them. "Go on an' tak' a good look. Fourteen o' you were headed for jail this morning, maybe for worse. They would ha'e tortured you, to get you to confess to whatever they needed from you. I ha'e nae doubt o' that. Fourteen of you, and only two of you had ever seen each other before. You were prisoners, wearing iron collars and being led like sheep to whatever they intended to do wi' you. But now ye're free men again, and we'll ha'e those collars off you before mornin'."

There was a chorus of muttering at that, and when it had died down he waved a hand towards his own men, grouped together on one side of the fire.

"The rest of us here number nine: myself, my dear wife, and my close friends. Come daylight tomorrow, we will be going home to Selkirk Forest." He glanced back at Rab Coulter. "Aye, Selkirk Forest."

His eyes moved again, and now he was smiling, though the bruises on his face masked most of his expression. "Dear God, you're probably thinkin', but yon's a big place, yon forest—it covers half the country, and it's wild. Well, it is, I'll grant ye. It is vast, and it is wild. But there are places in there that are no' wild at a', places so beautiful they'd make you cry wi' wonder, and the very hugeness o' the place makes people feared to go into it, for fear o' gettin' lost. And that suits us. Selkirk Forest is our home, teemin' wi' game and fowl, and every burn and river full o' fish. No one need ever starve in there. The place is one great larder."

There was silence again until someone asked, "Are ye sayin' we could go with ye, into the forest?"

"I don't see why not. There's plenty o' room."

"But what about our families, our wives and bairns?"

"What about them? Have you not been listening to me? Bring them wi' you."

"But will it be safe?" This was a different voice, from one of the men at the back, and it had a ring of panic to it.

"Will it be safe? I canna tell you that. But I can say wi' certainty it will be at least as safe as it was where you were living before you were arrested, and it could be a lot less dangerous. At least ye'd have no trouble wi' the English there, in the depths o' the greenwood. It's no' friendly country for armies in there." He drew a deep breath and began again, this time in a louder voice, speaking slowly and clearly.

"Look, I don't know what to tell ye, other than that things are changing here every day. Ye must have seen it for yourselves, and ye must know that if it werena so, none o' the things ye've been through in the last wheen o' days would ha'e happened. None o' ye would be outlawed, and ye'd all be livin' under your own roofs. Things are awfu' different here in Scotland since King Alexander died. When he was King, we lived well. We were at peace and folk kenned who they were and what the law demanded o' them. But that's a' different now. We ha'e changed in the space o' a few years frae a solid realm into a contested kingdom. The Bruces and the Balliols, the Comyns and the other magnates—the Buchans and the Stewarts and a' the rest o' them who'd like to wear the crown—ha'e set our country on its arse wi' their bickerin' and squabblin', and it's common folk like us who aey bear the brunt o' such foolery—except that this time it's no' foolery. Now they've brought in the English, and we're payin' the costs o' that, too. We've aey had to live wi' the Scots nobility and their pride and stupidity, but now we have the English to contend wi', too, lordin' it over us all, and these English are movin' a' the time, marchin' armies here and yonder and robbin' ordinary folk blind to keep their people and their horses fed.

"Well, some o' us have had enough o' it. We ha'e a new King now, we're told, King John. Mayhap he'll be a fine, strong King like Alexander, may God rest his soul, and we'll be happy if that's so. But we winna ken the truth o' that for years to come. And in the meantime there are folk out there, folk who should know, who'll tell ye Edward o' England has plans o' his own for Scotland, and the only strong King he'll countenance in this realm is himsel'." He stopped again, and no one sought to interrupt him.

"This much I believe," he continued. "Nothing in this land is going to get better soon, from the viewpoint o' folk like us. And that is why we ha'e chosen to live in the forest. We've lived there now for nigh on two years, and there were folk there when we arrived. We're a community there in the woods—there are several hundreds of us. We have our laws and rules, and they are much like the laws and rules we knew before, when we were ordinary folk, living within the law. And so I will say this to you: go back to your homes and find your families, then make your way, if you so wish, to the forest near Jedburgh. Ask there for William Wallace, o' anyone ye meet, and ye'll be directed to where we are. After that, ye'll be free to join us completely if you so wish. But ye'll have to live by our laws and rules, and if ye break those, you'll be banished back into the outside world." His mouth quirked in a smile. "But they're simple rules, and easy to keep.

"And now I'm going to go and sleep, and hope I don't stiffen too much in the night. We'll need to be away before dawn, so don't stay up too late around the fires just because you can. Those of you wi' collars should talk to Shoomy over there. He's our smith and will clip off your bindings."

Shoomy was ready to go to work immediately, and we knew the job of striking off the collars would not take long. They were temporary fetters, fastened with knotted wire, and even as Will and I were making our way back to his hut, Will with an arm around Mirren for support, I heard the loud *snip* as the first man was cut free.

When we reached the front of the hut, I bade Will and Mirren a good night, but as I turned to leave, Will stopped me, speaking in Latin.

"Ewan tells me you still remember how to swing a quarterstaff ..." I made no response, and he continued, "What time will you leave tomorrow?"

I looked at him in surprise. "When you do. Why would you even ask?"

"Because we'll be leaving practically in the middle of the night. I see no need for you to lose that much sleep. You can lie in."

"How can I lie in? I'm coming with you."

He eyed me strangely. "What gave you that idea?"

"It came to me when I remembered how to swing a quarterstaff. They'll be looking for me now, along with you."

"Ah! I see. And who would they be looking for? Did you tell them who you are?"

"No, but—"

"Who, then, might they think you are?"

I found myself blustering, somehow resenting what I took to be the implications of the question. "They saw me. They know my face. They know I was with you when you arrived."

"Who saw you? The men who saw you are all dead, from what I've heard."

"Except the Bishop himself."

He cocked his head. "And does he know your real name? Does he even know where to begin looking for you? You told him you were from Jedburgh. Jamie, all the Bishop saw when he rode by us was a grey-frocked cleric, a mendicant monk carrying the tools of a common scribe. He paid no more attention to you than he would to any other beggar in his path."

"He looked at you close enough."

"Ah. You saw that, did you? Good. And yes, he did. Did he look at you the same way?"

"No. He barely glanced at me that time, but he looked closely enough when we were face to face and he thought I had named him responsible for the men we were after. And that was before you called me Father James."

"Aye, but you are not Father James, are you? You're not even Brother James. You are Jamie Wallace, a mere student. And so at worst he will set his people to looking for a minor priest from Jedburgh. He will not instruct them to visit Paisley Abbey and interrogate the seminarians. I'm the one he wants, Jamie, the one he knows. I'm the marked man. He'll be at Uncle Malcolm's house looking for me at sunrise, so you stay well away from there and make your way back to Paisley alone. Do you understand what I am saying, Jamie? There is no safer place for you than at the Abbey, and it is time for you to take those vows and be ordained."

"But I sinned, Will. I sinned grievously. I broke a man's head."

"Aye, I've heard. And he would have broken yours had you not struck first. You regret it, I can see that. You are full of remorse, and that's good. So take your remorse and confess it to Father Peter when you get back to Paisley. Tell him everything that happened. He'll shrive you pure as the driven snow. Come here."

He pulled me into his embrace—though cautiously, with a mind to his injuries—and then he reached out again to Mirren, drawing her close to both of us.

"Wife," he said quietly, lapsing back into Scots with his forehead touching both of ours, "you havena yet known the joys of communing wi' my cousin Jamie here, but ye ha'e heard me talk of him many times. This is a man I love as I do myself, and nigh as much as I do you—though, thanks be to God, for far different reasons." He smothered a laugh with a grunt as his wife twisted in his arm and rapped him sharply in the ribs, but she was smiling as she did so, and he pulled her close again. "You two are my closest kin," he said. "My nearest and dearest, and so I will need you to be close wi' each other, supporting one another when I canna be here. I love you both." He hugged us close again, then straightened up and released me.

"Now, Cuz, get ye to your bed, and we'll try no' to wake ye when we leave. And get those vows taken this time. I might need a priest in the forest one o' these days."

3

Will was right about Father Peter's reaction to my confession. I went to him the day I arrived back at the Abbey and I told him everything I could recall about the events surrounding Will's meeting with Bek and the beating he had sustained afterwards. He listened in grim-faced silence, nodding only occasionally as I said something or other that appeared to fit with his own perceptions, and when I had finished he went straight into the rite of absolution without even delivering the normal warning against laxity. The penance he assessed me was a very light one, too, considering what I had believed to be the gravity of my sin, and when I voiced my surprise at it he waved his hand impatiently, giving thanks to God instead that I had not forgotten my boyhood lessons with the quarterstaff. Then, when he asked me if I had anything else that concerned me, I told him that I expected the English to come looking for me.

He laughed at that, much as Will had the previous night. "They would never dream of searching for you within the Abbey precincts," he said, "but while you are awaiting their arrival—for I know you will, no matter what I tell you—you should apply yourself to your studies and try hard to forget about the entire incident. Wait and work and watch," he said. "But work harder than anything else, because work will make the time fly quickly."

And so I worked hard, and the ensuing week passed quietly, albeit with agonizing slowness, without any English searchers coming to hunt me. The next week passed the same way, and by the end of the third week I found myself forgetting to listen for their clattering arrival. Then Christmas came and went without disruption. Because of King John's royal activities in the aftermath of his coronation, and King Edward of England's less than enthusiastic reactions to them, the ordination ceremony that would see me elevated to the priesthood was postponed yet again, this time until Eastertide of the new year.

On the last day of the year, Edward's ever-tenuous patience snapped. He repudiated all the promises he had made to the Scots Crown and realm during the interregnum. Two days after that, King John in return pronounced the recent Treaty of Birgham null and void and declared that all promises made to England during the same period, involving the marriage of the Maid of Norway to Edward's son, Prince Edward of Caernarvon, were no longer binding.

To the Scots folk in general, none of that meant anything that they could understand, but they understood very clearly that the magnates—the Norman-Scots nobility and the ancient Celtic earldoms—were fighting among themselves yet again and that the outcome would do nothing for the welfare of ordinary folk.

Then, in early February, in the ancient town of Scone, King John held his first parliament as monarch of the realm, and it went sufficiently well for him to demand, a fortnight later, that four of his most powerful liegemen, two from north and two from south of the River Forth, should pay formal, public homage to him at the close of Easter, swearing allegiance to his Crown and cause. The two northerners were Donald MacAngus, a Celtic chieftain from the western Highlands, and John, the Earl of Caithness, in the far north. Both were powerful men in their own territories, but their names were practically unknown south of the Forth. The names of the two southerners, on the other hand, rang resonantly with local significance to us. They were young Robert Bruce, Earl of Carrick, who had not yet turned nineteen, and Sir William Douglas, an arrogant autocrat who ruled his territories with an iron hand and was known to brook no interference from anyone. Douglas was notoriously his own man, and all who knew of Balliol's summons were waiting to see how he would respond to the demands of the new monarch.

I must have been one of very few who cared nothing for how Douglas and Balliol regarded each other, for I had matters of my own to attend to that late winter and early spring. I was almost entirely lost in preparing for my elevation to the priesthood, for I was to be ordained at Easter. Bishop Wishart, who would officiate at the ceremonies, had assured me in person that my ordination would take place at last, even if politics were to take precedence again and he were forced to arrange the matter privately at an ordinary Mass, without pomp or panoply.

My aunt Margaret fell sick early in February of that year, too, and we knew from the outset that there was little chance she would recover. It was clear to all of us that she welcomed the idea of death; she had simply lost the will to live and she looked forward to being reunited in Heaven with her beloved husband. Sir Malcolm's death almost two years earlier had taken a heavy toll upon her, and not even her youngest daughter's wedding or the prospect of new grandchildren could sway her from her need to be with him again.

The other matter that drew at least some of my attention over that year-end period between 1292 and 1293, of course, was the welfare of my cousin and his wife, now living in the wilds of Selkirk Forest. I seldom heard from them, although I did receive a message at least once each month from some stranger passing through Paisley, and from these I deduced that all was well with the Wallaces in the fastness of the greenwood; they appeared to be content with the life they were leading there, and I gathered that they lacked for little. From time to time memories of Will—his smile, a gesture, a remembered opinion—would pop into my mind, and I would find myself smiling at the recollection of one shared occasion or another. What I remembered most often, however, was one of the last things he had said to me, when he told me to finish studying and become a priest, because he might one day need one in his forest haunts. I would think of that and smile too, never for an instant believing that it might be realized.

4

There came a day when I found myself lying prostrate at the foot of the altar steps in the Abbey church, dressed all in white and listening to Bishop Wishart asking the attending brotherhood if any one of them knew of any good and proper reason why I should not be raised to the priesthood. Face down as I was on the thick bed of fresh rushes strewn in front of the altar, I could not look up, for the ritual in which we were engaged demanded immobility of me, but even had it not, I would not have dared to raise my head, for one of the men gazing down at me from above was Antony Bek, Bishop of Durham, who had last set eyes on me at his camp, the morning he had met with Will. I felt sure he must recognize me eventually, and so I kept my face down, waiting for his cry of condemnation.

The silence around me stretched and seemed to shiver, but the anticipated challenge did not come, and eventually, incredulously, I heard Bishop Wishart begin to intone the Litany of the Saints. The massed voices of the congregants broke over me in the first responses, and I knew that God had sheltered me. I allowed myself to breathe again and sagged with relief.

I had spent most of the previous day in isolation, preparing for the rites I was now undergoing, and had then passed the entire night in prayer, surrounded by my closest brethren as they stood vigil with me. Bek had arrived sometime in the evening, making an unexpected, diplomatic visit to the Abbey on his way to St. Andrews. He had not expected Wishart of Glasgow to be in residence, but when he discovered the veteran Bishop's presence, and the reason for it, he was most affable, I learned afterwards, and insisted upon attending the ordination ceremonies and assisting His Grace of Glasgow with the ritual. The two prelates had never liked each other from first meeting, when Bek of Durham first set foot in Scotland; their mutual antagonism was based solidly upon their opposed priorities, for each of them was dedicated solely to the welfare and security of his own realm.

The litany ended and Bishop Wishart raised me to my feet with his own hands, then blessed me and laid his hands on my head, calling upon the Holy Spirit to imbue me with the grace to conduct my duties thenceforth with *dignitas* and rectitude.

Bishop Bek stepped forward in his turn to bless me by laying his hands upon my head, and I stood frozen in wide-eyed terror, my heart almost bursting with fear. But he barely glanced at me, his eyes raised to the high altar as he laid his hands on my newly tonsured scalp, and I realized, incredulously, that I was safe and that he would never dream of associating the white-robed, purified novice in front of him with the filthy, grey-clad cleric he had cast out of his camp the day he had thrashed the upstart Scot who had so offended him. I stood slightly dazed and alone after that, in front of God's high altar, while Bishop Wishart anointed my head and hands with holy oils, then dressed me in the vestments of priesthood, the blessed stole and the heavy, cloak-like chasuble. I took the chalice from him for the first time, feeling the weight of the wine and water it contained as I gazed at the flat, square paten of stiffened cloth that covered it and held the bread of the host. Then, as the sounds of the offertory bells died away, Bishop Wishart seated himself in his chair in front of the altar, and I stepped forward, holding a lighted candle, my offering, as a newly ordained priest, of light and purity to him. He took it from my hands and rose again, and together we proceeded with the Mass until, in unison with him, I uttered the sacred words of consecration for the first time and transformed the bread and wine into the Body and Blood of Christ.

Thereafter, with the bright tang of the sacred Blood still tingling beneath my tongue, I bowed my head while the Bishop laid hands on me yet again and uttered the words that endowed me with the power to forgive men's sins and impose penance upon them: "Receive ye the Holy Spirit. Whose sins you shall forgive, they are forgiven them; and whose sins you shall retain, they are retained."

After waiting and studying for so long, I was now, with those words, a consecrated priest, and my heart swelled in my chest with joy and with love for my fellow men as Bishop Wishart finally turned me to face and be greeted and welcomed by the fellowship of the assembled congregation. And there, among the applauding crowd, the first two faces I saw clearly belonged to Will Wallace and Ewan Scrymgeour.

The shock hit me in the chest like a hammer blow, and I turned instinctively to look at Bek, fearing that he, too, must have seen Will, but he was still smiling his frosty, condescending little smile, politely tapping the fingers of one hand into the cupped palm of the other and looking nowhere near the massed monkish ranks in the pews.

And only then did I realize that there was even less reason for Bek to recognize my friend in this setting than there was for him to recognize me. He had met Will but once—the clean-shaven, fresh-faced Will that I myself had barely recognized at that time, now that I thought back to it. The Will Wallace in the pews today was another man altogether, heavily bearded and darkly tanned—his face, I suspected, artificially stained with walnut juice for the express purpose of altering his appearance—and he was dressed as a resident Abbey monk, wearing a full habit and standing comfortably in the front ranks of the brotherhood, among Brother Duncan and his librarians. He saw me looking and grinned at me, his teeth flashing white in the darkness of his face. Knowing him safe then, and feeling a surge of admiration at his daring, I grinned back at him and moved my eyes to include Ewan in my welcome. As he and I locked eyes, he raised his right thumb to me in a gesture of support I had known well as a boy but had not seen since.

More than half an hour of blessings, good wishes, and salutations passed before I could finally embrace my two friends, and when I did I could barely see them for the sudden tears that blinded me.

"Are you mad?" I asked Will, the emotion making my voice sound husky. "You take your lives in your hands coming here. Especially with Bek present. What if he had recognized you?"

My cousin shrugged. "Then it would have been a different kind of morning. Besides, he wasn't supposed to be here. You didn't invite him, did you?"

"No, Cuz, I did not. But the fact that he came here anyway is an example of how easily our finest plans may come undone. I am glad to see both of you here today, but you took an awful risk."

That earned me another shrug of those massive shoulders. "I took an oath to see you priested. D'you not recall?"

"Aye, I do. But that was before you were outlawed."

"An oath's an oath, even to an outlaw."

"True, but I believe God would have held you guilty of no sin had you been prudent and stayed safely away."

Ewan spoke up. "Remember who you're talkin' to, Jamie. When did you ever know this one to be prudent, or to do the sensible thing?"

I kept my face straight and nodded seriously. "True enough," I said. "I'm always hoping he will change his ways, though. I suppose the most I can hope for on a day like this is that he will keep his head down." I turned my eyes back to Will. "And how is your lady wife? I trust you left her in good health?"

"I did, and she sent you her cousinly love. She is well and thriving in the freedom of the greenwood, and she told me to tell you that you will be welcome any time you wish to come and visit us. So when will that be, now that you are priested at last?"

"I have no idea—but I hope it may be soon. Master Wishart's the one controlling that, though, for now that I'm ordained he must see to it that I am kept busy learning my new tasks. For the remainder of my life, I will be learning how to be a priest. I know I'll be leaving the Abbey, and that will grieve me, but His Grace has plans for me in Glasgow. He has said he wants me to be his amanuensis, and I suspect that will keep me constantly engaged for the next few years. But now that you are here, how long will you stay?"

Will slapped his flat belly with an open palm. "Another hour or so, no more. We will eat with you and be gone. We came to see you priested, Cuz, and now you are. There is nothing else to hold us here, and we have much to do when we return to Selkirk. So come and embrace us again, and we'll leave you to your cleric friends, by whom you are well regarded."

I walked with them to the gates after we ate, and on the way we came within two paces of Antony Bek, who nodded to us as we passed, then returned to his discussion with the men around him.

"Learn a lesson from Bek," Will said to me at the gates. "People see what they expect to see, rather than what is truly there to be seen. Be good, young Jamie, and when ye've become a seasoned priest, come and see us in the forest."

I promised I would, and my two oldest friends strode away, and then I went back into the Abbey to begin my new life as a priest.

CHAPTER ELEVEN

I

The remainder of that year, 1293, may have been uneventful for most of the realm of Scotland, but for me it was a hectic period, spent adapting to the practical reality of living daily as a priest. My new principal and superior, Bishop Wishart, was then the senior prelate of Scotland, and he went out of his way, from the outset of our relationship, to ensure that I became familiar with, and stood prepared to deal with, *all* the political developments that affected our lives, not only within the realm but even more dramatically in the closely associated circles of the Church in England as well as Scotland. It was an exhaustive field of activity, particularly in the early days, and he plunged me into it directly after my ordination, going so far as to provide me with a well-lit office cubicle so that I could study more effectively and apply myself to the tasks he set me without being interrupted.

Callow, inexperienced, and newly minted as I was, I knew nonetheless that I was being accorded extraordinary treatment for a tyro, and I braced myself to raise the matter with the Bishop, to discover why he should be at such pains before I even had a chance to prove myself to him.

But it was he himself who raised the matter. Soon after I had moved to Glasgow, exchanging my home in the Abbey for the new and ornate but yet unfinished cathedral there, he told me he had seen a talent in me years earlier, an ability that had impressed him sufficiently to ensure that he would keep a close eye on me thereafter. I must have looked truly perplexed.

"I don't understand you, my lord," I said. "Forgive me, but what are you talking about?"

"Your gift for reading people," he said. "It's quite amazing. I've never seen the like of it in one so young."

I laughed aloud, at a loss for words.

"Don't laugh, Father James," he said testily. "If I wished to be amusing I could find more beguiling topics with which to entertain you. You have a gift, God-sent. A talent, lodged deep within you and thrusting itself forward despite your own wishes. God has granted you a rare capacity to look at men and see through all the artifices they present to mask them from the world. You do it without even being aware of it, and you see straight to the heart of whomever you are dealing with at any time. That, Father, is a capability so rare as to be priceless to a man like me, who has to treat from day to day with people whose main concern is to conceal their own true motives."

He saw me begin to raise a hand in protest and swept my inter-jection aside before I could voice it. "Believe me, I am no fool babbling into my wine cup. I saw this in you years ago. And once I had noticed it, I watched for it increasingly, and I never saw it fail. But even then, I did not trust my own perceptions. I enlisted the help of others, telling them what I suspected and then bidding them observe you as I had, and they all concurred."

This time I did stop him. "Forgive me, my lord, but who are 'they,' these people you set to watch me?"

"No one who would do you harm or wish any ill upon you, Father James. Your cousins, Father Peter and Brother Duncan, were glad to assist me, as were both the Abbot and Sub-abbot of Paisley, and all of them agreed that this ability of yours, whatever its source, is real and strong." He shrugged. "So what would you have me do with such knowledge, holding as it does the certainty that your abil-ities can make my task as bishop and pastor much less arduous? I have no choice but to foster your talents, because I believe that once you have learned to direct and control them, they will be of immense value, not merely to me but to the realm itself."

I tried to argue with him, claiming that he had misjudged me and overestimated my supposed abilities, but he was adamant. Much to my own surprise, I quickly came to love the challenges involved as he instructed me patiently on how to assess the records and reports, some written but most of them oral, of men's past deeds; to look meticulously at their backgrounds and their previous activities for indications of their beliefs and motivations; and then, in face-to-face encounters, to look beyond their outer, public facades to divine their true motivations and intent.

I became something of an adept in an astonishingly short time, once I had conquered the difficulty of believing that I really had a natural acuity in such things. I soon found myself becoming increasingly aware, from day to day, of the subtle pressure being applied on all sides in normal daily commerce by the clerical community within which I lived and worked, and by the swarms of influence seekers who flocked to the cathedral as a centre of both spiritual and temporal power. More than that, though, I became acutely attuned to the predominantly malignant activities of the influence brokers who pandered to the wishes of all the others. To the Bishop alone I reported everything that came to my attention, and he reciprocated with an openness he rarely showed to others, discussing privately with me matters that he would seldom entrust to others of higher rank.

Thus I was able to observe at close range, from the earliest days of his reign, the inconsistency and the tragic need to please and to be liked that doomed John Balliol's kingship and brought about the events that followed his removal from the throne after less than four years.

The rot had set in as early as the spring of 1293, when William Douglas and young Robert Bruce were swearing their allegiance to him, for that was the year when the common folk everywhere in southern Scotland really began to suffer widespread injustice and indignity at the hands of the "visiting" soldiery, and when the constant English presence was generally accepted as a fact of life. No one had the slightest doubt that the former was caused by the latter, yet even then no one would have thought of applying the word *occupying* to the English forces that were everywhere in the land.

No one would have thought, that is, of saying it aloud. But the truth was that the arrogance and intransigence of the English soldiery, fostered by their commanders and allied with the indifference of the Scots nobility, gave rise that spring to widespread injustices against the Scots folk, abuses that stirred up local unrest that was put down in turn by ruthless military reprisals.

Men and women—cottagers and householders—were dragged from their homes and hanged out of hand, with no one ever being called to account. With increasing frequency, community leaders and solid, successful farmers had their lands and holdings confiscated after they were accused of heinous crimes by blatantly unscrupulous "witnesses." Such evidence was too often ludicrous, most particularly so when it was tendered—and accepted—in denial of verifiable testimony to the contrary offered by more reputable witnesses. In defiance of all sanity, and making a total mockery of Scotland's laws, those spurious accusations continued throughout the summer and autumn, and large accumulations of land and assets that had been held by local folk for generations were snatched up by heavily armed outsiders.

In the spring of the year that followed, petty Scots leaders began to emerge throughout southern Scotland, driven to inconsistently organized self-defence, and to aggressive resistance, out of frustration and desperation. Reports of bands of outlaws and rebels began to circulate widely. The English made no formal complaint to King John, however, since to do so would have drawn attention to what was really going on in the countryside. They chose instead to increase their troop concentrations in the troubled areas and to deal more and more harshly with the local people. King John himself heard nothing of the increasingly urgent reports of these reprisals from the people in the southern half of his kingdom, or if he did hear of them, he chose to remain deaf to the problems of his poorest subjects.

One particular band of outlaws came into prominence soon after Easter that year. It began quietly, making its presence known in its own small area by the end of April, but it seized the attention of everyone in the southern half of the country towards the middle of June. Tales of this band's activities began to be repeated along with the latest reports of atrocities against the people, and they seemed to offer hope in the face of despair: wherever the most blatant outrages of condoned robbery occurred—the perpetrators called it confiscation by the military administration, but it was barefaced pillaging—there occurred, too, sudden and unattributable instances of retribution.

Men who had sworn false testimony against their neighbours were found dead, with their tongues cut out and reinserted backwards; men who had seized houses and property rightfully belonging to others were found hanged within the charred ruins of the buildings they had stolen; and soldiers who had taken part in these dispossessions, beating and whipping innocent men and ravishing their women, met swift justice on the trails and pathways through the forest surrounding the places where such crimes had occurred. Most often, they were shot down from ambush and left to rot where they fell, but at other times, in deeply wooded areas where bows were ineffectual and death by a blade or club was not always assured, they were taken on the march, gathered together under stout trees, and dispatched with cut throats, and any survivors were hanged directly above them, lest anyone miss the significance of what had happened.

These outlaws became known as the Greens, because at the scene of every killing, whether of a single man or a large group, a scrap of green cloth was left pinned to the chest of one of the corpses by a knife blade.

By the end of June, rumours abounded about who these Greens were and whence they came, and more than a few young men left home, all across the south, in the hopes of finding them and joining their ranks. The English, it was said, were terrified of even going out to search for the Greens; they did not know where to start looking; and they did not even know who they were looking for, because no one had ever seen the faces of the outlaws.

Leadership of the Greens, it was said, appeared to be shared by a number of people—although no one could attest to that. There was no doubt, though, that the frequency and the far-flung nature of the band's activities indicated that more than one leader was involved, for new reports of their exploits came daily, many of them describing events that supposedly occurred on the same day, at similar times, but many miles apart.

Mystery piled upon mystery, and the only thing that could be said with certainty was that none of the Greens was ever seen without a mask or hood. Their identities were unknown, and, according to people who had seen and heard them do so, they took great and savage pleasure in pointing out to their enemies, loudly, what it was that had moved them to rebel so openly. They would point to their own hooded faces while fighting and taunt the English with chants of "Let's see you point out *this* face to your magistrates!"

I first heard of this behaviour in early June, from a travelling priest who stopped at Bishop Wishart's residence to deliver a pouch of correspondence to His Grace. This man, Father Malacchi, had spent some time in the depths of Selkirk Forest after he fell sick from eating something less than fresh. While recovering his health among a small community of forest dwellers, he had heard many tales of the Greens, and of how they hid their identity from everyone lest they be betrayed in return for English gold.

I had taken Father Malacchi to the kitchens that evening, after he delivered his dispatches to the Bishop, and I remained with him while he ate a large and obviously welcome meal. It was after that, while we were talking idly over a jug of the cathedral kitchens' wondrously mild ale, that he mentioned the anomaly of the hooded outlaws.

I knew who they were immediately, of course, and saw their faces in my mind: Will himself and Ewan standing to the fore, while at their backs ranged their five companions, Alan Crawford of Nithsdale and Robertson the archer, Long John of the Knives, Big Andrew with his crossbow, and Shoomy the Gael. I had no doubt there were others by this time, but these were the men I knew, and I had no difficulty imagining them all wearing hoods. None of them were fools, and facelessness would be a great asset in Scotland nowadays, particularly for a public thief. I found myself smiling—somewhat surprisingly when what was really called for was priestly disapproval—as I thought about big Ewan and how we had met, and I could immediately hear his soft, lisping voice pointing out the advantages of a concealing hood to a man as disfigured as he was, a man who had no wish to frighten children and even less wish to be identified later as having a hairless, smashed, all too memorable face.

From that time onward, I was a leap ahead of the burgeoning lore that sprang up around the band known as the Greens. They were known to be based "somewhere in Selkirk Forest," and I never ventured an opinion on that, even though I knew it to be true. The forest is enormous—it covers half the country—and to my mind, had Will Wallace wished his whereabouts to be common knowledge, he would have made it so. That folk were still unsure meant that he had good reason for being circumspect. What was solidly established, though, was that the Greens were better organized and more effective than any of the other groups active in Scotland's south. The band quickly gained a fearsome reputation for dealing death to any unprepared English force that came against it or attempted to pass through its territories. As for those forces that came against the Greens ready for mayhem and military vengeance, they came in vain, for the outlaws scattered into the forest ahead of them, as insubstantial as morning fog among dense brush.

By August, everyone was talking about the Greens of Selkirk Forest. The scope and range of their activities had broadened greatly by that time, too. Crimes against honest Scots folk had begun to diminish as soon as it was clearly understood that the penalties for such behaviour were swift, savage, merciless, and inescapable, and it was then that the Greens had begun venturing into military activities, setting out to prosecute acts of war against any English force that could not justify its presence in Scotland as being necessary to the requirements of the King of England. Deputies, earls, and barons held no legitimacy in such cases; their forces were judged unnecessary and therefore inimical to Scotland's good, and they were declared fair game for the bloodthirsty Scots insurgents.

It was also said of the Greens, before the end of that summer, that no Scots folk had ever been accosted by them, and that, from time to time, they passed surplus food from captured English supply trains on to families whose own food and possessions had been confiscated by the English. The proof of that came after two well-organized attacks by the Greens on English supply trains in the Dumfries area, when small raiding parties of English soldiers moved swiftly into surrounding villages, searching buildings for anything that might have been taken in the attacks. The Greens' retribution for that came swiftly, too, and subsequent raiding parties were wiped out before they could reach their objectives.

I had developed an ambivalence towards such tidings since they began to come to my attention, for they always brought my patriotism into conflict with my morality. As a priest, I knew what the Greens were doing was legally atrocious; they were defying the duly constituted authority of government, spurning and openly flouting the King's Peace. As a Scot, however, a member of the voiceless people whose lives were being trampled underfoot by those in power, I exulted in the victories of the Greens. They were defying the King's power, certainly, but the Scots King himself was doing nothing, and in fact the King whose power they were mainly defying was not their own. The Greens were resisting the illicit power of Edward Plantagenet, who had no right, divine or otherwise, to be exercising his regal powers or his military prowess within the realm of Scotland, despite the high-flown language of the treaties he cited in support of his activities. Scotland now had a King of its own. The Scots lords and magnates had given the English monarch legal licence for his behaviour during the interregnum, but that should mean nothing now. The interregnum was long since over, even though Scotland's King was being painfully slow to assert himself.

Looking back now from the distance of decades, I can see that my perspective on the entire affair of the Greens was distorted, naturally and probably inevitably, by the fact that I knew, respected, and even loved their leaders. They were my friends and family, and my trust in them was such that I could not think of them as malicious criminals. No matter how much supposed evidence was laid before me for inspection, I viewed it with suspicion and sometimes outright disbelief, knowing it had been fabricated by people whose bias against my kin and my very race was beyond question.

My sole error lay in thinking that I was the only one aware of that relationship.

2

"That cousin of yours is forging quite a reputation for himself."

It was an unexpected comment, coming as it did after a long period of silence, and my chest tightened with alarm. Of course I had no slightest indication that it heralded the single most important conversation I would ever have with my mentor, Robert Wishart, the Bishop of Glasgow and Primate of Scotland.

"My lord?" I asked, allowing the inflection of my voice to demonstrate my puzzlement.

"I said your cousin's making a name for himself among the folk." He used the Latin word *populi*, meaning the common people. "We should discuss it, you and I."

It was March 20th, 1295, and I had been working for Bishop Wishart in Glasgow for more than a year by that time, learning to cope with more and more responsibility as my duties grew increasingly complex and demanding. We were in his private study that morning, in the administrative wing of the cathedral buildings, and since before dawn we had been working our way through the mountain of correspondence awaiting his attention. Beyond the open window, a far-off thrush was singing, its enthusiasm whetted by pale March sunshine, and in the middle distance I could hear the regular, rhythmic sounds of the stonemasons and builders as they went about their daily work, adding to the Cathedral buildings. Construction had been under way now for more than forty years, and no one, not even the Bishop himself, could say when the work might be complete. The Cathedral would continue to be built until it was deemed pleasing to the Deity.

I realized that I was dawdling, avoiding eye contact, and hoping to deflect whatever was in His Grace's mind. Now I set aside my pen and looked him in the eye.

"What do you wish to discuss, my lord?"

"Will Wallace and his Greens." He pressed his shoulders back against the carved oaken back of his armed chair. "It's time we spoke of it openly."

Openly ... That was the last word I would ever have thought to apply to this matter, for Will's identity as the leader of the Greens was the sole secret I had withheld from this man. I sat still for several moments longer, then picked up an ink-stained rag and made a show of wiping my fingertips.

"Where shall we start, my lord?"

"We will start at the beginning, Father James. You didn't think I knew, did you?" Seeing the wide-eyed look on my face, he pressed onward. "You didn't think I'd see it, the straightforward sense of it. That only Will Wallace could be the leader of the Greens. But think for a moment, if you will. How could I not know, knowing you? Your very silence would have told me, even had I not known all along. I have known you now for ... how long, nigh on twenty years? Sixteen at least, and in all that time, the single person you have talked about, other than your fellows here and at the Abbey, has been your cousin Will, the outlawed verderer who dared to cross the English. And then along comes this group of thieves calling themselves the Greens, whose leader, an archer, is unknown, and all of a sudden you forget the name and even the existence of your cousin Will. Am I that big a fool, lad?"

I grimaced. "I was afraid that if I said anything, my lord, you might have to act upon it."

He gawped at me, perplexed. "Act upon it and do what?"

"I know not, my lord ... Report his name to the authorities?"

"Which authorities? And had I done so, what would that have achieved? He is an outlaw already, destined to hang if taken.

Knowing his name would make no difference to the Englishmen's incompetence. It would not affect their inability to catch him. But did you truly think I would divulge his identity?"

I half shrugged. "I thought you might have seen it as your duty, my lord."

"My duty is to my King and his realm, to my monarch and my country." The statement was delivered in a tone that left me in no doubt of the old man's sincerity. "To this point the Greens have done nothing that openly defies or attacks either one of those. Their crimes, if crimes in fact they be, have all been carried out against the English, whose presence in this land I deem an abomination."

I opened my mouth to respond but he cut me off with a short chop of his hand. "Abomination, I said, and I meant it. And we brought it upon ourselves. We have been dancing wi' the Devil for too long, Father James, and now I fear we'll have to pay a high price for our dalliance. We invited the Plantagenet to come here, and he came. I fear he will not leave as eagerly when we ask him to retire."

He rose abruptly from his chair and crossed to the open window, where he stood staring down into the courtyard below, one hand holding the window's metal edge, the other hooked by the thumb into the white rope girdle at his waist. The thrush I had heard in the distance was no longer singing.

"I blame myself," he said quietly, speaking into the emptiness in front of him, so that I had to listen hard to hear the words that drifted back over his shoulder. "It came to me that this might happen, but I put the thought aside and allowed myself to be gulled by the man's reputation as the foremost knight in Christendom, the arbiter of justice and confidant of kings and popes." He turned to look back at me, and rested his shoulders against the wall beside the window. "He was all of those things once, and widely honoured for it. But of late he has kept himself at home, nursing a growing hunger to increase his lands and his power."

He seated himself with an aging man's care for his comfort and appearance, arranging his clothes carefully before he spoke again. "He engineered the war against the Welsh, you know." The hesitation that followed was barely noticeable. "You did know that, I hope."

I nodded.

"Aye, but he did it consummately, with great skill. The Welsh fell to him like lambs to a rabid wolf. And now I fear he plans the same fate for Scotland."

Hearing him say that so matter-of-factly startled me out of my silence.

"But King John will never put up with that."

His back straightened again and he stared at me for a moment, expressionless. "I forget, sometimes, how young you are," he said eventually, "because you seldom show your inexperience. But then when you do, your youth leaps out at me. You are almost right, though. King John will attempt to prevent it. There is no doubt of that. But the damage that's already done is irreparable, and he will fail. It is already too late to counteract that. England's King is no man's fool and he has worn his crown for many years. He has also shown himself to be ten times the man John Balliol is."

He reached up and removed the crimson skullcap of his office, something I had never seen him do before, and then he fell silent, kneading the silken fabric between his fingers as he stared at it with narrowed eyes, and suddenly the crimson cap disappeared within his large, clenched fist.

"Balliol looks like a king, I'll grant you that. He has all that's necessary there—the bearing, the appearance and the posture and the gait. On top of that, he is affable and amiable, amusing and engaging, with great charm. And he has a regal air of *dignitas* about him, too. But he is weak, for all that. He is too *compliant*, too accommodating and too much at pains to be ingratiating. He lacks the iron, the savagery a true king must own, though he use it but seldom. Our King wants people to like him, and that is a fatal flaw in any leader, be he king or bandit chief.

"Edward knew all that when he had his myrmidons choose John. He knew he could control him, bend him to his will. Bruce he could never have controlled, and I believe that fact alone barred Robert

Bruce from ever being elected to the Crown. Balliol, though ...
Edward never had any doubt that he could control King John of
Scotland, and through him he could control the realm."

The Bishop placed the back of his fist on the oak tabletop and
slowly opened his fingers, allowing the red silken cap to open up
and cover his palm. He smoothed it into shape, then replaced it on
the crown of his head and turned to look me in the eye.

"The Plantagenet is ruthless and calculating, and I see clearly
now that he laid his plans for us long before we even knew he had a
plan. We were too concerned with keeping order among our own ...
we being the Bishops, Fraser of St. Andrews, myself, Dunkeld, and
a few others, along with the Abbots of Dunfermline, Dunblane,
Kelso, Arbroath, and Cambuskenneth, and a few of the lesser
magnates. We sought to avoid the crush of civil war between the
Bruces and the Balliol-Comyn alliance, and initially we thought we
had succeeded. Instead, though, we delivered ourselves into the
hands of the English."

I could barely bring myself to ask the question in my mind. "Do
you truly believe things to be that bad, my lord?"

He looked at me with eyes that seemed close to pitying. "I do,
my son. And you will, too, once you have considered all the details
I will add today. You might even ask yourself how much worse it
could be. We have been betrayed by those we implored to save us.
Our country is now occupied by a foreign force. *Occupied*, Father,
by an army that no one can doubt is hostile. Anyone who cannot see
the truth of that is a blind fool, bemused by wishful thinking.
English armies rule this land, and their leadership knows no restraint.
And for reasons of politics and expediency our own so-called
leaders—not the Church, but the civil leadership, including our new
King—do nothing. They think they have too much to lose if they
complain, beginning with the forfeiture of all their lands and holdings in England. They believe that would leave them impoverished.
They cannot see that it would leave them free. They cannot see the
value of this realm in which they live. They have no wish even to

consider such a thing. They think of themselves as Englishmen and Frenchmen living in exile here in the north."

"Aye," I said quietly, unable to find a single point in his outpouring with which to disagree. "And the damnable part of that is that they ignore their people. They do not think about the Scots *folk* at all, and that tells me that they themselves cannot lay claim to being Scots."

That brought His Grace's head up quickly. "Do you truly believe that, Father James? Surely not."

"Believe that they are not truly Scots? No, for they clearly are. But that their abuse and neglect is destructive? How can I not believe that, my lord? It is all around us, everywhere I look, in the arrogance of the English sneers and the suffering of our Scots folk. Were it not so, the Greens would not exist. The Greens were born of desperation, bred out of the people's neglect, if not abuse, by the very leaders who should have been protecting them."

"Your cousin and his Greens are protecting them. The people, I mean."

"Perhaps so," I concurred, too agitated to realize I was talking to the Bishop as though I were his equal. "But too few of them to really count, and not sufficiently to make a difference. Will is but one man, and a commoner to boot. His men are loyal and brave, but they are all outlawed, and no one in authority will heed him."

"Not so. Will Wallace has his own authority. The English are heeding him, Jamie. And the Scots folk are heeding him."

"Aye, but that's not what is needed. What's needed is for other, more powerful folk, here in the realm, to look at what he is doing and see that it's a necessary thing. The magnates need to see what he is doing, and then they need to aid him in achieving it."

The Bishop raised a hand, almost wearily. "They will, eventually, Father. The time is not yet right." He looked back towards the window as the tolling of a bell began to echo outside. "It is midday, and I'm hungry and I need to empty my bladder, so go you and send someone to fetch us something to eat, but come directly back."

3

Ireturned quickly, but to an empty room, and so I finished composing the letter I had been working on when the Bishop and I had begun to talk, and while I was doing so, two lay brothers from the kitchens brought in refreshments for us: a jug of small ale and a platter of bread and cold sliced beef, with crushed horseradish root in sweet whipped cream, and onions pickled in brine. I resisted the temptation to serve myself until my mentor returned. When he did, he was frowning.

"Forgive me, Father James," he muttered as he bustled in. "I detest being kept waiting, and I detest keeping others waiting for me even more. Three times I was waylaid by bustling busybodies on my way back from the latrines, and I sent a fourth accoster reeling with a flea in his ear when he sought to stop me over some petty griev- ance that he could have dealt with himself when it arose. What is wrong with people today? No one seems to dare to risk making a decision on his own without gaining approval from someone else first. Ah! We have food, I see. Excellent. Then let us eat."

We ate in appreciative silence, but as soon as he had devoured a second wedge of bread stuffed with beef and fiery horseradish and washed it down with a deep draft of ale, my mentor pushed away his platter and sat back, belching discreetly into his sleeve.

"We have talked about your gift many times," he began then, "and about how I first came to notice you. But why was it, think you, that I took such an interest in your cousin Will from the first time I saw him? Can you guess?"

I pushed away my bowl and shook my head. "Because he used a bow?"

"Aye, good man. It was precisely that. He used a bow. But not merely a flat bow. Those are commonplace. He had a bow of English yew, a longbow. In Scotland, and with him so young, that was remarkable, and I took note of it."

"So did Andrew Murray, my lord."

"Aye, so he did. But Andrew's awe of Will came from Will's skill with the quarterstaff, if I remember rightly. Andrew was obsessed with that weapon, and it served him well enough, if truth be told, but he was ever an indifferent bowman."

"Were you ever a bowman, my lord?"

"Me?" His laugh was a single bark, and he gestured towards the window corner closest to him, where his long, well-used old sword stood propped in the angle of the wall. "No, not I. Old Grey-Tongue there was the only weapon I ever needed when the time came to the do the Lord's work. Why would you ask me that?"

"I don't know, my lord. Perhaps because I thought that might be the reason you took note of Will."

"Hmm. No, I noticed your cousin purely because he was a Scot, in Scotland, carrying an English bow. It marked him either as a fool or as a man to watch. Some men will carry a weapon like that solely in the hope of setting themselves apart from the herd of their fellows, imagining that the mere appearance of being different will indicate that they are dangerous. Such men are fools, for anyone who cares to look will see right through their pretense. It was obvious from the outset that your cousin was not one of those. The very ease and casual respect with which he bore the weapon proclaimed his familiarity with its use. And that made him doubly impressive."

I waited, but he said no more, and so I prompted him. "Forgive me, my lord, but doubly impressive in what way?"

"His youth, and his indubitable prowess." He saw that I was still not following. "Think of what I said of the fool who carries such a bow for pure effect. His foolishness is evident in that he must lack the physique to use it properly. There is but one way to acquire those mighty archer's thews, that width and depth of back and shoulders so enormous in your cousin and his friend Ewan. They come from years of discipline and practice; hours and hours of repetitive pulling, day after day and month after month. Your cousin had those muscles when I first set eyes on him, and he was yet but a boy. That told me he had great and admirable self-discipline, but even more, it told me that young Wallace, boy though he might be, was yet his own man. It told me he possessed sufficient pride and confidence to care nothing for what others thought of him, and would bow his head to no man other than those he chose to acknowledge as being worthy. I saw all that in my first glimpse of him, the way he stood, and the manner in which his unstrung bow stave hung in a case from his shoulder. Owning and using such a weapon, and such an *English* weapon, would set him apart from all his fellows and practically force him to walk alone in every endeavour to which he turned his hand and mind, and he would turn to nothing lightly. It crossed my mind then and there that our realm would always have need of men like him.

"And now I would bid you go and find him for me, to take my blessing to him and to deliver a message, assuring him of my support and encouragement in what he is achieving. And tell me now, if you will, why you are scowling at me with so much disapproval."

I had not been aware that I was frowning. "Forgive me again, my lord. I am having difficulty understanding your point of view. What is it, precisely, that you see my cousin achieving?"

He gazed at me levelly. "Not quite accurate, Father, if I may say so. You understand clearly enough what I am saying, I believe. Your difficulty springs from being unable to believe that your Bishop could hold such unlawful, even sinful opinions, let alone give voice to them. Am I not right?"

"Yes, my lord. That is true."

"Of course it is. Listen—" He stopped short, plainly thinking about what he was about to say, then sat back. "Look you, I am a bishop, but that makes me no less a man. As a bishop, I am pastor to my flock and bound by my God-given duty to protect that flock with all my power. That means using my skills and my influence to ensure that their welfare is protected and their corporeal needs are as well tended as their spiritual ones. The soul, we are taught, is everlasting; the body merely temporal and therefore less important, its needs and requirements to be given less urgency than those of the soul. That is all well and good and theoretically splendid, but that is where my own opinions tend to diverge from those of my colleagues—more accurately, from those of my English colleagues.

"I believe our capacity for prayer, our very ability to worship God, depends heavily upon our having the time and opportunity to place our duties to Him ahead of everything else we do. And there is where my voice as a man overwhelms my voice as a bishop. I believe deeply that we cannot pay God His due when we are beset by worries about the welfare of our families, when we live in fear of being evicted or imprisoned or hanged at the whim of some passing stranger who assumes the power of life and death over us. Few decent men can live with such threats and still conscientiously donate their time and their attention to the worship of God. Those very few who can we call saints, and they seldom stay long on this earth. Most men, though, lack that kind of sanctity. They are too concerned with being decent husbands and fathers, friends and neighbours.

"That single realization—that *awareness*—has set me apart from most of my brethren and placed me in a moral situation the like of which I had never imagined. And it has led me to a reluctant accept-ance of the fact that all the sheep in my flock are *Scots* sheep, Father James. I had never thought of that until a few weeks ago, but I know now that it is true. Two months ago, had I been asked about my flock, I would have said they were all equal in God's eyes, each soul of them indistinguishable from the others. It would never have crossed my mind to look at them as Scots souls or English souls. To me they were all God's children, pure and simple.

"But my mind has been changed on that, and forcibly. I've been made to see a new reality, through English eyes—even the eyes of English churchmen—and to accept that they perceive us as being different, and inferior. And so I say now, all my flock are Scots. They are like the sheep of our local hills, wiry and sturdy, dark faced, largely silent, and easily shorn of the little wool they possess. That they should be cruelly shorn and abused as they are today by outlanders, English interlopers, grieves me more than I can say. It also infuriates me, though, and it has pushed me to a point where I had never thought to find myself. It has forced me to make a choice no bishop should ever have to make: to choose between being a Catholic and being a Scots Catholic, when there should be no such difference. But the choice is real. And I have made it. And having made it, I must now live with the consequences, one of which is that I may speak of it now to no one, other than you. You understand why that is so, do you not?"

I nodded, but he went on anyway, saying the words more for his own ears, I felt, than for mine.

"Aye. Were the word to get out that I have made this choice, taken sides where no one will admit that opposing sides exist, I would quickly be removed from my Bishop's Chair and from my responsibilities to my flock, and I cannot allow that to happen. As I am, in place here and able to act as an intermediary even if only to a limited extent, I can serve my people and look out for their interests for as long as I am permitted to remain Bishop of Glasgow. Were I to be removed, some English bishop would be installed in my place and my people would be in vastly greater peril than they are."

It was true, I knew, for by papal dispensation only a few years earlier, in 1291, Edward of England had been empowered to appoint bishops to the Church in Scotland, thereby seizing yet another advantage from the interregnum. Neither Wishart nor I had the slightest doubt that, were he to be removed, his replacement would be an Englishman chosen and appointed, in all probability, by Bishop Antony Bek of Durham.

"So now perhaps you can understand, to some extent, why I need you to find Will Wallace for me. He is become one of the few men in Scotland I can trust to look to Scotland's affairs ahead of his own advantage. There are others, similarly trustworthy, but very few of them, I fear, and I have not the time to go hunting for them one at a time. My hope—my devout and prayerful hope—is that men like your cousin Will here in the south and Andrew Murray in the north will be strong enough and clear enough in their summons, when the time comes, to unite others behind them in ways that I could not and dare not. This country of ours is hell-bent for war and slaughter, Father James. We were afeared for the longest time it would be between Bruce and Balliol, civil war setting kinsmen at each other's throats, but I hope we are beyond that now—or nearly so.

"The nobles shilly-shally still, and I make shift to understand that. They are like coy young women, flirting with strutting suitors, withholding favours and denying commitment in the hope of coming to understand in full the proposals being made. But the time must come, sooner now than later, when the scales will fall from their eyes and permit them to perceive Edward for what he is." His gaze sharpened. "You have a question."

"What makes you think, my lord, that this time must come soon?"

His eyes grew wide and his brows arched high. "Because it must! We live in changing times, Father James, and there are shifts afoot today, even as we speak, that will reshape our very world. Look at our towns here, our burghs. What do you see?"

I blinked at him. "Towns, my lord, nothing more. Though I can see from your face that I am in error. What should I see?"

"Burgesses, Father. Merchants with counting houses, traders with warehouses full of goods, skilled artisans everywhere, masons and manufacturers. They are everywhere."

"I know they are, my lord. But I still don't understand what you are talking about."

He bent forward, and there was an intensity about him that made me feel apprehensive. "Ask yourself where they came from, Father," he said in a low voice, "and what their presence means."

"Their presence in the burghs, my lord? They live there. What else should it mean? Forgive me, for I am not accustomed to feeling stupid, but I still don't follow you."

He grinned fiercely, a very un-bishoplike grin. "I know you don't. Nor does King John, nor do his magnates, and King Edward and all his earls and barons are no more enlightened than any of those. These *people*, Father James, these merchants, traders, and their like, are calling themselves *burgesses* nowadays. Burgesses! Is that not a wondrous name? Perhaps not, you might think, but it is a *new* one. They were not here a hundred years ago—burgesses did not *exist* at that time. Nor sixty, nor even fifty years ago. But now every town in the land has its burgesses, and they all build and own guildhalls and craft centres and fraternal lodges. They are all solid, upstanding, and prosperous citizens, too wealthy to be thought of, or treated, as peasants.

"These are men of *substance* now, Father James. An entire new breed, a new kind of man. And they conduct their daily affairs— commercial enterprises, they call them—in every land throughout Christendom and even beyond, dealing in every kind of commerce you could imagine. Ours deal mainly in wool, shipping hundreds of bales each year to places like Lubeck and Amsterdam that have none, in return for finished cloth. But some of them send glazed bricks to Brussels, and others ship metal and ores of tin and lead and iron to France and Burgundy, and bring back wines in payment. Most of them use the good offices of the Temple bankers to conduct their business, and they pay heavy taxes in return for the rights to maintain trading premises and safe quarters in their various ports of call.

"And as they grow and prosper, their voices are being raised in the affairs of all the burghs throughout this land. They are demanding and receiving more and more say in how their towns are governed and maintained, and from year to year, as their good influence continues to expand, our burghs are being governed by their own burgh councils."

He stopped, clearly waiting for me to respond, and when I failed to do so he succeeded in achieving the improbable, frowning and smiling at the same time. "You cannot see it."

I was floundering in my failure to grasp his meaning, and I saw him shrug.

"Well," he said quietly, sounding vaguely disappointed, "that is hardly surprising, I suppose. You are the first person with whom I have tried to talk about this, and I know I looked at it for years myself without seeing it for what it is."

He coughed, clearing his throat, then began again.

"Now listen closely to me, Father James, for I am about to open a new window and show you a world you have never thought of and could never imagine. Are you listening?" I nodded. "This world of ours is changing, as I have said. It is changing visibly, from day to day. We are witnessing an upheaval that will rival the fall of Rome. Believe me when I tell you that the burgesses of our towns—and of all the other towns throughout Christendom—will change the very world as we know it."

I confess I was half afraid that my mentor was losing his mind.

"The system cannot coexist with these new burgesses, Father James, and it cannot survive without them. And therefore it must perish. Not today, and probably not within our lifetimes, but the system will perish. Of that I have no doubt."

"What system, my lord Bishop?" I asked. I felt like a fool.

"The system that governs the world, my son. The system within which we live and work, the one by which we have survived these hundreds of years. There is always a system governing men's existence. The Church is one; the pagan Roman Empire was another. We have no proper name for the one that governs us now, other than the system of fealty, in which society is bound by the laws of lord and liegeman, duty and allegiance, and honour is defined by loyalty and common service. But these burgesses are a new phenomenon and they exist outside the commonality. They are beholden to no one but themselves for their success, which means they owe fealty and allegiance to no one but themselves. They *have* no sworn lieges to whom they are committed, for their entire commitment is to their own commerce. They cannot be levied to fight for any lord and master, for they are their own men, and therein lies their threat. Think upon that, Father, if you will: *they are their own men*. That is a concept that has not been heard of since the days of Republican Rome. These are men without allegiance! Imagine, if you can, what that means."

I was aware that somewhere outside, among the trees surrounding the cathedral grounds, the thrush had begun to sing again in a soaring crescendo of magnificent sound, but though I heard it, it was as if through a thick fog. I shifted in discomfort.

"It seems to me, my lord, that should what you are suggesting become known, these burgesses would all be wiped from the face of the earth, for the nobles could not live with such knowledge. They could not afford to countenance the possibility of people living within their lands who pay them no allegiance."

"Ah, but you are wrong, Father James. The nobles cannot simply wipe the burgesses out, for they are already too dependent upon them. These burgesses all pay taxes on the profits of their enterprises. They pay them, albeit indirectly, to the nobles, and those taxes amount to vast sums of money. The nobles, on the other hand, produce nothing. They merely own the land on which others live and work. That is news to no one.

"But now, with the emergence of these burgesses, there are different elements in play, and they refuse to fit within the system's status quo. The towns themselves, the burghs of Scotland—Glasgow and Edinburgh, Perth and Berwick, Aberdeen and St. Andrews and even Paisley—have grown too big and much too prosperous to be controlled by any single man, no matter how powerful a lord he may be in name. They are owned now by their burgesses and citizens—part of the realm still, but no longer part of the old system. No nobleman, be he earl or baron, chief or mere laird, can dictate anything but his displeasure to the citizens of Scotland's burghs today. The burgesses have outgrown—not yet thrown off, but definitely outgrown—the power of the nobles."

"What does that mean?" I asked eventually. "The King and his Council of Guardians yet govern the realm."

"What it means, Father James, is that sooner or later—and I mean not tomorrow or even a decade or a century from now, but inevitably—the common folk of this land of ours will wrest control of it from the nobility who own it now in its entirety."

I tried to grasp that thought, but it was too large and too tenuous for me to grapple with at that moment. I did make the leap, though, from what the Bishop had just finished saying to what he had said at the start.

"You believe Will Wallace will be a part of this great change you foresee. That's why you want me to find him for you."

"Hmm." The old fox hesitated, then shook his head. "No. Your cousin will have a part to play in what transpires, I have no doubt of that, but he will be part of the *process* of change, not necessarily a part of the change itself. No, Father, I want you to find him because I have gained information that I must pass on to him, vitally important information concerning the welfare of this realm, and you are the sole means I have of delivering it to him without anyone else being aware of it."

Then why all the obscure digression? I thought. "Information. I see. Shall I write it down, Your Grace?"

"No. No, it is too … sensitive, too delicate and dangerous to put into writing, I suspect, and a letter can be stolen and traced. This information is but newly arrived and I must think it through. And I intend to think it through with you as my witness and sounding board, Father, so that, familiar with it and all its implications, you might then go on alone to meet with your cousin, carrying the information in your head. Would you agree to that?"

"Of course, my lord."

"Good. Excellent. Listen, then. I received this word last night, roused from my sleep in the dead of night, the middle watches before matins. It was brought by a wandering priest whom I have known for years and trust completely. He had divined its import and brought it directly to me with all the speed he could achieve on foot. He was in Norham Castle one night nigh on two weeks ago and overheard a conversation that should never have occurred. He had arrived there late, after curfew, and unable to enter the castle proper, he had curled up in a gatehouse to sleep for a few hours out of the wind.

"Edward Plantagenet was in residence there that night, as was Bek of Durham, and they chose to walk together out of doors in the dead of the night, presumably to discuss matters of grave import without the danger of being overheard. Fortunately for us, that was not how things transpired, for they ended up walking a great distance from safety, outside the castle walls, only to have their discussion within a few paces of my visitor, who froze in place, fearing for his life.

"He told me that their entire conversation was about Scots bandits and their thieving activities in the Selkirk area—your cousin Will and his people. The stories that we hear of them up here in Glasgow are simple stories told by simple folk who enjoy having someone champion them even from afar, moral tales of wicked English trespassers brought to grief by intrepid Scots avengers. The reality, though, according to what my informant overheard, is far more potent. These Greens—and that is what the English King himself called them—are causing Edward much grief with their raids and depredations, far more so than any of us might have imagined. But it is Edward's inability either to capture them or bring them to battle that is goading him to madness. He is faced with mutiny among his troops."

He cut me off with a wave of his hand before I could even begin to react.

"I know there is nothing new in that rumour. That is precisely the point I wish you to make to your cousin, so listen closely. We have been hearing for years that Edward is having troubles among his own people in England, that his barons are on the point of rebelling against his incessant demands for more and more funds and fighting men for his campaigns in Aquitaine and Normandy and Gascony. That is a given of Edward's life in governing his realm, and until now he has been able to cope with it and look after his affairs here in Scotland.

"But this ... this situation here and now is different. This is in Scotland, and it is *not* a rebellion against unjust or overweening demands. This is a rebellion over money—gold, silver, and copper coins. The English soldiers in Scotland have not been paid in months, because three consecutive baggage convoys, northward bound from England and laden with payrolls and paymasters, have been intercepted by the Greens, their goods stolen and their armed escorts slaughtered. Each one in turn, according to English sources, was hit in overwhelming strength by outlaw forces from the forest as they passed. But now it appears that each of the last two convoys was accompanied by a military escort twice as strong as the force accompanying its predecessor, and still they were overwhelmed. Edward's intelligence estimates an enemy force numbering upwards of five hundred in the last attack."

"Five hundred …"

"Aye, that's what I am told. So now the English are considering bringing their payrolls in by ship, establishing a military treasury in Leith or Edinburgh itself, and off-loading their paymasters' cargo there. But setting up an English treasury on Scottish soil will take time to arrange, and it will involve a deal of negotiating with King John and the Guardians. It will not happen overnight."

"No, I see no way that it could. So what will Edward do in the meantime? From what you have said, he will need to do something to change the situation as it stands."

"He intends to. That was the purpose of such a secretive meeting between him and Bek. He will attempt to achieve by subterfuge what he cannot achieve by force."

He hesitated but a moment, then launched into the details of the English plan.

The following morning, before dawn, I left Glasgow and headed south and east, towards Selkirk and its great forest.

CHAPTER TWELVE

I

I stretched my leg slowly and cautiously, I thought, to relieve a mild cramp in my calf, but the movement was sufficiently visible to startle the small herd of deer in the clearing in front of me. Barely a heartbeat after I had stirred, the entire herd was bounding away to vanish into the thick undergrowth that edged the glade. I cursed myself in silence and glanced guiltily at Shoomy, who lay beside me, but he did no more than purse his lips and frown gently, moving his head almost imperceptibly from side to side and spreading the fingers of his hand in a warning to be still. I lowered my head to the grass again, closing my eyes and straining to hear beyond my own heartbeat as I waited.

We had been in place for four hours by then, having arrived in the dead of night when there was little chance of being detected, and daylight had crept up around us as we sat or lay there, snugly wrapped in waxed woollen blankets, within the dense fringe of bushes that edged the glade, so that from the blackness of pre-dawn we had emerged almost imperceptibly into one of those unpredictable, seemingly magical mornings that sometimes come along without warning. In all that time together in the night-chilled darkness, save for the muted responses to the Mass I celebrated by torchlight when we first arrived, we had barely spoken, not because of any fear of making noise, but simply out of the human need to think without sharing what we were thinking.

Now, however, our stillness had a purpose. Shoomy had chosen this spot with care, deeming it most likely to yield rewards, and now we were waiting for someone to appear, and the need for silent immobility was absolute.

I was unsure what the first sound I heard actually was. It was too distant and indistinct to identify, but mere moments later it came again, and this time I recognized it as the fluttering sound of air being snorted through a horse's nostrils. I knew the others must have heard it, too, and I forced myself not to move. A long time passed, it seemed, before the next sound came, and then it was the heavy, muffled thump of a stamped hoof on soft ground, and it was accompanied by a whispered shushing as the animal's rider sought to keep it calm. Another long silence followed that, with none of us daring to breathe, lest the sound be too loud, but eventually there came another sound of movement, accompanied by the unmistakable creak of leather saddlery. The screen of leaves near where I lay shivered, then parted infinitely slowly, pushed aside by an extended hand, to reveal a man leaning far forward over the neck of a horse, his chin almost against its mane and his eyes peering between the beast's twitching ears.

Nothing moved as the scout examined everything he could see ahead of him and on each side. He wore a conical steel helmet, which forced him to keep his head tilted severely back, and he was highly alert and vigilant, his very life dependent upon both. He examined everything minutely, meticulous and unhurried in his inspection, so that long before his questing eyes turned in my direction I had pulled myself down into the smallest possible bulk, hugging the ground as I sought to keep my head and the curve of my back beneath the gentle ridge that separated me from his line of sight. I waited to be discovered, but nothing happened, and then I heard him move again, the soft fall of hooves as he walked his horse quietly away. I heard no sound of sweeping branches, though, and so I raised my head again as slowly as I could and looked for him. He had vanished, evidently circling the clearing behind the screen of leaves that marked its edges.

I caught sight of him again moments later, emerging as before from the screening bushes, too far away now to see me easily even had he been looking in my direction. This time, however, he came through the screen, peering carefully about him as he rode into the green-shaded glade. His shield was slung diagonally across his back, and he held the reins easily in his left hand, his right grasping the hilt of a long-bladed sword in a grip that allowed the bare blade to lie along his thigh and rest gently against his knee, featherlight and unobtrusive, yet ready for instant action at the first flicker of movement.

Clear of the bushes, he drew rein for a moment at the very edge of the clearing, his eyes sweeping the open, seemingly innocuous space on both sides of him. Then he nudged his mount on again, leaning forward in the saddle as before and seeming to shrink even lower as he passed beneath the low-hanging branches of the huge elm that dominated the glade. He was in no danger from the over-hanging boughs, for the lowest of them cleared his head by almost two feet, but his reaction was an instinctive avoidance of a sensed, potential threat. I remember thinking, though, that it clearly had not occurred to him that he might be attacked from above, for he did not once look up, and in consequence the man who leapt down on him caught him completely unprepared and drove him crashing to the ground and into unconsciousness. The only sound we watchers heard was the abrupt, wrenching thud of two bodies colliding and then hitting the earth concussively before the startled horse could even snort in fright.

The attacker rolled and rose quickly to his feet, and I saw that it was Alan Crawford, now one of Will's senior lieutenants. He spun back to the unhorsed man, crouching over him quickly with a bared dagger in his upraised fist. But a moment later he straightened up and sheathed the weapon, then summoned the others to come forward, giving orders to some to secure the prisoner and to others to fan out into the forest from which the rider had come. Now, as two of his men gagged the fallen man and bound him at wrists and ankles, Alan crossed to where I crouched beside Mirren and two other women.

"Right," he said quietly. "This should have been the point man on our side. The others, four of them, will be behind him, spread out on either flank. They may not have met our people yet, but when they do, if anything goes wrong, we'll hear about it quickly enough. Keep your ears open for noises on both sides of the road. We'll give them another quarter of an hour to reach us, and if they don't appear, we'll know they've been dealt with. Then we'll head across the road and join Long John and the others."

The main north–south road lay to our right, little more than fifty paces away but hidden from us by the woods. The remaining scouts, we knew, would be riding on both sides of it, four now on this side, five on the other, searching for people like us, people who might pose a threat to the train they were escorting.

Our group, of which we were but one-fifth, faced south, commanding the eastern side of the roadway. Across the road, five more groups hunted the scouts on the western side, prepared to kill all of them if required. In the entire party of fifty dispatched to neutralize the ten scouts, only Mirren, her two women, and myself were unarmed, and we were there in the first place simply because it was the safest spot Will had been able to think of for this morning's work, far enough removed from what would happen where he was to ensure that Mirren would be in no danger. My task, ostensibly, was to guard her, but the mere idea of that was ludicrous, and I knew I was there only because Will had been seeking some means of protecting my priestly sensibilities against the kind of murder and mayhem that was likely to erupt in the confrontation that lay ahead.

I had arrived unannounced in his camp four days earlier, bearing strange tidings and urgent instructions from Bishop Wishart to which Will had listened initially in slack-jawed astonishment. That bemused wonder, though, had been supplanted within moments by the realities of the looming situation, and from then on everything had taken place at breakneck speed in Will's forest camp. Edward of England had moved decisively, far more quickly than even Wishart, with his privileged knowledge, had imagined. As always, by seizing the initiative, Edward had left no opportunity for anyone else—most particularly enemies like Will and his band—to do anything other than react to what he had already set in motion. I watched with awe in the hours that followed my delivery of Bishop Wishart's tidings as messengers were dispersed at speed to summon fighting men from all across the southeastern region of the country. Large numbers of other men soon began appearing, too, obviously summoned from close by, and I could see these were all commanders of varying rank. They wore no insignia, but there was no disguising the air of confident authority that hung about them. They were unmistakably leaders of men, set apart by their very bearing. These men vanished almost as soon as they arrived, into gatherings that were clearly planning sessions; and as those sessions progressed, more and more orders began to be issued, and activity throughout the encampment increased visibly.

I learned within the space of that first day that my cousin's following was far greater and his authority more far-reaching than I had ever imagined, and that made me aware, too, that my very presence there at such a time must be a distraction to him and might soon become a nuisance, and so I sought to efface myself by simply keeping out of his sight.

Out of sight, however, did not mean out of mind, and as word reached us the next day that Edward's messengers had already passed Berwick town, little more than thirty miles to the south of where we were, Will turned his attention to the safety of his wife, who was, he informed me, newly pregnant, and to me, his favourite, younger cousin. He knew me better than I knew myself, knew the strengths and weaknesses of my character and thus knew that the greatest of these, in both respects, was my immense regard for the sanctity of the Church. He knew I would have great difficulty in accepting what was now afoot, and so he guarded me from it by entrusting me with the care and safety of his wife and his future family, forcing me to take them away and out of danger.

Thinking of that, I found myself smirking at the irony of what had happened just moments earlier. Had we not fled Will's camp, we would have been nowhere near the enemy scout who had come so close to us with his long, bare blade. But the thought was overwhelmed by a sudden commotion in the trees at my back. I heard a muffled grunt, an explosive breath, and then the lethal clang of steel on steel, followed by a scream that was cut off in mid utterance. Then came the plunging, stamping sounds of a heavy horse forcing its way through thick growth, and the bushes split apart, yielding to the advance of a heavily mailed and helmeted rider on an enormous destrier, the largest animal I had ever seen. My first, fleeting impressions were of an upraised visor and a red-bearded face with bright, glowering eyes. Then I saw a broad-bladed sword sweeping down, its bright steel fouled with blood, and as it fell it seemed as though someone leapt to meet it, springing effortlessly up towards the blade to counter its thrust. Blade and body met and seemed to melt together, motionless for a flicker of time, and then in a leaping spray of blood the sword continued its downward slash, taking the body with it and casting it aside, severed and broken.

The rider now stood up in his stirrups, ignoring his victim and looking about him. He slammed his visor closed with the cross-guard of his sword and pulled his horse up into a rearing dance before launching it forward, and I found myself face to face with a charging knight at a distance of less than forty paces. He was enormous, as was the armoured creature beneath him, and the high crest on his visored helm made him look even larger. The crest was a rampant green lion, and the rider's shield and surcoat were pale blue with the green lion, jarringly familiar, blazoned across the front of both. I knew this knight, had seen him somewhere before, perhaps even met him, but that faded to insignificance as he set spurs to his mount with a savage, rowelling kick and came thundering towards me and the three women huddled beside me. It never crossed my mind that he had seen us. I knew that with his head encased in his massive steel helm, his vision was severely restricted. He could see solely what was directly ahead of him, and that imperfectly, his sight constrained by the slits in his visor, and this close to me and my three charges, thundering directly towards us, he was no more than a blind and lethal juggernaut. His enormous warhorse, though, trained to kick down and kill any assailants in its path, was Death incarnate.

I started to crouch down, to cry to the women to get out of the creature's way, but even as I did so I hesitated, appalled by the lumbering spectacle of the beast's approach, and so I merely crouched there, wide-eyed with terror and unable to move, watching death come towards us.

But then an arrow struck squarely in the centre of the knight's breastplate with a clean, violently metallic clang.

Bodkin, I thought. The bodkin was a war arrow with a solid, cylindrical head that tapered to a point, and it was designed to pierce plate armour. That they seldom did nowadays was due, I knew, to their being deflected more often than not by the newer, harder steel being forged by smiths today. Sure enough, in less time than it took for its impact to register in my awareness, the missile had vanished, spinning off into the distance. Nonetheless, the mounted man felt the full brunt of the impact and reeled in his saddle, almost unhorsed by the savage weight of the strike. He threw both arms up, fighting against the thrust of the missile's impetus, and his shield went whirling away, end over end, ripped from his grasp. His horse, too, went down on its haunches, driven backward by its rider's rapidly shifting weight. The horse quickly regained its balance and heaved itself back up onto all fours with a triumphant scream, and precisely at the moment when it looked as though the knight had won and would wrest back control of his animal, a second arrow struck, entering one of the slits in the rider's visor and piercing his skull, killing him instantly and hurling him out of the saddle.

I stood stunned, weaving in shock. Someone grasped me by the shoulder and pressed me down towards the ground, and I sank gratefully to sit beside the women, my legs shaking. The man standing above me, his hand still on my shoulder, was an archer called Jinkin' Geordie, so named because of an affliction that rendered him incapable of remaining still for any length of time without twitching. Even as I looked up at him, he twitched nervously. But it was plainly true, as I had heard before, that his affliction failed to affect his prowess in a fight.

"Was that you?" I asked him, a little breathlessly.

"Was what me?"

"The knight … Did you shoot him?"

"Aye. Can I ask ye somethin'?"

I was staring at the fallen knight, and I assumed that the fellow wanted to ask me something about him. "Of course," I said, asking myself already what I could possibly know about the slain man. "Ask."

He fixed me with an intense, furtive look. "I've been hearin' folk talk, about what we're to do. Sounds to me as though we'll be killin' priests afore this day's oot, and I don't know if I like that."

I felt my jaw fall in shock. "Killing *priests*? In God's holy name, Geordie, how can you even think such a thing? Of course we won't be killing priests. The very thought is an abomination."

The archer jinked—there really was no other word to describe it—his chin twitching down towards his right shoulder, which jerked forward to meet it as though in sympathy. "Aye, maybe so, right or no'," he added. "But that's what folk are sayin'. We're goin' to be killin' priests this very day. I ken they're there, too, the priests. I saw them mysel', last night, frae up on the cliffs, aboon their camp. There was half a hunnerd o' them." He nodded emphatically. "Aye, easy," he added. "Frae a' the noise they were makin', a' the singin' an' chantin', easy half a hunnerd."

I forced myself to smile at him with a serenity I suddenly did not feel, and highly aware that others, including Mirren and her two women, were listening to our exchange.

"No, Geordie," I told him, waving a hand dismissively and trying hard to keep my voice sounding relaxed and confident. "There's nowhere near as many. There might be half a hundred men in that whole train, give or take a handful, but few of them are priests. We counted them last night, from the top of the same cliff. There are twenty-eight clerics in all. Two of them are bishops, six are priests, and the remaining score are Cistercian monks. And on top of that, there are these ten scouts, five on each side of the road, and this knight who was in charge of them, and perhaps half or three-quarters of a score of servants."

He cocked his head like a bird, one eye glittering as it caught the light and adding subtly to the birdlike resemblance. "Cistercian monks, ye say?" His voice took on a conspiratorial tone. "Are they no' French, tha'e Cistercians? Aye, they are …What are French monks doin' ower here?"

This Geordie was a curious soul, and simple, and I glanced down at Mirren, who was looking back up at me. She rolled her eyes as though to let me know I would receive no help from her.

"Geordie, I can't tell you that. You know more about them than I do, so shush you now and let me go. I have to see to the knight there."

I was less than ten paces distant from the fallen rider, and no one moved to join me as I walked over and stood looking down at him. I suppose there must have been some thought in my head of baring his face and identifying the man, for I was still convinced I had seen him somewhere before, but long before I reached him I knew I would do no such thing. He was unmistakably dead, reeking with the stench of voided bowels, and his face would remain unseen. The arrow that had killed him, travelling with incomprehensible speed and force, had hammered diagonally up through the front of his war helm and lodged inside, twisting the visor violently out of true and jamming it shut, and blood and grey matter from the shattered skull within had filled the helm and now oozed, thick and obscene, through the openings in the metal.

My stomach lurched and I snatched my gaze away, trying to empty my mind and resisting the urge to vomit, and as I did so my eyes fell on the man the knight had killed. The difference was startling, and somehow pitiful. The knight appeared largely unbloodied. The man he had killed, though, had been unarmoured, and the knight's broad-bladed sword had split him wide open, carving him like a slaughtered deer and sending his lifeblood flying in all directions to stain the grass and the bushes for yards around the spot where he had fallen. I crossed to where he lay, holding the skirts of my robe high to avoid staining them with his blood, then bent forward slightly so I could see his face. He was a stranger to me, heavily bearded and poorly dressed in a tunic-like garment of rough homespun wool, and I could see no weapon anywhere near him. I wondered what had possessed him to attack a heavily armed and armoured mounted knight, alone as he was, on foot and unarmed, for I remembered seeing him springing high towards the falling sword.

I found myself suddenly seething with outrage. Will had sent me away from the coming day's activities, with the women, in order to protect my feelings, because he knew I was uncomfortable with anything that smacked of defiance of Holy Mother Church. Now, though, with this single instance of mindless violence and unnecessary slaughter, a new understanding of what was happening everywhere in my country crashed down upon me. I saw that what I had been objecting to—what Will had tried to protect me from—was nothing less than an atrocity, an atrocity carried out against my fellow countrymen by a cynical foreign king using the Church's name and privilege to abet a damnable war of aggression.

Bishops and senior clerics, indeed all clerics, by general consent, had no need to fear travelling alone, for no one in his right mind would ever dream of robbing a priest. But the two English Bishops whose presence here today had demanded our attention were engaged in activities that set them apart from their peers, and priestly innocence played no role in what they were about. They had a screen of killers thrown out ahead of them, purely to ensure that no profane eyes would gaze upon whatever it was that they were transporting. And I had been puling and fretting like a callow, unformed boy because I was afraid that Will was doing something that might draw down the displeasure of the Church upon my head. I stood there for some time, feeling my flesh crawl with the sickness of self-loathing and thinking about what that voluntary and wilful blindness said about me, and then I swung around and strode back to where Mirren, alone, stood watching me.

"What happened to you?" she asked as I reached her. "Did you know that man?"

"No. Scales from my eyes," I answered, not caring whether she understood me or not.

"Aye? So where are you goin' now? It's plain to see you're goin' somewhere."

I looked at her, and then beyond her to where one of our party held the reins of her horse and my own. "I'm going back to Will. You'll be fine without me … Better off, in fact, for we both know how feckless I'd be in a fight."

Her eyes had narrowed and she looked at me now with a completely different expression than the slightly scornful one that she habitually reserved for me. "And what will you do when you find Will? He'll have no need of a priest under his feet, Jamie. D'ye not know that's why he sent you away in the first place?"

"Aye, I do. And I'll stay out of his way. But first I'll give him the absolution I've been withholding."

Her frown was quick. "Absolution for what?"

"For what he's about to do. It needs to be done and he's the one to do it, but it's taken me until now to see that. Now I need to give him my support and my blessing."

"D'ye think he needs those?"

"I don't care, Mirren, and I didn't say *he* needs anything. *I* need to give them to him, freely. I've been wrong. Stubborn and stupid and short-sighted." I pointed with my thumb to the blood-drenched corpse on the grass behind me. "I see it now, my eyes washed clean by the blood of the sacrificial lamb there."

"That sounds blasphemous," she said more quietly.

"What's happening in this land is blasphemous, and my Church has been perverted to make it possible. I've only now come to see that. So now I'm going to try to help change things."

She nodded, a single dip of her head. "Aye, well, ye'd better hurry, or it'll all be done when you get there. Away wi' ye, and tell my man he's in my mind and heart. Run now."

2

Less than half an hour later, I walked out of the woods into full daylight again, leading my horse, and allowed my gaze to slide across the scene in front of me, marvelling at the rich brightness of it. The uneven surface of the rocky escarpment beneath my feet was sparsely carpeted with short, springy, startlingly green grass and striped in places by slanted, inch-high ridges of silvery-white, flaky stone. The sky was blindingly blue and cloudless. The sun had been climbing it now for nigh on two hours, yet in the valley below, the fog was still thick and solid. Directly ahead of me, seemingly just a short leap down from where I stood, a thick, flat blanket of greyish white stretched away from me. It had appeared solid mere moments earlier, but as I looked at it now I could see the topmost, budding twigs of the trees beneath it showing through, the mist that had concealed them eddying gently and dissipating in the tiny breeze. Across from me, half a mile to the south, a twin bluff loomed straight up from the fog-shrouded trees at its feet. Beyond that, stretching away like a string of green and silver beads, other hilltops sparkled in the strengthening sunlight.

"Fog doesn't often stay this long," a voice said beside me, and I turned and nodded to Will, who had been standing with three of his people, gazing down into the carpet of mist when I arrived. "But the wind's coming up now, so it'll all be gone soon." He turned his head slightly to look me in the eye. "What brings you back here, and where's Mirren?"

"She's with Shoomy and the others. She's fine. They've cleared away the scouts along the road, so you don't need to worry about being taken from behind."

"That's good, but you didn't answer my other question. What brings you back here?"

"Conviction, but not in the way you're probably thinking. I'm here to tell you I'm sorry for the way I've been … stubborn and stiff-necked and arrogant."

"Arrogant?" The expression on my cousin's face was almost but not quite a smile, for there was uncertainty in his gaze, too. "Am I hearing aright? A priest, admitting to arrogance?"

I ignored the jibe and merely nodded. "An epiphany is what you're seeing. I've had a change of heart in the past hour. I watched a man die and I saw the pity and the sickness of it all. And with that, I came to see that I have been wrong. Ever since he first told me about this, about what was in his mind and what he intended to ask you to do, I've been angry and afraid of my own Bishop's motives and I've been questioning what I saw as his mutiny against the Church. But now I can see he's right—has been right all along. This trickery that's afoot is sinful, betraying the Church's trust for the benefit of a mere man, no matter that he be a king."

Will looked at me wryly. "So? What are you telling me?"

"That I am here to stand with you, as a representative of God's Holy Church, on behalf of men of goodwill everywhere."

Will stared at me for some time, his face unreadable, and then he turned away to look down into the valley at our feet. "And these men of goodwill, think you there are such creatures in England, Jamie, when the talk turns to Scotland?"

"Aye, Will. I do."

"Right," he said then, nodding. "Look, it's clearing quickly down there. Look at it blow!"

Sure enough, the remaining fog was vanishing even as we looked, whipped to tatters and blown into nothingness by a strong breeze we could not feel, and as it cleared we saw the activity below us where the group we were waiting for had made camp late the previous afternoon. This party of churchmen was making a leisurely progress of the journey northward, its members secure in their safety as clerics in the service of God. They had crossed the border at Berwick three days earlier, and we had received word of their arrival within hours. Since then, they had travelled less than twenty miles, beginning each day's journey after celebrating Mass and eating a substantial breakfast. Thereafter, at a pace set by the cows they had brought with them for their breakfast milk and matched by the horses pulling the upholstered wagon in which the Bishops rode, they had made their way steadily along the broad, beaten path that served as the high road into Scotland from England, eating their midday meal while on the move, and stopping at roadside camp-sites, selected by their scouts, long before the afternoon shadows began to stretch towards nightfall. Then, while the priests prepared for evening services, their servitors set up an elaborate camp with spacious leather tents and ample cooking fires, and the episcopal household staff busied themselves preparing the evening meal. The soldiers of the scouting party maintained a separate camp, a short way from the main one.

Now, in the open glades between copses, we could see the horse handlers leading two large, heavy wagons into place below us, in what would be the middle of their line of march. The two Bishops in their upholstered carriage would ride in front, and behind would come the two heavily laden supply wagons. Behind those, in turn, would come the priests and acolytes, walking with the Cistercian monks.

"They're fine," Will muttered. "Their Graces should be on their holy way any moment now. Did you recognize them?" I shook my head, and he looked back towards the group in the distance. "Aye, there they go. And now it's our turn. Let's get down there." He swung himself up onto his horse and kicked it into motion as I mounted my own and fell into place behind him, following him down a narrow, twisting goat path until we reached the road. The three men who had been talking with Will when I arrived struck out on foot, making their way down separately by a far steeper route.

It took us no more than a few minutes to reach the spot Will had chosen for what he intended to do that morning, but the path we had taken down from the escarpment was vastly different from the winding route the Bishops' train would follow through the valley bottom. It would be half an hour before they reached us, and in the meantime, Will had some final dispositions to see to.

The place we came to, the narrow end of the funnel-shaped valley we had been overlooking, had been burned out years earlier in a summer fire and was now a long, narrow clearing extending twenty to thirty paces along each side of the road for more than a hundred yards. It contained a rolling sea of waist-high grasses and a scattering of saplings, plus, on this particular morning, an army of at least a hundred men, all of them wearing hoods or masks and carrying bows of one kind or another. A large, recently felled tree, one of only a few to have escaped the fire of years before, lay by the roadside at the northern end of the exposed road, and broken branches and debris from its collapse littered the road. Beside it, drawn up close to a makeshift saw pit, a high-sided dray blocked the narrow roadway completely. It had been there since the previous day and was half-filled with sawn logs. The two draft horses that had brought it there were cropping idly at the rank grass by the roadside, some distance from the work area.

Will and I stood side by side in the bed of the cart, Will shrugging and twisting to settle a long, ragged cloak about his shoulders. It altered his appearance miraculously, because it had been made to do precisely that. Someone, working with great skill, had sewn a construct of woven willow twigs into the voluminous garment so that when it was properly in place, it turned its wearer into a grotesque hunchback. I watched him as he shifted and hauled for a few moments until he had the garment comfortably draped over his shoulders, and although I had seen him wearing it several times in the previous few days, I was amazed anew by how effective it was.

Ahead of us, emerging from the woods and running straight north towards where we waited, the road from England stretched like the shaft of a spear. Hardly anyone among the hundred standing in the grass moved at all, I noticed, and the air of tense expectancy was almost palpable. Eventually, though, a runner appeared at the far end of the path, waving to announce the imminent arrival of the quarry. Will gave a last signal, and everyone except him and me sank into the waist-high grass and disappeared from view.

He and I moved to the driver's bench then and sat down, lounging comfortably and facing west, our backs towards the steep, rocky face of the escarpment we had just left. We made ourselves comfortable and I opened a cloth-wrapped bundle of bread and hard cheese, which we began to eat as though we had earned it, and there we remained as the first of the Bishops' wagons, carrying the two prelates themselves, emerged from the forest and began to approach us.

As it drew closer and its accompanying party continued to spill out from the forest behind it, Will pretended to hear them coming and sat up straight, turning and leaning towards them. I followed his lead, both of us striving to look like dullards, uncomprehending but reverent and slightly awestruck by the richness of the train coming towards us so unexpectedly.

The leading wagon creaked to a halt about ten paces from where we sat, and for a moment nothing happened. But then the driver raised his voice, addressing us in passable Scots, though with a heavy, broad-vowelled, English intonation.

"Well? Are you going to sit there all day and do nothing? Move your cart aside and let us through. Didn't the soldiers ahead of us tell you to clear the way?"

Beside me Will raised his eyebrows and his face became a portrait of innocent astonishment. "No," he answered. "They tell't me to move, right enough, and I said I wad, but they didna say onythin' about you comin' ahent them. Haud ye there, now, and I'll move." He stood up stiffly, muttering under his breath and bundling the remainder of our food clumsily into its cloth before setting it on the driver's bench between us, seeming to ignore me completely. "Stay here," he murmured so that only I heard him, and then he lowered himself over the cart's side and moved deliberately to collect the grazing horses and lead them back by their halters, mumbling all the time to himself in a voice that was barely audible. He took his time about lifting the heavy draft collars over the animals' heads before backing the team into place and starting to attach its harness. I watched in silence as the occupants of the other wagon fought to contain their impatience. There were three of them there, the one in the rear plainly a priest and the two in front even more evidently Bishops. None of them even deigned to glance in my direction.

The two Bishops were almost laughably dissimilar to each other in every respect. One of them was much younger than his companion, taller and with a red face and a big belly. His face-concealing beard yet failed to hide a pouting, petulant mouth. It was plain at a glance that this lord of the Church, whoever he was, had no intention of being mistaken for anything less. His robes were imperially striking, heavy and opulent with texture and bright colours, and the fingers of his big, meaty hands were festooned with heavily jewelled rings. I decided, without ever looking into his eyes or hearing him speak, that I disliked him intensely.

I disliked his companion even more, though, and I also assumed him to be the superior in rank, if for no other reason than the disparity in their ages. In the older man's eyes, naked and undisguised, was unmistakable contempt for anyone he considered beneath him, and it was clear he thought us far, far beneath him. This man wore black edged with crimson, and though the stuff of his vestments was probably no whit less costly than the younger man's, the cut of it combined with the severity of its blackness to suggest a cynical attempt to appear austere and perhaps even thrifty. He wore no rings, save for a single episcopal ruby, and the crimson-edged black velvet of his pileolus, or bishop's cap—a recent innovation from Rome, larger, heavier, and thicker than the traditional red silk skullcap, that had caused much discussion before being rejected by our community in Glasgow—marked him as a man who paid close attention to the drifting currents of theology and Church politics. Beneath the cap, his face was gaunt and devoid of humour. He never took his eyes off Will, from the moment he leapt down from the driver's bench until he had the team properly harnessed and had pulled himself up to sit beside me again.

"Good," he said quietly as he settled himself on the bench. "They're all here."

As indeed they were. In the time it had taken Will to harness the dray's team, the rear elements of the Bishops' train, the monks and servants, had had time to assemble around the wagons. Will stood up then and gathered the reins of our team in one hand while picking up the whip from its holder by his seat, preparing to drive us out of the way. But on the point of cracking the whip, he hesitated and turned towards the Bishops again.

"Ye'll be Bishops, then, I'm thinkin', by the dress o' ye. English Bishops?"

No one deigned to answer him, but he had not expected a response. He half turned and indicated me with his whip. "This is a Scots priest. A priest, mind ye, no' a monk. A *real* priest. Said Mass for us this mornin', before dawn. And we had nothin' to pay him wi' for his services. But we fed him. He disna' need much else. He's a priest. He kens God will look after him, ye ken?"

I had to stifle the urge to smile at Will's acting the dimwit. His mix of English and simple Scots should have been intelligible even to an Englishman, but both Bishops were staring at him blankly, the younger in astonishment, the elder in disgust. The priest in the back seat leaned forward and spoke to me in Latin, not even glancing at Will.

"Have your man move aside, Father. Their lordships here are not to be kept waiting by the likes of him or you. Quickly now."

The peremptory, intolerant snap of his voice released something inside me and permitted me to smile openly at the man, who was tall and clean shaven, balding yet broad shouldered and fit looking, with narrowed, pale blue eyes and a stern, humourless look about him.

"You are a Scot," I said courteously in the same tongue, permitting but a hint of my surprise to show through.

"Of course I am. What has that to do with anything? I am here to serve as translator for their lordships."

"In their dealings with the untutored savages, you mean."

"You are impertinent, Father."

"No, I am merely truthful … and powerless here, Father, as are you. In the first place, this man is not mine to command. He is very much his own keeper. And if their lordships are to be kept waiting at all, I doubt they could improve upon being kept by the likes of him. Look at him, Father. This man speaks for Scotland."

"You've been away from civilization for too long. Your wits are scattered!" The glance the priest threw at Will was withering. "A hunchback woodcutter, to speak for Scotland?"

"Aye," Will said in English, suddenly and clearly. "If need be, for it seems no one else will." Then, ignoring the slack-jawed expression of surprise that had sprung to the priest's face, he raised his voice to a shout, in the command his hundred had been waiting for among the grass. "Up, Greens!"

Within the space of two heartbeats the train on the road was surrounded by a ring of standing bowmen, and every monk, priest, and bishop in the gathering was the target of at least one levelled arrow. Will's men had risen up in utter silence from the chest-high grass, their weapons at the ready, and their appearance wrung a chorus of dismay from the clerics as the threat sank home. Without being ordered to, men everywhere in the throng began raising their hands in bewildered surrender. Will watched them until there was no one, monk, priest, or servant, who did not have his hands in the air, and then he said, still in English, "Everyone down from the wagons. Now."

As the Bishops' driver and his bench companion scrambled down and away, their passengers moved to follow them, but Will waved them back into their padded seats. "Not you three. You stay there for now." All movement had ceased on the other two wagons as people watched to see what would happen next, but Will merely waved a pointing finger. "The rest of you, off. Move!"

To his credit, the elder of the Bishops was the first to regain his composure. As his servants and retainers began clambering down from the wagons at his back, he stood up again quickly and stepped forward as far as he could in the confined space of the wagon. There he raised a peremptory hand, pointing at Will. "Take heed, Hunchback, lest you imperil your immortal soul! Would you dare molest and rob God's servants in the solemn execution of their duty?"

"Dare to molest and rob God's servants in the doing of their duty?" replied Will in Latin as clear and fluent. The Bishop's skeletal face registered sheer disbelief. "No, Bishop, I would not. But dare to rob thieving rogues and lying scoundrels who usurp God's good name and privilege unlawfully in the name of England's King within the realm of Scotland? Aye, that I will, and with pleasure. Those I would molest and rob at any opportunity, and I thank you for this one."

"You blaspheme, woodsman!"

Will had not moved since this exchange began, holding the reins in his left hand while the other gripped the teamster's whip loosely, but now he raised the long whip and pointed its drooping end at the black-clad Bishop, and his voice took on a biting, steely edge.

"No, Churchman, I do not. *You* are the blasphemous party here, wearing the robes of sanctity and episcopal privilege while playing the serpent. Your very *presence* here is a lie that turns to blasphemy as you pursue it." He glanced down at his own men and indicated the black-clad prelate with a jerk of the head. "Watch him. Watch all of them. If any of them tries to speak again, pull him down and stifle him."

A number of his own men, several of them his lieutenants, had already approached the Bishops' wagon, and now some raised their bows at full extension towards the trio in the cart while others lowered theirs to rest their arms. As they did so, Will shook out the reins and cracked his whip expertly between the heads of his team. The animals leaned forward instantly into their harness and Will handled them surely, bringing them around easily until the two vehicles were wheel to wheel, though facing in opposite directions. The younger Bishop opened his mouth to speak, but Will cut him off.

"Did you not hear what I ordered done to you if you dare to speak? I meant it. Shut your mouth, Englishman, and keep it shut."

The man froze, his mouth gaping, and he made no other attempt to speak, though his face writhed with fury and loathing. Will's eyes moved to the Scots priest on the rear bench.

"You," he said. "In God's name, man, what are you doing? Have you no honour, no self-worth? How can you lend yourself to such a travesty as this and yet call yourself a Scot, let alone a priest?" He tilted his head sharply to one side as he saw something in the man's eyes, something I had not seen because I had been watching Will.

The other man's answer was swift and forceful. "I do not know what you are talking about, fellow, but I have done nothing other than my duty. I was dispatched by my superior, Bishop Henry of Galloway, to meet their lordships when they arrived in Berwick, my function to assist them in their dealings with whomever they might meet upon the road from there to Whithorn. You are the first person we have met since then, and it shames me to be named a fellow Scot with such as you." He looked around him at the faces of the crowd staring up at him. "It's evident that you are thieves and outlaws—the Greens of whom I have heard spoken. But most of you are masked and unrecognizable, and to this point you have done nothing irremediable. You are misguided, and I regret having witnessed your folly, but you might yet escape from this error without blood being shed." He looked back at Will. "Let me ask you once again to stand aside and permit us to pass unmolested."

I could see Will nibbling at his inner cheek, an indication that he was thinking rapidly, and when he spoke again his tone was less accusatory.

"You're no craven, Priest, I'll grant you that. But do you truly not know what's afoot here? Is that possible?" He watched the Scots priest, and then nodded. "Aye, it would appear it is. Well, listen closely, Father. What's your name? Father what?"

It looked for a moment as though the priest would refuse to answer, but then he shrugged slightly. "Constantine."

"Constantine … A distinguished and imperious name. Listen then, Father Constantine, and do not interrupt me until you have heard everything I have to say. You will know when you have, because I will inform you. Do you understand me?"

The priest inclined his head and Will returned the gesture.

"Good. Scotland is teeming with English soldiery. You were aware o' that, of course. They swarm like fleas on a hedgehog and they are causing us Scots much grief. They should not be here at all, no matter how the English try to justify their presence, for we have a King of our own again, King John of Scotland, of whom you must have heard, since he is from your own diocese of Galloway, as was his mother, Devorguilla. Well, see you, the fact that John now rules in Scotland means that Edward of England has no lawful place here, save as an invited guest bound by, and beholden to, the laws of hospitality. Yet Edward maintains an army on our soil and in defiance of our country's ancient laws."

Will paused, gazing directly into the priest's eyes before continuing. "Edward is facing mutiny today, though, because his merce-
nary dogs have not been paid. Three times now his quartermasters
have attempted to bring English money into Scotland to pay their
troops, and three times have those quartermasters' trains been intercepted and—*taxed*—their contents confiscated. I know that to be
true, Father Constantine, because it was we who took the money,
levying the taxes against Scotland's future needs.

"In so doing, we sought to teach the English King a lesson: that
this land is ours, an ancient realm secure in its own legal right and
beyond his grasp. His armies are unwelcome here and we will not
allow him to maintain them here unlawfully. He seeks to make our
Scottish laws conform to his own wishes, but no man, not even the
divinely anointed and legally enthroned King of Scots, can do that.
And so we have thrice denied Edward permission to pay his troops
within this realm by denying him the means with which to do it,
knowing that if the troops remain unpaid, they will return to
England, one way or another, in search of payment. And that is our
intent: to send Edward's army back to plague him rather than us."

Every man in the surrounding throng was rapt, caught up in
Will's explanation as the Latin speakers among them translated what
he had said. Even the English prisoners appeared interested in what
he was saying. He looked about him slowly now, aware of the hush
awaiting his next words.

"That has been the truth in recent months, and for a while now
we have been awaiting Edward's next response. And here, this day,
we have it. A new ruse being attempted. A scheme involving trickery
and treachery, in which you are involved. A devious and under-
handed ploy that will have far-reaching implications for everyone
because it betrays an understanding that has governed this world of
ours since first the Word of Christ came to these shores."

Another pause stretched out as he moved his gaze from face to
face among his listeners. "It has always been the truth that
churchmen, being humble servants of the Christ, may travel unmolested throughout all the lands of Britain and elsewhere. None but

the most depraved of madmen would ever stoop to rob a priest, because in doing so he would be seen as robbing and insulting God Himself. But there is honour and responsibility involved in that covenant, my friends, on *both* sides. In return for that freedom of movement and the lack of fear in which they travel, all churchmen bear a sacred trust of honesty in their travels and endeavours. They may transport the Church's goods without molestation, so be it they are engaged upon the Church's affairs and in the sole interest of the Church itself."

Will turned back to the priest. "Tell me, Father Constantine, what do you think is in those chests in the wagon at your back?"

The priest frowned. "You mean the kitchen supplies and provisions?"

"No, Father, not those. The others. The locked chests."

A terse headshake from the priest. "I do not know what you mean."

Will pointed to two small groups of his men who stood listening beside the wagons. "You and you. Find them."

Several men hoisted themselves into each of the two draft wagons, and for a time there was much pushing and shoving as cargo was uncovered and dragged aside. The shout of discovery came from the second wagon, directly behind the Bishops' own, and a moment later one of the men straightened up.

"They're all in this one!" he shouted.

Will nodded. "How many?"

"Eight o' them. Wee ones, but they're ..." The fellow stooped again and there came a series of grunts and scraping noises. "Heavy whoresons ... all padlocked."

"Break one open. Any one of them."

"No! In God's holy name, I—"

It was the older Bishop who shouted, and before he could say more than the Lord's name, Will had dropped the reins and whip and leapt into the other wagon. He seized the Bishop in one hand by the front of his robe, pulled him up onto his toes, and then slapped him hard, sending the man's pileolus flying. While every one of the watching clerics gasped in horror, he hauled the grimacing cleric up to within inches of his own face and snarled, "And now I have laid violent hands on one of God's anointed. Well, we will test the truth of that in time to come, Bishop Weasel. In the interim, though, I have too much to do and lack the time to waste on you. Catch him," he growled and threw the cleric like a child's straw doll down into the waiting arms of his men. They caught him with a shout, and before it had died away Will had turned to the other prelate, who flinched and scrambled over the side of the wagon, almost falling to the ground in his hurry to escape. Will raised his arms, pointing and shouting orders in Scots.

"Line them all up over there. Keep them close and watch them, but don't abuse them. These two here—the fat one and the black crow—I want them on their knees and bare headed. Bare arsed, too, if they give ye any trouble. I'll come back to them." He looked over to the wagon with the chests. "Sully, have you got it open yet?"

His answer was a loud, splintering blow. "Aye, it's open now. Sweet Jesu!"

Will pointed at Father Constantine. "You. Come with me. Here, take my hand." He took the priest's proffered hand and steadied him across the gap between the Bishops' wagon and our own, and when he was sure he had him safely across, he took the reins again and moved our vehicle to flank the next one in line.

He did not even have to speak, for the sight in the other wagon needed no words to explain it. Sully's crew had smashed the lid of the small iron-bound chest that lay in the wagon bed in front of others exactly like it, and in doing so had scattered some of the densely packed coinage that the chest contained, so that large silver coins and smaller golden ones were strewn across the planking, gleaming and glittering in the sunlight that had now penetrated the clearing.

The startled priest began to speak, but he immediately bit down on his outburst, the muscles along his jaw standing out clearly. He turned his head to look at the two Bishops, his expression unread-able. The two Englishmen kneeling side by side in the road glared back at him, wild eyed, but neither one of them dared breathe a word. And finally he turned to me.

"Clearly there are grounds for suspicion here. As to whether what your companion alleges is true, I cannot say with certainty."

"Then ask yourself why we are here, Father, and how we knew these chests would be here." Will's voice was a growl. "And weigh your own response against this one: I learned four days ago that this train would be coming from the south, and I was told what it would be carrying. I was also told how the plan to send it came about. My informant was a prelate of the Church in Scotland, warned by an associate in England who saw the perfidy in what was being done. Not all English bishops, it seems, are as duplicitous as these two. Some understand the difference between right and wrong and between honour and infamy."

Father Constantine nodded slowly. "It may be as you say, and truth to tell, it looks that way. The fact remains, though, that I knew nothing of this, nor, I am sure, did Bishop Henry."

He looked at Will again, before addressing the two English Bishops in a voice filled with genuine concern.

"My lords," he began, "I may not help you here, for this is clearly beyond the scope of my duties to you, even did it not bring my personal honour and my loyalty to my King and realm into question. It does all of those things, though, and I intend to throw myself upon the mercy of King John, even though I know that, in allowing myself to be duped, I have been guilty in my failure to see what was going on beneath my nose. As for you and your case, I would recommend clemency in almost any other circumstances—penance and absolution—but I see no contrition in either one of you, and penance without contrition is pointless. It pains me to say that, my lords, but there is nothing I may do to change it. And so I must wash my hands of you." He turned away from them and looked Will straight in the eye. "I am now in your hands, Master Woodsman."

"Hmm. My hands are full, I fear, but I will think on that. In the meantime, come you and sit here, by our good Father James."

As the priest began to make his way to join me, Will looked down at the two Bishops, who, as he had ordered, had been stripped of their outer garments. The larger man was kneeling dejectedly, staring down at his own knees, but the smaller, older man knelt upright, his head cocked as though he was listening for something.

"Now," Will said, his voice addressed to no one in particular, "to business, for that is what this is, and let no man mistake it for anything else. We are dealing here with a sordid matter of trade and monies that has nothing to do with churchly offices or duties, save in the deliberate abuse of both." He turned to the older Bishop. "You there, the Crow. If you are waiting for your mounted escort to come charging from the woods and rescue you, you wait in vain. Young de Presmuir and his scouts lost interest in your cause hours ago. In fact they lost all interest in everything."

I saw the Bishop's eyes narrow with bitter disappointment, but my mind was full of the young knight's name, for my instinct had been correct. I had met the man. Henri de Presmuir, the knight of the Green Lion, had been a guest of Bishop Wishart on an evening soon after my arrival in Glasgow. He had been unarmoured, of course, but I recalled his livery of green on blue, and now I remembered that I had liked the young man, finding him amiable and pleasant to be with. Small wonder, then, that I had not recognized him in the murderous figure who had come charging at me through the misty trees that morning.

3

Try as I might I could see no smallest sign of shame or contrition in either of the two Bishops, who knelt on the ground glaring up at the enormous figure who loomed over them from the wagon's height. Will raised his eyes to look towards the group of monks clustered behind them.

"Who is your leader? Who speaks for you?"

"I do," someone answered in a deep, resonant voice, and a tall, lean man stepped forward. "My name is Richard of Helensburgh."

"Helensburgh? Another Scot?" The tall monk nodded, and Will continued. "These Englishmen are well supplied with Scots to help them in whate'er they are about. And you are Cistercians, are you not? What are you doing here, then, with such as these? Are you a part of this charade?"

The monk's face remained expressionless and dignified. "No, Master Woodsman, not at all. We belong to the community of the Abbey of the Holy Trinity, near Newcastle, and we have been travelling with their lordships since they passed through our Abbey lands, but we are not part of their expedition. We were commanded by our holy Father Abbot to travel with them for safety's sake, and we have been obedient to his orders. We have barely spoken with any of their group, keeping ourselves to ourselves. Our task is to reach Lanark town, where we are to reclaim and refurbish a priory of our order that burned down some years ago and has lain abandoned ever since. Many of us resided there at that time, and after the fire we were received by our brethren in the Abbey of the Trinity. We have been there ever since, awaiting the proper time to return to our priory."

"And that time is now?"

The monk dipped his head. "So says our Abbot Nicodemus, and we are bound to obey him in all things."

"Then you may go in peace to find and rebuild your priory, Brother Richard, but ere you do, I require of you, in the name of King John and the realm of Scotland, that you bear witness to what is happening here."

"As you wish," came the quiet reply, and Will turned back to the kneeling men.

"What are your names?"

Both men stared through him, defiantly.

Will turned to Father Constantine. "Father? Do you know their names?"

"Aye, I do. Both are named John, but only one is a bishop. The elder is John Romanus, a bishop of south England. The other one is Brother John, Prior of Whithorn in Galloway."

Will looked at the priest in surprise. "A Prior in *Galloway*? But he's an Englishman, is he not? I thought all you Galloway people were close-knit and jealous of your holdings."

Constantine shrugged. "We are, by nature … close-knit and close-mouthed. But the truth is that Edward's people gained the right to appoint English bishops and priors to Scots benefices five years ago. Pope Nicholas saw to that. As for me, I'm but a simple priest. I do my duty, celebrate Mass daily, tend for the people in my care, and keep my nose clear of politics. But the Diocese of Galloway, and with it the Priory of Whithorn, has been subservient to the Archdiocese of York for a hundred years and more. That's a fight that has been going on for years now, with the Scots Bishops wanting to keep England out and the English equally determined to rule Scotland's Church."

"That's right. Of *course!*" The suddenness of my interjection brought both men round to look at me in surprise. "John Romanus, you said? A bishop of southern England?"

"Aye." The priest was looking at me warily, as though expecting me to do something violent.

"What diocese would that be?"

"How would I know that? I never met the man until three days ago. The south of England was all he said when he named himself to me."

"And you did not think that strange?"

"Why should I think it strange? Does England not *have* a south?"

Will interrupted. "What's wrong, Jamie?"

I threw up my hands. "I cannot believe he does not know who this man is. We have a noble prisoner, it seems. The man is John le Romayne, Lord Archbishop of York. He holds primacy over the Diocese of Galloway and its Bishop, Henry, as well as over the Priory of Whithorn and his companion there, its prior. How could this man, a priest of Galloway, not know who he is?"

Constantine spun to face the English bishop, then turned angrily back to me. "I do not know him because I *am* a priest of Galloway! A priest, nothing more. I have never seen the man before. I know him by name and by repute, I know his status as primate of Galloway. But I had never set eyes on him until I joined his party at the border."

Will ignored both of us and turned slowly to the kneeling Bishop. "Is this true? You are Archbishop of York? Then what, in God's great and holy name, are you doing here?"

"I can answer that," I said. "For it's plain he isn't going to."

Romayne's head swivelled towards me, his expression baleful. I felt my stomach stir with anger, but my mind was racing as bits and pieces learned and overheard fell into place. I took a step forward and looked down on him from Will's side.

"The Archbishop is wealthy, as you might expect," I said. "And that is fortunate for him, because were it not for the depths of his own pockets he would be in prison now, locked up in London Tower."

I sensed rather than saw Will's frown. "What are you saying? In *prison*, an archbishop?"

"Aye, an archbishop who dared, less than a year ago, to excommunicate King Edward's most loyal friend and servant, Antony Bek, Bishop of Durham." I let the words hang there, knowing they would bring a gasp of disbelief from all who heard them. "Bishop Bek, it seems, committed an indiscretion: he permitted the civil arrest of two miscreant priests of his diocese in Durham. That was unprecedented, for only the Church may arrest and imprison a priest. No civil body has ever had the right to challenge that. And therefore the Archbishop, as was his right in canon law, deemed Bishop Bek's actions to be both detrimental and threatening to that law's validity. The King himself intervened in Bishop Bek's favour, though, and the case went before parliament for judgment."

"And parliament found in favour of the King," Will said.

"It did. It decided that Antony Bek, in calling for the arrests, had acted in his vice-regal capacity as earl palatine, not as Bishop of

Durham. Parliament called for the imprisonment of Archbishop le Romayne on charges of impiety and *lèse majesté* in challenging the King's earl palatine. As it transpired, though, in return for a princely fine of four thousand marks of silver from Master le Romayne's own purse, the prison term was set in abeyance and the Archbishop was returned to his duties, though not to royal favour."

The watching crowd began muttering as the translators caught up with what I had said. Men turned to each other with questions and comments, and the noise grew quickly until Will raised an arm to quell it.

"Enough!" he shouted in Scots, and the crowd fell silent. "Stand quiet now. There's mair here than meets the eye and it could be important. Haud your noise, then, till we find out what it a' means." He looked back at me and lowered his voice. "What does it mean?"

"It means that the Archbishop badly wants to be back in the King's high regard." I could *taste* the truth of what was in my mind. "He wants it badly enough to ignore all the rules of episcopal conduct and to prostitute himself and his sacred office in trade for the King's good graces. Few bishops would condone what he has done here, and none, I dare say, would stoop to it themselves. This foul man has suborned and betrayed the Church to win the mortal favours of a King, undoing the work of centuries with the betrayal of a sacred trust. Think about it, Will—about what's involved here. This … this betrayal represents an awful, unsuspected sin. A sin, perhaps, such as has never been before." I was speaking quietly, for Will's ears alone, but I knew that Father Constantine could hear what I was saying, and now Will glanced across at him.

"Do you agree, Father?"

The priest nodded immediately. "I do. Completely. This frightens me with its power to change things forever … to destroy the Church's trust. I am afraid to think on what might happen now."

"Don't be," Will said, "because it's already done. You cannot change it now." He turned back to the watching crowd and held up his hands, commanding and receiving instant silence.

"All of you," he said in Latin, looking from face to face and speaking slowly enough for the interpreters in the crowd to translate what he was saying. "Listen closely to me, because I am going to tell you what all this means—this treachery we have discovered. And make no mistake, any of you. It *is* treachery." He glanced around him, catching eyes here and there in the throng that faced him. "Father Constantine has just told me that he fears what has happened here may have the power to destroy men's trust in Holy Church, and I believe it will do just that, because much has changed today. And even if most of us seeing it cannot clearly understand it, it is there in plain view of anyone with the eyes to look.

"You wonder what I am talking about, what I mean. I see it in your faces. Well, I mean this: from this day forward, because of what we have discovered here today, no priest of any rank, anywhere in this realm or any other, can ever again claim the right to travel unquestioned. All may now be stopped and searched at any time, their goods and stores inspected in the search for contraband, for on this day this Arch*bishop* that you see in front of you has been taken in perfidy and has destroyed the faith all men have always had in priests and in their Church. He has destroyed the universal faith that all priests are trustworthy by their very rank, that they can be relied upon, without question, to put the welfare of each living soul above all else, and to value God's holy will and wishes for mankind ahead of all worldly considerations.

"The perpetrator of this sin, one of the highest ranking members of the Church in all England, stands exposed as a liar and a panderer, having betrayed his God, his Church, and his high office in return for the worldly status offered him by a petty king. By cynically smuggling England's gold into another realm under the auspices of Holy Church and for the sole purpose of paying and sustaining an invading army, this *priest* has chosen worldly profit over the loss of his own soul, using his position of trust and privilege to undermine a peaceful foreign realm and its people.

"This is politics, my friends, in the guise of holiness. Treachery and depravity under the appearance of dignity and solemnity.

Blatant hypocrisy unveiled as the writhing mass of maggots that it is." He looked directly down at Romayne then. "John le Romayne, Lord Archbishop of York, you have won yourself a place in the annals of infamy. Until the end of time you will be the man who destroyed the Catholic Church's probity. May God have mercy on your crawling deformities, though I doubt that Edward Plantagenet will once he learns that you have cost him yet another paymaster's train. For the present, hear my decree: in recognition of your treachery in thus attempting to smuggle Edward's gold into Scotland, we now impound not only Edward's money but yours, too. Those rich clothes of yours will keep cold bodies warm in winter, even though they serve as simple bedclothing, and the jewels that festoon your hands and bodies will buy food for starving folk." He nodded to one of his men. "Strip them of everything. We will send them naked into the world, as they arrived. It may serve to remind them what poverty and humility mean to most people."

He raised his eyes to address Brother Richard and his assembled monks. "You brothers may leave now, but go at once and waste not a moment in pity for these two. They will come to no more harm at our hands, for nothing we might do to them could injure them more than the maladies they have brought upon themselves. You all *know* what they have done and so you know they deserve no pity. Talk of it as you go, though. Tell everyone you meet along the road what you have seen today and make sure they all understand the gravity of what was done." He stopped short then and surveyed the crowd. "It occurs to me, brethren, that there is a lesson here to be learned by all of us."

He looked back down at the Archbishop, who had sunk onto his thighs and now appeared beaten and dejected.

"You all saw two Bishops here, where in fact there were none. You saw them with your own eyes, and you believed. Yet one was an Archbishop and the other but a Prior. Sleek and well dressed, the two of them, and looking like anything but what we now know they are in fact. And so the lesson is, Judge not by appearances. Yet we all do, and we tailor our appearances to suit our needs." He paused.

"Me, for example, with my hooded cloak draped and arranged just so, to conceal my hunched back, and my men around you, with their masks in place to hide their faces. But will they need masks once word of this little adventure reaches Edward Plantagenet? I doubt it. When Edward hears of this, he will come ravening, seeking blood and vengeance in addition to his lost coin, and the presence or absence of a mask or two will make little difference to who is hanged or slaughtered.

"And so I say to you the time for masks and hoods is past. Bishops, plain to behold, are not bishops, and the men around you, who have been the Greens, will go masked no more. They will stand from this day forth as Scots, united in their stance against the tyranny and treachery of England and its King. And as for me, the hunchback?"

He slowly removed the hooded cloak, pushing the cowl back off his head and then throwing the heavy garment aside. He straightened his back and flexed his huge shoulders and raised his voice into a shout, shifting from Latin to Scots. "My name is William Wallace, of Scotland, and I dinna care wha kens it, so be damned to them a'. So tell them that when ye go out to spread the word o' what has happened here, the shame and the disgrace o' it. Tell them that Scotland has a voice amang the trees o' Selkirk Forest. And tell them that *their* voices will be heard as long as we in Selkirk stand and fight. Tell them my name, too, and tell the English that, 'gin they want to tak' me, I'm here waitin' for them. An outlaw, aye, but a Scot first and last, and ready to fight to my last breath."

In all my life I had never heard anything like the roar unleashed by that gathering. It swelled and expanded and changed shape as it grew to a sustained chant of "Wall-*ISS*! Wall-*ISS*! Wall-*ISS*!"

CHAPTER THIRTEEN

I

The year that followed was unlike any other I ever experienced, and I think of it now as the happiest time of my adult life. I remember it as a time of freedom and great beauty, of soaring hope amidst increasing desperation, and, for me at least, a time of liberation and fulfillment, spent as a forest chaplain, ministering to the folk—the families and assorted misfits and strange, often wonderful characters—who were attracted, for a multitude of reasons, to the man William Wallace.

Foremost among those reasons, of course, was the fact that Will had stepped forward and declared himself as he did that day when he took the English paymasters' gold from the Archbishop. No one had ever stood up boldly in the face of both Church and state and declared himself to be representing and defending the common folk of Scotland, and word of it spread throughout the land like fire in dry grass.

The nobility condemned him, of course, but everyone else dismissed that as unimportant, for in their view, by their indifference to what was happening to their countrymen, the nobility had abdicated their right to take offence. What was significant was that Wallace's action lit a fire in the breasts of the countless hundreds of ordinary men who had grown sick of the incessant bullying and chronic injustice bred of the system they were forced to live under. In a development that no one could have foreseen, they chose, overwhelmingly, to join William Wallace in his forest domain and to stand beside him as free men, beholden to no masters and responsible for their own destiny.

It was this burgeoning of small but vibrant communities within the greenwood that led to my being delegated to work there as a priest, ministering to the needs of Will's followers. I had returned quickly to Glasgow and Bishop Wishart after the raid on the English paymasters' wagons, bearing tidings of the outcome of my mission to Will, and His Grace had listened, stone faced. When I had finished my report, he nodded once, thanked me, and dismissed me. Had anyone asked me later, even under torture, to describe his reaction to what I had told him, I would not have been able to say.

Then word came to us, with all the condemnatory wrath of an outraged clergy, of a heinous crime against a nameless bishop during the prosecution of his divine duties. That report spoke of the impious and blasphemous theft of unnamed but invaluable Church property. I had been back for two weeks by then, so it was evident to both the Bishop and me that people had spent considerable time colluding on the details of what had actually happened and what would be released for public consumption. Once again, Bishop Wishart listened grim faced and offered no comment.

Two weeks after that, though, during the Friday-evening communal meal in the cathedral refectory, when I was deep in thought and shamelessly ignoring the droning voice of the visiting friar who was reading that evening's scriptural selection, I was interrupted by one of the secretariat and summoned immediately into the Bishop's presence.

He was alone in a corner by his window when I arrived, sitting with his feet propped up on a cushioned stool and tapping a flattened, much-misshapen scroll against his chin as he stared into the blackness beyond the window's tiny, diamond-shaped panes. He looked up at me and grunted, then waved for me to pull forward another chair and join him, and as soon as I was seated he handed me the scroll. Someone had flattened it roughly, cracking its seal in folding it to fit into a pouch or pocket. I unfolded it and immediately recognized Will's penmanship, which made me smile.

"Does this not make you wish, my lord, that everyone was capable of being his own scribe? How much clearer everything would be, were that the case."

"Aye, but wishing for that would be a waste of God's time, Father James, for such never will be the case. Your cousin is one of the three or four literate men I know outside of our clerical ranks. Read it."

The missive was brief and to the point: in the space of a month, Will had written, the situation in the greenwood had changed greatly. People had begun to gather there from every direction, lured by the promise of freedom, whatever that might be, and their numbers were growing daily and showing no signs of abating. He had underscored *freedom*, but aside from adding *whatever that might be*, he spent no more time attempting to define what they were seeking. He and his people were coping, he wrote. Food was plentiful, and they had made sure people were living far from the main road, deep in the forest and beyond reach of attack.

The largest need he could foresee, Will wrote, was for priests. He had a few people among his followers with rudimentary knowledge of the healing crafts, but not one single monk or priest. Children were already being born, elders were dying, and young people were exchanging marriage vows. He needed priests now, he said, to live among his people and minister to them.

I lowered the letter and looked wordlessly at Bishop Wishart, who was staring back at me. He had pouted his lips and was picking and plucking at them with a fingertip.

"You want me to go."

He stopped what he was doing and sat up straight, removing his feet from the stool. "Aye," he said. "At once. Take Declan and Jacobus with you. They can both use the experience to advantage. They will be in your charge and will answer to you as their superior."

I nodded, content with the authority he had granted me. The two priests he had named were respectively the youngest and the eldest in the cathedral chapter, and both would undoubtedly benefit from escaping the daily sameness of the cathedral's regimen. Father Declan had been ordained with me. He was two years older than I was, but there were years of difference between us in experience and temperament, for Declan, orphaned since birth, had been cloistered all his life. He was a true Innocent, his most heinous sin, I would have wagered, no more serious than a sometime tendency to daydream. Now, however, he needed to learn to deal with real, living people, the sheep for whom God had made him responsible as a shepherd, charging him to lead them to Salvation.

Father Jacobus had been crippled for decades by a mysterious infirmity that had barred him physically from serving as a normal priest, making it impossible for him to mix with people and share their daily lives. And then his affliction had miraculously vanished, between one day and the next, shortly before I came to Glasgow. His return to health had been complete, so that now he positively glowed with vigour and devotion, but like Declan, he had been immured for many years, and the time had come for him, too, to step beyond the bounds of a regulated, monastic existence and reacquaint himself with the bountiful and wondrous world of God's creation.

"When do you wish us to leave, my lord?"

"As soon as you can. Gather all you think you might need, including medicines and supplies, and have it loaded on a wagon— two wagons, if you need them—but don't tell me or any of my people what you take, or how much you take, or where it's going. That way, no one will be able to betray anything, even by accident. As soon as you are ready, come and find me. By then I will have written a reply to your cousin, and you can take it with you."

"Of course, my lord. How long will we be gone?"

He had already started to look about him, his attention shifting to his next task, but now he looked back at me, his eyes showing his surprise. He gave a grunt, then answered in Scots. "For as long as ye're needed. So dinna fret about returnin'. 'Gin I ha'e need o' you i' the interim, I'll send for you. But until then, think o' the Selkirk Forest as your kirk."

He smiled then, a small sideways twisting of his mouth accompanying the softening of his fierce old eyes, and reverted to Latin. "A vast, green cathedral of your own, Father James … I know you will not abuse it, and I will pray for your success and happiness among the beauties of God's wilderness." He paused again, then added, "I envy you this, you know, this freedom you now have. Were

I much younger, I would jump at the chance to do what I am now instructing you to do. Ah, well … We are what and who we are and we live in the here and now, so there's an end of that nonsense. Go now, with my blessing, and make a start on what you have to do."

I knelt quickly, and as he made the sign of the cross over my bent head, I was aware of a sensation of lightness in my chest.

2

The guards at the turnoff point recognized me as I approached and remained hidden, only one of them stepping out from his hiding place to wave us forward. He was one of Will's sergeants, as they were known, soldier leaders chosen from among the ranks, who wore a coloured shoulder patch to mark their status. They were responsible for maintaining discipline among the wild men who formed Will's active units. He threw me a casual salute as I passed by, running his eye over my loaded pack horse and the wagon at my back. I knew that he had already passed the signal on to the watchers at his back that we were friends. Without that signal, we would not have survived the first mile beyond his post.

From where we had turned, a long, narrow, tightly winding path protected Will's main encampment from attack. It took an hour to travel, twisting and turning through evil-looking bogs that threatened to suck our wheels down into the mud, and sometimes snaking between impenetrable thickets of tangled blackthorn and hawthorn. These thorn thickets were not high, but they were dense and unyielding, forcing everyone who came this way to keep to the narrow path.

I knew, without ever setting eyes on any of them, that we were being watched constantly as we rode by within arrow shot of ever-vigilant guards, and I knew beyond doubt that men were also watching us from the high branches of the scattered, massive trees that towered above the growth on both sides. And so we rode in silence until the path emerged into a spacious water meadow, straightening into a long, grassy avenue that led directly to the cluster of solid-looking log buildings along the edge of a small lake.

From the moment of our arrival at Will's camp, I felt at home and ready to tackle anything that might be thrown at me. Will came out to greet us when he heard someone shout my name, and when he saw me sitting my horse with another, laden, at my back and a wagonload of goods behind that, his face split into an enormous smile and he spread his arms wide, waiting to embrace me. I swung down from my mount and he swept me up into a mighty hug, threatening to crush my ribs as he swung me around in a circle.

"Damn, Jamie, you look good," he said, holding me by the shoulders, and then his face went serious as his eyes moved to take in my two fellow priests watching us from their wagon. "I swear there's nothing more unwelcome to an unsuspecting host than the sight of an empty-handed visitor," he said, then laughed again and punched me on the shoulder. "Welcome, Cousin. Bid your fellows climb down and have a drink with us. Patrick will take care of your horses and the wagon."

He shouted to the man Patrick and rattled off a string of orders, and in no time at all Fathers Declan and Jacobus had been helped down and willing hands were busy with the disposition of the supplies we had brought. I introduced Will to Declan and Jacobus, and he welcomed them cordially, then herded us towards the rear of the camp, where I saw more buildings than had been there on my previous visit.

"Here," he said, ushering us into a pleasant little clearing at the back of one of the new buildings and directing us to one of several tables with benches attached. "Sit here. It's comfortable and it smells good, with the smoke from the kitchens there making everyone hungry."

"Those are the kitchens?" My surprise was unfeigned, for these buildings were more than twice the size of the kitchens I had seen before.

"Aye. I've heard it said we are raising an army here, but I tell you, Cuz, if we are, it's an army of gulls and gannets—save that gulls and gannets fly away once their bellies are full. I swear, I've never seen so many hungry people." He leaned back, stretching out his legs and crossing his hands over his belly. "But the food is good and plentiful, thank God, and we yet have room to sit and spread our legs. And here's Tearlaigh. Ewan has taught our cooks to make a passable beer from local hops, and Tearlaigh's been his best pupil. His beer is almost as good as Ewan's. You'll find it goes down smoothly."

A giant of a man had come bustling towards us carrying a leather bucket and with a loop of wooden beer tankards strung around his neck, and now he served us, unhooking tankards from his string and filling them with foaming beer.

"So where is Ewan?" I asked, having taken my first gulp of what was a truly excellent brew.

"He's around somewhere. I saw him a while ago." He stood up and looked around, but sat down again immediately. "He won't be far away. He never is."

"And Mirren, she is well?"

"Aye, blooming like a flower. She'll be glad to see you, Cuz."

I had my own ideas on that, for Mirren, I believed, had little time or liking for me, but I smiled and brought my two companions back into the conversation.

It was good to be off the road after the long journey, and as the sun went down fires began to appear between the scattered tables, and soon we moved to sit by one of them, enjoying the heat, the drifting smoke, and the dancing firelight. The beer was excellent, and some time later I woke myself up by nodding forward and tipping the brew into my lap. I know the three of us slept that night in one of the new huts by the kitchens, but I barely remember moving from the fire, and when I awoke the next morning before dawn, I had no idea where I was.

My two charges and I spent several hours after morning Mass sorting through our clerical provisions and selecting the items we would need in our first week in our new communities. Those included basic liturgical vestments for ceremonial occasions like the consecration of the new churches we would build, and sacramental items like chalices and ciboria used for the Eucharist, as well as mundane but necessary clerical supplies like writing materials. Each of us had his own consecrated altar stone, of course, but we needed bread and wine, for the consecration of the Mass, and salt, holy oil, and chrism for dispensing the other sacraments. We knew we could restock our supplies simply by walking back to the main encampment, but we knew, too, that we would have enough to do in the days ahead of us to waste time fretting over supplies.

Afterwards, Will walked us the length and breadth of the territories that his men now commanded, an area almost two full miles in length and close to a mile in width, comprising a rough oval of low, rolling, tree-covered terrain containing three primitive settlements surrounded by a wide belt of undisturbed, heavy-growth forest. Building was under way in all three settlements, and people were already living in the newest dwellings.

Having left Declan and Jacobus to begin their new ministries in the first two settlements, I was at the mercy of whatever I might find at the third. Any fears I might have had were soon proven groundless, though, for the last site was the most beautiful of the three, and I felt at peace there from the moment I saw it. It lay the farthest from Will's main encampment, a full half-hour's walk, but it was set in a tranquil and lovely place, a gently sloping, oak-grown, and moss-covered hillside above a wide, rocky stream. The rocky hilltop above the settlement was split by a yawning ravine, exposing sheer sides where great slabs of stone, stained by lichen and moss, appeared to be bound together by a network of massive, mossy tree roots. I could see several cave openings up there, and guessed that people had been using these natural shelters for habitation long before Will Wallace and his outlaws came this way.

Today, the caves were being used by Alan Crawford of Nithsdale and the crew of men assigned to him to build shelter for the newcomers. Alan's was the largest of the crews I had seen, and their work was well in hand when we arrived. I counted six sturdy military-style barrack buildings made of heavy, new-cut logs. Four of those already bore thick roofs, and the remaining two were raftered and being covered with planking that would soon be covered with a thin coating of sod.

Alan remembered me and greeted me cordially as soon as I dismounted.

"Well met again," I said to him, shaking his hand. "If this is to be my new home—and it appears it is—I thank you for preparing it against my coming. But where is everyone else?"

Alan pointed a thumb towards his men, who were already back at work. "We're a' there is for now. The new settlers winna start comin' till tomorrow. That's whit wey we're tryin' to get these last twa huts finished afore it gets dark. That first group will a' be men, mind—about twa score o' them—and we'll put them to work the minute they get here. They'll build mair huts, bigger yins, for families, weemin and bairns."

"Ah. And at what time do you start work in the morning?"

He looked at me blankly. "Why, when we ha'e broken fast."

"*Prayed* and broken fast, you mean, do you not?" I said.

He grinned. "Aye, of course … now that you're here, Father James."

"Good. Mass will be at daybreak. You can let your men know."

He nodded, still smiling, and walked away, and I turned to Will.

"What? You've got that old Will Wallace look on your face. What are you thinking?"

He gave a small shrug. "Nothing. I was just wondering where you will say your first Mass. You'll need an altar."

"No, I won't. Not a real one, not at first. You know that as well as I do. Any flat surface will do—any tabletop, anywhere, as long as it's big enough to hold the altar stone."

"Fine. But you *will* need a church of some description, sooner or later, even if it's no more than a roof on pillars, a shelter to keep your people dry in foul weather. We can build you a real altar then. But you'll have to tell Alan's builder yourself what you need. Don't leave it to Alan to instruct him, or you'll be sorry. Alan's a fine organizer and driver of men, but he's none too good with abstract notions. The builder's name is Davie Ogilvie, and he's a northerner like Shoomy. You'll do well to put yourself in his good graces, for he can build anything you can describe to him. He'll build you a cathedral out of kindling, if that's what you ask for."

"I'll settle for a solid little chapel, but I'm grateful for the advice. In the meantime, though, where should I sleep tonight? Do you know or care?"

"Neither one nor the other, Cuz. Alan's people are sleeping in the finished huts over there, but I think that might not suit your needs anyway ... nor theirs, now that I think about it. A priest should have a place to be alone and do whatever priests do when they're alone." He paused, then waved towards the nearest cave. "Were I you, I'd throw my belongings in there. It's dry, and it's warm and draft free, with a couple of separate chambers, and Alan has told me it has a natural chimney that draws smoke right up through the roof."

"So if it's that good, why isn't Alan himself using it?"

Will grinned and ducked his head. "Because I told him to leave it for you. I knew you'd be coming, sooner or later."

"You sly snake! You asked Wishart to send me here, didn't you?"

"Not in so many words. It was more of a suggestion, a word of encouragement. I knew he'd send you anyway. He needs you as a go-between from him to me, so it makes sense to have you billeted with me, where you can do the most good."

I shook my head in mock disgust and hoisted my heavy pack. "Right, then, show me this cave and you can light a fire while I unpack."

3

Ever since we left Glasgow, I had been fretting privately about our collective inexperience. All three of us had been cloistered in the sanctified atmosphere of the cathedral, yet now, of a sudden, we would be living and working with a real congregation, men, women, and children of all ages and descriptions who would look up to us as God's own representatives. They would

depend upon us for their sacraments and for their moral and spiritual guidance and welfare, and they would have a never-ending need
for help in clinging to their faith in the midst of their daily lives. It
was a terrifying prospect, and I entered into the experience like a
boy dropping into a swimming hole from an overhanging branch,
remembering Will's exhortation from years earlier when he and I
had discovered the deep hole in the river by Paisley Abbey. "Jump
in," he had told me, "and swim out."

I hung up my liturgical vestments in an alcove dug into one wall
of my cave on that first night, thinking that by the time I had need
of them, they would have had a few days for the wrinkles to smooth
out. A full month later, those garments were still where I had hung
them. In all that time, I had worn the same hooded, monkish robe—
a single, dark grey, ankle-length garment, ragged beyond belief and
tied with a rope at the waist. I had gone barefoot, too, most of that
time, while building my own church side by side with Davie Ogilvie
the builder. He was an immensely strong man, though he did not
look large, and I quickly developed a great regard for his skills,
which included the astonishing ability to visualize complex
constructions in his mind and then translate them into charts and
drawings from which others could work.

I used up my supply of Communion bread very quickly, but that
was easy to replace. Bread is bread, plentiful at most times. Wine,
however, is an entirely different matter, scarce and difficult to come
by in rural Scotland. I was not short of it to begin with, but I knew I
had little prospect of renewing my supply easily, and so I quickly cut
down the amount we used in the Mass and found that, by diluting
even that fastidiously, I could stretch my supply well enough.

For the first week I celebrated Mass each morning as the first of
our new settlers began to trickle in, but by the end of the second
week I had to schedule a second Mass on the Sunday, and soon after
that I was saying Mass twice a day, every day. By the third Sunday,
I found myself exchanging nods with those faces among my congregation that had already grown familiar, and by the fourth, I knew
most of the people's names. We were one hundred and twelve souls

by that time, and our numbers would exceed two hundred within the year. From the moment I awoke in my cave that first day and went to celebrate Mass with Alan Crawford's work crew, I never again had time to fret about being capable of fulfilling my obligations.

I was celebrating the second nuptial Mass among my congregants, early in June, when Will stalked into the roofed building we called a church, and as soon as I saw the set of his shoulders and the cast of his face I knew something was gravely wrong. It had been raining intermittently all morning, and he wore a heavy cloak of wool, waterproofed with a thin coat of brushed-on wax. He made a place for himself at the rear of the congregation, where he stood with his head bowed while I continued with the service. The young couple I was marrying that day were a delightful pair, well thought of by everyone, and the church was filled with well-wishers, so I put Will out of my mind as well as I could for the time being and returned my attention to the sacrament I was conferring on the young pair, not wishing to give them anything less than a ceremony they could recall throughout their lives. I distributed Communion to the throng, Will included, and then brought the service to a close by leading the radiant new wife and her goodman out to meet their families, friends, and neighbours. I stood at the threshold of my poor little church and watched the parade weave away, with great hilarity and jubilation, to enjoy their wedding feast.

When Will and I were once more alone, I stepped to the altar and carefully cleaned and wrapped my precious chalice and ciborium, then packed them carefully into their leather case and carried them with me as I led Will to the cave that was my home. One of the women who insisted on caring for my few comforts had built a roaring fire against the day's dampness, and as we reached the fire, Will threw back his cloak and unslung a fat, heavy wineskin from where it had hung beneath his shoulder.

"One of my fellows took this from a knight he and his men stopped this side o' Selkirk town. It's miraculous wine, they say."

"Miraculous?" I took the skin from him and hefted it appreciatively. "This will be put to good use, I promise you. I've been thinking I would have to send Father Declan back to Glasgow for a fresh supply, because we are already on the last of what we brought with us. My gratitude, then, to whoever was responsible. But miraculous? What's that supposed to mean?"

"Miraculous, for one thing, that he and his men didn't drink it themselves. But also that they brought it back because they knew that you and the other priests are short … I confess, Cuz, that astonished me. Tousle-arsed forest outlaws saving good wine for a priest? Impossible, I would have said."

I smiled. "Well, take off your hat and offer thanks to God for your enlightenment, and have more charity in future. Would you like a cup of it?"

"After all that? I would to God I could, but I would feel like a thief, so, no."

I had started to remove my vestments and now I paused, eyeing him and smiling to take any sting out of my words. "But you *are* a thief, Cuz. That's why you are here in the forest, after all."

"That is true, Cousin Priest, and I had no need to hear it. But I am grateful, nonetheless, for the thought about the cup of wine and I'll gladly drink some ale if you have any."

"In the chest there, between the chairs. Pour one for me, too."

I finished taking off my chasuble and stole and hung the garments carefully in the niche I used for them, and then I stripped off my long, white alb and folded it meticulously into its box on the floor of the niche. I had but the one and I seldom wore it because it was almost impossible to keep clean and fresh looking, and so I reserved it for special occasions like this morning's Nuptial Mass. Normally, I celebrated the Sacrifice in my plain monk's robe, believing that God cared little how I dressed so long as I served him in the spirit of love and piety.

By the time I turned back to the fire, Will had poured ale for both of us and set a flagon for me on the rough table between the two chairs that flanked the fireplace. I drank deeply, then set the vessel down before looking across at my cousin.

"All right, what's wrong, Will? You're plainly angry over something. What brings you here? Apart from bringing the wine, I mean."

"Reprisals."

I heard the word, and understood it, but for several moments it meant nothing to me.

"From the English," Will said. "They're punishing folk for what I did last April."

"April! That was months ago."

"Aye, it was, but they're taking payment now. Plainly they took a while to think about what to do next, that's all. And now they're doing it."

"Doing what, Will? Are they coming here?"

"No. They'd never dare, unless they came in strength, to wipe us out, and they won't risk that … unless they have permission from King John, and I don't see that coming. Nothing would please Edward more than to have right of passage from the border to here, but there's too much going on between the two kingdoms and their Kings right now to permit our wee affairs to take on that kind of import. But reprisals are being carried out against us, Jamie. I've had reports, and we have had casualties coming in, to bear witness to what's going on. Farms and whole villages laid waste and burned, their people hanged or slaughtered. Men taken on the road, about their own affairs, and hanged without trial. Their women ravaged, sometimes spared, sometimes not … And no one, anywhere, able to identify the killers." He dragged his hands down over his face and mouthed a formless moan of weariness and frustration.

"I want to send some of them here, the survivors, to the main camp, but we can't handle them. We've no room, and we're too close to any enemy that comes against us. Close enough to fight them, certainly—that's why we're there. But there's no safety for any but ourselves, the fighting men. Can you take some of the others, d'you think? Have you room?"

"Of course we can take them, and we'll make room if need be. Where are these people from?"

"They're plain folk from around here, on the outskirts of the forest."

"Which outskirts?"

He shrugged. "Nowhere, everywhere. Some attacks were close by our territories, others were farther afield, near places like Selkirk village. But none were actually within our reach for retaliations. Most were in the southwest, though … west and southwest."

"How far?"

That made him frown. "Ten miles? No, more than that." He hesitated, thinking rapidly. "Twenty miles at least, perhaps more."

"Twenty miles south and southwest of your main camp. That's Bruce country."

"Aye. It is." He glanced at me and nodded. "They would ne'er ha'e dared try such a thing when old Bruce the Competitor was alive, God rest his soul. The old man would ha'e gone to war over it. But now his son, the Lord o' Annandale, sits in England's Carlisle Castle as its custodian, and his grandson, the Earl of Carrick, is in London, playing the popinjay at Edward's court. So you'll hear no complaints from the Bruces."

"And why have these survivors come to you?"

"Because they have no other place to go, why else?"

"Do you know them? And if the answer to that is yes, then *how* do you know them, that they should come to you?"

"I don't know them. They are just folk who had heard of us, that we were in the greenwood, and who came to us when they lost everything. I knew none of them before they came, and none of them knew me."

"But if that's so, if they had no connection to you, why were they harmed?"

"Come on now, Jamie, don't vex me. We're dealing with Englishmen here! Think you they need a reason to be as they are? To behave the way they do? Have you forgotten Ellerslie and what they did to us and our kin?"

"No, Will, I have not. But this is different—"

"*How* is it *different*? How can you sit there, knowing nothing about what is going on, and say it is *different*? Different to what? I'll send you three wee boys who watched their parents being butchered like stirks. Three wee boys younger than we were, with ravaged arses sorer than ours were! Tell *them* how different this is, then watch how they walk, hobbling in pain and shame, and how they look around them at the men they meet, waiting to be jumped upon again. Different? The only difference I see is in the time. When they did it to us, we were children, weak and helpless. Now, by the living Christ, I am a man grown, and I will meet these English whoresons with a man's strength and judgment."

My mind had filled with the image of two other small boys, running in endless terror for days on end, and I held up my hand to stem his words.

Now he checked himself. "What?"

"I hear what you are saying. And I understand. I disagree, but that is neither here nor there. But tell me about the logic behind these attacks. How can you be sure they have anything to do with the robbery in April?" I watched the frown that came over his face. "From what you have said, or from what I think I've *heard* you say, none of these … reprisals has taken place anywhere near the scene of the April robbery. Is that correct?" I could see in his eyes that it was, and so I continued. "But you are convinced beyond doubt that whatever is going on has to do with what you did that day." Once again, reading his face, I could see that I was right. "Yet where is the connection? Why would you not simply believe these are random raids, like the one that cost us our home in Ellerslie? Why are you so sure they are linked to the April theft?"

He frowned again, briefly, then sat up straighter and looked me in the eye. "Because they have to be. No other explanation makes sense. Besides, it fits the nature of the beast. Edward Plantagenet is not a passive enemy. We created havoc with that raid—absolute havoc that no one, he least of all, had dreamed of. We destroyed all of his carefully structured plans, smashed them to splinters just when he must have thought he had been supremely clever. Can you imagine how he must have raged when he heard of it? But the most infuriating goad of all must have been that he could not breathe a word about *any* of it. How could he complain about the theft of illegal funds, funds that should never have been brought into Scotland in the first place and should never have been smuggled across the border under the protection of Holy Church under *any* circumstances? He would have been condemned by everyone, publicly disgraced. Mind you, I am not saying that, in itself, would have deterred him. I've no doubt he would have been prepared to defy the whole world had his stratagem been successful. But once his funds were lost, he had no hope of winning anything but scorn, condemnation, and harsh judgment … perhaps even excommunication."

As I listened to his words, the scope of what William Wallace had personally done to England's King sank home to me as it had never done before. Until that moment, I had seen the events of that now distant day in April solely from a clerical perspective, assessing the damage done to the fabric of Holy Church by the actions of the renegade Archbishop of York. Other than the physical bulk of the royal specie we confiscated—and I had not seen so much as the image of his regal head on a single captured coin— there had been no visible trace of Edward of England present that day, and I had somehow lost sight of his overwhelming influence in the entire affair. It had never crossed my mind until that moment, listening to Will, that Edward Plantagenet, the implacable and remorseless conqueror of Ewan's people in Wales, might come looking, in person, for vengeance against my cousin for having dared to defy him. It appalled me now to see how blind and wilfully stupid I had been, living in a fool's paradise.

"You're right," I whispered, fighting down a surge of nausea. "Edward can't let that go unavenged. He will have you killed."

"He might try, Cuz, but he'll have to come and get me himself if he wants to see me dead …" His voice died away, then resumed more quietly. "In the meantime, though, he's serving notice."

"Notice? I don't understand what you mean."

"Killing these simple folk is what I mean. There's no reason for it, other than to make me notice. Women and children, innocent of any crime, die or are evicted with their men. Their slaughter is a signal, nothing more. A signal to me, from him, that he knows I'm here and would have words with me. Words." He grunted. "I'd hear few words from him, other than 'Die,' and he would have some other speak for him before he'd soil his tongue by using it on me. He's a savage man, I've heard. D'you remember the tales of what the Turks did to Christian pilgrims, before the Great Crusade?"

"No. I mean, I've heard many tales, but I don't know which ones you mean."

"I'm thinking of the one Pope Urban used when first he raised the Cross in France. He told of how the Mussulmans would take a Christian man and slit his belly, then tie his entrails to a stake and chase the man around the stake until he died, gutted. I never really believed that happened, but Edward of England could do such a thing. He is that kind of man. A dire enemy."

"God forbid!" I shuddered and blessed myself with the sign of the cross. "No Christian king would ever kill a man in such a barbaric fashion."

My cousin looked at me and smiled a grim little smile. "Edward Plantagenet would, if he thought it necessary. He thinks these raids against the folk are necessary, to capture my attention."

I gazed down into my empty flagon. "Can you stop it, this slaughter?"

"Aye. I can ride into Lanark, or to some other English garrison, and give myself up."

"No, Will. Apart from that. Can you stop the slaughter?"

"Probably not." He bent forward and picked out a log from the pile by the hearth, then laid it on the embers and pushed it into place with his booted foot. "But I can make it hazardous for any Englishman foolish enough to step out of doors to take a piss in southern Scotland. It will take the like of an army of men to achieve that, but Edward Longshanks and his English bullies have provided us with just such an army. At last count, we had close to nine hundred men throughout the south, most of them bowmen and all of them willing to rise at the blast of a horn."

"Nine *hundred*?"

"Aye, from Selkirk to Teviotdale to Dumfries and as far west as Galloway. Had you asked me yesterday if it was feasible to field so many, I would have said no." His lips quirked, but there was no humour in his eyes. "But now I say yes. It will take planning, but we can do it. We have to stop this obscenity, this wanton slaughter. And if that means killing them to stop them killing ours, then so be it. We will do what needs to be done. And we will do it as soon as it can be arranged. We'll flood the entire south with patrols, strong foot patrols, three hundred men on any given day, and woe betide any stranger with as much as a knife who can't appease them with good reasons for being armed and where he is. We will be declaring war on England. Let there be no misunderstanding. It will not be open war, and it will not be knightly war, or chivalrous, but it will be war—bloody and brutal and unforgiving, for as long as Longshanks wants it."

CHAPTER FOURTEEN

I

I have asked myself a hundred times, over the years that have passed since that afternoon, if I could really have changed any of the things that happened afterwards, had I behaved even slightly differently as we spoke by the fire in my cave. Could I have influenced any of what occurred, had I planted my feet firmly and objected to what Will was proposing? What might he have done, had I ranted and admonished him, reminding him that he was endangering his immortal soul? Would he have relented? Would he have chosen some other way to proceed in order to achieve his goal?

I know, of course, that he would not. He would have done nothing differently and the outcome would have been unchanged. I have always known that, I suppose, even though I have fought against admitting it to myself. Simply by being who and what he was, William Wallace had preordained that he and the Plantagenet King would collide. The ancients would have said that it was written in the stars. They would also have said that I was committing the sin of hubris, overweening pride, by even thinking I might have had the power to alter any vestige of what happened. But it was not hubris. The curiosity I dwelt upon for all those years was merely wishful thinking. The truth is that I was but a humble priest, eclipsed by the titanic figures of Edward Plantagenet and William Wallace, both of whom History already regards as giants. When Will left me that June day, to launch his patrols to protect the common folk, his mind was already set beyond changing. His plans had been set before he told me about them, and their preparations were already under way.

And so the struggle that I once heard a powerful Scots nobleman refer to as "Wallace's dirty wee war" began, and I bore witness to it, impotent to change a single part of it, appalled by its ferocity, and yet paradoxically thrilled and proud to be a part of it, even as a mere observer. When I first heard that nobleman's description, years afterwards, I took umbrage, thinking it an insult, but then I saw its truth. The conflict *was* a small one, for the first two years at least, a series of skirmishes rather than a full-blown war, and it was certainly dirty—dingy and dire and destructive to everyone involved.

I have always found it strange, though, that Wallace's reputation as a dishonourable, disreputable fighter emerged from that time. From the perspective of those who yet adhere to the chivalric code, his methods are seen to this day as outrageous and unacceptable, no different from brigandage and lawless savagery. But when, in war, has savagery ever been unacceptable as a means to victory? When, for that matter, has the strict code of chivalry ever been respected or observed in the chaos of battle, amid spilling blood and entrails and shattered flesh? William Wallace, in those earliest days of his struggle, was an unknown, a desperate man fighting for his beliefs at the head of a small band of willing but untrained followers who were ill equipped for the task they faced and were therefore, on the surface at least, utterly incapable of withstanding the forces ranged against them. There was never any possibility that he and his ragamuffin outlaws might hope to stand toe-to-toe against the enemy that threatened them. The mere thought of such a thing was laughable; they would have been slaughtered instantly, obliterated under the hooves and booted feet of the disciplined ranks opposing them.

Wallace's men were peasants, farmers for the most part, but while they lacked the weapons and armour their opponents had, their supposed impotence was misleading. They were fighting on their home ground and they knew every fold and wrinkle of the land around them, and so they turned the land itself into a weapon, picking their fighting sites and then striking from ambush, their actions predictable only in the certainty that they would be unpredictable. Thus they fought, and thus they won consistently, in defiance of all the maxims of warfare, proving themselves to be adaptable, elusive, and ultimately invincible.

Over the decades between then and now, I have found it both
ironic and tragic that Wallace is condemned as a base-born, ignoble
brigand for the way in which he waged war and the methods that he
used, while King Robert himself, who perfected those same
methods in the two ensuing decades and carried them to unprecedented extremes both on and off the field of battle, is universally
hailed as the Hero King. Yet it is true; Wallace's methods appalled
his enemies, not all of whom were English, whereas Bruce used
precisely the same methods and emerged victorious, his reputation
unblemished.

The reason, of course, lies in the perceptions of jealous and
embittered men. William Wallace was not a belted knight. He
became one later, knighted in order to allow him to assume the
mantle of Guardian after the death of his friend and fellow leader,
Sir Andrew Murray, but when he first moved to challenge England's
power, he was not. No matter that his father's brother Malcolm had
been a knight, or that his own elder brother wore the silver spurs.
William Wallace himself did not, and that alone was sufficient to
demean him in the eyes of lesser, spiteful men who set store by such
things as birth ahead of ability. It laid him open to their sneering
disdain and to accusations—though always from a distance well
beyond his hearing—of being an upstart. He was deemed a
commoner, ignoble from the outset and therefore, in the eyes of his
self-styled betters, entitled neither to hold nor to voice an opinion on
anything that mattered.

They were all wrong, of course, for as history has demonstrated,
my cousin had one attribute that enabled him to rise above his
detractors and to capture the attention, the love, and the admiration
of a society comprising many races: he was William Wallace, the
only man of his time with the God-given strength and natural ability
to offer hope to his broken, strife-ridden homeland and to instill in
his people a sense of pride, and something greater yet, an unprecedented sense of unity and *nationality*.

I saw that process begun in Selkirk Forest, with the dispatching
of the first patrols sent out against the English. Yet even in writing

those words, I am contributing to the general inaccuracy that surrounds that entire time. To speak of patrols *sent out against the English* suggests that the English were *there*, formally, and that Wallace fought against them formally. But in the hair-splitting language of Edward of England's lawyers, that is demonstrably untrue. In terms of strict legality, enshrined with great formality in the annals of the English court, there were no English troops, *per se*, abroad in our land at that time. That term, *abroad*, is all-important, because it connotes mobility and far-ranging activity. Scotland's south was swarming with English soldiers that June, and had been for more than a year, but every man of them, ostensibly at least, had a sound and defensible reason, set down on parchment by the Plantagenet's lawyers, for being there, *in residence* upon their royal master's behalf, but not *abroad in the land*.

Add to that the fact that the great majority of the Scots noble families were bound by double bonds of fealty to Edward, tied to him as much by the simple truth that they all held spacious lands and rich estates in England by his grace and favour as by the ancient laws of Norman-French feudality. And of course these same Scots nobles benefited greatly from having Edward's well-equipped fighting men conveniently at hand to assist them with policing their own lands, since they did not then have to hire and equip costly men-at-arms of their own.

And so it becomes clear what was in truth afoot in the Scottish lands north of the border: Scots magnates, in return for the privilege of using English soldiers at no cost other than food and drink, were being induced to turn a blind eye to "irregularities" in the activities of certain of those visiting troops, even at the cost of hardship to their own Scots people. Not all the Scots noble houses were involved, and some may not have been comfortable with what was taking place, but they must all have known of it. And the alternative—the loss of well-trained auxiliary troops and a very real loss of privilege and royal favour for refusing to cooperate and be compliant—intimidated many of them and overcame the consciences of others.

Thus, English infantry and mounted men-at-arms roamed at will throughout Scotland's border country in that period of 1294 and 1295, free to behave as they wished, whether it was called reprisals, policing, or the collection of rents and taxes by the Scots landlords, and no Scots magnate, anywhere, spoke of abuse of power, or unprovoked aggression, or royal English displeasure and revenge.

The first patrols we sent out late that spring were a complete success: unanticipated, rapid, and thorough. Fully five hundred men were dispatched on the first sweep, most of them bowmen, although none of them were limited to the bow alone. They dispersed from Will's main camp, moving west and south in groups of fifty, with five ten-man squads in each group. One hundred men bound for Galloway, the farthest end of the sweep to the west, twenty-five miles distant, went first in the grey light of pre-dawn, and they were followed at two-hour intervals by the remaining groups, the last of which headed directly south to the open Annandale lands. All were ordered to proceed at speed but keeping themselves out of sight, and to be in place by nightfall, ready to mount a coordinated attack at dawn the next day.

I celebrated Mass with them before dawn on the day they left and distributed Communion to them all, and I remember that I was not in the least upset that they were setting off to do what they would do, for by then I had seen for myself the ravages inflicted by the people they were setting out to stop, and my own righteous anger overrode my priestly training sufficiently to permit me to wish them well in their assault.

On that first morning of the sweep two groups were found, a score of miles apart from each other, in the act of committing atrocities against Scots people. In one location they had already killed a farmer and his two sons and were venting their lust on the three women of the place when our patrol arrived; in the other they had killed the householder and his wife, an elderly couple who had been granted their lands as freeholds by the late Lord Robert Bruce as a reward for decades of faithful service as his personal retainers. In both instances, the attackers were taken and hanged from the closest big tree, side by side and still wearing their identifying armour, and the corpses of their companions killed in the fight were hung up beside them.

Elsewhere on the patrol routes, there were numerous encounters with other bands of armed men, nine of those with groups of ten or more, on foot, and six more with mounted men-at-arms. The large groups and the mounted groups were challenged and destroyed, their animals, weapons, and armour confiscated and the dead laid out and left in the care of the survivors, whole and wounded, with a warning to whoever had sent them that no further abuses would be tolerated. Smaller parties, of ten men or fewer, if they appeared belligerent, were treated accordingly. If, on the other hand, they could explain themselves and their presence, and were able to convince their interrogators that they were being truthful and had broken no laws, then they might be permitted to go free. Many of them were, and were released bearing warnings about future penalties for breaking King John of Scotland's laws concerning trespass and molestation of the lawful populace.

In all, seventy-eight men died that first day in June. None of them were ours. Thus the word was spread, in the name of King John Balliol, that a new presence was active in Scotland's border country and to the north of it; a vengeful presence, bent upon the protection of the common folk.

For a time after that, the entire border territory lay quiet while the harriers who had provoked Will's anger took stock of their situations and debated how next to proceed, for it transpired that they had larger matters than an outbreak of border warfare to concern them, and far more to worry about than the threats of a ragtag collection of bare-arsed outlaws snarling at them from the shadows of Selkirk Forest. And so, hesitant and probably afraid to aggravate a situation that they did not yet fully understand, the oppressors at the local levels of the reprisals held their forces in check while they waited for further instructions from their masters.

Tension had been building for more than a year between the new Scots monarch and his increasingly impatient and domineering

English counterpart, who had for all intents and purposes placed him on the throne and now saw no reason to disguise the fact that he considered John of Scotland to be in his debt and in his pocket thereafter. The pressure of an impending confrontation between the two monarchs had every political opportunist in Scotland on tenterhooks that summer of 1295, wondering which way to jump next in order to safeguard his own wealth and welfare. It was obvious that choices would soon have to be made, by every noble house and nobleman in Scotland. Which of the two kings was most like to win in this contest—a battle of wills but not necessarily a war? The odds greatly favoured Edward, but John was a relatively unknown quantity, and no one had any desire to commit to either monarch prematurely, or to be seen to pick sides too soon, lest he lose everything on a wrong bounce of the dice.

Throughout that entire period Bishop Wishart kept us informed, to the best of his considerable abilities, on what was happening politically within and even beyond his territories as the various families, houses, and personalities of the magnates manoeuvred for power and position. The Bishop's network of clerical spies and agents, as I knew from close experience, grew ever larger and more complex, fuelled by the fierce, protective ardour of Wishart's concern for the Church's welfare in Scotland, its integrity and very identity within the Scots realm. Even with that backing, though, His Grace could not supply us with all the knowledge we required in such fluid conditions, for the nature of the information we needed most urgently was not the kind that lent itself to discussion in the company of priests or strangers. Men who spoke of such topics were dealing in grave risk, entailing treachery and even treason, with dispossession, imprisonment, and death looming over them. That amount of risk, aligned with such dire penalty, tightened men's tongues, so it was unsurprising that our sources all dried up in short order as that summer settled in.

2

Every now and then, in the life of each of us, a day comes along that seduces us with its unusual delights and leads us far astray from where our so-called better judgment warns us we should be, and yet so attractive are the fruits it offers us that we can set our consciences aside for a while and give ourselves over to unaccustomed pleasures.

On the eighteenth morning of July that year I found myself in such a situation. I remember the date precisely because Ewan laughed about it when he came to visit me that morning, after attending my pre-dawn Mass. It was his natal day, he told me. He was now forty-three years old, and he and his cousin Alec had decided to celebrate the date properly for the first time in years, by spending the entire day in activities that no one, anywhere, would be able to call useful.

The statement was so astonishingly unlike anything that I had ever heard Ewan say that I had to smile when I heard it, knowing exactly whence it had sprung. I was at loose ends that morning, by merest chance and for the first time in weeks, and I can still recall the surge of high spirits with which I laughed in return and told Ewan I would be glad to assist them with their celebrations on such a beautiful day.

Alec, whom I had met weeks earlier and liked immediately, was a newly discovered cousin, another Scrymgeour. Younger than Ewan but older than Will, he had come into the forest a few months earlier, announcing loudly that he had come seeking the warrior William Wallace, to offer him his sword and services. He had been taken to meet Will, who had greeted him with cautious reserve and more than a little suspicion, wondering how anyone from Argyll could legitimately claim to have heard of activities in a forest so far to the south. Those suspicions, though, had been short lived, and the two men had become close and trusting friends within mere days. From the perspective of years I can see it was inevitable that, with his imposing size, ferocious loyalty, and formidable fighting skills, Alexander Scrymgeour would, in a very short space of time, become one of Will's staunchest and most distinguished followers.

"When did you last draw a bow?" Ewan asked me.

I had to think, calculating rapidly. "Two years ago, at least. Why?"

"Because I think it's time for you to reintroduce yourself to the discipline. You're growing soft and pudgy."

"I am not! There's no fat on this frame, if you would care to test it." I stopped. "Besides, I have no choice there, Ewan, and you know it. I am a priest. I cannot carry a weapon."

"Pshaw! You could if you wanted to. Your own Bishop Wishart has no fear of carrying a sword—nor of using it if he has to."

"But His Grace—"

"Oh, relax. I said it's time for you to reintroduce yourself to the *discipline*. I did not say to *killing*. It's the training, Jamie, that will keep you fit and hale. Come with us now. I'm going to try to teach Alec here to use a quarterstaff. Too late for him to hope to learn to draw a bow."

"Mind your mouth, Cousin. I can draw a bow."

Ewan responded without even looking at his cousin, speaking quietly as always. "Too late to mind my mouth, it's ruined. And too late for you to learn to draw a bow—a *real* bow, I mean, like mine, a round yew bow. The other kind, the kind your folk use, can barely throw an arrow half the length of mine. You'll see, Cousin. You too, Jamie, come along."

"I'll come, but I no longer have a bow. I have a staff, but it's for walking and not heavy enough for fighting, even if I wished to."

"I know that. We brought two with us. You may use mine. I'll wager you've not lost the knack of it. Now then, we have food and even a flask of wine, and it's a fine day and we have no demands on us, so come, let's waste no more of it."

Three hours later, I awoke from a doze with the sun burning my face through a gap in the canopy of leaves above my head. We had found a pleasant spot on the banks of a wide stream that had once been a wider river, and had made man-sized targets from a couple of ancient logs that we dragged from the stream bed and lodged upright against the flank of the former riverbank. Ewan had quickly demonstrated the truth of what he had told Alexander, for the big Scot, despite his enormous muscles and breadth of shoulder, had been unable to draw Ewan's longbow to its full extent. He had tried manfully for almost half an hour, but had finally slumped down on the stream bank without having been able to send a single arrow effectively towards the two targets.

I had fared little better, though somehow my muscles still seemed to remember the knack of combining the series of movements that produced the archer's pull. I managed to cast three arrows with a degree of accuracy, though I hit neither target, but then my performance deteriorated rapidly as my body rebelled against the unaccustomed stresses. For another half-hour after that, we tried one another with the quarterstaves, and I was the one who proved most useless there, my muscles long unused to the efforts and tensions of wielding the weapon. And then, eventually, we had eaten, washing the food down with some of the wine we had brought with us and diluted with clear stream water, and dozed off on the grassy bank, beneath the shade of a towering elm tree.

I rolled onto my side to escape the direct heat of the sun and saw Ewan sitting on the edge of the bank, his feet dangling in the water as he concentrated, head down, on something in his fingers.

"What are you doing?"

He cocked his head towards me without taking his eyes off whatever he was holding. "I'm getting ready to catch our dinner. There's a deep hole not far downstream and it looks to be a haven for fine, juicy trout. I remembered I had some hooks in my scrip, but they had strings attached and now they're all a-tangle and I'm trying to unsnarl them. If I succeed, I shall go fishing. If I do not, I'll throw the whole mess into the river."

"And which will it be, think you?" Alec had sat up, too, and now sat squinting towards where Ewan worked meticulously, his tongue protruding as he frowned in concentration over his hooks.

"Probably the river, the way things are looking now," Ewan growled.

"Aye. Well, keep trying, and I'll go and try my hand at the guddlin'."

Smiling to myself, I rose to my feet and followed Alec, intrigued to see how he would fare. I had seen many try but few succeed at guddling, for it involved stroking the belly of a fish and lulling it until you could grasp it and flip it up onto the bank. It was not easy to do, but neither was it impossible—it merely required endless patience and an ability to lie still and move one's questing hand slowly and imperceptibly once it was in the water.

It was clear from the outset that Alec was a master guddler. Within minutes he located a low spot on the riverbank, with a deep channel beneath it, and was soon bare from the waist up, lying full length on the grass with his arm sunk almost to the shoulder beneath the water and his gaze fixed on the large, fat trout that hovered below him. In mere minutes, it seemed to me, he surged up and threw the sparkling fish high into the air to land on the grass behind him, and by the time I had scrambled after it and killed it with a sharp blow to the head from my knife hilt, he was back on his side again, peering down into the water in search of his next catch.

Ewan, in the meantime, had untangled his hooks and was paying us no attention as he pulled up clods of earth in the hunt for worms. I watched idly as he caught one fat grub and threaded it carefully onto a hook attached to a long length of twine, then cast it out into the gentle current of the stream. He, too, had Fortuna on his side that afternoon, and between his efforts and Alec's, we ended up with six fine trout, all about a foot in length. I foraged for firewood and suitable firestones, then kindled and tended the fire while Ewan mixed a dough for bannocks and set them to bake on a flat stone among the coals. When the time was right, Alec, who had cleaned the fish and flavoured them with salt and wild onions, spitted them expertly on sticks and arranged them over the fire, tending them carefully.

We ate surrounded by a magnificent panoply of birdsong, and none of us spoke a single word throughout the meal; we were too appreciative of God's bounty, savouring every delicious mouthful, and when nothing remained but the fish heads, skins, and bones, Alec sighed blissfully and tipped those into the fire.

It was yet early, with a good six hours of July daylight left to us, and we decided to walk again, for the sheer pleasure of it, and so I shouldered Ewan's quarterstaff, leaving him to carry his bow in its long case. Alec had his own staff, and so we walked for an hour or so, seldom speaking but enjoying our companionship and the beauty of the terrain that surrounded us as the deer path we were following led us gradually higher until we reached a rock-strewn hilltop from which we could look down on the greenwood spread out at our feet.

"Look at yon beauty," Alec said, nodding downhill to our right, to where a fine stag stood poised in an open glade, his head high as he sniffed at the breeze for any hint of danger. He sensed none, and we watched as he lowered his head eventually and grazed, following the lure of the richest plants until he vanished among the surrounding trees. I was turning to look behind me when I saw Ewan freeze. "What?" Alec asked before I could even think to speak. "You see something?"

"Aye, but I don't know what ... Something, though. A flash, yonder between the hills, about two miles out."

"Hmm. Jamie, did you see anything?"

"No, but I saw Ewan see it."

"Right, then. Between the two hills. Three pairs of eyes are better than one ..."

Several minutes passed before the next visible stirring occurred, but I saw it instantly.

"There!"

"Aye," Alec growled. "What did you see?"

"It was a man, I think, but it might have been two."

"Two it was," Ewan said in his soft voice. "Two men, one right behind the other, coming towards us. They crested a small ridge, I believe. One head visible for a speck of time, followed by the other. Coming this way now, but headed where, I wonder ..." He coughed gently, clearing his throat. "I don't know the path they're on, don't know where it goes or whether or not it forks, but if it keeps coming straight this way, then it will have to go down there to our left, parallel to the way we came. We'll stay here and wait for a closer look, and if we think that's where they're going, we can cut back down and catch them as they come out into the water meadow where we ate." He shook his head. "Two men? Alone? They're either mad or they're looking for Will's lads."

A short time later, the two appeared again.

"One of them is wearing armour."

"Aye, and the other is not. And one's on a horse, the other on a mule."

Alec jerked his head around to stare at his cousin. "How can you tell that?"

"I can see its ears. Can't you?"

The other man looked at me and rolled his eyes. "No, but I'll take your word for it. A horse and a mule. That means a knight and his servant."

"It might," Ewan said. "Then again, it might not. The man is muffled in a heavy cloak, so his armour might be no more than a breastplate, and the servant might be a woman. Would you care to make a wager?"

I had been half listening to the pair of them, keeping my eyes on the newcomers. "They turned right," I said. "Their right, our left. I saw them go, and then they disappeared. If we're to be in place by the time they arrive down there, we had better go now."

Within moments we were striding back along the path we had followed on the way up, moving twice as fast as we had earlier.

"Damnation," Alec growled. "We only have the one bow."

"It's all we'll need, believe me," Ewan answered. "Give me an open space in which to aim and shoot, and this bow against two men is far more than we'll need."

We reached the point where the path had started to climb, and bore right from there, leaving the path and skirting a fringe of hawthorn trees and willows until we came again to the path, where it entered the water meadow. Ewan looked around quickly and pointed to a copse less than twenty paces from the pathway, and we followed him as he made straight towards it. The strange pair, whoever they were, would have to come along the path behind us and would pass us in the open, providing us with an unobstructed view of them. None of us spoke as we entered the trees and took up positions from which we could see the pathway without being seen ourselves, and we settled down to wait. Ewan, the only one of us with a weapon, strung his bow carefully and then thrust three arrows, point down, into the ground in front of him.

Mere minutes later, the two riders came into view from the north, and at the sight of the one wearing armour I straightened up. "It's His Grace," I said. "Bishop Wishart, in his other guise." I stepped from hiding and walked out into the open.

Wishart called out my name and kicked his mount to a canter as soon as he recognized me, and the man behind him on the mule attempted to follow suit, but his mount had a mind of its own and refused to change its plodding gait, so that the gap between the two men widened rapidly.

"Who did you say this is? A bishop?"

Alec sounded skeptical, and I glanced at him, grinning. "*The* Bishop, Alec. You are about to meet His Grace Robert Wishart, the formidable Bishop of Glasgow. He is a grouchy old terror who has no time for fools or folderols, so smile, man, for I promise you will enjoy him."

His Grace of Glasgow rode right up to us before drawing rein and scanning each of us from head to foot as we each bowed to show him our respect. Ewan and I bent more deeply than did Alec, who watched to see what we would do before he committed himself, then bent forward stiffly from the waist and lowered his chin. The Bishop merely eyed us during his examination; offered no greeting; expressed no opinion until he had completed his scrutiny. Finally he grunted.

"An unlikely trio at first glance, but not entirely unsuited to escort a prince of Holy Church. You look well, Father James. And you, Ewan Scrymgeour, look … like yourself." He turned slightly to eye Alec again. "This one, though, I have never seen before."

"My cousin Alec, Your Grace. Alexander Scrymgeour, lately come from Argyll to join us."

Wishart's eyebrows rose. "From Argyll? Then it is little wonder that I have never seen his face." He looked directly at Alec. "And how is my old colleague Bishop Laurence? I knew him well at one time, though we have seldom met these past two decades. He has been Bishop of Argyll for nigh on thirty years ... But of course, you know that, being one of his flock. I trust he is still hale?"

Alec dipped his head, clearly less than comfortable in making small talk with a bishop. "I have never met His Grace, my lord, but I know he is yet hale—old, as you say, and growing frail, but he yet governs his flock from Lismore and keeps them in order."

"Aye. He was ever strong in that regard."

What neither man mentioned, yet all of us knew, was that there was little love lost between the two Bishops. Bishop Laurence was a native MacDougall of Argyll and, as such, his sympathies coincided with those of the all-powerful House of Comyn, which was enough by itself to set him at odds with Wishart and several other bishops who aligned themselves with the House of Bruce. Wishart's comment about having known the other Bishop well at one time was a reference to the period, twenty years earlier, when he himself had come into harsh conflict with his own cathedral chapter over a disciplinary matter, and Laurence of Argyll had been one of the two judges chosen by papal mandate—the other being the Bishop of Dunblane—to try to resolve the case. His Grace never spoke of the matter, and it had become one of those arcane little secrets known of, but never discussed, by the cathedral community.

The Bishop raised a hand and beckoned his companion forward.

"Father William," he said, "I present to you two at least, and probably three, of William Wallace's closest friends and supporters. Father James here, of whom you have heard me speak, is another Wallace, William's cousin and close friend since early childhood. The hairless one is Ewan Scrymgeour, an archer but much more than simply that. Ewan is the man who inspired Will Wallace and taught him how to use the long yew bow. Thus, in many ways this man is directly responsible for our having travelled to be here today. About the third man you will have just heard." He waved a hand then to include all three of us. "And may I present to you, in turn, Father William Lamberton, newly returned from France and installed this last week as chancellor of Glasgow Cathedral."

The man on the mule had nudged his mount forward and now smiled at us, and I studied him closely, for William Lamberton was very well known to me by repute. He was much younger than I had expected, though, and I judged him now to be no more than two or three years older than myself, which surprised me greatly, considering what he had already accomplished. I liked his smile. It was open and easy, showing both humour and intelligence, and his eyes were bright and wide. He sat erect in the mule's saddle and I judged him to be tall, perhaps taller than I was, with wide, straight shoulders emphasized by the robe he wore, which was the plain grey habit of a monk.

As soon as the greetings were over, His Grace asked us to take him directly to Will, and he was not happy when I told him that Will would be away until at least the following day. He muttered something about having ridden for more than two days to get here, and I could see from his face that he really wanted to shout and complain, but there was nothing he or we could do about the misfortune of his timing, and so he set his jaw, bit down hard on his disappointment, and decided to make the best of the situation. He asked me about my mission in the forest, and about the small communities that Jacobus, Declan, and I tended among us, and he even managed to sound interested in my response, but he frowned with quick impatience when he detected something in my gaze.

"You find it amusing, Father James, that I should be frustrated in my failure to find your cousin here when I have travelled so far to speak with him?"

I heard a cold acerbity in his tone that was new to me. Something inside me flared with alarm, and in one moment of frightening clarity I sensed danger and a need for great caution. And then sanity returned and I remembered that here was a man who had learned,

from hard and often brutal experience, to trust few men and to share
his thoughts but sparingly even with those. This was a man, I knew,
who had no friends, as other people thought of friends; a man to
whom most people lied, in hopes of pleasing him and winning
favour; and above all a man who detested hypocrisy and could smell
a liar and a flatterer from another room.

I looked him straight in the eye. "No, Your Grace, I do not. I
regret your frustration deeply and I know that had Will been aware
you were coming, nothing could have taken him away from here.
But I was smiling, inwardly I thought, at how you managed, after
such a bitter and unexpected disappointment, to feign an interest in
me and my activities so quickly, and to do it convincingly. I found it
admirable, and typical. If that offends you, then I regret that, too."

Robert Wishart hesitated, glaring at me with those ferocious eyes
of his, so formidable beneath his shaggy, unkempt brows, and then
he made the loud, harrumphing sound that I had come to recognize
over the years as the announcement of a change of mind. One corner
of his mouth twitched upward, and he turned his head to look at the
man Lamberton.

"He is not merely impertinent, as you can see, he verges on the
impious," he growled to the chancellor, but then he reached out and
dug his fingers deeply but not cruelly into the muscles of my
shoulder. "It might have made me smile, too, lad, had I but thought
of it, for it's a sad prospect, after endless days of riding, to contemplate long hours of talking about nothing more exciting than the
misadventures of my three most junior priests. Walk with me now."
He tossed the reins of his horse to Alec, who caught them easily and
returned a bob of his head in acknowledgment. "I will accept the
listening to your report as a penance, though, for my hubris in
expecting that your cousin would be waiting to welcome me when I
arrived." He began to walk, slightly stooped, his hands clasped
loosely at the small of his back and his bare head bowed and tilted
towards me, the better to hear what I would say. "Tell me, then,
about your three new parishes …"

3

"Will it disturb you if I share your fire?"

The sound of his voice startled me because it was very close and I had been unaware of his approach. I know I jumped, because Father William reared back and brought up his hands quickly to pacify me. I laughed, slightly embarrassed, as I waved him forward.

"Of course not, Father. You startled me, but I was dreaming when I should have been paying more attention."

He smiled then, moving to sit on an upended log close by me. His eyes sparkled with humour and sympathy in the reflected light of the flames.

"To what should you have been paying attention, sitting alone by a cheerful fire in a guarded camp at this time of night? Plainly you had other matters on your mind. Would you prefer that I leave you with them?"

"No, not at all. I shall be glad of your company." I glanced over in the direction from which he had approached and saw nothing moving. "Is His Grace asleep, then?"

He chuckled. "Aye, these good two hours, which is a blessing approaching the miraculous. And it will do him good. He is no longer young and he sleeps too little nowadays—too little and too seldom. There is always someone waiting close by him with matters demanding his attention. I went to bed when he did, but I lay awake until now. I was hoping to walk myself into tiredness, until I saw you sitting here, staring into the fire."

"And nodding."

He cocked his head, unsmiling now. "No, you were not nodding. You were deep in thought."

I nodded then. "Very perceptive of you." I wondered for a moment if I was being too familiar with him, considering who and what he was, the chancellor of Glasgow Cathedral, but then I remembered who and what he was in truth: a young priest, not too long since ordained and only slightly older than I was. "I was concerned—I *am* concerned. You met Mistress Wallace tonight, so you will have seen that she is with child. She is expected to be delivered of it within the week, but tonight, after Lady Mirren had retired, I saw the midwife emerge from her hut and huddle in conversation with several of the other women. I was too far away to hear what they were saying, but they all looked ill at ease—almost afraid, I thought. I sought to ask them if anything was amiss, but as I started towards them they saw me and exchanged what I took to be warning glances among themselves, and then they all sped away."

Lamberton was frowning slightly. "You suspect there might be something wrong with Mistress Wallace?"

"No, Father, not really. But I have a reluctant and fearful respect for the way things tend to go wrong at the worst, most inconvenient times, and I should hate it if anything untoward occurred while Will was not here to know of it."

"Aye. I know what you mean. Believe me, though, the best thing you can do is leave such things to God. All your fretting and concerns will influence nothing when the time comes for the infant to be born. I know, because I have been present at a birth—delivered the child, in fact—and I had no other option that day than to adapt to what had been thrust upon me."

He saw the astonishment in my eyes and laughed aloud. "Upon my word as a canon of Glasgow, Father, I swear to you it's true." He held up his hands as though he had washed but not yet dried them. "I delivered a child with these two hands, alone and unassisted. It happened in France, not one full year ago, on a journey from Paris to a nearby village called Versailles. I was on my way to visit a monastery there, riding in grand estate in a coach owned by Maitre René St. Cyr, a prominent goldsmith of Paris—goldsmith by appointment to King Philip, in fact. Maitre St. Cyr's wife shared the coach with me, along with her maidservant, Yvette. Madame St. Cyr was *enceinte*, as they say over there—with child—and was on her way to stay with her mother and sisters in Versailles until her confinement was completed the following month. Her husband's affairs had unexpectedly obliged him to remain in Paris, and when he found out that I would be travelling to Versailles on foot at that very time—it is little more than ten miles from Paris—he insisted that I should take his place in the carriage and accompany his young wife to her mother's home.

"Such was the intent with which we set out, on what would normally be a journey of but a few hours, but the route, although otherwise an excellent road, runs through heavy forest, and deep within the woods we were overtaken by a violent storm and met disaster when a large tree, struck by lightning, fell right atop our carriage, smashing two wheels and throwing the vehicle over on its side. The trauma of the incident triggered something within the goldsmith's wife, for she went into labour then and there, even though she was supposedly a full month short of her term."

"And you were *there*?" I was horrified, and I tried to picture what must have happened.

"There?" Again he snorted with half-smothered laughter, shaking his head at the recollection. "Yes, Father, I was there. Right there, by the grace of God, conveniently in the overturned carriage where it all took place, and apart from Madame St. Cyr herself, I was the only person conscious and able to assist with the birth. The maidservant was unconscious, the driver and his footman had been killed by the falling tree, and the full weight of the tree's trunk lay across the carriage door and window, preventing me from climbing out. And so I stayed, and with God's own help I delivered a baby boy who lives and thrives today in Versailles and is named Guillaume, in honour of his godfather, who also baptized him."

He smiled at me. "None of us knows, when we join the priesthood, Father James, that the major disadvantage of our priestly life will be that we are invariably and perennially useless when it comes to involvement in the matters of women." He laughed again, enjoying my wide-eyed discomfiture immensely. "I fear I have scandalized you, but let me reassure you of one thing." He sobered slightly. "I can tell that you were raised as I was, in the company of men and monks and priests, in terror of the sins of carnality and the wiles of scheming women. That is true, is it not?"

I nodded.

"Therefore, on hearing what I have just told you, your mind must have filled with ill-imagined visions of that same carnality, with me among them in my priestly robes. Am I correct?"

Again I nodded, unable to speak.

"Aye, well, nothing could be further from the truth, I swear to you. No slightest trace, not the merest *tinge* of carnality entered my mind—I was too afraid to think of anything other than what I must do to save the lives of that woman and her child, and the other woman, too. I was so unworldly, I did not even know what was happening with the child until the woman slapped me and told me what I had to do. And from that moment on, I behaved as though I were in a dream. There was nothing remotely sexual or sinful in what ensued. The world inside that shattered carriage was a seething cauldron of pain and fear and blood and anguish—and the terrifying awareness that one careless move by me could cost at least one life and possibly more. And yet, in the midst of all that horror, all the fear, instead of death and tragedy I saw the mystery of God's creation being enacted right in front of me, and I received a newborn child into my hands, covered in blood and watery fluids and howling in protest at being thrust into this sinful world ..."

He fell silent, gazing into the fire for a while, but then he straightened. "I can say to you honestly, Father James, there is nothing to be gained by fretting over the time or circumstances of a birth. God has decreed that it will take place, and He alone will decide when and where it does, and how it proceeds. What hope, then, does a mere man, any man, have of influencing any tittle of what will be?"

He saw me still gazing at him slack-mouthed, and he grinned. "What I am telling you, my friend in Christ, is that with women, as with everything else, you merely need to have faith and place your trust in God. I swear, Father, sinful as it may be, I sometimes find it helpful to think of women as another species altogether. They resemble men in no way at all, and men will never come to understand them. It matters not if they be nuns or one's own closest kin or honest wives or bawds—they all have an infallible propensity to make all of us men feel, and appear, and *be* as ineffectual as mewling babes in arms."

The obvious truth of what he had said left me floundering, until he saved me by changing the subject.

"Tell me about your cousin."

"What do you want to know?"

"Everything. I have a hunger to know all there is to know about this man, for I believe he is remarkable. I have heard the Bishop speak of him many times, but always using both his names, naming him William Wallace. And I have met others who have met *Wallace*, but no one who speaks of him the way you do, as plain Will. You, Father James, are the one who has been closest to him throughout his life, so I would like to know what *you* know about him, as a cousin and a friend."

"Well," I began, "he is more like a brother than a cousin, to be truthful. From around the time of my eighth birthday, for the next eight years until Will was eighteen, we lived together, most of the time with Ewan the archer, and shared everything we did every day. We learned to use a quarterstaff together, and though I was never good enough or strong enough to beat him, there was a time when I could hold my own against him, for a while at least, until he wore me down ..."

I talked incessantly for an hour or more, aware that he replenished the fire twice while I was regaling him with all my favourite recollections of Will and the boyhood we had shared. When eventually I fell silent, he was still sitting across the fire from me, smiling at me.

"You love the man. That is plain to see. And I find it heartening because it speaks to his humanity."

"There's much about our Will to love," I answered. "Yet I know there is no lack of folk who would disagree with me. He can be wild, I'll grant, and that is all some ever seem to see in him. And when he's crossed—particularly in things he believes to be right and necessary—he can be hard, and even violent if he perceives that violence is called for. In addition to that, he has no love for Englishmen—indeed he hates them, for good and sufficient reason in his own eyes and, truth to tell, in the eyes of others. But with his friends and loved ones he is the gentlest of creatures."

"You have the same reasons for hating the English that he has, Father, but you do not hate them."

His inflection made a question of the statement. "No, I do not, but neither do I love them greatly. I am a priest, though. Turning the other cheek is part of my life. Will, on the other hand, is a warrior and an avenger."

"Hmm … Think you he will return tomorrow, this warrior cousin of yours?"

"He won't stay away longer than he needs to, not with Mirren so close to her time. May I ask you a question now?"

"Of course. What would you like to know?"

"Tell me a little about France, if you will, about your time there, what you learned. Is it exotic?" I knew that within two years of his early ordination, Lamberton had been selected by a cadre of Scotland's senior bishops to attend university in Paris.

"Well, goodness, where to begin? It is beautiful, heavily forested, and it has unimaginably long, straight roads that run without a bend for score upon score of miles, joining together far-flung cities. The roads were all built by the Romans, of course, as were the great roads of England. But the French have more of them, and better, because the Romans were in Gaul for hundreds of years longer than they were in Britain. Here in Scotland, of course, we had little to attract the Romans, and so although we have some of their roads, we have no great ones.

"Is France exotic?" He thought on that for a moment and then shook his head decisively. "No, not, I think, in the way you mean. It is not strikingly foreign, in the way that Africa and Greece are foreign, visibly and tangibly. France is much like England, in fact, but not quite so green and not quite so wet all the time."

"What did you learn there?"

"Much that you might expect. I studied canon law with some of the finest teachers in the world. But much, too, that I had not anticipated. That sprang from being exposed to brilliant and inquiring minds."

"Such as whose?"

He pursed his lips and looked at me as though he was considering a choice of options. "There is a man called John Duns. They call him Duns the Scot. Have you heard of him?"

"I have heard the name—Duns Scotus is what they call him here. He is a Franciscan, is he not? He is earning a reputation for himself as a free and unique thinker."

Lamberton nodded. "That's the same man. He has been resident at Oxford now for more than a decade, beginning as a very young student, and is now a teacher of philosophy and theology. He is surprisingly young, considering his accomplishments."

That made me smile, as it echoed what I had been thinking about Lamberton himself a short time earlier. "No, I'm serious," he went on. "The man is no more than three or four years older than I am and already he is revered. His ideas are … I am tempted to use the word *exciting*, even though it is not a word normally applied to theology or philosophy. Nevertheless, his opinions are vibrant, and some of them have set the world of scholarship reeling, without scandalizing the orthodox majority—a signal accomplishment."

"It sounds as though you know the man, Father. Have you been, then, to Oxford?"

"No." Lamberton almost laughed at the thought. "But I do know him. I met him in Paris, when he came to debate with several of the faculty at the university, and I had the privilege of spending many pleasant hours listening to him speak, and speaking with him, during the few weeks that he remained in Paris."

I tried to imagine what it must be like to sit in the presence of a truly brilliant and original thinker and to drink in his words. "What a privilege, to meet and speak with such a man," I said.

"He impressed me greatly. But there was yet one other man I met there whose ideas stirred me even more, in some ways, than Father Duns's, perhaps because I sensed a connection between their ideas that had not, and may not yet have, occurred to them. This second man made no attempt to formalize his ideas; he merely spoke to and from his personal convictions. Yet I was convinced, merely by listening to him on one sole occasion, that he lives by and would die for his ideas, and that they will forever direct his life." The corner of his mouth flickered in a tiny grin. "His name, too, you will have heard."

"From Paris? I think not, Father. You overestimate my knowledge of the world. I doubt if I could name a single person in all the city there."

"Then you must expand the city to embrace the realm. I was speaking of Philip Capet."

"Capet?" I blinked at him in astonishment. "You met King Philip of France?"

"I did. He came to speak with Father Duns one night when I was visiting him, and I was graciously permitted to remain with them."

"That surprises me. From all I have heard, Philip the Fair prefers to hold himself aloof from human contact."

"Aha! Then, my friend, you have been listening to people who are but repeating hearsay. All men need human contact, and there are no exceptions to that rule. Even the strictest anchorites must communicate with other men from time to time, or risk going mad. I am not saying Philip is a hearty and gregarious companion, or even that he is particularly hospitable, but he has a certain personal amiability when he chooses to display it. Yet he is a man conscious of owning a destiny. And men of destiny, I am told, are seldom easy to deal with, requiring great finesse and circumspection, even dedication, in the handling."

"What was it that caught your attention so quickly in the discourse of the King of France?"

He smiled briefly. "It is late, now—it must be close to midnight—and this simple-seeming question of yours could take much answering. Are you sure you wish to hear my response?"

"Very sure, and I am not the slightest bit tired, so if you are prepared to think and talk at this hour of night, I am more than ready to listen. Why don't you find some wine for us while I replenish the fire?"

4

I went in search of split logs from the neighbouring fires, for we had burned up the supply closest to us. I made short work of the quest, gathering unused logs from several dead or dying fires close by, and by the time I had emptied my arms of the fourth load of plundered fuel and came back to sit down again, there was a cup of lightly watered wine waiting for me on the log that was my seat. I picked it up, tipped it slightly towards Father Lamberton in salute, and sipped at it appreciatively, finding it far more palatable than the rough, raw wine we used for Communion purposes. Lamberton sipped at his, too, then stooped and placed his cup carefully by his feet, where it would not tip over.

"Our system is broken," he said.

"Which system?"

"There is only one."

"You mean the Church's system? But that is God's own and therefore perfect and unbreakable. What other system is there?"

"The one by which the whole world lives, outside the Church. I am talking about Christendom—more accurately, about the hierarchical system by which all of Christendom is governed."

"Strange," I said. "The Bishop himself once described Christendom thus to me, as a vast and complex system of governance, functioning everywhere under the same principles, yet among different peoples."

"Aye, it is, and all of it is based upon property: land, territory, possessions—wealth. Think of it: Scotland, England, France, Norway, Italia, Germany—all *land* and all of it owned and operating along the same lines, radiating outward from the central landholder, who may be king or prince or duke or earl or chief. Each of these— let us call them rulers—has deputies, whom we will call barons, to whom he parcels out the land he holds, in return for their services. Those barons, in their turn, split up their holdings equally among *their* liegemen in return for fealty, and then the liegemen parcel out their lands to knights who will support them for the privileges they receive. The knights, the lowest rank upon the social ladder, employ freemen and serfs and mesnes and bondsmen to tend and till and harvest the tiny plots of land they have within their grant, and they garner rents and fees into their own hands, portions of which they pass up the ladder."

I nodded. "And surprisingly, when you look at it thus closely, it all works. So why would you say it is broken?"

He grinned at me then. "I can see the crack in the edifice from where I sit."

I looked quickly around the clearing, but we were the only people there, and there was nothing else to be seen except the darkened shapes of the huts and tents beneath the trees. "What crack in which edifice?"

"Those huts. The fact that we are sitting in this sleeping village filled with outlaws, all of whom might be hanged out of hand were they unfortunate enough to be taken. That is one end of the crack, if you can perceive it. The other end is Glasgow, or Jedburgh, Berwick, Roxburgh, Edinburgh, Stirling."

I shook my head. "Now you really have lost me."

"I know, you and nine-and-ninety out of any hundred men to whom I might speak of it. *I* know what I am saying because I have thought much about it and discussed it with men like Father Duns and King Philip of France." He grimaced, shaking his head in what I took for regret. "Our earthly world is changing rapidly, Father. The changes are not visible to everyone who looks, but to those who know exactly where to look, the signs are unmistakable. And here in Scotland, the place to look is here, and in the burghs."

"Here and in the burghs." I knew I sounded dull, because that was precisely how I felt. "You mean … here among the outlaws?"

"Aye, and elsewhere among the burgesses, though I will grant the burgesses may be the more important."

The burgesses may be the more important *what?* I had never considered the burgesses as anything more than they appeared to be, the townspeople of our land, the merchants and manufacturers and craftsmen, the shopkeepers and traders who lived in the seaports and centres of commerce throughout Scotland. Now, however, I recalled the mystifying conversation I had had with Bishop Wishart on the same topic a year earlier, and I could see—though the comparison itself struck me as being perverse—that the burgesses were, in fact, the opposing face of the coin to Will's outlaws; each group took great pride, albeit for widely differing reasons, in being self-sufficient and accountable to no one.

I realized that my companion had fallen silent and was staring at me, clearly waiting for me to say something in response.

"Frankly, Father," I told him, "I find it difficult to see any connection between outlaws and burgesses."

"And that is as it should be, at this point. But the connection is there—merely obscured for now. Think how the system works: the land being handed downward from the rulers, and the feudal services and fruits of the harvest being fed back up the various levels to sustain them. Neither of those processes takes into account the presence of the outlaws or the burgesses. That is a new development."

"Hardly new," I said. "There have always been outlaws."

"Granted. But until recently they were always—*always*—outcasts in the truest sense, banished beyond the limits of society, shunned and condemned by everyone, and quick to die in consequence. Now, though, we have outlaws like your cousin and his followers, entire communities of them—still proscribed and banished, still condemned to execution upon capture, but *organized* into social groups, and widely acclaimed by their countrymen because of this unprecedented claim of theirs to what they are calling freedom, and their determination to live their lives according to their own wishes, paying fealty to no one other than the leader of their choice. That would have been inconceivable when you and I were boys, a few short years ago."

"And to me it so remains. Do you really believe that's what my cousin Will is saying to the world?"

The eyes gazing at me from across the fire became, quite suddenly, the grave eyes of the cathedral chancellor. "Aye, Father

James, I do, because it *is* what he is saying. And loudly, too, if you but stop to listen."

"Which I have evidently failed to do. But where do the burgesses fit into this vision of yours, this break in the system?"

Lamberton reached down to his feet and picked up his cup of wine, sipping at it before he answered me, and when he spoke, his voice was calm. "The system is hundreds of years old. Would you agree?"

"Of course. It grew out of the chaos left behind when the Roman Empire fell here in the West, seven or eight hundred years ago."

"There were no burgesses *one* hundred years ago."

I blinked at him. "The Bishop himself said the selfsame thing to me more than a year ago. And I find it as incomprehensible now as I did then, even though I know it to be true. But still I keep thinking there must have been burgesses of some description."

"Oh, they were there a hundred years ago, and they lived in burghs, but they were simple traders—fishermen, merchants perhaps, not burgesses as we know them today. You see, it has only been within the past hundred years that the traders and merchants of this realm, and every other realm, have organized themselves. Before they organized, they were single traders, merchants, whatever you wish to call them. Each was responsible for amassing his own trading goods and finding his own markets, and each bore the entire cost of protecting his own interests. Then they saw the benefits of cooperation, and they began forming guilds and brotherhoods and trading associations. Soon after that, pooling their efforts and working together, they began to prosper. They amassed greater and greater profits, in greater safety and at less expense, and once that change had begun, it continued, *because it was meant to be*!

"But nowhere do they fit within the *corpus* of the system."

"I know. I can see that now. The Bishop explained it all to me, as I said. I did not fully understand what he was talking about at the time, and I'm not sure I understand it now, but I can accept that these people are their own men. They thrive or perish by their own efforts. And they hold themselves beholden to no other because of some accident of birth. Their burghs, too, belong to no overlord. They have emerged as public lands, free of lien or debts to the nobility ..."

I broke off as I realized my companion was staring at me, looking slightly baffled. "I can see you understand what I've been saying, Father, but it's obvious something is troubling you about what I've been saying. May I ask you what it is?"

My lips had gone numb and my tongue felt wooden in my mouth, because I remembered how I had felt on hearing all this on that first occasion, when I had anticipated chaos and disaster.

"War," I said aloud, struggling to articulate the single word.

"*What*?" He bent forward quickly, peering at me. "Why would you say that?"

"How could I not? What else is there to think? Bishop Wishart reacted the same way when I said as much to him, and I thought he was wrong then. And now I think you are equally wrong. You both say no one yet sees the world you describe, the crack in the edifice, but it seems clear to me that when they do, it will bring chaos. Few things have the power to unite the magnates of the noble houses into a single force, but this threatens all they are and all they stand for. They will unite to wipe out the burgesses and their towns. And they will scour the whole land, looking for those who might stand against them."

"Nonsense, Father James. No nobleman will move against the burgesses, for the simple reason that the townsmen of the burghs now generate more riches with their local industry than all the nobles together can raise from their vast estates. And so the nobility borrows from the wealthy burgesses and becomes ever more indebted to them. They cannot move against them, for they would be depriving themselves of their main source of income.

"And besides, it is already far too late for them to alter any of what I have described. All they can do now is wait, like every other living soul of us, for the changes that must surely come, for the world of Christendom will never revert to what it once was." He stood up suddenly and shook out the skirts of his robe, rearranging them more comfortably before sitting down again. "The system under which we all live now will wither and die and be replaced by another, just as did Rome, the supposedly eternal city, and the empire it created."

"Aye, but Rome was pagan and benighted. We are speaking here of *Christendom*, Father Lamberton. How can you—?" I paused, seeking the words to express my fear and confusion, and stooped to retrieve my cup, raising it to my mouth only to discover that it was empty, and I bent quickly and put it down again by my feet more forcefully than I intended. "How can you say such a thing, when you have barely finished saying that not one person in a hundred knows what is happening?"

The chancellor gazed at me levelly. "Fewer than that," he said. "One in ten thousand might be closer to the truth at this time, but nevertheless, the changes are happening. You are a priest, Father. Need I remind you that in the days when our Blessed Jesus walked the earth there were not twenty men in all the world who knew Him as the Son of God? Yet there He was, and the changes He had wrought were already all in place. I believe we are experiencing something similar today. For His own good reasons, my friend, God has decided that this world must change. And therefore, change it will."

"And what about the King? Does he know about these changes?"

"Ah, the King. King John, may God bless him, should he live and prosper and emerge the victor in his struggle with the King of England, may end up absorbing the wisdom and long-headedness of the King of France on such matters. Philip has known of it for years, since soon after he assumed the French throne. His kingdom is tiny, although it is growing constantly these days. And he is bankrupt, several times over, if one is to heed his critics. Were it not for the largesse of the Templars and their inexhaustible wealth, the realm of France would be incapable of functioning in any manner."

He stood up again and arched his back, massaging his behind with both hands.

"Do you not find these logs supremely uncomfortable? I know they are logs, and not chairs, and I generally have little trouble with them. Then again, though, I seldom sit like this for hours at a time, and I have little padding on my bones at the best of times ... and virtually none on my buttocks, where I could most use it. Will it vex you if I stand for a while?"

"Vex me? Not at all. In fact, if you wish to walk and stretch your legs I will come with you. We'll throw some fresh logs on the fire and then walk the camp's perimeter, checking the guards for vigilance along the way. It takes about an hour to make the circuit and we can talk as we walk. By the time we get back, the fire should be at its prime. Shall we?"

The night grew noticeably cooler once we had left the fire, and we were soon walking briskly against the chill in the air, each of us well wrapped up in our long cloaks.

"You were talking about France," I resumed as we approached the nearest edge of the tree line around the camp and the first guard post on our route. "You say it is growing. How can that be?"

"By absorption." He was looking at the ground ahead of him in the darkness "Philip Capet is a hard man to deny. He believes God truly wants him to consolidate under one crown the entire territory of what once was Roman Gaul. France, as you know, is but one of many duchies, and not at all the largest of them. Their names are lustrous, some of them more famous, even, than the name of France itself: Burgundy, Aquitaine, Languedoc, Flanders, Champagne, Anjou, Poitou, Picardy, Lorraine, and the rebellious Gascony, of course, currently the cause of so much grief to King Edward. All of them are in turmoil today, and Philip is determined to unite them all beneath his banners. He sees himself as King of one great entity that he has named the Nation State."

That term meant nothing to me and I said as much, and for the ensuing part of our walk my companion held forth on the wonders of this nation state that Philip Capet dreamed of ruling. We visited two more sentries in the course of that time, but I was barely aware of them, so completely was I caught up in what I was hearing. It was a vaunting vision that my new friend described for me in sweeping words, entailing elements of politics that sounded revolutionary and impossible to me: talk of a unified state built along new and radical lines, where the state itself would become an active entity in its own governance, and the people of the state would come to think of themselves as something new—a *nation*, a single people united by ties of race, language, government, and common interests. They would forge this nation out of Philip's dream, and in time their new creation, their new nation state, would dictate the behaviour of all of Christendom, for Christendom itself would be unable to withstand the threat posed by the united resources of the new nation state.

"It is an ambitious idea," Lamberton said. "But I have thought much about it since the night Philip spoke of it to Duns and me, and I am not convinced it is as preposterous as once I thought. Now, in fact, I think he might achieve his goal."

"But how can he do that, any of it, if, as you say, his treasury is bankrupt?"

Lamberton tilted his head in an unmistakable indication that he considered my point to be moot. "Edward of England's treasury is bankrupt, too, but that has not prevented him from continuing to wage war against his Gascon rebels, or conducting an illicit campaign against this realm. Monarchs fight wars for widely differing reasons, but almost all of them *do* it—incessantly, it seems—and nothing is more ruinously expensive than conducting a war. Yet by that very token, no route to conquest and expansion or dominion is more direct or more effective than the one offered by war. A successful war results in massive riches, which, in return, defray the enormous costs incurred in waging war. It becomes a never-ending cycle."

"Granted," I said, nodding in agreement. "But you indicated that Philip had a new viewpoint, did you not? I interpreted that to mean he believes he can achieve this melding of all the duchies and territories where no one has done so since the days of the Caesars."

"Aye, that is what I meant. And I believe there are several reasons why he might succeed. The first of those being that all the duchies share a common language. A common *root* language, that is. They all speak variants of the old Frankish tongue. We call it French, but many of them continue to call it by their local names—Angevin in Anjou, Poitevin in Poitiers, Oc in the Languedoc, and so on. There are regional differences, some of them profound, but fundamentally the tongue is French and they can all speak it and understand each other. Which means a newly conquered territory can be absorbed without great disruption."

I stepped into the shadows beneath a dense stand of trees, where I hoped we would be challenged by the fourth and last of the guardsmen on duty. Lamberton followed at my heels, and within moments a voice rang out ahead of us, challenging us to stand where we were. I identified myself quickly, addressing the guardsman by name and telling him we were two priests with much to talk about and no desire to sleep, and after a brief exchange of greetings he waved us on, no doubt glad to have had the opportunity to speak with someone even for mere moments and even gladder, I was sure, to have been awake and at his post when we approached him.

"Tell me," I asked as soon as he had fallen out of hearing behind us. "Are there burgesses in Philip's France?"

"Heavens, yes—more than there are in Scotland, and they may even be wealthier, which means Philip's problem there is more pronounced than ours yet is. Philip, gazing into his empty treasury and needy as he always is and ever was, is seeing the returns from his royal lands and holdings growing smaller from year to year, while more and more people are thriving without having to pay tribute, in the form of rent and revenues, to their so-called betters. Yet under the existing system he has no means of redress, other than to increase those holdings by any means available—namely, wars and conquest. But the riches of his burgesses must make him gag, because their wealth is laid out before his eyes in every town and city of his realm."

"So how will he change that?"

"By changing the way things stand—by enacting new laws that will allow him to apply new taxes in ways that have never been seen before. He has already set his lawyers to work. He will tax merchants for the premises they own within his kingdom and for the use of the roads within his realm. He will tax them for their use of those ports and storage facilities they need in order to pursue their ventures. Rest assured, his lawyers will eventually find ways of taxing merchants for the nails that hold horseshoes in place. And in return he will offer them his royal protection—the protection of the state—against outside interference in their operations. Far more important, though, will be his offer to include them in the country's governance."

"Governance? To what extent?"

"To whatever extent he sees fit, though that will be subjected to his divine right to rule. But at least he is speaking of giving his merchants—his mercantile citizens—a voice for the first time. And that may be the single largest and most significant change in the coming new order. Like our burgesses, these men are commoners. The call themselves *bourgeois* in France, and it means exactly the same thing, burgh-dwellers. They have never had any voice, or any influence, in anything. But now they will. They may not speak out as loudly or as effectively as they do here in Scotland, where there is no divinely entitled monarch, but the French bourgeois will nevertheless be heard from more and more as they grow richer. Philip needs their wealth, but more than that, he needs their support. He cannot simply plunder their vaults, for they would quickly move away to a safer place where they could continue working beyond his influence, and that would be fatal to all his hopes. So he must keep them on his side. He must tax them in such a way that they will submit to his taxation, however grudgingly, and continue in their commerce. He has no choice. He will be forced to compromise, and *that* is a new phenomenon."

We followed the moonlit footpath around one more bend and found ourselves back where we had started. Ahead of us the fire I had built up before we left had dwindled to a glowing pile of embers, and we made our way straight towards it.

"Have we been gone an hour?" Lamberton asked as I pushed and prodded new fuel into the coals, stirring up a storm of sparks and blue- and purple-tinted flames.

"Close to it. When was the last time you were awake this late by choice?"

He laughed. "Other than in all-night vigil, I have no idea. And I cannot even remember my last vigil, so it has been a long time. We will probably both regret it tomorrow."

"I think not. The time has not been wasted—not from my viewpoint, at least. The discussion of ideas is never a waste of time. Tell me, if you will … It seems to me we lost sight of the importance of Will's outlaws in all we were discussing. Where do they fit into all of this?"

"They do not, and that is precisely why they are important. Their importance here in Scotland echoes that of the French burgesses: they have never had a voice before, but from now on they will. Make no mistake, Father James, the outlaws living here today—in Will's community, certainly—are historically different from the outlaws who once hid from justice in these woods. Most of those people had set themselves outside the law by their own actions. They were criminals at least, and some of them were monsters. But most of the people living here in the greenwood with Will are outlaws through oppression, not through choice. They have been dispossessed and uprooted, cast out of their homes and villages through no fault of their own. They are victims themselves, not victimizers."

"I understand that. But how will they have a voice?"

"Because they are the *people*, Father James, and their voice is a new one, and once it has been raised, it will never die away. The people of this land are making themselves heard as they have never been before. The burgesses are demanding a new place in the scheme of things, and so are the common folk, and once that has begun, nothing can stop it. People here in Scotland are talking about themselves as a *community*—the 'community of the realm' has become a common phrase today. For the first time in history there is talk everywhere of the will of the people—the *people*, Father. *All* the people, not merely the landowners, the magnates, or the earls and barons. The *people*!"

He rose to his feet. "I think I might sleep now, for an hour or two. My eyelids are grown heavy suddenly. And tomorrow I will meet your cousin Will, who, though he does not yet know it, represents— or, I believe, soon will represent—the voice of the people of Scotland. Think upon that before you fall asleep yourself, tonight, if you sleep at all—William Wallace, *vox populi*, the voice of a people."

CHAPTER FIFTEEN

I

Bishop Wishart officiated at Mass before dawn the next day, with Lamberton and myself as co-celebrants, and as soon as we had broken our fast afterwards, he set out with Canon Lamberton to visit my two junior colleagues, Declan and Jacobus. Aware that part of the Bishop's objective that morning would be to assess my performance and general fitness through the observations of my two subordinates, I settled down to read my breviary, and I was still deep in meditation when a messenger arrived to tell me Will had returned and wanted to see me.

I was glad to see Mirren standing with Will in their doorway, glowing with health and smiling happily up at her husband from the crook of his arm. Her belly was enormous, but there was no doubting her well-being, and I offered a swift prayer of thanks that my misgivings of the previous evening had been baseless. Will had seen me as soon as I emerged from the trees, and he waved, beckoning me to follow them as he turned and moved into the hut, his wife still held close. By the time I stepped inside, though, Mirren had disappeared. I assumed that she had withdrawn behind the painted screen of reeds that separated their sleeping chamber from the remainder of the dwelling and called a greeting to her, but I received no answer and so looked at Will, raising one eyebrow in inquiry.

"She went out through the other door. She's meeting with her women. Come and sit." He was already sitting in the large, padded chair he had built for himself in the corner by the empty stone hearth, and he waved me to the chair facing it.

"Wishart's here, I'm told," he said as I moved to sit. "What does he want, d'you know?"

"I have no idea. You'll have to ask him that yourself. But he was none too happy when he found out you weren't here, so it might be urgent."

"Who's the other fellow with him?"

"One of the cathedral canons, a man called Lamberton. He's been in France these past two years. Came back a short time ago and was raised to chancellor of the cathedral. He's a clever lad."

"Lad? How old is he?"

"Your age, I would guess. Not much more, perhaps a little less. But he has talents beyond his years."

"He must have, to be chancellor already." He frowned. "We never had a chancellor at the Abbey, did we? What does he *do*?"

"He regulates the daily life of the cathedral. It's an administrative post."

"So why is he here?"

"He's here to meet you." I stopped short, looking in wonder at the thing that had just caught my eye. "What is *that*?"

Will twisted in his seat to see what I was staring at. "What's it look like? It's a sword. Why does this … Lamberton, you said? Why does he want to meet me? Or will I have to ask that, too, myself?"

"You will. He would not tell me. Not that I asked." I was still gazing at the sword in the corner behind him, propped upright beside the long leather cylinder of his bow case. "That's the biggest sword I've ever seen in my life. It's enormous. Where did it come from?"

"It's a gift, from Shoomy. He brought it from his brother's smithy last week."

"Shoomy's brother is a smith? I didn't even know he had a brother."

Will sniffed. "I didn't know, either, until Shoomy brought me this. When I asked him where he had got it, he told me it had been gathering dust in his brother Malachy's forge. Apparently the brother is well known, the finest sword crafter in all the northwest.

But Shoomy is so close-mouthed, I had to drag that out of him. Never says more than he has to, our Shoomy. Most of the time that can be a blessing. At other times, though, it can be damned annoying."

I had walked over to the weapon and now stood admiring the craftsmanship and skill of the man who had fashioned it. It was resting, point down, in the corner, and its long, bare blade gleamed dully in the light from the window. "May I handle it?"

"If you wish, but you won't be able to swing it in here."

"I can see that, but I have no intention of swinging the thing, Cuz. It's huge … I would gladly settle for being able to lift it." I reached out to touch the pommel, and had to raise my hand to the level of my head to do so. From its large, acorn-shaped pommel to its pointed tip, the weapon was as tall as I was, which made it just under six feet long. I estimated the hilt, which was covered in leather and bound with spirals of what appeared to be bronze wire, to be about a foot and a half in length. The slender, twisted, downward-curving cross-guard, of the same gleaming metal as the blade, was as wide as my shoulders but no more than a thumb's width in section, and it had been turned throughout its entire length to give it the appearance of a length of corded metal rope, with decorative quatrefoils at each end. But there was much more to the defences for the wielder's hands than I had seen on any other sword. I had to step in close to see how it had been done, but the swordmaker had taken great pains with the metal cross-block over the top of the blade, which was a palm wide at that end. He had hammer-welded one-half of an oval steel ring onto each side of the thick block, then bent the twin pieces down until they lay almost flush with the flat of the blade on either side, leaving just enough space between ring and blade to trap the blade of an unwary opponent.

I ran my finger down the addition and hooked the first joint into the space between guard and blade. "This is fine workmanship. Is it sharp?"

Will had come to stand beside me. "Not there, that part's for gripping, but the cutting edge is lethal. Be careful if you touch the blade lower down."

I had suspected as much, simply from the way the light caught the lower edges of the blade; it had that unmistakable twinkling look of razor-sharpness. The edges of the first ten inches of the blade below the guard were hammered flat to provide a guiding grip for fighting at close quarters, permitting the swordsman to wield the weapon as a stabbing spear rather than a slashing blade. Below that, at the top of the blade proper, which was tapered and double-edged for its remaining three-and-a-half feet, twin spurs projected from the edges of the blade, and though they were not long, they were thick and strong, hooking towards the point, their purpose to catch and break the impetus of an opponent's hard-swung blow. I had almost no experience of swords or of the knightly art of swordsmanship, but I knew that the weapon I was looking at was magnificent by any standard and was too long and cumbersome to be used easily from horseback.

"So Shoomy's brother made this thing for *you*?"

"No, not a bit of it! How could he? He had never heard of me, any more than I had of him. I said Shoomy found it in his brother's forge. He made the hilt and guard, Shoomy said, for that is what he does best. The blade itself, though, was made elsewhere, probably in Germania for one of those Teutonic Knights you sometimes hear about. How it ended up in Malachy's forge, I don't know. It lay there for several years, it seems, before Malachy fashioned a new hilt, pommel, and guard for it, and *then* he discovered he couldn't sell it. It was too big ... bigger than any sword around and made for a giant, folk said. And so it lay there for two years until Shoomy set eyes on it and brought it back for me."

"I see ... And what made Shoomy think you needed a sword— you, the bowman? Or was this a mere whim prompted by the size of the thing?"

My cousin grinned at me, though without much humour. I could see it mostly in the crinkling around his eyes; that was enough, nevertheless, to allow me to imagine the wry quirk of the lips concealed beneath the thick growth of his beard. "You should have been here six weeks ago. Then you'd have no need to ask that question."

"Why? What happened?"

"We met some strangers in the woods … unfriendly strangers."

"Englishmen?"

"A few, but most of them were Scots. We know that because we heard them shouting to one another, back and forth, but to this day we don't know who they were. A score of them, give or take one or two, and all horsed. They had seen us coming. Attacked us from hiding, with crossbows. Killed four of us before we even knew we were being watched."

"How many were you, against their score?"

"Eight of us, until that first volley—four thereafter. That we got out at all was a miracle. They hit us as we were passing through the edges of a bog, surrounded by thickets of osier willow. We had no room to do anything, least of all to draw a longbow, and the few shots we were able to loose were deflected by the dense growth around us. They, on the other hand, were on higher, drier ground, clear of the bog, unhampered in their aim, and shooting short steel bolts."

"How did you get out?"

"We ran away, into the bog, and we were fortunate they chose not to follow us. They could have picked us off one by one out there, floundering in the mud as we tried to wade across. I don't know why they didn't follow us. They should have. I would have, had I been them. And thanks be to God they didn't. I'd be dead otherwise."

"What would you have done if you had this sword with you that day?"

He bared his teeth, white flashing through the darkness of his beard. "I might have charged at our attackers and died trying to reach them before they could shoot me down."

"That's what I thought. So why do you now need a sword? To enable you to be killed more easily?"

He smiled again, but this time the smile was genuinely amused, warming his eyes. "No, Cuz. If I wear it at all, it will be as a symbol."

"A symbol … Very well, then, let's accept that it could be a symbol. Heaven knows it's big enough. But a symbol of what? Outlawry?"

His smile did not falter. "No, of leadership. Bear in mind, though, that I said '*if* I wear it at all.'"

"If … Is there doubt that you might?"

"Enormous doubt, Jamie."

"Enormous is more than merely large. What causes such great doubt, may I ask?"

"Aye, you may ask. It's caused by the fact that I'm about to be a father. I am to have a son, Jamie, or perhaps a daughter. It matters not which to me, but either one will be a responsibility I've never had before. A small wee person, wide-eyed and alive and hungry for knowledge, and dependent upon me for his or her existence. For that reason alone I will be steering well clear of any more leadership in future. If God permits me, I intend to stay here safely in the greenwood with my wife and child, providing for them and getting more of them."

I found myself grinning at him inanely, wondering where this new Will had come from. In all the years I had known and loved him I had never seen this aspect of him, never even suspected its existence. I had always known he loved Mirren, that he had loved her from the first time he set eyes on her, but I had never suspected that he might love her dearly enough to shut himself off voluntarily from the entire world on her behalf.

"Believe me, Cousin," I told him, "if you were fortunate enough to be able to do such a thing, I would count myself blessed to be able to travel here from Glasgow to minister to you and your family once each month."

A tiny frown grew instantly between his brows. "But you don't think it is likely to happen. I can hear it in your voice … see it in your eyes."

"No, I did not say that, Will, but you yourself will have to admit, if you but think on it, that the odds against your winning that peaceful isolation are great. Your name is too well known now for you to simply disappear, especially after your announcement of your name and your intentions to His Lordship of York in April. I am not saying you could not vanish from the ken of men, because of course you could, but it would not be easily arranged. Nor easily maintained."

"The ease of doing it and the difficulties of sustaining it do not concern me," he said slowly. "It will be done, if I wish it to be done. Determination to stay hidden is what I'll require most—that, and a place where no one will find me accidentally. Will you help me with that, if I call upon you?"

"Of course I will, and happily. And I will apply myself from this time on to making it possible. This will be a worthwhile task."

He lowered his head. "My thanks, Cousin."

"Don't thank me yet. Wait until I've found the way to make it work. In the meantime, though, take my advice and keep this sword well hidden. Thank Shoomy for it, but ask his leave to hold it safe against a time when you might really need it. It will attract too much attention if you wear it openly, for it smacks too much of something a leader might carry for effect. And that brings us around in a complete circle to what we were talking about when we began. Whence did this all spring, this notion of symbols and leadership?"

"Murray," he said, and I did not know whether he meant Andrew Murray or the place called Moray, for they both sounded the same when spoken.

He grimaced then and clawed at his beard with hooked fingers, scratching deeply as he continued speaking. "This has to come off. I swear it's full of fleas. And I should know better than to sleep with the dogs when I'm on the road. Mirren will flay me." He paused, collecting his thoughts. "Where did this thing about leadership and symbols come from?" He shrugged. "I first heard of it from Andrew Murray, when I saw him in the north a few years ago, on that errand for the Bishop. He carries a battle-axe with him everywhere now because it has become his emblem. He even has one blazoned on his standard, which is laughable. Murray is a swordsman, as you know—always has been. And because he's trained all his life on the English quarterstaff, there is no one in Scotland who can best him face to face and toe to toe with a sword in his hand.

"Several years ago, though, when his father's lands were invaded by raiders from the far northeast, he won a dire fight using an axe against a mounted raider after he himself had been unhorsed. The axe was all he had, he told me, for when he was knocked from the saddle, he had fallen on his sword and shattered the blade. When his opponent charged him for the kill, Andrew managed to dodge aside and hooked the end of his axe blade behind the knee joint of the fellow's armour. He couldn't say afterwards if it actually hooked behind the fellow's knee brace or caught in a flaw in his chain mail, but he knew it was a fluke, the sheerest accident, and he told me he could never have done it again. It worked, though, for when the fellow's horse spun away, Andrew's weight on the lodged axe pulled the rider from its back. The fellow hit the ground hard and Andrew split his helm with a single blow. The word spread that Andrew Murray was a peerless axe man. He has never used an axe in a fight since then, he says, but he carries one with him everywhere he goes, because his people expect to see it. And he rides beneath a yellow banner marked with a blood red axe head, a symbol of his *puissance*, as the French call it."

"And he thought you might wish to bear one, too, someday?"

"No, it was not quite that straightforward." He crossed the tiny room in a few strides to where a jug stood, covered with a white cloth, beside a quartet of earthen mugs. He poured a mug of ale for each of us and brought one to me, waiting until I raised it in a salute that he returned before bringing the rim of his mug to his own lips. He drank deeply, then lowered his cup and belched softly. "There, now that tasted good." He reached out to touch the cross-guard of the great sword, his hand side by side with mine.

"What Murray said was that every leader, great or small, needs a recognizable emblem—a symbol of his leadership. His became a battle-axe, irrespective of what he himself might have wished for, and that led him to wonder what mine might be, if ever I should become a leader of men here in the south." He flicked his thumb against the metal of the guard, then turned away and moved back to his big chair. "It was whimsical thing, of no real import, and we were but passing idle time. I had forgotten all about it until I came in here one day and saw that great thing leaning in the corner. It came to me then that Andrew's symbol should have been a sword but ended up being an axe, and I knew that my own should be a bow, but that *as a symbol*, a bow, contrary to all my love and respect for it as a weapon, now seemed somehow … insubstantial. Slender and slight looking and not at all weighty or solid.

"That thought, in turn, reminded me of something else Andrew had said that day. We had been talking about battle tactics and leadership and the worth of infantry as opposed to cavalry and of both together in the face of massed archery. The English use their Welsh archers to great effect, as you know, and in the last twenty years, under Edward, they have been working hard to train their own men in the Welsh techniques. Massed bowmen, properly deployed, can rout the finest army ever fielded, for modern armies have no defence against them."

He fell silent, and I waited for him to finish, but he was clearly thinking about something else by then.

"So?" I prompted. "What was his point?"

"Eh? Oh, that we have neither sufficient bowmen nor adequate cavalry in Scotland, so any fighting that we have to do in years ahead will be left to our foot soldiers." He saw the expression on my face and spoke quickly to forestall what I might say. "We have fine bowmen. I'm not denying that. Excellent archers, and I am one of them. But we have nowhere near *enough* of them, Jamie. Where we can turn out a hundred archers, the English can field a thousand in half the time, and they can keep doing the same for every other hundred we can raise. The same goes for heavy chivalry—armoured knights and the mounts to carry them. We have numerous and noble knights as well, but they wear mail, not solid plate armour, because nowhere, nowhere in all Scotland, do we have a single horse as big as those the English breed and train to fight. They call them destriers. Murray calls them destroyers—destroyers of infantry. I agree with him. Frankly, Cuz, we have nothing we can field against an English army with a hope of winning."

"And you believe it will come to that, to fielding men against them. Is that what you are saying?"

"Aye, it might. It could. But we would do little fielding, in the true sense of the word. We might find ourselves having to fight them, but we will not be confronting them in battle. That would be madness, self-destructive folly. If we are to fight them with any hope of winning, it will have to be as outlaws and brigands, fighting the way we fight them now, using the land itself against them, then hitting them hard and fast and withdrawing before they can strike back at us."

"But we do not fight them now, Will."

"Yes, Cuz, we do. Not often yet, and not to any great extent. But we do fight them. What else would you call the patrols we've been sending out since April but fighting? And it is going to get worse. As the English grow more confident in their ability to bully the folk here with impunity, those of us who can will be forced to strike back against them more and more often. And understand this: it will be men like us for the most part, the common folk and the so-called outlaws, who will have to bear the brunt of it, for we can put no trust in the magnates' willingness to defend us. Some will stand by us, people like Sir William Douglas of Douglasdale—more of an outlaw himself than we are—and Murray, too, in the north. But men like those, whether they be influenced by principles or politics, are few and far between. That leaves common folk like us with but two choices: we can lie down like sheep and let them all, English and Scots nobility alike, trample us under their feet, or we can fight for what we have and what we hold, uncaring who has legal title to the ownership."

"But, Will, we *have nothing*. We have no land, we have no rights, and we have no voice."

My cousin shrugged. "I said both 'have' and 'hold,' Jamie. We *hold* the lands in which we live and we will not relinquish them meekly. And until God Himself takes the field against us and stamps us out, we will have our pride, our integrity as men, and our freedom. All of them worth fighting for."

"And will you lead your folk, Will, beneath the symbol of a sword? This sword?"

His teeth flashed again behind his beard. "Did you not hear a word I said about what I intend to do from this time on? I meant it, Jamie, every word of it. I am not the only man in Selkirk Forest capable of swinging a blade or casting an arrow. I can name you half a score, right here and now, who could step over me and take command were I shot down in battle. Only one man was ever irreplaceable, Jamie, and He died for all of us. As for the rest, the common leaders, kings and generals, there's always someone, and often someone better, waiting to step in and take command. I will be gone, lost in the forest, and the matter of who will replace me is for God to decide, but I do not believe for a minute that He will abandon us." He straightened up, head cocked. "Who's there?"

The door swung open and one of the guards stuck his head inside. "Yon Bishop's back, Will. Riding in now."

"Thank ye, Alistair. I'll be right out. Tell the Bishop that and bid him make himself comfortable in the gathering hut." He turned back to me. "Well, shall we go and find out what this visit is about?"

"Not I, Cuz. I was not invited. Go you alone, for now. If they then send for me, I'll come, but for the time being, I believe their business is with you."

He narrowed his eyes and regarded me for several moments before nodding slightly. "So be it, then. You'll dine with us tonight?"

I said I would, then he nodded again and glanced around him as though looking idly for something he did not find, before he crossed quickly to the door and left me there alone.

2

As soon as Will was gone, I stepped back to the big sword and reached up to grasp the hilt. It fell heavily towards me when I tugged at it, but as I stepped quickly back, tightening my grip and hefting it properly, the weapon settled into my grasp, and I felt the beautiful, integral balance of the thing. I lifted it higher, holding it with both hands, and the long blade rose effortlessly, reflected light from the small window nearby flickering along the watermark patterns on the blade as it moved. I decided that it must weigh somewhere between seven and eight pounds, with most of the mass centred in the upper third of the weapon to provide a fulcrum for the long, lethal beauty of the blade. I was concentrating so deeply on what I was doing that the sound of Mirren's voice at my back made me jump and turn towards her reflexively, still clutching the sword.

She had been in the act of taking off the light shawl that had covered her head, but she released it and threw up her hands in mock horror as the long blade swept towards her, even though it came nowhere near where she stood. "Heavens! Will you kill me, Father James?"

I lowered the point to the floor immediately, mortified, and began to bluster an apology.

"Jamie Wallace, you're blushin' like a wee boy caught stealin' honey. I startled you, and I'm sorry. I didna know you would be here." She hesitated, then added, "But now that you are, I want to ask you something. D'ye mind?"

"No, of course not. Let me put this back where it belongs." I turned away and replaced the sword in its corner, and as I did so I heard her lowering herself slowly and carefully into her chair. "This is a fine weapon," I said over my shoulder, giving her time to settle herself decorously.

"It's for killing men," she answered dismissively. "I'm surprised to hear you, of all people, finding something good to say about it. We will a' die some day soon enough. I canna see any beauty in a thing made to bring that time closer."

I turned to face her, bowing my head respectfully. "Forgive me, Mirren. You're right, of course. I was admiring the form of it, the symmetry and proportion, not thinking of its purpose. Now, what do you wish to ask me?"

She finished adjusting the light shawl over her hair, apparently having decided to retain it, then looked at me with narrowed eyes. "What does Robert Wishart want from my Will?"

I was caught off kilter by her hard tone, and she continued before I could say anything. "I'm asking Jamie the cousin, not Father James the priest, and I want you to sit down and talk to me, eye to eye, Jamie Wallace. What does that old schemer want from my man? And don't try to tell me he doesna want anythin', for I'll no' believe you any more than ye'll believe yersel'."

I raised my hands in surrender. "I swear to you, Mirren, I don't know. I didn't even know the Bishop was coming. We met him by accident yesterday, Ewan and Alec and me, in the forest. We could just as easily have missed him. I really think, though, that you might be doing him an injustice …" My voice died when I saw the look that came into her eyes, and I felt a tide of blood colour my face.

"Aye," she said, "ye may well blush. Ye were about to tell a lie that would shame a hardened liar, let alone a priest. You know as well as I do that Robert Wishart does nothing, ever, wi'out reason, and his reasoning is often as twisted as the top o' that big, curly staff he carries when he's fully robed. What's it called?"

"The crozier, the pastoral staff."

"Aye, that. It's braw, I suppose, but naebody would ever ca' it plain or simple. Just like his thinkin'. Everything that man does is to a purpose. I've heard tell, to his credit, that everything he does is for the good o' Scotland's realm. I ken that, and it's fine and good. But my concern is that he's planning to use my Will for something I don't like, and I've a deathly fear o' what that might be."

"There's no need for that, Mirren," I said. "Bishop Wishart would never ask Will to do anything dishonourable."

"Dishonourable? Are ye daft, Jamie Wallace? What in the name o' God do you think I'm talking about here? What does *honour* have to do wi' anything ither than the witlessness o' stupid men strutting like fighting cockerels?" She looked at me wild eyed, as though she could not believe that I could be so obtuse as to miss her meaning, and continued in a voice that was little louder than a sustained hiss. "I'm no' talking about that kind o' rubbish. I'm talking about puttin' my man's *life* in danger, about sending him out to do something brave and stupid that could get him killed and leave me here wi' a

newborn babby an' nobody to raise him. I'm talking about my Will,
your cousin and closest friend, *dyin'* for that auld man's notions o'
what's right for Scotland. And I'll tell you, Jamie Wallace, I
wouldna gi'e a handful o' acorns for this whole holy realm o'
Scotland and a' the bishops in it if it came down to a choice between
its life and my Will's." She stopped, breathing deeply.

I raised a placatory hand, but only half-heartedly, because I truly
did not know what to say to her. "That will not happen, Mirren," I
said, hearing the uncertainty in my own voice. "It would never come
to that, or anywhere close to that."

"Close to what? Close to *what*, Jamie? To fighting? To war? To
my Will getting killed?" Her voice was granite hard, her eyes
scornful. "Tell me ye dinna seriously believe that tripe."

"Of course I believe it, Mirren. It's true."

"*True?* Sweet Jesus, Jamie Wallace, listen to yourself! There's
been mair folk killed around here in the past three years than in the
thirty years afore that, when King Alexander was alive. And that's
just plain Scots folk. When ye start addin' in strangers and English
sodgery on top o' that, it doesna bear thinkin' about."

"But that's all banditry, Mirren, not war. And besides, the worst
of it seems to be over now."

"Oh, is it? Och, I'm so glad ye told me that." The contempt in her
voice was chilling, and even though I knew her scorn was not aimed
at me, I cringed inside. "I'm sure a' they dead folk would be glad to
ken it was banditry that killed them and no' war."

"What do you want me to do, Mirren? What can I do that will
help?" I had to swallow my impatience forcefully.

I don't know what she had expected me to say, but her head
jerked up and her eyes went wide. And then, to my absolute horror,
she began to weep, not noisily or even audibly, but hopelessly. She
was staring at me and her eyes were enormous, the helpless agony
in them spearing through me as her tears welled up and spilled
profusely down her face to drip from her chin. She simply sat there,
letting them flow.

I had not spent much time alone with Mirren, but as I had slowly come to know her I had learned to appreciate and respect her strength of character and will as being truly extraordinary, and I had heard Will himself say, many times, that she was the strongest woman he had ever known. To see her reduced to tears like this was, therefore, appalling to me. I knew, of course, that her condition, so close to being brought to childbed, was precarious and that her behaviour could be expected to vary from what was normal, but so pathetic was my ignorance that I had no appreciation of what *normal* was supposed to be. And so I merely sat there, praying for inspiration and assistance.

The assistance came first and was provided by Mirren herself when her tears dried up spontaneously and she raised a hand as though to bless me. "Forgive me, Father James, I shouldna be sayin' such things to you." It was the first time she had addressed me by my title. "I know you're no' to blame for any o' this," she was saying as I collected myself again. "Auld Bishop Wishart formed his interest in my Will long afore you were ever in a position to influence him one way or the other. But, God forgive me, I'm feared o' losin' my man ... losin' my babby's father."

I sat down resolutely in front of her and leaned towards her, looking her straight in the eye. "Listen to me, Mirren. Listen carefully to what I'm going to tell you. I swear it's true and it is something you might never have heard before. Will you listen to me? I'm going to tell you something Will confessed to me ... swore to me, in fact." I saw her eyes flare with surprise and I knew instantly she had misunderstood. "No, no, no." I reached out and took hold of her wrist. "It was a personal confession between friends, not a sacramental confession binding me to silence. Do you understand the difference?"

I knew she must, but I waited for her to nod her head in acknowledgment.

"Good." I squeezed her wrist, reassuringly I hoped, but did not relinquish it. "Well then, we have talked about this, Will and I, since you"—I floundered for a moment, then pressed on—"since you became with child. And in fact we first talked about it soon after the raids along the border lands, when word came back that Tam Elliott the weaver had had his hamstring cut during the fighting at Selkirk town. Do you remember that?"

She nodded soberly. "I do, because his wife had just had twin baby boys, an' it near killed her. All o' it, I mean—the birth o' the bairns and then the word that Tam had lost his leg."

"Aye. Well, Will and I talked about what was to be done for them, and the talk turned to you and Will and what might happen to you were he ever crippled or, God forbid, killed in a fight. I know now that Will has been thinking deeply about it ever since, and he has made a decision that, quite frankly, I would not have believed three months ago."

She did not ask, although her eyes grew even wider. She merely waited, unmoving, until I continued.

"Will has decided that his duty—but even more than that, his *heart*—lies with you and your child, Mirren. He has told me that you and his son, or the daughter you will bear him, are more valuable and far more important to him than anything else could ever be."

She asked in a tiny voice, "What does that mean?"

I had to smile at her, at the tremulous hope in her voice, the half-formed awareness that her fears might yet prove groundless.

"It means that your man has decided that you and the child you carry, and the others you will bear him in the years ahead, *are* his world and his life. And he has chosen to believe that nothing else, especially not the political haverings and squabbling of men who would not deign to bid him the time of day in person, can ever be permitted to threaten the love and the esteem he has for you and what you mean to him. Those other men may think of themselves as Will's *betters*, his superiors, his masters—poor benighted creatures that they are—but you know and I know that not a one of them approaches Will Wallace in stature or dignity or goodness. And the strange part is that, somewhere deep inside himself, Will is beginning to see that, too. Strange, I mean, because he is a modest, self-effacing man, with little idea of how highly other men esteem him.

But be that as it may, Mistress Wallace, I believe you can dry your tears, for Will is going nowhere that will grieve you."

Her eyes flared again with something resembling panic. "But he's in wi' the Bishop now. What if—?"

"Bishop Wishart will not change Will's mind, no matter how persuasively he tries, and we all know how persuasive he can be. But Will has made his decision, and you know your goodman. Once his mind is made up, nothing, not even you, can change it."

As I finished speaking, someone knocked at the door, and Mirren answered immediately.

"Come in."

Ewan leaned inside, his face lighting with pleasure as he saw me. "Ah, there y' are. God bless this house and good day to you, Mirren. Jamie, the Bishop sent me to fetch you."

"Aye, I'll be right there, Ewan." I turned back to Mirren. "I have to leave for home tomorrow morning, so you and I should talk about this again later, perhaps before dinner. Will that be possible?"

She smiled at me then, the most open and friendly smile she had ever bestowed on me, and crossed her hands over her belly. "Aye, or perhaps after we eat. After all, I have to play the hostess and entertain the Bishop and his ... companion."

"He's a canon, Canon Lamberton, chancellor of Glasgow Cathedral. You'll like him."

"Thank you for this, Jamie. You have eased my soul."

I blessed her quickly and left.

3

The three faces grouped around the smallest of the tables in the hut that served as an assembly hall were all serious when I walked in, and the greetings we exchanged were no more than perfunctory nods.

"Did someone die?" I asked and immediately regretted my levity. "Your pardon, my lord Bishop, I meant no disrespect."

Wishart turned his gaze on me, his eyes distinctly unfriendly. "No, Father James," he said, so quietly that I almost had to strain to hear him. I had worked closely with him for almost two full years by then, and I knew that Bishop Wishart whispering straight-faced was the equivalent of other men raving while they destroyed buildings and slaughtered innocents. "No one has yet died today. But preparations are afoot in numerous places that should see a profusion of death in times to come. We are entering dire times here in Scotland, times that will test the mettle of each one of us, and now your cousin has informed us that he will be removing himself from any possibility of conflict."

I winced, despite knowing it was not a wise thing to do. I looked back at Will to try to guess at what had been said already, but he seemed unruffled.

"Aye, well," I said, struggling to find my tongue and straighten out my thoughts. "His wife will make a father of him within the next few days. Events like that have been known to make men re-evaluate their lives and how they live them."

"We are aware of that, Father James." Now the icy chill in that quiet voice was radiating towards me. "I find Will's motives admirable, and his desire to be with his wife and child could not be more laudable. The timing of all this, however, could not be more unfortunate."

"Forgive me, my lord. The timing of all what?"

The Bishop moved his head to look at me, a quirk of annoyance appearing between his brows. "Must I lay it all out like a map in front of you?"

I felt my chin go up in spite of knowing I should not react. "I fear you must, my lord, for I have been in these woods for nigh on four months, and we hear little of the outside world here."

I saw Will bend forward slightly, and when I glanced at him, I found him looking at me and he closed one eye in a long, approving wink. The Bishop, though, had gone stock-still, staring straight ahead. And then the stiffness left his posture and he sank back into his chair.

"Forgive me, Father James. You have every right to chastise me. Come, then, and sit down, and I will bring you up to date on all that has been going on in Scotland and in England."

He waited until I was seated across from him and then he raised one hand, fingers spread, preparing to enumerate points as he made them.

"You left Glasgow to come down here as minister to your new flock soon after the Old Robert Bruce died, towards the end of April, did you not?"

"Aye, my lord, the twenty-eighth of April."

"Right. And then in June, Will's men launched several actions in response to the illegal activities of certain … people in these parts. That created a stir at the time, but though much was achieved here, it was regarded by the powers in the land to be a local issue, a minor disturbance that faded to insignificance against the backdrop of what was taking place elsewhere. And then came July, and many matters came to a head. The first ten days of July of the year of our Lord 1295 will prove, I believe, to have been a memorable time.

"On the third of the month, I set my name and episcopal seal, in the company of others, as witness to a royal charter from King John of Scotland. Those others were four belted earls—Buchan, Strathearn, Dunbar, and Mar—along with Patrick de Graham and John Comyn, Lord of Badenoch. An illustrious group of witnesses, by any gauge. The import of the charter was to grant lands in Douglasdale, forfeited by the rebellious Sir William Douglas, to the Englishman Antony Bek, Prince Bishop of Durham and King Edward of England's former deputy in Scotland."

I was aware that my mouth was hanging open. "Bek?" I said eventually. "They gave Douglas's lands to Bek?"

"Aye, they did." The Bishop's voice was flat. "Sir William Douglas stands convicted of sedition and rebellion and all his lands and goods are forfeit to the Crown. It is regrettable, but the man brought this judgment down upon himself through his own obstinacy. He was warned often enough, advised to pull in his horns, but he always was a bull, headstrong and wilful and heedless of what others thought. He behaved like a tyrant king within his own lands, and some argue that was his right, but he crossed the true King elsewhere in the realm, acting as though he were a law unto himself, and that was his undoing. His behaviour was little short of brigandage and treason, and he has paid the price for it."

"But *Bek*, my lord! What folly is there, to make a gift of Scots lands to a man whose hatred of the realm is common knowledge—"

"Consider, Father James." Wishart's voice was minatory but not impatient, warning me to say no more. "The gifting was King John's, a gesture of goodwill towards his royal cousin, England's King. Would you take issue with your monarch over it?" I closed my mouth, restricting my protest to a frown as the Bishop continued. "The wishes of the likes of we four here weigh nothing in such matters, and besides, the gifting of Bek was rendered insignificant two days later, on the fifth of July."

Lamberton cleared his throat quietly, steepling his fingers beneath his nose as though to pray and gazing at me from beneath a slightly raised eyebrow. I could almost *feel* the question hovering on my lips, and I knew they were waiting for me to ask it. I turned slightly to look directly at the Bishop.

"It seems to me, my lord, that anything capable of reducing such a grotesque gesture to insignificance must, in itself, have been earth shaking."

"It was," came Wishart's reply. "It was indeed, although the effects of what occurred that day have not yet come to pass."

Damnation, I thought. *He is determined to make me ask.* "I see. What took place, then? What was this earth-shaking occurrence?"

"Another charter from King John, but more significant by far than the temporary awarding of the title of some lands to a visiting potentate. *This* charter has great substance ... or it has the potential to acquire great substance. On July fifth, His Grace the King appointed a delegation of senior representatives of both the Church and the laity of the realm to travel to France with plenary authority there to negotiate a formal alliance with the French Crown. The terms of the alliance, as drafted by King John, will set both realms, shoulder to shoulder, against any aggression against either party by the Crown of England. The chosen delegates were William Fraser, Bishop of St. Andrews, Matthew de Crambeth, Bishop of Dunkeld, Sir John de Soulis, and Sir Ingram de Umfraville. They left for France within two days and have since arrived in Paris, where they are currently in negotiations with King Philip and his advisers." He paused. "How significant is that development, think you, as opposed to the granting of the Douglas lands to Bek?"

I nodded slowly. "It places an entire new meaning on the word," I said. "And I can see, too, what you meant by saying that the earth-shaking effects of it have not yet been felt. Does England have any inkling of what's afoot?"

"Not yet. But they will, soon enough. Events of such magnitude cannot be easily concealed, especially in a place like France, where Philip keeps a court filled with foreigners and has been at war with England for years. Edward will have spies aplenty there, safe-guarding his interests in the war over Gascony, and it will not take long for word of what is happening to reach him in England. When it does, then I have no doubt the earth will start to tremble."

"How *will* he react, think you, my lord?"

"Noisily, I suspect, but not violently. Not yet, before he has taken time to assess the situation."

"And what of King John? What does he hope to gain by this?"

"Time. Time and a strong ally. The approach to the French King is to work hand in hand with the other development that occurred in that same week. The following day, in fact."

Canon Lamberton must have seen my confusion, for he dropped his hands into his lap and bent forward to speak to me directly. "The delegates to France were formally appointed in Stirling early on the morning of July the fifth, Father James. They left that same day for St. Andrews and sailed thence to France on the seventh, while on the sixth, King John's seventh parliament opened in Stirling. My lord Bishop?" He shifted his gaze to Wishart, but the Bishop merely waggled his fingers at him in a signal to proceed.

"It is no secret that King John has had increasing troubles with King Edward since his assumption of the throne. The Plantagenet clearly believes that having made it possible for John to claim the crown, he now retains the right to dictate how the new King should wear it, and he has made it more than evident that he believes himself entitled to impose *his* will upon the entire realm of Scotland. Witness his continuing insistence that he be granted occupancy of all our castles. He wants them all, to garrison at his leisure and to his own purposes. And what could such purposes entail other than domination and suppression of this land? He seeks to cloak it all under the guise of diplomatic words: that he is entitled to be recognized as overlord of Scotland because most of our Scots magnates owe him some form of allegiance. That most, if not all, of Scotland disagrees with him matters naught to this man. He sees no impediment to imposing his regal will on all of us. But we will not permit that. *Scotland* will not permit it."

I shifted my eyes sideways to Will and found him listening closely, his eyes narrowed to slits as he concentrated upon every word being spoken, and as I looked, he spoke up.

"*How* will Scotland not permit it? Who is this 'we' you speak of, and what do they intend to do, to change anything?"

It was the Bishop who responded this time. "We are the community of the realm. The description is new—"

"I've heard of it," Will said.

"Aye, you have, for the idea is not new. It has been around for years, being talked about by everyone. Recently, though, it has begun taking hard form, in the persons of those most involved."

"The magnates." There was a flat, dismissive quality to Will's voice, but the Bishop appeared not to notice it.

"The magnates, aye, but not alone … no longer alone. These are changing times. In recent years we have been seeing the emergence of an addition to the three main estates of the realm. A fourth is coming into being. The first three still hold sway: the bishops of the Church, the earls of the ancient Celtic kingdom, and the barons of the current realm. But a strong new voice is now making itself heard in the land—the voice of the burgesses, some of whom are beginning to call themselves the fourth estate. For the time being, though, and in the case we are discussing, the vested power is unchanged. The parliament in Stirling appointed a council of twelve governors—four bishops, four earls, and four barons—to assist King John wholeheartedly in his dealings with England, to provide visible and formidable support for the King's grace in the face of bullying and bluster."

Will muttered something tinged with disgust, and Wishart cocked his head sideways, eyeing him. "Have you something to add, Will?"

"Aye," came the low response, "but nothing new. How long, think ye, before Edward yanks the chain and threatens to deprive your magnates of their lands in England? That has never failed to bring them obediently to heel before, and I see no reason why things should be different now."

"But things *are* different now. These men have accepted full responsibility for their new tasks in the eyes of parliament."

"And have they willingly agreed to forfeit their estates in England?"

That brought no answer, and the silence stretched until Will spoke again.

"That's what I thought. And that, my lord, is why I will not fight. As long as these men rely on the wealth of their estates in England, England's King will have them on a choke leash. Tell me this, and be truthful: why should I, why should *any* man of ability or worth, be expected to endanger and abandon his own family and step forward to fight for, or with, or beside these ... these posturing buffoons, knowing them likely to skip sideways in the middle of the measure and end up dancing on the other side, accepting table scraps from England and leaving us to die for our folly in trusting them?"

He was glaring at the Bishop, defying him to interrupt him, and when Wishart said nothing he continued. "Magnates! Magnates, my arse. *Maggots* suits them better. Sir William Douglas may be a brigand and a bully and a rebel, but at least no one doubts where he stands. That kind of man I can deal with. But until these *maggots* can make up their mind about whether they're Scots or English, they'll get no support from me or any of my kind. And until then, be damned to them." He dropped his voice dramatically and spoke his next words slowly and clearly. "I will not fight to enrich some faceless, half-bred mongrel magnate at my own expense and risk."

He permitted that to linger in the air, then sat back in his chair. "On the other hand," he said, "the moment the Scots noble houses wash their hands of all they held in England and commit themselves to being Scots and to caring for their folk and for this realm, I will stand prepared to change my mind. And if it comes to waging war, united one and all against Edward's greedy grasp, I will come quickly out of Ettrick, with every outlaw I can muster, and join the fight."

"And you are determined not to fight until then?"

Will laid his hands flat on the table, fingers spread. "I have explained my situation, my lord, as clearly as I am able, but I will do so again. I have a wife big with child. Within days we will have a son or a daughter, the first of many, I hope and pray. I will not endanger the welfare of my family needlessly. If it should come to a just war, properly led by trustworthy commanders for the common good, then I will march with everyone else. But I will risk nothing for, nor will I support in any way, anyone who has no care for me or mine and no interests in his mind but his own welfare."

He appeared to suck at something lodged in his teeth, then shrugged. "An honest man can serve only one master—in this case, one King. Any fool knows that. And Scotland *has* a King, crowned with all the blessings of Church and state. The allegiance of our so-called magnates is clear—their monarch is King John. Yet they fear to give offence to Longshanks, lest they lose wealth and privilege. Bluntly, they are duplicitous and treasonous, and I intend to keep myself and my family as far removed as I can be from all the stink of their corruption."

He stood up and bowed stiffly to Bishop Wishart and the canon. Then, without another word, he was gone, closing the door quietly behind him. No one spoke for a long time, but then Wishart sighed and looked over at Lamberton.

"You did not even get to speak with him. *Mea culpa*. I pushed him too hard."

Lamberton shook his head. "No, my lord. Master Wallace had passed the point at which anyone could push him further long before we came here. But no matter. I will seek him out later, once he has had time to cool down." He glanced then at me, and his mouth twisted in a wry grin. "Your cousin is a man of strong opinions."

"Aye, he is. But you always know precisely where you stand in your dealings with him. He is just and level headed. And he will talk to you later, so be it you do not attempt to change his mind or make him feel guilty about the decision he has made."

"I have no intention of attempting either one. I merely wish to talk to him about a mutual friend, Sir Andrew Murray."

"You are a friend of Andrew's? Then he *will* talk to you, gladly."

The Bishop cleared his throat and rose to his feet, pulling his breviary from his scrip. "I think there is little to be gained by remaining here now … in this room, I mean. I think I would enjoy walking alone for a while." He nodded a farewell to both of us and made his way out into the encampment, deep in thought. Lamberton and I exchanged glances and then, with nothing further to say to each other, we went our separate ways.

4

From the moment I heard that the birthing had begun, I was swept up in a spate of fearful imaginings that I would not have thought, two hours earlier, could exist within me. Will himself fared little better. After being told that Mirren had collapsed and been taken indoors to the shadowy domain of the hovering midwives, my virile, assertive cousin was transformed: the colour vanished from his face, he appeared to shrink in size and bulk, and his very movements, normally firm and decisive, took on an aspect of uncertainty and timidity. The Bishop and his chancellor offered Masses for the welfare and safety of mother and child, but their presence had no real relevance for any of the rest of us. People like Ewan and Shoomy and Alan and Long John, faces familiar and ever-present, were far more comforting and supportive at such times than mere clerics could ever be.

Throughout that long, moonless, seemingly endless night we waited, huddled in cloaks around a leaping fire while shapeless, faceless women scurried back and forth among the shadows, on errands we were not equipped to guess at. From time to time we would hear noises, some of them loud but all muffled and meaning-less, that made us squirm with discomfort over our own ignorance of what was happening. Then came a succession of harrowing screams that left us all chilled, afraid to look at one another. Thanks be to God, though, the last of those awful screams was closely followed by the wail of a newborn.

Shoomy barked a laugh and punched the new father lightly on the shoulder.

"Dada," he growled, and everyone laughed and started to talk all at once in the welcome release of tension. Everyone, that is, except Will. He sat as tensely as before, staring towards the cluster of huts housing the midwives, unable to forget, I was sure, those last agonized screams. I crossed to where he sat and gripped him firmly by the shoulder.

"Stay here," I said. "I'll go and find out how she is."

As I approached the nearest of the midwives' huts, I saw a stir-ring in the shadows, and one of the elder wives stepped towards me.

"Father," she said, neither questioning nor inviting comment.

"Mistress Wallace," I said. "How is she?"

The woman raised one brow as she stared at me, and I knew exactly what she was thinking. A priest, asking after the welfare of the mother of a newborn child, was something rare, for in the matter of a newborn's life, the greeting and harvesting of a new soul, the welfare of the mother was never a priority. If a choice became neces-sary between the survival of the mother and the life of the child, the child's life took precedence.

"They are both well," she said eventually. "Mother and son are both hale and strong. Permit us time to clean the chamber and prepare the child, and then you may bring the father." She nodded, graciously enough, then glided away into the shadows.

I went back to where Will still sat by the fire, every angle of his body radiating stiffness and tension. Long John and Ewan stood close by.

"God bless all here," I said as I approached. "He has already blessed your newborn son and his mother. Both are well. Strong and healthy. God be praised."

Will had raised his head, staring at me wide-eyed. "Mirren?"

"She is well, I'm told, and anxious to have you meet your son."

He stood up slowly, holding my gaze, and reached out to touch me. I felt his hands grasping the front of my robe, and then he drew me towards him, without even being aware that he had taken hold of me. "She's well, Jamie? She lives?"

"And waits to show you your new son, Cuz. Come now, by the time we walk over there they should be ready to receive us."

Ready they were, too, and my throat swelled up with love and pleasure and gratitude to God in His goodness as I watched my cousin's introduction to his first-born son. Mirren was startlingly, radiantly beautiful, and it was impossible for me to imagine her as the source of those appalling screams that had so frightened us a short time earlier. She was regally wrapped in furs and brightly coloured woollen shawls, and she held her son in the crook of one elbow, the fingers of her free hand tucked gently under his chin. As Will stepped forward shyly to stoop and kiss the top of her head, she reached up and tugged at the side of his beard with her fingertips, a gentle, loving gesture of tender affection, after which she held the swaddled child up to him with both hands. He took the small bundle from her as though it held the most precious substance in all the world—which, of course, it did—and raised it up in front of his face to where he could stare at the wondrous creature inside, and then he stood rapt, for long, long minutes, transfixed by what he saw.

It was also on that night of the child's birth that I had the most memorable discussion of that entire visit with Canon Lamberton. Bishop Wishart had retired early yet again, but Will sat with us until long into the night, finally able to relax and enjoy himself, and I was

glad to see him and William Lamberton warm to each other over a
flagon of ale by the side of a leaping fire. The two Williams
compared their experiences of having met and come to know their
mutual friend Andrew Murray, and I was surprised to learn that
Lamberton had met Murray in Paris. I did not know that Andrew had
been in Paris, and neither did Will, but Lamberton told us he had
been there on business for his father, a man of great power in the
north.

Both Will and I knew that Sir Andrew Murray of Petty had been
justiciar in the north about the time of King Alexander's death and
that he was closely connected by marriage to the all-powerful
Comyn family. Those things were common knowledge, if little
understood, in south Scotland, and now that the name of Murray is
renowned, and has been for decades, it may seem strange to younger
people that it was not always thus.

In the days before Wallace emerged from his woody lair,
Scotland was a vastly different place, and the division of the
kingdom into north and south, separated by the Firth of Forth, was
real and alienating. The English called the Firth of Forth "the
Scottish Sea," and in fact it separated north Scotland from the south
the way the narrow sea the English call the Channel divides France
from England. The analogy is not inapt, for the folk north and south
of the Forth spoke vastly different tongues and appeared to be even
racially different, with Erse-speaking Gaels and Norse-descended
folk of Danish and Norwegian Viking stock making up the bulk of
the northern populace, while the inhabitants of the south spoke
mainly English and a polyglot trading language that was becoming
known as Scots. Between the two regions there lay a huge cultural
gulf and a mutual sense of distrust that was tenuously held in
suspension by the intermediary efforts of the Church.

Now, when Canon Lamberton raised the name of Andrew's
father, the senior Andrew de Moray, both Will and I began to question him.

"He's a famous man," Will said. "But I am not sure *why* he
should be so famous. D'you know?"

Lamberton sat back and laughed. "How does any man become famous, Will? He is rich, above and beyond all else, wealthy on a scale that folk like us cannot imagine." He sipped at his ale pot before continuing. "He is the Lord of Petty, which means small, as you know, but there is nothing remotely petty about His Lordship, for he owns most of the enormous lands of Moray, which is unimaginably vast. His primary seat, from which he controls what most people would call his empire, is Hallhill Castle, a giant stronghold on the south bank of the Moray Firth, but he also holds the lordship of Avoch in the Black Isle, which is controlled from Avoch Castle, another huge fortress, said to be impregnable, that sits east of Inverness and overlooks the Moray Firth. He is also lord of Boharm, which is governed from Gauldwell Castle and contains the estates of Arndilly and Botriphni. Oh, and he also owns other lands and estates at Alturile, Brachlie, and Croy, in the Petty region. Young Andrew is heir to all of it."

When he saw we were bereft of words, he chuckled. "Are you not glad you asked me that? Can you imagine what it must be like to own such wealth? No, of course you can't. I can't, and I'm a cathedral canon." He sat up quickly and placed his hand over his lips, peering around as if looking for eavesdroppers. "Did I say that? Well, I'll deny it if I'm accused of it. But quite seriously, you must be aware that such wealth brings with it great political influence. Sir Andrew served for years as the justiciar of the north and he is married to one of the Comyns of Buchan. The House of Comyn is the most powerful family in Scottish society, as I know you are well aware. But it is one thing to be *connected* to the Comyns. It is quite another to be connected as de Moray is. Sir Andrew's second wife, young Andrew's stepmother, is Euphemia Comyn, the niece of King John Balliol himself. She is also the sister of John Comyn, the Lord of Badenoch, one of the most politically influential men in Scotland. So there you have our mutual friend's connections: Balliol, Buchan, Comyn, and de Moray. And, of course, the Church. The young man does not lack for influence."

"What mean you, the Church? What influence has he there?"

"The name de Moray is well known within the Church in Scotland, and has been for years. There was an Andrew Moray who was Bishop of Moray early in this century. He was the man responsible for the transfer of the seat of the bishopric to Elgin about sixty years ago, if my memory is accurate. He built the town's cathedral. A man well thought of by his peers in his own time, and his memory is revered today."

"I dare say it is," Will said, slightly awestruck, as was I. "Pity that the family has no friends or relatives here in the south. That way, we might have known more about them."

Lamberton raised an eyebrow. "Did I give you that impression? Then I must ask you to forgive me, or to pour me some more of this excellent ale." I replenished his mug, raising a lively head on it that he blew off before sipping reflectively and nodding his approval. "Let's see," he mused. "The south. Are you familiar with a place called Bothwell?"

"Aye, in Strathclyde," I said. "I've been there. It's but a hamlet."

"No, it is the seat in Scotland of Sir Andrew de Moray's brother, Sir William Moray. Sir William is almost as wealthy as his younger brother Andrew—in fact he's known as *le riche* because he's so rich. He has another younger brother, too, who is also in holy orders. Father David de Moray is rector of Bothwell church. He is also a canon of Moray.

"William *le riche* is currently pouring his fortune into the construction of a castle there, to be known as Bothwell Castle, overlooking the River Clyde, and in the manner of the truly rich, he has spent huge sums importing the latest knowledge of scientific fortress construction from all over Christendom. He is reportedly determined that his castle will set a new standard for all of Britain and the world."

"He sounds like a braggart fool," Will muttered. "You said this Bothwell place is his seat in Scotland. Does that mean he has seats elsewhere?"

"Heavens, yes. He owns extensive lands at Lilleford in England, near Lincoln."

"Ah, I should have known. Another Scots magnate dependent upon Edward's largesse. The bane of this poor land."

"No, I think not, in this instance … at least, I am not sure. But I seem to remember Andrew telling me that the Lilleford lands have been in William *le riche*'s ownership for generations. And of course the lands will one day belong to him."

"*Andrew?* They will be *his*?"

"Yes. Sir William has no heirs. So young Andrew will inherit all his uncle's wealth, along with his father's."

"Good God! Pardon me, Fathers both. But is there anyone Andrew is *not* connected to?"

"Aye, certainly. He has no connection to the House of Bruce. He is, however, connected to the Douglases of Clydesdale. Sir William Douglas is a distant cousin of his, I believe."

Will merely looked at me and shook his head at that, then said no more, and Lamberton moved on to talk about what I was beginning to believe was his favourite topic: the burgesses of Scotland and how they were beginning to make themselves recognized as owning a voice to be listened to. Although I had heard all this explained before, the essence of it continued to elude me. I can only suppose that my slowness to appreciate its import was tied in to the generally limited scope of my vision at that time, living as I was in the greenwood and ministering daily to the needs of a small and very local congregation.

Will, however, took to the new ideas Lamberton was presenting to him much as dry grass will take to an igniting spark. And marvelling at the briefness of the time it took Will to progress from polite interest to raging ardour, I saw, suddenly, why both my companions were so excited about this new idea, and I finally understood why it was so important, and inevitable, that Bishop Wishart, through this younger, vibrant intermediary, should bring this message directly to William Wallace.

In the eyes of Robert Wishart, William Wallace was a bellwether, whether he knew it or not. He was a flock leader, and his peers would follow him naturally, without being exhorted by him or anyone else. Will had always stood alone and had never been afraid to be different from those around him. And in the entrenched scorn he held for the Scots magnates, William Wallace had been saying for years that the system under which we lived was broken.

As I thought those precise words, I felt myself shiver with a rush of gooseflesh, remembering that it was William Lamberton, not William Wallace, whom I had heard use that expression the night before, and that the two men had not yet met when Lamberton said it. Now they were together, talking about that mutually recognized notion, and I knew that God Himself had brought them together for a purpose. Will, in his own quiet, unassuming way, had been living in political despair and disillusionment, bereft of any hope of repairing whatever it was that had broken down in the system that controlled the affairs of men. The nobility had been rendered impotent by time and change, incapable any longer of stimulating or inspiring the realm and its people, and the Church appeared to have been equally impaired. But now, miraculously, here was the Church itself, championing the emergence of a new social order, a new estate that was strong and virile and puissant, the voices and wealth of the burgesses of the combined burghs of the entire realm. Small wonder that Will Wallace embraced the notion like a breath of springtime air; and small wonder that he and his new companion completely forgot about my presence.

From that evening until the two churchmen left to return to Glasgow three days later, they talked incessantly of politics and probabilities, and for the most part, I was content to leave them to it, happy to see my cousin walking again with that spring in his gait that I remembered from our boyhood.

§

The year that followed, the first year of little William's life, was the happiest I ever knew, for as Will and Mirren settled into their new life, so, too, did I in mine, and the child became almost as much a part of my life as he was of theirs. I quickly came to love him and to dote on him as though he were my own son, and as his mother learned to trust me with him, I came to know the delights of the milky, sweet smell of his skin just after feeding, and learned to clean and tend him at both ends, changing his swaddling and generally luxuriating in the miracle that he was.

Surprisingly, too, the transition from bandit leader to simple forest dweller was far easier for Will than we had all anticipated. From the moment of the boy's birth, Will let it be known among his people that he no longer sought to lead men, or to fight. He made no secret of the fact that he considered nothing more important than his family, and that all he wished to do was live with them, undisturbed, and provide for them in the best way he could. And unsurprisingly, his people accepted his wishes.

Looking back, I can see that the change was greatly helped by the fact that, for a period of months, from mid-July until October of that year, there was almost no outlawed activity within the greenwood. Troop movements continued, of course, mostly from south to north as English soldiery continued to advance into the realm, but the numbers of men on the move were invariably too large, and their composition too powerful, to draw any kind of interference from the forest outlaws. Furthermore, any pickings that might have been gleaned from robbing passing baggage trains were rendered unattractive, not so much by the difficulty of winning them as by the certainty of grief thereafter as large numbers of English were loosed into the woods to punish anyone they could find and recover the stolen property by any means available.

Will moved quickly to change his role as it was perceived by the people around him. He rapidly established himself as verderer for the thriving community that had grown up around his original encampment in the forest, and he did it simply by convening a gathering of all the local folk and talking to them seriously about the need for conservation and the careful husbandry of the wild forest animals, to avoid depleting the health and numbers of the deer herds. He undertook to become the warden of the forest marches for the outlawed folk, exactly as he had been for his uncle Malcolm in Elderslie, gathering tallies of the local herds and their territories, marking their patterns and their breeding numbers, and culling them for food without being wasteful. He then selected six men, each of whom had had some degree of training as either verderers or foresters, to work with him in organizing new coppices and culti-vating arable plots in suitably isolated areas of the forest.

That done, he casually appointed three of his former lieutenants as joint commanders of the local forces and publicly relinquished his duties to them. Long John of the Knives, Robertson the archer, and Big Andrew Miller, the wiry little fighter with the ever-present crossbow, quietly took over the responsibilities that had gradually become Will's over the preceding few years. The transformation was well on its way to being achieved.

By October of that year, relations between Scotland and England had deteriorated almost beyond redemption. Edward Plantagenet had not relented for a moment in his quest to have the Scottish castles passed into his jurisdiction as overlord of Scotland, and King John, backed by his council of the strongest and most powerful earls and barons in his realm, had been equally intransigent in his refusal to cede a single stronghold, despite the increasingly bellicose English threats of reprisals aimed at enforcing their King's docu-mented rights in that matter. It mattered nothing to Edward and his barons that the "legal" statutes they brandished had been prepared by English lawyers upon the self-important instructions of England's King; or that the rights of overlordship to which they referred so pompously were the self-assumed rights of that same English King; or that the application of such rights in Scotland, the sovereign realm of another, legally anointed monarch, was illegal. Such minor details had no relevance at all in the matter of Edward Longshanks's drive to subsume Scotland as he had Wales mere decades earlier. That became abundantly self-evident as September came to an end amid rattling drums and the braying of recruiters' horns in England.

But Longshanks had overplayed his hand this time. The collec-tive awareness of his determination drove the Scots nobility to unite, at last, behind their own King at a parliament of the realm—the eighth and last of King John's reign—held in Edinburgh that October. They were unanimous in their formal refusal to give up a single Scottish castle to the English.

Barely a week later, the delegates King John had sent to France on his behalf months earlier signed a treaty of alliance with Philip IV and the realm of France. It was a treaty of mutual support and assistance in all things military, commercial, and diplomatic, designed to bring the two realms together in mutual amity and interests. To mark the grandeur and historic significance of the treaty, the parties agreed that Prince Edward Balliol, King John's eldest son, would marry the Princess Jeanne de Valois, whose father was Charles Capet, Count de Valois, brother to King Philip IV and titular Emperor of Constantinople. The treaty would have to go before the Scots parliament to be ratified, and until it had done so nothing could yet be certain, but no one doubted that the ratification would occur.

Edward Longshanks, of course, was incensed. And when that happened, someone—or someplace—invariably was made to suffer.

The news of his rage had barely been spread when more word arrived from the south, unconfirmed but barely questioned, since it merely added flesh to the stories that had been filtering up from England since September. Edward, according to these reports, was assembling an enormous army in northern England, at Newcastle on the River Tyne. No one doubted the tidings, for that was the historic gathering point for any army planning to march north into Scotland.

Yuletide came and went, as did the start of the New Year, 1296. That winter was a cold and brutal one for soldiers under tents, for it was windy and sleety and sustainedly miserable, never quite cold enough for snow or freezing temperatures but never warming up sufficiently to dry out sodden clothing and footwear. But since the soldiers enduring the misery and freezing in their rusting armour were Englishmen preparing to invade us, no one felt any sympathy for their plight, and those who thought of it at all might reasonably have wished for the weather to deteriorate even further.

In the meantime, little William was the delight of his parents and admirers, including his priestly godfather. His long, black tresses had vanished soon after his birth to be replaced by a thicker, more substantial growth, tinged this time with a fiery chestnut red that emphasized his deep blue eyes and drew involuntary gasps of delight from every woman encountering him for the first time. Added to that, his ready grin, infectious in its appeal and challenging in its bright-eyed directness, attracted everyone who encountered it, men and women both, cajoling them to come and play with him and pay no attention to the tiresome details of what was transpiring in the unseen world beyond the iron-hinged doors of solid oaken planks that kept him and his family safe.

He was industriously studying locomotion, crawling everywhere before he was fully six months old and endlessly exploring the wonders of every place where he was not supposed to venture, so that, one morning in January, after early Mass, I found him at the entrance to the byre, eyeing the cattle with delight. He had escaped, somehow, out from under the eye of his mother or the cook in whose charge he had been left, and, clad in nothing but a loincloth, had made his way right across the inner yard, which was inches deep in icy muck. I stopped short, because he was doing something I had never seen him do before. He had pulled himself upright, using the chinks in the rough, narrow logging of the door, and was standing on his own, barefoot but heedless of discomfort and swaying slightly as he peered into the beast-warmed gloom of the cowshed, gurgling to himself in enjoyment. He caught sight of me from the corner of his eye and swung to face me, crowing ecstatically over his own cleverness. But even as I began to move towards him he tottered alarmingly, fighting to retain his balance for at least two steps before landing flush in a pile of wet dung. His howls of outrage were spectacular. I carried him home very carefully, attempting to keep him at arm's length to protect my priestly robes, but it was a hopeless task, because he was so slippery with mud and dung that I had to hold him close to prevent him from slipping right through my fingers.

A very different kind of crisis occurred the following month, when Bishop Wishart and Canon Lamberton once again turned up unexpectedly on our doorstep. Will was the first to see them coming, and he set aside the arrow he was fletching and strode into the middle of the clearing that served us as a village square. He gave a shout of welcome and stood awaiting them, hands on hips and a broad grin on his face. I had heard his shout and come outside to see what had occasioned it, and I was in time to watch his face settle into lines of apprehension and even trepidation to match the look on our visitors' faces.

We stood silent as they dismounted with the merest nod of greeting, and then Will gestured wordlessly and spun on his heel to lead us into his hut. As soon as we were all inside, he closed the door and leaned against it.

"What?" he growled, looking directly at Wishart. "What's happened?"

"We are at war with England."

"*What? We're at war?* Sweet Jesus, has Balliol gone mad? We are not fit to fight among ourselves, let alone go to war with England! What happened?"

Wishart was shaking his head. "John had little to do with it, Will. It was Edward who declared war, on us. He's had an army gathering at Newcastle for months. We all knew that, but we assumed he was merely flaunting his displeasure, threatening us. We didn't seriously think he would invade."

"But he did. What caused him to?"

Wishart glanced at Lamberton and nodded to him to respond, and the younger man straightened up and sucked in a quick breath. "Displeasure with King John," he said quietly. "John summoned an assembly of nobles to Dunfermline to ratify the French alliance."

"A parliament? Then he must have done it in secrecy. We would have heard of such a thing even here in Selkirk."

"It was not a parliament," Wishart muttered. "It was an assembly, far less formal."

"Formal enough yet to involve the nobility and offend Edward of England sufficiently to launch a war. What happened at this *assembly* that prompted such a response?"

Lamberton cleared his throat discreetly. "Perhaps I can answer that. His Grace is correct, this was not a parliament. Those who were there referred to it as a gathering of the community of the realm. But the truth is that in certain respects it proved to be more noteworthy, and perhaps more important in terms of influence, than a true parliament might have been."

"Evidently so, given the result." Will's voice was redolent of disgust.

"It achieved what it was intended to achieve, and quickly. In a matter of hours, the new treaty with France was ratified and a marriage proposal between King John's son Prince Edward and the Princess Jeanne de Valois of France was approved and witnessed in writing by all present, including four earls of the realm, eleven barons, four bishops, and five abbots. All of which is well and good, but something far more significant occurred in Dunfermline. This truly was a gathering of the community of the realm. For the first time official representatives of the burghs of Aberdeen, Berwick, Edinburgh, Perth, Roxburgh, and Stirling were invited to participate, and for the first time the voice of the burgesses was officially added to the public record."

Will nodded. "And Longshanks responded with war."

"Almost instantly," Wishart said. "He must have had a spy there, because the word went back to him as though on wings. His reaction was spectacular, I'm told. He upended his table and cried upon God to witness that these ingrate Scots upstarts had finally exhausted his long-suffering patience. He declared war on us then and there and summoned his dukes and barons to invade."

"Hmm ..." Will crossed the room to the nearest chair and sank into it, his eyes gazing into nothingness, and the silence stretched, broken only by the sounds of movement as the rest of us seated ourselves, too, each one of us momentarily lost in his own thoughts.

Finally Will straightened up again. "So what happens next? Where are my people to go? We're practically astride the main invasion route."

Wishart glanced at Lamberton. "Father William, you might like to answer that, since you and I were talking about it on the way here."

Lamberton nodded, solemn faced, then spoke directly to Will. "The honest answer is that we don't know. You might be perfectly safe here—and by you I mean, of course, your womenfolk and children. You are a mile or two off the main road, and that might be enough to safeguard your settlements. The English armies will be moving quickly—at least through the thickest parts of the forest here—so they won't have much temptation to stray from the high road. And it's safe to say that the English commanders will be taking precautions against desertion, so they won't be letting their people into the woods, for fear of losing them. So your distance from the road certainly makes your situation quite promising. But it is also precisely the kind of situation than no one can judge in advance." He paused.

"Were I in your shoes, Will, I would prepare for the worst while hoping for the best. I would get the women and children safely away from these settlements and into defensible, out-of-the-way areas, and I would set up a strong but mobile screen of bowmen between them and the road. That way, if the English pass by without stopping, you will be able to move back into your homes in a matter of hours, and if anyone does come into the woods looking for you, the bowmen can deal with them."

Will nodded. "Aye, that is much like what I had already decided to do. Have you any other tidings?"

Lamberton turned to Wishart, and the older man spoke up quickly. "Of course, as you might imagine, we have been taking advantage of our foreknowledge of Edward's preparations and making arrangements of our own to counteract his threats."

"We being the maggots, you mean."

"Of course. Who else should I mean? This new community of ours may speak with one unanimous voice, but it cannot yet fight with one unanimous incentive. The armies must still be raised by the earls who control them, and commanded by the barons whose responsibility such things have ever been. But I am happy to be able to tell you, Will, that matters have improved in that respect since last we spoke. The commanders of the realm stand united today, and they are confident, as am I, that we, under the banner of King John and with the blessing of God, will acquit ourselves more than honourably in the fight ahead."

Will blew a puff of air from his cheeks, dismissing the opinions of the magnates. "That is all very fine, my lord, but can we *win*? Acquitting ourselves well and losing in spite of that has no appeal for me. And I know it will not appeal to any of the men who have to march through rain and mud, carrying spears and pikes. Besides, the English share our God with us, and they will swear, to a man, that He is on their side. What about the Bruces?"

The Bishop blinked. "What about them?"

"Annandale and Carrick are two of the most powerful men in Scotland. Where do they stand on all of this? For I tell you frankly, if Bruce is not with us in this war, then it were best to sue for Edward's peace this minute. Where do they stand? More simply, where is the young pup Carrick?"

"The Earl of Carrick ..." The Bishop cleared his throat, looking away into a corner. "I do not know his exact location."

"Nor do I, my lord, but I would be willing to wager that you would find him in King Edward's court, for that is more home to him than is Scotland. The earl, whose title makes him one of this realm's most illustrious peers, is a popinjay, a spoiled brat who enjoys draping himself in outlandish clothes and disporting himself with other men's wives, playing at being a man himself while spending his sponsor's money like a fool. There's precious little of the Scot in him, from what I hear. He is young—what, twenty, one and twenty? And I have been told he is engaging, pleasant, and amiable when he wishes so to be, but he is also completely irrespon-

sible. Edward dotes on him as though he were a favourite son and
spoils him ruinously. He gives him leave to abuse anything and
anyone he wishes to. And when he tires of indulging the young
earl's rebelliousness, he summons him back into the fold with a
click of his fingers. You mark my words, my lord. Bruce is an ill
name to employ in demonstrating solidarity, or anything purely
Scottish and admirable, on the part of the magnates."

The Bishop opened his mouth to speak, but Will ignored him.

"The Houses of Bruce and Comyn have been at daggers drawn
for long years now, and the Bruces, God knows, are no great
supporters of King John Balliol. They see in him, right or wrong, an
upstart and a weakling, thrust into kingship by England and held in
place only by the power and support of the Comyns. And the young
earl is not the only one we need to be concerned about. His father is
another matter altogether. The Lord of Annandale is currently
castellan of Carlisle, is he not?"

When the Bishop nodded, Will grunted. "Very well, then. Let us
consider the unthinkable. Now that the two realms are at war, one of
our first moves must be to march against Carlisle, to shut off the
English approach to the Solway Firth and neutralize the threat of
invasion from that direction. So the question becomes this: which
way will Robert Bruce of Annandale declare himself? Will he
support his anointed King and open Carlisle to a Scots army? Or
will he cleave to his much-acknowledged overlord and benefactor
and defend Edward's Carlisle Castle against his true King's
advance? I have my own opinion on that matter, but yours, my lord
Bishop, is the one that matters here. Until you and your advisers can
answer that single question, beyond a doubt and without reservation,
I suggest you would be foolish to trust the fate of this realm to any
assumptions having to do with the name of Bruce. I do not enjoy
saying that, for my family have always been Bruce men, and I have
no doubt that you are not happy to hear me bring my doubts to your
attention, but that is the truth as I see it today."

Robert Wishart rubbed at his eyes. "I know, my friend, I know.
But that, at least, is a matter that will not take long to resolve, for we

must put it to the test sooner than later, and by the time we do, we will know how to proceed in either circumstance. In the meantime, I am assured that the earls have matters well in hand. John Comyn, Earl of Buchan, is fortifying Annandale, since Bruce himself is in the English camp for the time being. Lord John de Soulis's nephew Nicholas commands in Liddesdale, and between the two of them, the south is well cared for. Sir William Douglas holds the castle at Berwick, and Sir James the Stewart has charge of Roxburgh Keep. We are well prepared and in good hands."

Wallace stood up and moved to a cupboard against the wall, from which he withdrew a jug of wine and a pair of cups, signalling to me to bring out more. He placed a cup in front of the bishop, but before he could pour any wine the old man waved him away, and so he stood there for a few moments, holding the jug between his hands and looking from one to the other of us. "Well," he said eventually, "I hope you're right and that the hands in which we rest are truly good, for if they hesitate or fumble, this land of ours will go down into chaos, and the groans of the folk crushed under England's heel will assault the gates of Heaven itself." He placed the jug carefully on the table, untouched. "I hope you're right, and I will pray that you are."

"But you won't fight." Wishart's voice was bleak, and Will sat down and gazed at him levelly. I could see that he was fighting against his temper and I found myself wondering if the Bishop had any idea of how close he was to receiving the full benediction of my cousin's wrath. But as the moments passed, the danger of an explosion passed with them, and soon Will raised his hand, almost in a blessing.

"I told you, on the last occasion that we met, that if a just cause ever came along and the folk of Scotland marched to war united, I would join them. I have not since changed my mind. I am not yet convinced, though, that the unity of which I spoke is firmly in place … and yet on the other hand, I am greatly encouraged by what you told me today about the power of the burghs and the burgesses. That, I believe, is a mighty step towards what we had hoped to achieve, for if the burgesses can speak with one independent voice, then someday this country of ours could stand on its own as an independent land, governed by its own community for the welfare of *all* its people."

William Lamberton studied him carefully. "What are you saying, Will?"

"That I am half convinced. That is what I am saying, I think." He scratched at his beard. "I am half convinced; the other half remains in doubt. And so I shall half prepare for war; I will half fight. I will stay here in the forest with my folk and watch what happens, and if the English come to me in search of pain and grief and sorrow, I will supply them with all they can take, and more atop that. But I will not yet march away to war." He straightened up and looked directly at the Bishop. "Show me a leader worth following and a war worth dying in, and I will fight. That I swear to you."

CHAPTER SIXTEEN

I

"Thae priests are back, chappin' at wir yetts," was how Alec Scrymgeour put it five days later, when he interrupted Will and me to announce that the Bishop and the canon had returned. By "knocking at our gates," we understood him to mean that they were close to arriving, approaching along the winding bog path from the south.

Will's brows crooked in a small frown as he looked at me, but he said nothing. We had expected the two clerics to stop by on their return journey, but nowhere near as soon as this. They had left in search of the Earl of Buchan, who had last been heard of as being somewhere south and west of us, in the territories of Annandale, and we had anticipated it would take them at least a full day, and more likely twice or even three times that long, to find him. Given that the Bishop had ridden all the way from Glasgow to meet with Buchan and must therefore have had matters of great import to discuss with the Comyn earl, Wishart and Lamberton should not have been expected to return this way for at least another three days.

"Perhaps they ran into the earl on the road," I suggested, and Will shrugged.

"Aye, and mayhap they missed him completely. He might not even have come south yet. That wouldn't surprise me. The man's a Comyn and an earl, unpredictable on both counts. Considers himself beholden to no one and answerable to even fewer. We'll find out soon enough."

Our visitors arrived less than half an hour later, and we were waiting for them as they emerged from the serpentine path into the water meadow at the southern edge of the encampment. They were evidently glad to reach us—especially when Will informed them there was wine awaiting them in his house and a young deer already turning on the spit in their honour—and they seemed cheerful enough, with no air of dejection about them to indicate a failed mission. But the protocol of the day dictated that nothing be said until the proper time, and so no one asked any questions or ventured any comments until the rituals of hospitality had been observed around the shallow fire pit outside Will's hut, after which the casual attendees departed about their own affairs and the four of us were left alone to talk without interruption.

Lamberton started by explaining that they had, in fact, encountered Buchan on the road, no more than half a day after leaving us, to the great surprise of both parties. The earl, it transpired, had sent his main army of several hundred men marching south and west into Annandale while he himself had taken a small escort of horsemen and made a diversionary cross-country journey to the east, to visit briefly with James Stewart the High Steward, who had garrisoned and was holding Roxburgh Castle. Through Stewart he had passed on dispatches to Sir William Douglas in Berwick, and then, on the road back towards Annandale to rejoin his army, he and his men had run into Bishop Wishart's little group at a fork in the road. They had set up a camp close by the road junction so they could conduct their business.

When Lamberton had finished, Will turned to Wishart. "And all went well? You achieved everything you sought?" The canny old churchman raised an eyebrow, the merest flicker of response, but Will carried right on. "I know you went in search of something from Buchan, my lord. You would hardly have ridden all the way from Glasgow merely to wish him well. Am I permitted to ask what it was?"

The older man sighed, and I thought he looked more frail than he had seemed a mere half year earlier, when he had first brought Lamberton to visit us around the time of young Will's birth. He looked exhausted and dispirited, but even as the thought came to me, he straightened his shoulders and pulled himself up straighter, visibly shaking off the appearance of listlessness.

"Aye, William," he said, "you are permitted to ask. And I can even answer you now, which I could not have done before we left to meet with John Comyn. There are plans afoot to send an army of mounted skirmishers over the border into England at the first sign of hostilities. It will be led by a number of earls—"

"Now *there's* an error at the outset, my lord, if I may say so. No *group* can be a leader. It sounds fine and noble, but it's nonsense. All your group of earls will do is fight with one another for command."

"No, not so!" The Bishop's voice was whip-like. "Bear in mind, my son, that the Church itself is such a group, and leads the entire world." He paused, and then resumed in a milder tone. "Granted, the Pope is the leader of the Church, but the cardinals are effectively His Holiness's earls, and they wield their powers effectively. So it will be in this case. The earls will share joint command, each leader commanding his own men, as has ever been the case within this realm when the earls raise the Scots feudal host, calling every able-bodied fighting man in the realm to arm himself and answer the summons. They will act separately but in unison, in accordance with a carefully prepared plan in which every earl will have a role to play. It is the way our forefathers have fought for centuries."

"Aye, for centuries … and there's another point I wish to raise in time to come." Will glanced sideways at me. "Jamie, remind me of that if I forget to bring it up—*the way they have fought for centuries*." He turned back to Wishart, who sat blinking at him, his lips moving, but Will himself appeared unfazed. "Pardon me, my lord. Which earls will be involved in this cross-border attack?"

"Six at this point. Stewart of Menteith, Malise of Strathearn, Strathbogie of Atholl, Donald of Mar, Malcolm of Lennox, and William of Ross. And, of course, Comyn of Buchan, newly named Lord of Annandale after Bruce's defection and failure to answer the call to arms, will now make a seventh."

"The Comyns are well represented, I see—Ross, Buchan, and Mar."

"Aye, and don't forget John Comyn the Younger of Badenoch, son of the Guardian. He rides with them."

"Hmmph. And where will they ride to, can you tell me?"

"They will begin with a three-pronged raid into Cumberland, from south of Jedburgh, striking at Hexham and Corbridge. Farther west, under the command of Buchan, they will attack Carlisle itself."

"Carlisle. You will pit Comyn against Bruce. Think you that is wise?"

The Bishop sighed deeply and peered into his drinking cup. "I do now, though I would not have thought so before you asked me your question about Bruce's loyalties the other night. Before that, I would not have doubted Bruce's commitment to this realm. But then I looked at your question through different eyes—the eyes of a discerning and often disapproving cleric, rather than the wishful, self-deluding eyes of an optimist and a patriot—and what I saw unsettled me. Bruce is for Bruce. His commitment has never been otherwise. And if Bruce has to stoop to using Edward's power to open up the route to Scotland's throne on his behalf, against the Comyns, why then, that is what Bruce will do …"

His voice faded, and then he resumed, in a firmer tone. "Not all men in this realm are as we are, Will. They do not all share our vision, for though you and I are far apart in our opinions and judgment on many things, we do share a grand vision, and one, I believe, that is God-sent. We dream—you and I and other folk like us—of a new and different world. We dream of freedom and of independence as a people—a single people united by our shared place in this land that mothers us, a people with the right to stand up tall and free, beholden to no foreign king or outside power, free to designate and control our own united future, our destiny, according to the people's will."

He turned his head slightly to include me.

"We call ourselves Scots, and nowadays we talk about the community of the realm, and we seek to redefine ourselves and our role in our own lives and living." One corner of his mouth twitched as though he might smile a little, but all he did was jerk his head in a tiny gesture of regret. "We may all be Scots—we *are* all Scots, in name at least—but we are not yet one people. Not by any measure. We are a folk greatly divided by and among ourselves, by language and race, Highlands and Lowlands, Isles and forests. But the greatest of all our divisions, I believe, lies between our magnates and our common folk, and that is the one I fear most as an obstacle to commonality and unity."

"How so, my lord?" I thought I knew the answer, but I could not resist asking the question.

He looked at me, his face expressionless. "Because the common folk and the magnates are two different creatures. The common folk of this land, including us in Holy Mother Church, perceive ourselves as Scots, plain and simple. The magnates have no such belief and no such certainty. If anything, most of them see themselves as English at root. But Bruce is for Bruce, Father James," he said. "Make no mistake about that. And similarly, Comyn is for Comyn. And all the other noble houses, comprising every magnate in the land, support one or the other. The others are all for themselves as well, be it understood, but fundamentally the two houses of Bruce and Comyn split the land between them. King John's hold on the crown, on the realm itself, is faltering. If he should fall and fail—which God forbid—then Bruce and Comyn will divide the land between them yet again, and until that balance of power is rendered null, Scotland will have but little chance of knowing peace and prosperity, and none at all of ever knowing independence."

He turned back to Will. "And so, by pitting Buchan against Bruce, I have chosen to gamble with the fate of this realm. I now believe Bruce will stand for Edward Plantagenet and bar the gates of Carlisle against us. If he does, I doubt that we'll be able to dislodge him. But if he sees his ancient enemy, the House of Comyn, descending upon him from his own lands of Annandale, he might be tempted to come out and fight, and if he does that, then our odds of taking Carlisle are greatly improved. That is my hope, and it is why I asked John Comyn of Buchan to take the lead in the southwest." He stopped short, eyeing Will. "You look skeptical."

"I *am* skeptical. We are speaking of Robert Bruce V here, the new Lord of Annandale. Were we dealing with his father, the old Competitor, then your hope would be a certainty. *That* Robert Bruce would bring his men howling out of Carlisle's gates like a swarm of vengeful wasps. The son, though, is made of different stuff. He is no poltroon, that is not what I am saying. From what I have heard, he does not fear a fight, but he will not fight merely for the love of fighting. He lacks his father's balls of steel and the fiery temper that went with them. *This* Robert Bruce thinks before he acts, every time, and he will never act rashly. He won't come out of Carlisle, I fear."

Bishop Wishart stared at Will for a long time, then twisted his mouth wryly. "And I fear I agree with you. Damn the man."

I could see Will was on the point of twitting His Lordship about such an utterly un-episcopal wish, and I held my breath, but the temptation evidently passed and he changed the subject instead.

"What will the Steward do, my lord? Does he intend to remain pent up in Roxburgh?"

"Sir James will do what he must. He has already left the castle in the hands of a lieutenant and is posting north to join King John. As the Crown's most senior officer, his duty is to raise the Scots host in defence of the realm. He is about that now, and when the time comes, he will lead the host as instructed by the King's grace."

"Then he is not yet committed."

"He is committed to act. That is why he now rides north without rest. But he has not yet moved against England. When he does, I myself will ride with him, representing Mother Church … And what will you do, William Wallace?"

Will peered down at his hands, digging some ingrained dirt from the side of one fingernail with the nail of his thumb.

"I have been thinking about that, my lord, and I have reached a decision. I told you I would fight, if it came to war and if you gave me a leader to follow, but though the war is here, I have yet to hear of such a leader. Frankly, this matter of the earls raiding into England bothers me. It seems too … indeterminate, with too much left to chance. Edward's army stands ready at Newcastle. He will march north from there, towards Berwick. Why, then, are the earls striking at Carlisle? What is to be gained there?" He threw up his hands. "Nothing, except the business of Bruce and Comyn, making war upon each other for the benefit of England, when they should be marching to reinforce Berwick."

The Bishop hawked loudly, then spat into the fire. "You might well be right, William, but we can influence none of that from here. Besides, Berwick wants and needs no help. They have the strongest burgh walls in all Scotland, and they are determined they will hold William at the border."

"Perhaps," Will growled. "Aye. Perhaps, indeed. We can but hope so. But I mislike the smell of all this, and I would like to see more solid planning, for the need to fight is clear. Edward of England has declared a war against this realm without just cause, and every man in Scotland must stand up and fight for it."

The Bishop raised a hand. "Edward believes his cause is just, William. I have no doubt of that. He believes absolutely that his status as overlord of Scotland is valid and that this realm is his fiefdom. By extension, King John is his feudal vassal and is now squarely in open rebellion against his lord by having made alliance with Edward's enemy, Philip of France. That is why Edward has declared war: to depose his faithless vassal, John Balliol, King of Scotland."

"But that is—"

"That is what? Outrageous? Infamous? Damnable?"

"Aye, all of those."

"It is indeed, from where we look at it, but it is none of those if you believe as Edward does. But his claim is based on ancient Norman law, law that has never been enshrined or observed in Scotland since William the Bastard first landed in England, two hundred and thirty years ago. Norman lawmakers might wish it otherwise, but Scots law is far older than theirs, and the realm of Scotland has never been Norman. That is the fallacy underlying Edward's claims, and that is why his lawyers, both civil and canonical, have worked so hard to cloak his every action in a veil of legal-seeming obscurities.

"And that, I suggest to you, is the main reason for what you see as the shiftiness and unreliability of the magnates—and most particularly the Norman-Scots magnates—in this matter of loyalties. They live in a state of constant confusion, not because they are stupid or untrustworthy but simply because they do not know *what* to believe, Will. Their family histories and traditions are strongly rooted in the ancient system of feudalism and chivalry, wherein everything was clearly defined and there was no room for doubt. Now my brethren and I are telling them otherwise, preaching from a book of new ideas, proposing new values that fly in the face of everything they have been taught and are predisposed to believe in. *That* is why they vacillate so much, Will."

My cousin sat listening blank-faced, his chin resting on his steepled fingers.

"These are not learned men, but neither are they inept. They are not ignorant in the laws of duty and chivalry, but they are unlettered and unread. They believe in actions, not ideas, and they respond to actions, not to words written on paper or recited by clerics. That is the truth, Will, and we cannot alter it within mere weeks or months. That is the way this world of ours functions. And I believe the magnates, for all their supposed powers, are afraid of the way their world is changing. Their way of life requires stability and permanence, but even the positive changes nowadays, such as the emergence of the burgesses, must seem threatening to the old guard. In their world, where change is anathema, everything now seems to be in flux."

Will grunted, and I saw Lamberton's eyebrows go up as Wishart's came down in a frown.

"And what is *that* supposed to mean?" the Bishop growled.

"It means that I agree with you," Will said, his eyes unfocused. "And that must be the first time on that topic. I confess I find it hard to imagine the Earl of Buchan being afraid of change. Still, I'll not dispute what you have said, except to say that not everything in their world is in flux. I can see one thing that is dangerously static, and I see it very clearly."

"Aye? And what is that?"

"Their military experience. And that is what I meant when I spoke of the way they have fought for centuries. It comes to me that they have learned nothing through all those centuries and have no time to learn anything new now. They have great confidence in their own abilities, God knows, but how valid is it?" He held up one hand to prevent anyone interrupting. "I bring it up only because I've been worrying over it since you left to hunt for Buchan. I do not like what I have been thinking, my lord Bishop, but this matter has sunk into my head and would not leave me alone until I came to grips with it. I am a verderer—a forester and not a soldier, as you know. But even so, I can see what is there to be seen and I find that I cannot ignore it, no matter how many others can. And the first thing that I see is numbers. The English outnumber us by ten to one, at least. For every hundred men we can march to battle, they can field a thousand, and if they lose a thousand men, they can make good that thousand losses where we may not, and they can do it ten times over." He grunted again, his jaw working. "Now, it's fine to say they're naught but Englishmen and any Scot is worth a score of them, but that is hardly credible when blows are to be traded. We all bleed the same red blood and we all feed the same black earth.

"But the simplest, plainest truth, the thing that frightens me and dominates my thoughts at all times now, is that the English are in solid fighting trim and we are not. They are focused and tight, disciplined and battle hardened. Their forces are keenly edged and toughened after years of sustained warfare in France, in Gascony, and in Wales. Their morale is high, with ample reason, whereas our swaggering has nothing to back it up or sustain it. The Welsh and English archers are well trained and well equipped, furnished with arrows by the hundreds of thousands, produced incessantly by fletching manufactories set up throughout England to keep the country's bowmen armed and ready to fight instantly and anywhere. Their infantry is equally well equipped, and tempered by years of fighting in scores of battles. And their cavalry is something which we simply cannot match. We lack the enormous horses that the English breed, and because our horses are smaller, our armour must be lighter, so we have no knights who can withstand the might of England's chivalry.

"But even were we able, by some divine magic, to erase those differences, we would still be facing disaster, for we have not fought—I mean really *fought*, hard battles in the field—for more than thirty years. No Scots army has taken the field since the fight to throw out the Norwegians, at Largs, more than thirty years ago. And even that was no real battle by any standards. Since then, the closest our leaders have come to formal battlefield experience, the closest in *decades*, is on short raids into neighbouring territories against their own kind. That does not fill me with hope about the outcome of this new war."

"Let us pray you are wrong, Will."

"Pray all you wish, my lord, but prayer will not alter the fact that we are outweighed and outdistanced on every front. Pray hard, and have your people pray hard, too, for we'll have need of every prayer they can muster. As for myself, I intend to fight, but I will do it here, where I can serve best by protecting the rear of our forces against incursions from the south. The English host will doubtless invade across the flats of Solway, striking into Annandale and Galloway, but there will be a constant progress of supplies and reinforcements coming north by way of Berwick and by the roads through Coldstream and Jedburgh. My men will keep those roads secure and bar all interference by those routes. You have my word on that."

2

The Bishop and his chancellor left us to return to the cathedral in Glasgow on the morning of the fifteenth of March, the day the ancients called the Ides. I remember warning them to travel with care that day, which had not been a propitious one for Julius Caesar. I recall clearly, too, that it seemed to take a long time for them to reach the end of the long avenue and veer from sight. It was the last thing I can remember that happened slowly from that day forward.

"I like that man Lamberton," Will said as we walked back towards his hut. "He has a good head and a stout heart and he loves this land of ours. I would follow him, were he a fighter."

"He is a fighter, Cuz, but he's a warrior of God. He'll fight savagely for those things he believes in, but he will do it with nerve and sinew, and his only weapons will be his mind, which is formidable, and his will. He would never spill blood, though, unless it be his own, in sacrifice. He has the makings of a fine bishop, and I have not the slightest doubt he will be one someday."

"If he survives this war."

I glanced at my cousin in surprise. "Of course he will survive. Edward does not make war on clerics."

"Hmm. Edward has not made war on clerics *yet*. But it seems Edward is breaking new ground everywhere he goes these days, and he does not enjoy being crossed. I would not like to cross him in person. Mind you, I'm no bishop."

As he said the words, we heard Mirren calling his name, and we turned as one to see her watching us, her body tilted to hold her son on her hip as she beckoned.

"Is she not grand, Jamie? Look at her, the stance and the pride of her. Truthfully, I have to thank God I'm no bishop ... and to thank Him even more that I'm no saint. Let's find out what she wants."

The following day brought word of English troop movements in the fringes of the forest to the south of us, between the towns of Selkirk and Wark and Coldstream, and Will summoned his three appointed leaders to his camp to discuss what they would do to intercept and harass the Englishmen. Within days Will's men were involved in hostilities, provoked by a seemingly unwarranted attack on a village no more than five miles from his main camp. Word of it came to us from one of the villagers, who had escaped into the woods for long enough to watch the brutality escalate to the point where women and children were being slaughtered as they tried to flee, shot down by bowmen who bet among themselves over how each running target would be hit—in the arm, leg, torso, or head. I was appalled, not so much by the attack itself as by the borderless abyss I sensed yawning ahead of all of us.

Will questioned the man closely for some time, searching for anything that might provide a reason for the attack. But once he had satisfied himself that it was brigandage and murder, pure and simple, he called in Long John and the others and sent a contingent of forty archers off towards the village with orders to bring back as many of the raiders as they could find. Two injured prisoners, both of them English, were brought back within a matter of days; their party of five men, three of whom had died rather than surrender, had been the only people found. There had to have been many more involved in the raid, but they had obviously been under orders to scatter widely after the attack.

The two prisoners had been questioned extensively before they were brought in, and so we knew who had employed them. They were truculent and they were afraid, and the booty they had been carrying when they were taken was enough to leave no doubt in anyone's mind that they were guilty.

The case against them was laid out by one of our own, Alan Crawford of Nithsdale, and the elder of the pair was identified under oath by Walter Armstrong, the survivor who had brought the tale to us. He recognized the archer as the man he had seen shoot two arrows into his cousin Willie, the village blacksmith. The two were judged by a quartet of judges and found guilty, after which the judges met together to determine their punishment. The deliberations were short and the judgment unanimous. Each man had the middle finger of his right hand severed with a single chisel blow. They retained their lives but lost their livelihood, since neither of them would ever again be able to draw a nocked arrow. Their wounds were cauterized roughly, and they were set free.

As soon as they were gone, Will called his leaders into conference again and set them to organizing patrols, morning and evening, to ensure that all traffic moving through the greenwood for a twenty-mile radius would be tracked.

Later that day, when Mirren was called away by one of the women, she left Will and me alone with the baby for a few minutes. He was eight months old by then, as burly and agile as a badger and almost impossible to restrain, even for his father. Will finally hoisted the boy high into the air, then held him out to me.

"Here, then. Away and see your holy Uncle Jamie."

I caught the child under the arms, instantly aware as I always was nowadays of the weighty, solid, squirming bulk of him and the speed with which his hands moved to whatever he identified as worthy of examination. This time it was my nether lip, and his tiny fingers grasped it before I could avoid them. I winced in anticipation of the pain, but before he could tighten his killing grip, I was saved by the sudden swoop of one of the women who doted on the boy. She whipped him up and away from me, carrying him off towards the women's quarters, doubtless to be fed something warm and delicious.

"I thought he was going to rip that bottom lip of yours right off," Will said, and his grin spread wider. "I don't know what the reason for it is, but my son seems fascinated by your mouth."

"Aye, as I am by yours."

"What's *that* supposed to mean?"

"Are you going to fight?"

All the animation left his eyes and he sat staring at me, willing me to continue but unwilling himself to respond.

I kept going. "A week ago you told Bishop Wishart you would not fight. Since then, you've sent out men to fight."

"Only in defence of our own peace."

"Perhaps, but now you are arranging day and night patrols. I am not saying they are unnecessary, but I am wondering if you are changing your mind about your involvement in this affair that's bubbling on the hob."

He continued to gaze at me, his face unreadable, and after a while I began to think he was not going to answer me at all, but then he shook his head, a short, sharp, impatient gesture.

"If you are asking me if I am going marching off to war, then no, I am not. I meant every word of what I said to Wishart. So no, I'll not fight. Not without solid reason. The magnates will not miss my presence, and the realm of Scotland, needy though it might be, has no great need of William Wallace. None grand enough, at least, to outweigh the need my wife and children have of me."

"Children?" I heard the surprise in my own voice.

Will grinned almost shamefacedly and lapsed into Scots. "Aye. Mirren's expecting again. The women say she's three months along already." He flipped a hand and made a face, as though asking me what else he could have done. "I would ha'e waited longer, y' know? But she would ha'e none o' it. No need to wait, she said. She's as strong as a horse and likes the thought o' twa wee ones close enough together to be company for one anither. A lad and a lass, she wants, and close thegither, so what was I to say—or dae, for that matter?"

He shrugged and dipped his head. "Anyway, that's the way o' it, and I intend to see them safe through whatever lies ahead o' us. War is no fitting pastime for a man wi' bairns and a comely wife. So what I said to the Bishop holds true. I'll take no part in fighting for some magnate—*any* magnate—who canna make up his mind whether he's Scots or no'. I ha'e no such doubts. I'm a Scot, as were my grandsires and theirs before them. I ken wha and what I am, and I ken wha my King is. 'Gin he calls upon me directly, then I'll go to war. For him. But for naebody else, Jamie."

The rough accent of the local people vanished again beneath the lustre of the Church's tongue. "In the meantime, I intend to keep my family safe and hidden from marauding eyes here in the forest. Should any seek to threaten them or me, then I will fight, and those I fight will rue the day they sought to find me. But that is all. So be the English keep themselves and their evil presence far from me, then I will keep myself away from them."

I felt a blossoming relief well up in me and raised my hand to bless him. "Then so mote it be, Cousin William, and may God keep you and yours in safety in such times."

It was a heartfelt prayer, and at the time I felt sure it must have flown directly from my lips to God's all-hearing ear.

3

War.
In merely setting those three letters down here, hours ago, penning each of them with increasing slowness, I found myself fascinated by the contradiction between the brevity of the word itself and its overwhelming, cataclysmic meaning. It is a commonplace little word, seldom truly understood by those who use it daily. Even to speak it aloud, or even shout it at the top of one's lungs, in the context of *going to* war, or *being at* war, fails to elicit more than a mild stirring of interest. That is because in most instances—thanks be to God—war in the abstract has no real significance for ordinary, peaceable, law-abiding folk. To those unfortunate enough to know otherwise, that is both extraordinary and incredible, but unless we have been personally touched by its insanity and brutality, its monstrous, crushing inhumanity, we remain armoured in the innocence of hope and the blithe assumption that it could never happen to us.

The people of Scotland were that way in the springtime of the year of our Lord 1296. They heard the talk of war with England and they knew that matters had been set in motion that were beyond their control, grave matters that would affect them and change the very way their land was governed. And yet they did not grow unduly alarmed. An entire generation had come to middle age without ever knowing the dangers, the risks, or the enormous tragedy of extensive warfare, and the men whose duty it would now become to fight this new war and confront the English approached the task with a wide-eyed confidence that reflected their innocence and ignorance. That innocence was about to be rudely shattered.

On the twenty-sixth of March, under the command of Sir John Comyn, Earl of Buchan and High Constable of Scotland, King John's army, jointly led by seven earls of the realm, marched south from Annandale and crossed the sands of the Solway Firth at low tide to strike at the English stronghold of Carlisle, forcing Robert Bruce, the castellan there, to declare his loyalties. Bruce chose the side of Edward Plantagenet and barred his city gates against the Scots, who set fire to the town outside the castle walls. The word that came to us in Selkirk Forest later was that Buchan had miscalculated, assuming Carlisle would fall to his first surprise assault. Instead, his attack came as no surprise at all, and Bruce's resistance was unwavering.

As Buchan had been moving against Carlisle, though, Edward himself had arrived at Newcastle, in the northeast, and advanced with his main army to the border town of Berwick, Scotland's most prosperous burgh, on the River Tweed, where he demanded entry. It was a demand that must have been foreseen, but the citizens of Berwick made a grievous error, born of the overconfidence engendered by too many years of peace. They overestimated their own defensive strength, and they underestimated the power and temper of the man whom they defied. They made no secret of their contempt for the English King and his army, and openly laughed and jeered at Edward himself when he rode forward to inspect their walls. Infuriated by this treatment, the like of which he had never been shown by any enemy in a lifetime of warfare, Edward unleashed his full power on the burgh and trampled over its vaunted defences, bringing them down within a single day. When the burgesses and town fathers sued for peace after that, he ignored them, and set out to teach Scotland a lesson on the foolishness of attempting to withstand England's power. Mercilessly determined to avenge what he perceived to be an insult to his personal honour, he turned his army loose on the populace, and they burned the burgh down, butchering fifteen thousand citizens of all ages and both sexes. Edward permitted the rape of the burgh to go on for three days before calling a halt to it solely because the bodies clogging the streets had begun to rot sufficiently to become a hazard to his own men.

The sack of Berwick was a deliberate, royally condoned atrocity that appalled every person in Scotland, north and south of the Firth of Forth, and so I expected to find Will in a towering rage when I arrived in his camp. But he was quite the opposite, evidently the only man in his entire encampment who was not up in arms. When

I asked him for his opinion of the reports we had received, he simply looked away.

"Which reports are you talking about?"

"Why, the Berwick reports," I said tentatively. "Are there others?"

"Aye. We have reports out of Carlisle, too."

"Great God! They burned Carlisle?"

His headshake was terse. "Nah. Not them. *We* burnt it, or we tried to. We set it afire on the outskirts, and it was going well, I'm told, but then the defenders threw us out and tackled the blaze before it could destroy the whole town."

"They threw us out ..."

"Aye, they did, just the way you said they would. It was Robert Bruce we were attacking, and him behind strong walls with his own Annandale men and a garrison of English veterans to back them. The mere sight of Buchan's Comyn banners coming south at him out of his own lands of Annandale would have been enough to guarantee he'd hold Carlisle forever against such an attack."

"So what happened to the Scots host?"

Will shrugged. "They turned aside and went raiding south of the border. From what I've heard, the five earls split their forces and set out in search of booty. Buchan himself came back to Scotland, and promptly wrote to Bishop Wishart and Bishop Fraser of St. Andrews, reporting Bruce's perfidy in repulsing the army of his anointed King."

"You mean they simply split up and disbanded the host? How could they be so irresponsible? They could have ridden to save Berwick."

"They knew nothing about Berwick, Jamie. In all probability they didn't even know Edward had come north. The English had already surrounded Berwick by the time Buchan reached Galloway."

"Dear God in Heaven! What a waste ..."

Will shrugged. "Perhaps, but no useful purpose would have been served by dashing across the north to Berwick, even had they known of it. The men of Berwick itself thought they were invincible behind their walls, so we may hardly blame the earls for thinking they could win some time and land and booty while leaving Berwick to fend for itself and hold the English at the border crossing. They had all lost sight—every one of them—of the true savagery and treachery of their enemy."

I seldom saw my cousin smile in the days that followed, and then it was solely for Mirren or little William. Like the rest of us in Scotland at that time, he saw little in the land to smile about. I knew he was chafing at the restraints he had imposed upon himself, but he also knew there was nothing he could have done to influence what was going on beyond the forest. He had sworn publicly that for as long as the English left him alone, he would leave them alone, and during that spring and early summer, no one came to disturb his tranquility. The English had far more important matters to attend to elsewhere in Scotland.

Three weeks after that talk of ours, on April 27th, Edward's army, commanded in the King's name by John de Warenne, the second Earl of Surrey, met and smashed the army of the Scots magnates at Dunbar. John Comyn the Constable was captured and sent to England to be imprisoned there, along with the Earls of Atholl, Menteith, and Ross and, much to the chagrin of Will and me when we heard of it, Sir Andrew Murray of Petty and his son, Andrew Murray the Younger, our greatly admired friend. The day after the battle, Edward himself arrived at the head of his army to demand the surrender of Dunbar Castle, which capitulated without a blow being struck. Three weeks later, Edward arrived in the burgh of Perth, having bypassed Stirling on the landward side on his way north, and while he was there, King John Balliol wrote to him in person, suing for peace.

Ten days later, in his own royal castle of Kincardine, John Balliol, the King of Scotland, bent the knee to Edward Plantagenet and begged his English cousin's royal pardon for rebelling against him. Five days after that, at Stracathro in Angus, where he had been taken as a prisoner under escort, John Balliol, a broken man by then, formally and publicly renounced his alliance with King Philip IV of France. The next day, July 8th, 1296, under the merciless eyes of his royal tormentor, he was formally deposed as King, the royal insignia torn from his gold-encrusted tabard by no less a person than Antony Bek, Prince Bishop of Durham.

Scotland was without a king again; the throne lay vacant and the entire country waited to see who would be first to claim it. In that year of 1296, however, no one did, and the weather grew colder as the months lurched towards winter. To be sure, Edward of England called himself nothing more than the feudal overlord of Scotland, and he made no slightest mention of any claim to the kingship, but in truth he behaved like a despotic monarch, and his behaviour left no one in Scotland in any doubt of how he saw himself. He went to great lengths to subjugate the kingdom and humiliate and stifle its contentious leaders, and in his determination to achieve that he confiscated the Stone of Destiny, upon which every legitimate King of Scots, including King John himself, had been crowned since time immemorial, and shipped it back to England, to his palace in Westminster.

Edward also summoned a parliament at Berwick, where he demanded, and received, a written oath of allegiance from more than two thousand Scots freeholders: knights, lairds, earls, barons, lords, chieftains, and burgesses. The resulting document, in the form of four huge parchment rolls comprising thirty-five pieces, each of those a list signed and sealed under duress, was known as the Ragman's Roll, meaning, according to whom you ask, the Witnesses' Roll, or more popularly, the Devil's Roll. No matter which it meant, though, no one who signed the roll was glad to have done so. More significantly, few who had signed it felt constrained by having done so, and Edward bought himself no loyalty or well-wishers by forcing the Scots freemen to comply with his arbitrary wishes.

Will himself put it best of all, I believe, when he said to me later, mere weeks before he flung down the gauntlet in cold fury and set out to destroy England's presence in our land, "Edward Plantagenet.

Can you believe the folly and the hubris of the man? He surpassed
the boast of Julius Caesar, for he came, he saw, he conquered, and
then he went home again without making sure he had won. He
should have stayed here and ground the spurs on his boot heels into
our throats when he had us down. He should have crushed us, killed
us all then and there, while he yet could. But he went home instead,
and left us to recover, and now he'll rue it."

CHAPTER SEVENTEEN

I

Edward Plantagenet carried his war into Scotland from the border town of Berwick, which he had ordained should be rebuilt as the administrative centre for his overlordship of Scotland. He populated the town with English burgesses, having created sufficient room for them through the slaughter of fifteen thousand former residents, and brought in English engineers and architects to redesign its defences as he garrisoned the newly fortified burgh with English troops. He then established a special branch of the royal exchequer in the town and appointed a man called Hugh Cressingham to administer it as treasurer of Scotland. Cressingham, a senior royal clerk who had been, before that, an itinerant justice in the northern counties of England, threw himself into his new post with a voracious eagerness that within two years earned him the reputation of being the most hated man in Scotland.

Edward also used the months following the battle at Dunbar to seed the entire realm of Scotland with his own personnel, placing trusted functionaries of his own to fill positions left vacant by those imprisoned rebels—Edward's own word—who had dared to oppose his invasion of their land. Then, for the last five months of that year, he and his armies trampled Scotland under their heavily mailed feet. They confiscated the realm's crown jewels and insignia and they despoiled the countryside and its populace everywhere they went. Few could withstand them. Among those few, however, William Wallace, and the outlaws of Selkirk Forest whom he led, ranked first and foremost.

Every army lives at the mercy of its lines of supply, and Edward, as aware of that as any good general must be, had taken steps to ship supplies into northern Scotland by sea, using the port of Leith on the Firth of Forth. However, most of the supplies that fed and sustained the garrisons of western and central Scotland were channelled directly through the new administrative centre of Berwick on the east coast, because the northern route from there into Scotland was the only viable route for large numbers of personnel and heavy trains of wagons entering from England. The sole western route, north from Carlisle across the sea sands of the Solway Firth into Galloway and Annandale, was little better than a track, ill maintained at the best of times, dependent upon tides and weather, and vulnerable to attack all the way north from Carlisle. For that reason, every supply train, every reinforcing troop body, every important communication that came north from England by way of Berwick passed through Selkirk Forest, either on the high road itself or through the greenwood byways, and for the last half of 1296 and the first half of the year that followed, all of them were at hazard from the threat of attack and plunder by the Selkirk outlaws.

Cressingham, whose jurisdiction covered all things fiscal in Scotland, felt himself constantly under attack, and he took every threat of interference as a personal insult. He resorted to reprisals soon after his appointment as treasurer, taking hostages from among the populace and hanging scores of them out of hand as punishment for attacks against the King's property and personnel. Others he executed by public beheading, irrespective of age or sex. The more people he killed, though, the greater the resistance and aggression he provoked, and by the end of the year, less than three months after his appointment, he was offering a reward to anyone who would bring him the head of any forest outlaw, and a premium in gold to any who would bring him the killer, William Wallace.

A chant of "William Wallace, Laird o' the Forest" was popular that autumn, when some wag suggested that as *de facto* lord of his own woodland domain, Wallace demanded a toll of everyone who set foot upon his property. The toll for a Scot was a pledge of loyalty and silence; for an Englishman, it was forfeiture of everything he possessed; for English clergymen, it was forfeiture of everything they professed not to have at all; and for Hugh Cressingham, it was everything that bore the stink of his presence. And as the faceless forest bandit became the Forest Laird, and the fame of William Wallace spread, yet still he maintained the role of planner and supervisor and, true to his promise, did not fight in person.

I stayed in the forest with him and Mirren throughout that time, until September, when a messenger arrived to summon me back to Glasgow, where Bishop Wishart apparently had need of me, and during that time we often spoke of the imprisoned Scots leaders from Dunbar, and in particular about the calamitous effect Andrew Murray's imprisonment in England would have on his northern people. The magnates had proved themselves to be as overconfident and ineffectual as Will had feared they might be, and he wasted no time mourning their absence now. Andrew Murray's removal, though, was another matter altogether, for Murray was one of the few competent military leaders in all of Scotland. Edward Plantagenet was known to be whimsical when it came to forgiving rebellion and disobedience among his people, and it was generally conceded by those who knew him that he was not normally vindictive towards his own nobles. In this instance of the Scottish Rebellion, though, he was being obdurate, and when he refused his royal pardon to Sir Andrew Murray of Petty, one of the richest and most influential lords of Scotland, it boded ill for the probability of any leniency being offered to his rebellious and high-minded son. We regretted the loss of Murray, as we knew Bishop Wishart must be regretting it, but there was nothing we could do to change things.

The courier who came to fetch me also brought instructions that before I left I should divide my duties equally between my two subordinate priests, Fathers Declan and Jacobus, both of whom had flourished and matured wonderfully since moving out of the cloisters and into the world of ordinary men and women. They were both flattered to be thought worthy of increased responsibility, and I, in turn, felt confident in leaving them to tend to my erstwhile flock, and glad at the same time to be returning to my duties in the cathedral, though I knew I would miss my forest-dwelling kin greatly—

most particularly my sturdy, stalwart, year-old godson—in the months ahead.

I met Cressingham, not at all coincidentally, soon after my return to Glasgow, when he presented himself at the cathedral to announce formally, for the benefit of Scotland's clergy, his appointment to the post of King Edward's treasurer for Scotland, and I immediately discovered that the name of Wallace was already anathema, not only to him but to all the Englishmen who accompanied him on that occasion. As senior bishop of the realm at the time, since Fraser of St. Andrews had been in France at King Philip's court for more than a year by then, Bishop Wishart hosted the gathering at his episcopal seat in Glasgow. The Bishops of Dunkeld, Aberdeen, Moray, and Argyll all attended, hastily summoned, along with half a dozen of the country's most distinguished abbots upon notice that the King's party sought audience with Scotland's senior prelates. The English contingent included several bishops and abbots, too, the most senior among them being Antony Bek, still King Edward's deputy in Scotland. Besides the new treasurer himself and a few of his senior functionaries, a number of intermediately ranked nobles made up the English lay presence, led by one Robert Fitz Hugh, a baron from the region south of Newcastle. There were also two representatives of the Order of the Temple among the group, and I found that mildly surprising, since I had always believed—albeit without specific reason for so doing—that the Templars owed their allegiance solely to the Pope.

Hugh Cressingham, the centre of all the activity on that occasion, was a big man—not merely large or stout, but gross in his bigness, corpulent to the point of being grotesque, and crass in the hectoring loudness of his grating voice. He was tall, too, several inches over six feet in height, and the first thought that entered my mind on meeting him was that he dressed *voluminously*. His clothing was rich, and richly tailored, but it all seemed too much, as though it had been shaped and fashioned to make its wearer look even bigger and more important than he actually was. His face, swarthy and coarse skinned, was framed by lank, blond hair, greasy and lustreless. He barely took the time to acknowledge me when Canon Lamberton made me known to him, for he was far more concerned with speaking to another member of the visiting group, the Templar called Brian le Jay, and so he ignored me beyond a dismissive nod when I was presented to him as Bishop Wishart's amanuensis.

All in all, Scotland's new treasurer was an unprepossessing man, with a personality and a disposition to match, and although it may have been unsacerdotal and uncharitable of me to think so, as a purported man of God, I was never surprised afterwards to hear him widely condemned as the most hated man in Scotland, because it struck me at that first encounter that he possessed an innate gift for alienating everyone around him—including, I noted, the very men who had been dispatched to escort and introduce him.

Sir Brian le Jay, on the other hand, looked precisely like what he was, a senior commander of the Order of the Knights of the Temple of Solomon. Sumptuously dressed and equipped, he exuded confidence, arrogance, and wealth with a complete disregard for any possible restriction caused by his vow of poverty. He had a haughty tilt to his head that spoke of intolerance and little patience, and the hectic colour of his cheeks suggested a fondness for good red wine. I had met him once before, five or six years earlier at Paisley Abbey, during his term as preceptor of the Temple in Scotland, but since then he had been reassigned by his superiors to England as preceptor there, and the Templars' overall role in Scotland had been downgraded to a mere military presence, commanded by the other Templar in the gathering that night, Sir John de Sautre, Master of Cavalry. Watching le Jay then as he listened, frowning, to something Cressingham was saying to him, it came to me that I would have a hard time, had anyone asked me, deciding which of the two of them I disliked less than the other.

Among the dozen or so in the English party, though, I did find one man I liked, and I liked him immediately and wholeheartedly. His name was William Hazelrig, and he was another of Edward's new political appointees, having been named only recently as sheriff of Lanark, with full control of the English garrison there and a mandate to keep the King's Peace in that jurisdiction. I heard him laughing at some sally made by one of the company, and the warmth and spontaneity of the sound attracted me to the man immediately. He saw me looking, and when our eyes met he winked at me. I nodded and smiled back at him, wondering what he found to laugh about so easily in conversation with the Bishop of Moray, whom I had judged to be a humourless pedant with the conversational skills of a tree trunk.

It was during dinner, as usual, that I discovered more about, and developed a greater appreciation of, the discussions and the delicate manoeuvring that would continue over the ensuing few days. Nothing had yet been decided upon at that stage, and therefore no one yet felt constrained to speak or behave in any particular way; people were getting to know one another, and at the dinner table, where the wine flowed freely, the atmosphere grew increasingly informal as the evening progressed, and I listened carefully to everything I could overhear. Bishop Wishart had invited me to be there with that in mind, and it was no accident that his finest wines were being served.

Mathew de Crambeth, the mercurial and outspoken Bishop of Dunkeld, asked the question that set the mood of the gathering for the remainder of that night. Master Crambeth had returned mere days earlier from France, where he had been among the party sent almost two years earlier by King John to negotiate the alliance treaty. On his return, he had received a peremptory summons to present himself before King Edward and explain his atrocious conduct in daring to make alliance with the King of France. Crambeth had mentioned this to Wishart that very afternoon in my hearing and said that he would go and eat his humble pie when he got around to it, but not before he had set his own affairs in Dunkeld in order after his sixteen-month absence. Now, at dinner, he was seated across the table from me, next to the young English sheriff, William Hazelrig, with whom I had seen him talking on their way into the dining hall.

The seating at Bishop Wishart's "intimate" table for gatherings such as these was notoriously and deliberately informal, the Bishop believing that people in small gatherings would interact more easily and honestly if they were able to seat themselves where they wished. Protocol and formality were therefore ignored more often than not, and although I saw a few raised eyebrows at first among the English guests, the word was quickly passed among them that this informality was one of their host's episcopal idiosyncrasies, and they accepted the convention without demur.

During a brief lull in the general conversation, one of those odd moments when everyone falls silent at the same time as though at some unseen signal, Bishop Crambeth leaned forward and spoke across the table to the Templar le Jay, who was sitting a few places to my left.

"Sir Brian, *Brother* Brian, how are you finding life in England nowadays, as opposed to Scotland, I mean, seeing that you are, in fact, Scots born? I have not seen you since you were transferred south, what was it, five years ago? And therefore I admit, frankly, to being curious. Is the air more beneficial down there for a man such as yourself?"

All eyes turned to the dark-faced Templar, who found the grace to smile. "I find it pleasant there, my lord Bishop, and very little different from my former posting here, since the preceptor's duties remain the same irrespective of where they apply. To those of us in holy orders, as you know yourself, it matters less where we live than how we live."

"Well said," Crambeth replied mildly. "Well said. But on that very topic, I have a question for you, if you would not consider me impertinent to ask it."

"Ask away, my lord."

"It concerns your support of King Edward … your support, and that of your order, of course. You yourself swore allegiance openly to Edward when you moved south five years ago, did you not?" He waited for le Jay's nod. "Would you explain to me, then, how that could be so? You are a Temple Knight, and it has always been my understanding that the Knights of the Temple were forbidden to swear fealty to any temporal monarch. They owe their allegiance directly to the Pope alone. Has that changed, then?"

Le Jay's smile did not waver, and he gave a sideways dip of his head. "Aye, you are correct, my lord, as ever … to the Pope and, of course, to our Grand Master."

"But not to Edward of England—" Crambeth held up one hand to forestall a response. "I have no intent here to embarrass you, my friend, nor do I wish to discomfit you in any way, but there is something here I plainly do not understand."

"I must point out," le Jay said, ostensibly responding to Bishop Crambeth but clearly, from the pitch of his voice, addressing the whole gathering, "that Edward Plantagenet is no man's idea of a normal, temporal monarch. He is unique, distinguished from all others in several respects, and the oath of which you spoke, my lord Bishop, was not undertaken lightly. Quite bluntly, I could not have undertaken it at all had my obeisance not been authorized by our Grand Master at the time, Sieur Tibauld de Godin. I was merely the vehicle on that auspicious occasion. It was the Order of the Temple itself that extended the privilege of its fealty to King Edward, in recognition of his outstanding exploits and achievements on behalf of the Church and the Pope."

Aware of the effect of his words upon those to whom this information came as a revelation, le Jay sat silent for a moment before he continued. "Edward crusaded as a Prince, in the Holy Land, in Acre to be precise, on the Ninth Crusade. He stood with our order and fought beside us there against the Turkish heathen. And in his Christian monarchy, he espouses the principles of feudalism, in which it is decreed that all Christian society is hierarchical, extending upwards through monarchs to the Pope himself. Edward Plantagenet has proved his devotion and commitment to the Pope, every bit as completely as we in the Order of the Temple have proved ours, and therefore we Templars see no contradiction between our fealty to this particular King and our loyalty to the Pope."

"Hmm." Crambeth nodded. "So be it. I thank you for resolving that for me." He turned away to talk to Hazelrig again, but then hesitated and swung back towards the Templar. "So, and again I beg your indulgence, but would I be correct in saying that although your sworn duties as a Temple Knight forbid you to bear arms against another Christian, your sworn fealty to England's King might send you here to fight your fellow Scots in his name?"

A profound silence fell over the table. Le Jay sat open mouthed. His face flushed and then just as quickly grew pale, his fingers curled motionless in the fork of his great black beard. Finally, though, he found his voice and spoke in a cold monotone.

"I would not do such a thing. The King would not demand that of me."

Crambeth sighed. "The King, if you will forgive my saying so, Sir Brian, is a king, and an oath of fealty may never be retracted. If times and your King's needs were to become desperate enough, you could be required to fight—and kill—your fellow Scots."

Cressingham's harsh voice filled the room like the braying of an ass. "Aye, and you might well be called upon to do precisely that, Sir Knight, if this miscreant Wallace continues his outrages against the King's Peace. *Him* you might be asked to apprehend and bring to justice. The man is an outlaw—a thief and a murderer, with a following of like-minded vermin little better than a swarm of rats." The treasurer rose to his feet. "I have already written to King Edward, requesting his permission to stamp out this pestilence of outlaws that pollutes this ungrateful land, and to make the forests safe for honest English travellers again. I wrote most eloquently of the need for haste and vehemence."

Amid the furor that followed, I looked down the length of the table to where Antony Bek, the King's deputy, sat glowering, his florid face the very picture of fury and discomfiture. His frown grew ever deeper, and I could see the effort it was costing him not to raise his voice and savage everyone, including the fool Cressingham, but he clenched his fists and took them off the table, lowering them to where no one could see the whiteness of his knuckles.

Beside him at the head of the table, Bishop Wishart sat silent, his eyes moving from face to face around the gathering. When they reached me, he raised one eyebrow, very slightly, and I nodded to him, signifying my understanding of what had taken place. Will's name was on everyone's lips, and none of the English party had anything good to say about him, the consensus being that he should be taken into custody as soon as possible, his punishment used as an example to others of the folly of attempting to defy English rule.

I caught Sheriff Hazelrig's eye and thought he looked amused, so I leaned across the table and asked him what his opinion was on the matter of Wallace and the forest outlaws.

"Too much smoke and not enough fire," he said with a casual shrug. "The man is an outlaw, beyond the law and beyond the protection of Church or state. He has managed somehow to acquire a reputation and has gained a small amount of fame among the local peasants. But he is a nonentity and a common criminal, and someone simply has to make a decision to put an end to him, and then go out and do it. He and his rabble cannot be expected to prevail against a strong force of disciplined soldiers. And his past activities, from what I have heard, are of the kind that can neither be condoned nor forgiven. I do not think he has been active within my territories of Lanark, but I might be wrong. I have not been here long enough to ask about that, but I will. Then, if I find he has transgressed against my jurisdiction, I shall move against him and destroy him without hesitation. If it is not me, it will be someone else. Sooner or later, all such nuisances are dealt with properly and finally. And legally." He smiled, good-naturedly, I thought. "You'll see. Someone will get him, soon."

2

"Father."
I was striding quickly, heavily muffled in my warmest winter cloak, but something about the voice stopped

me in mid-step, and I turned around carefully to peer into the shadows beneath the walls on my right. It was dark and bone-achingly cold, a wet, dismal, chilly night in November, and I was on my way back to my room after a late-night visit to the cathedral's infirmary, where one of our oldest and most beloved brethren lay dying, beyond any aid that our medical fraternity could offer him.

"Who's there?" Strain as I would I could see no one within the blackness facing me. I knew that there was a row of four rowan trees in front of me, between the footpath on which I stood and the wall of the building, but they, too, were swallowed by the blackness. I was alone in the darkness, facing someone, at least one man, whom I could not see and whose voice was filled with strain and wariness, but I sensed no threat to myself. I was about to repeat my question when the answer reached me.

"I am a stranger here, but I mean you no harm. I but seek your help."

"My help in what, exactly?" The voice was coming from straight ahead of me and it was close enough that I felt I ought to be able to see something of the speaker, if only a darker or lighter shade of blackness, but still I saw nothing.

"In finding shelter. Sanctuary."

I hesitated, thinking quickly about how I should best proceed.

"Shelter is simple to provide, especially on a night like this, but sanctuary? That might be more complicated. Who are you, and why would you seek sanctuary here?"

The voice that came back was stronger this time. "My name is common enough, but I am a fugitive, a wanted man."

"Wanted by whom?"

"By England."

"By *England*? That sounds very grand. Have you offended the entire country, then? Or do you mean England's King, in person?"

"I do. Edward Plantagenet of ill renown. Is Robert Wishart yet Bishop here?"

"He is, and has been for years. Where have you been, that you should wonder such a thing?"

"In England. Imprisoned. Can you inform him that I am here?"

"I can. But not if you are nameless."

"Tell him Andrew Murray of Petty seeks audience with him. Murray the Younger."

It seemed to me then that I actually felt my heart knock, physically, against my chest. "Andrew?" I asked, stunned. "You are supposed to be in England, in prison."

"And I was. Have you not been listening? And who are you, to know me by my name?"

"Jamie Wallace. Will's cousin. We met in Paisley years ago, you and I."

"Aye, when Will broke my head and you pulled me from the river. I remember. Well met, then, Father James. Will told me you were to be ordained the last time we two spoke. I thought you would still be in Paisley."

The blackness moved and he stepped forward, pushing back a hood to bare his head and show the paleness of his face, and I saw why I had not been able to see him before. Like the huge man who now moved up to stand silently by his side, he was wearing the black robe of a Dominican friar, a single, cowled garment that covered him from head to foot and rendered him invisible on a night like this. But the shock of seeing his face revealed reminded me sharply that he was indeed a fugitive and that it would be best to take him and his man indoors and out of sight as quickly as possible.

The two hours that followed passed by very quickly, notwithstanding that Bishop Wishart required a full hour of it alone with Andrew. I had plenty to do in the interim, though, organizing hot food and dry clothing and airing fresh bedding for our unheralded guests. By the time Andrew emerged from the Bishop's quarters, and despite my own busyness, I had grown acquainted with his travelling companion, a gentle soul whose name, he told me, was Wee Mungo. Mungo himself appeared to see nothing incongruous in his name, but he was even taller and broader and thicker through the chest than my cousin Will, and I had only ever met three men that big. I had no doubt he was a warrior, probably impressive in his wrath if he were provoked, and I knew he would not otherwise be accompanying Andrew Murray under such dire circumstances. But he was a simple soul, with the gentle disposition and demeanour of a backward child. I enjoyed the way his eyes grew wide when I told him that this great cathedral was named after the saint who had first settled here and built the first church by the side of the Molendinar Burn, his own patron, Saint Mungo, whom the Islesmen called Kentigern. It was Mungo the saint, I told him, who had named this place, calling it Glasgow, which meant "the dear, green place" in the old tongue.

The big man sat enraptured while I told him the story, and when Andrew Murray joined us and stood quietly by the fire, he tousled the big man's hair fondly and asked him if he had enjoyed the tale. Wee Mungo nodded, still wide-eyed with the wonder of what he had heard, and then went obediently to bed when Murray dispatched him as quietly and firmly as a fond father would a beloved son.

"Wine, Jamie Wallace," Murray said as soon as we were alone. "I'll sell you my birthright for a cup of wine."

"There's a mess of pottage involved, too," I said, grinning at him. "I raided the kitchens and fed myself and Wee Mungo while you were with His Lordship. There's a pot of stew on the hob there, and some fresh bread. Serve yourself and I'll go and rob the sacramental wine store."

"You won't!" The shock in his voice was real, and I felt my grin grow wider.

"Of course I won't. We keep the good stuff in the Bishop's pantry. I'll be back in a moment."

Later, while we disposed of half a jug of excellent wine between us, I learned that he had been detained in Chester Castle in north Wales, more than a hundred miles from the Tower of London where his father was imprisoned. Once the hostilities had died down, however, his guards' initial vigilance and zeal had changed into laxity bred of the awareness that their stronghold was the oldest in England, built as the headquarters of the 22nd Legion in the time of the Caesars, and occupied continuously by garrisons thereafter. No one ever escaped from Chester. That truth was so universally accepted that Murray had found it easy to plan his escape.

Wee Mungo had been the only one of his retainers left with him, and he had managed to achieve that by demonstrating to his English captors that the big man was utterly harmless and could be left to himself all day long without ever getting into any more mischief than a young boy would. And so when the time came to escape, Andrew Murray and his giant companion walked out through the fortress's main gate as part of a work party, as they did every day, but on this day they had surprised and overcome their lackadaisical guard, tied the fellow up, and simply walked away. From Chester, the two men had made their way north and east to the Solway Firth, and thence north to Glasgow. It had taken them seven days.

"But didn't they come after you? They must have tried to catch you, surely?"

Andrew sipped at his wine, his face serious. "Aye. They did. They were in better condition than we were from the outset, and seven of them caught up to us between Carlisle and the Firth."

"They caught you, but you're here. How did you escape?"

"They didn't catch us. I said they caught up to us. Mungo killed them. All of them. He does that sometimes."

That silenced me for a spell, as I thought about the childlike giant who had sat so bemusedly in front of me just a short while before. I stared hard at Andrew Murray and he stared equally hard into his cup, as though examining his reflection in the wine.

"Mungo is two very different people," Murray explained. "One of those is the innocent, gentle soul you met tonight. The other is the antithesis of the first. A warrior, but a warrior unlike any you have ever seen. When that person takes over, Mungo becomes a killer, savage, merciless, and implacable."

"To everyone?"

"God, no, Heaven forbid! No, he knows which side he is on at all times, and he would never turn on a comrade, but to anyone facing him on the wrong side, he is Death incarnate."

I made the sign of the cross upon my breast. "May God forgive him." I reached down and collected the wine jug, and divided what remained between us. "So what will you do now that you're back in Scotland?"

"Back in Scotland and outlawed, you mean. I'm a fugitive from the King's Peace."

"The King of England's Peace."

He grinned. "Aye, but to Edward, there's no difference. What will I do? I'll fight him to my last breath. My lands in Moray and elsewhere are vast, and largely empty, with ample space for fighting. If Edward of England wants to seize them, he will have to come and do so in person, and I will not be standing idly by, watching him from some far mountaintop. So I am heading home, as quickly as I can, and once I'm there I intend to raise the men of Moray and stir up Hell itself against these arrogant English overlords, as they like to call themselves. I intend to teach them that Scotland is ours, that they have no place in it, and that they never have had legitimate claim to any part of it. Who do they think they are, these strutting bantam cocks? And who does this benighted king of theirs believe gave him the right to come up here and impose his will upon free folk who have no need of his interference, no desire to suffer his attentions, and no intention of lying down and allowing him and his thieving, ignorant bullies to trample them and their rights? I swear to you, Jamie, by the living God, that if no other man in Scotland will stand up against this aging, braggart crusader from a bygone day, I, Andrew Murray, will defy him alone and die, if I must, with my spittle soaking his grizzled beard—" He broke off and laughed. "Do I sound overeager? You did ask me! First, though, before I tackle any of that, I have to talk to Will Wallace. The Bishop tells me you can take me to him."

"Aye, I can. But why do you need to talk to him?"

"Can you not guess, Father James? I need to conscript him to my cause, to help me drive these English oafs out of my country."

"But he cannot." It came out as a blurt, and it earned me a disconcerting look from his level blue eyes.

"He cannot?"

I flapped my hands, feeling foolish. "He cannot. He has sworn an oath not to become involved in the fighting—"

"Until Scotland produces a leader he can trust and follow. Yes, yes, Bishop Wishart did tell me." He grinned, and the sight of his flashing white teeth almost made me feel better about what I instinctively knew he was going to say next. "Well, that has been taken care of, because Scotland now has a leader whom I will swear William Wallace can trust, a leader born on the battlefield at Dunbar, this year, and raised to maturity these past few months in England's prisons. Andrew Murray of Petty, Lord of Avoch and Moray and commander of at least five thousand fighting men, every one of them dedicated to watching the arse of the last Englishman in Scotland vanish back over the border into England. Let us drink to that, Father James." He raised his cup and emptied it at a gulp, then set it down and smiled at me again. "Now, when can we leave for Selkirk?"

3

I was sitting back in comfort in Will and Mirren's hut, marvelling at the astonishing relationship that existed between the two men I admired most in the world. It had always been thus, ever since the three of us had met as boys in Paisley.

That evening, though, listening to the easy banter the two of them traded, I was unusually aware of Mirren, knowing without ever looking at her that she was watching me closely, with that secretive, inscrutable half smile that I imagined on her lips every time I thought of her when she was not around. Now, as Will and Andrew waxed enthusiastic about something, some element of training or of fighting that was less than interesting to me, she rose quietly and made her way to the small stone sink Will had installed next to a built-in cooking stove close to the window. Moved by some prompting that I did not even pause to think about, I followed her, and she cocked her head to look at me as I approached.

"What?" she asked. "You look as though you have a question to ask me."

She was correct, but suddenly I felt awkward, almost abashed by her perceptiveness, and instead of saying what I had intended to say, I shrugged. "You like him, don't you?" I asked, adding, needlessly, "Andrew."

She smiled and began to stack the platters from which we had eaten earlier. "Of course I like him. Why should I not?"

I shrugged again. "You didn't like me when first we met. What is so different about him?"

She looked at me and laughed quietly, and my breast filled up with the familiar, comfortable warmth of the respect and esteem that I had always had for her. "Jamie Wallace," she said teasingly, and I heard the fondness in her voice. "If I didna ken ye were a priest, I'd think ye were jealous o' the man. But why should I no' like him? My goodman loves him like a brother ... and you do, too, forbye. With two such as you on his side, how could I be foolish enough to dislike him?" She tilted her head to one side, looking at me with sudden seriousness through narrowed eyes. "What's wrong, Jamie? Ye have a strange look about you."

I shook my head again, but she was not about to be dismissed that easily. She stepped closer to me and lowered her voice. "Tell me."

I squirmed, and she reached out and plucked at my bearded chin, jerking it up so that I had to meet her eye. "Tell me," she said again.

"I think he's here to take Will to war," I said.

"No. He's here to *try* to tak' Will to war. I have nae doubt o' that, but he'll ha'e nae joy there. Will winna go. He tell't me that again last night, just afore you two arrived. He'll play the general, he says, but he'll no' fight himsel'. He swore."

I found myself unable to look her in the eye, for Andrew Murray had been right: Will had said he would follow a worthwhile leader if Scotland could produce one. I turned and moved away to join the other two again, leaving her to her household tasks.

From then on I sat and listened closely as Will Wallace and Andrew Murray drew up their dreams and schemes for Scotland's future. Will's championship of nameless, faceless folk did not surprise me at all, for he had lived his life among them and was deeply solicitous of their welfare. That he came of a knightly family was true, but he himself had had no training in the ways of chivalry and he had never considered any possibility of being raised to knighthood someday. I found it amazing, though, that Andrew Murray should be voicing such ideas, let alone championing them so enthusiastically, for his makeup contained nothing that anyone could describe as common stock. Nevertheless, he appeared to accept, willingly, that aligning himself at the head of his fellow Scots, in defence of their common interests, must entail the forfeiture of his vast English holdings and the revenues that flowed from them, and he dismissed the loss as insignificant.

He stayed with us for three days, and I spent every moment I could find listening to their conversations. I was fascinated by the way their minds worked in concert. Every idea advanced by one or the other of them—and they appeared to feed off each other voraciously—generated a cascade of others, the way a smith's hammer scatters sparks from a glowing iron bar. I listened admiringly as they discussed strategy and tactics in grand, sweeping terms, comparing possibilities of attack and manoeuvre in order to wring every advantage possible from the land itself in fighting and beating the English forces whose own disciplined formations might be—and would be, had these two anything to do with it—hampered and disadvantaged on mountainous or boggy Scots terrain.

I listened open mouthed as my cousin expounded on current political and philosophical theories that I had not even known he knew about and with which I would never have guessed he might be familiar; yet there he was, stating strongly held and obviously long considered opinions on free will and the morality of restitution and atonement, citing Edward of England's lack of contrition for his deliberate intent to usurp the throne of Scotland after undermining and destroying its rightful occupant. I sat awestruck as he demonstrated, using flawless logic, that the King of England's behaviour was unconscionable and indefensible and that he was therefore morally unfit to function as a truly Christian king. I knew whence those ideas had come, for I had often heard them voiced by William Lamberton, who had absorbed them in his turn from John Duns during his visits with the scholar in Paris, but I had never suspected that Lamberton and Will had been spending the amount of time together that Will's grasp of his subject indicated.

Then, late one night, I listened to the two of them debate the propriety of the hit-and-run battle techniques advocated by Murray as opposed to the "honourable" and time-honoured system of chivalric warfare championed by Will. That confrontation, mild though it was, provided me with further cause to shake my head over the incongruities and contradictions of their alliance. Andrew, born to the nobility and to the strictures and traditions of chivalry and the feudal ways, and trained for years in the customs and the lore of the chivalric code, should have been the champion of the status quo in warfare, calling for things to be done as they had always been done and looking for ways to bring the Scots forces as close as might be feasible to parity with the English. Instead, he declared that to be impossible and committed himself to the idea of training his fighting men to use every possible advantage they could find in the terrain and the topography of the countryside to outwit, outmanoeuvre, and ultimately outfight and destroy the armies brought against them. He refused even to pay lip service to the old, "honourable" style of warfare, calling it suicidal and immoral. A man forced to fight, he said, should fight as though his life depended upon winning, because it did. Winning, he said—victory and survival—was the only measure of success in war. Everything else was failure since, even if it did not result in death, it involved defeat and the loss of liberty, which he maintained was worse than death.

My cousin, on the other hand, argued strongly in favour of formal battle between ranked armies as the most legitimate and generally accepted means of resolving conflict. He ignored Murray's immediate heaping of scorn on that notion, holding his peace as the other denounced the rampant folly of sending hundreds or even thousands of poorly trained and equipped men to die needlessly against superior formations when far more success could be achieved, at far less cost, by using much more versatile methods of isolating, stranding, and then defeating depleted enemy battalions. When his opponent fell silent, Will merely nodded and acknowledged that the other might be right, in fact, but from the viewpoint of political reality, he believed that was ultimately unimportant. His primary concern lay, he maintained, with legitimacy and the appearance of propriety. I blinked when I heard that, and for the first time in many hours of discussion I interjected.

"Are you serious, Will? *The appearance of propriety?* What bearing does that have on throwing the English out of Scotland? Forgive me, but that strikes me as being the most mindless thing I have heard."

I thought he was going to give me the rough edge of his tongue, but then he twitched his shoulders in the beginnings of a shrug. "Mindless," he said. "You think speaking of propriety is mindless? No, Jamie. Let me tell you what mindlessness is about. Mindlessness is the ability to accept things without thought simply because they are familiar. Mindlessness is the condition of going through life without ever questioning the right or wrong of general custom. It is seeing things that frequently are wrong in the moral sense and ignoring the wrongness purely because it has become so familiar that we are no longer aware of it—or because, were we to notice it and pay attention, we would be forced to do something to change it. That is mindlessness, Cousin." He sucked at something caught in his teeth.

"And then there is another kind of mindlessness," he continued, "comparable perhaps, but different. The mindlessness of seeing something happen and being able to deny that it is happening—and not only that, but going ahead then and basing a set of expectations on that denial of what you actually saw." He nodded in the direction of Andrew. "If our friend here will forgive me, I will point out to you that the group to which he belongs subscribes to that. A knight is not required to be literate or educated, except in the ways of war. The knightly code requires only adherence to the laws of chivalry. It makes no demands otherwise. It ignores logic, by and large, and it expects no moral judgments. And yet judgments are made all the time, based on the expectations it engenders, irrespective of logic. Do you have any idea what I am talking about?"

I shook my head, and he shook his in return, his mouth twisting downwards. "Aye. Well … What I am saying is that every ignorant, thick-skulled, witless bully capable of carrying a sword or swinging a club, be he knight, pikeman, or man-at-arms, will condemn us as brigands and barbarians for not fighting in accordance with their rules of combat." He saw my lips quirk. "Don't laugh! There is nothing even mildly amusing in what I am saying." He paused, looking from Andrew to me and back to Andrew. "No matter how hard we fight in this struggle, no matter how many men we mobilize against them, no matter how long we fight against them or how many of them we kill, these people will afford us no legitimacy until we meet them face to face on the field of battle and defeat them according to the rules of chivalry."

"Thereby committing suicide," Andrew added. "That is obscene, Will. We've been over this before. No army that Scotland can field would be equipped to defeat the English host in battle. We might as well lay down our weapons and surrender ourselves to them right now."

And so the argument began again.

There is no defining military word for what Will was, or for what his methods were. In those days when he and Andrew Murray first took up the sword against the English, there was only one accepted way of waging war, and that was the way of chivalry, the way wars had been fought between Christian armies for hundreds of years. There were conventions to be observed therein and rules to be followed, and a battle—any battle—was as likely to be decided by negotiation and bargaining between leaders as it was by physical combat. All of which appeared highly civilized and carefully struc-tured to avoid unnecessary killing, until the observer took note that the only people who ever benefited from these negotiations were the leaders from each side. The remainder of the people involved, probably ninety-nine out of every hundred people in the field, were unimportant and insignificant. There at the behest of their leaders and under pain of forfeiture and punishment should they refuse, they were expected to die happily should their leaders not be able to arrive at a satisfactory settlement of their troubles.

Will and Andrew changed all that, although the doing of it all was far less simple than that plainly written statement suggests. For the first time, though, between the pair of them they raised an army of the common Scots folk led by men whose sole qualification for leadership was their ability as warriors and leaders. None of these new commanders were high born or titled or otherwise privileged, and none had anything to influence their conduct other than a will to defeat the English invaders. That, in turn, resulted in their having an unprecedented awareness of, and a dedication to, the welfare of the men who followed them and shared their dreams of victory.

I know people today, less than thirty years later, who would dispute that loudly, pointing as evidence to the large number of magnates and high-born lords present at the Battle of Stirling Bridge. But that was later, and their support had materialized with painful slowness during the first long months of the "rebellious" activities of Wallace and Murray. Only when it had become undeniable that the entire populace of Scotland had come out in support of the two rebel leaders, and that no one could hope to stand against them, did the situation change, and then it changed radically, with a sudden and total shift of support among the nobility. In the beginning, though, in the months after I sat there and listened to them talk, there were only Wallace and Murray, two disdained and widely disparaged voices crying, like the Baptist, in the wilderness.

The two men had not yet settled their differences by the time Andrew Murray left to return to the north, but they had arrived at an agreement. Will himself would not appear as a leader in the fighting. His oath to remain with his family precluded that. But otherwise he warranted that he would commit his full support, using his name, his

influence, and his outlawed followers to raise the standard of resistance and rebellion in the south, should Andrew Murray ask it of him
in the months ahead.

And the months ahead were active months, since John de
Warenne, the English Earl of Surrey whom Edward had appointed
military governor of Scotland, seemed determined to pacify the
whole country within the first few months of his tenure, sending out
large bodies of English troops to patrol the entire land and stamp out
any signs of rebellion before they could begin to flourish. Towards
that goal, he also set out to reinforce and amplify the English
garrisons in various strongholds throughout the land, and Lanark,
the jurisdiction of the young sheriff I had met in Glasgow, was one
such place. Spurred no doubt by his officious superior, William
Hazelrig let it be known that he would not tolerate outlawry, in any
sense, in his lands.

CHAPTER EIGHTEEN

I

At about the same time that Will and Andrew Murray were debating so earnestly with each other in Selkirk Forest, King Edward's new treasurer for Scotland, Hugh Cressingham, began to assert his noxious presence more and more visibly. He treated Scotland as a conquered fiefdom, levying taxes here, there, and everywhere in order to pay for England's foreign wars, and fomenting widespread anger and frustration with his high-handed arrogance. Encouraged perhaps by the overt signs of a widespread English military presence that would back him should the need ever arise, and recognizing that the international trade in wool was the economic engine that had made Scotland prosperous over the past hundred years, he imposed crippling taxes on the gathering, processing, and exporting of wool and thereby came nigh to killing the entire industry within his first year in office. Nurturing Scots trade was of no importance to him, but he smiled with satisfaction as he shipped off enormous sums of Scots money to fill his master's coffers.

Mirren's father was one of the Scots merchants most direly affected by these outrageous taxes, because they obliterated his commercial enterprises almost overnight. Hugh Braidfoot had become a prosperous wool trader and broker and a wealthy, respected burgess of Lanark, where his enterprises were headquartered, but his eastern operations, all of them involving the warehousing of wool and its transportation from the eastern Scottish ports to the countries across the North Sea, were vulnerable to Cressingham's most punitive taxes, and Braidfoot was rendered close to penury within months of the treasurer's arrival in Scotland.

However, Braidfoot was neither fool nor craven. He determined to
fight what he saw as this Englishman's fiduciary madness, and he
set off for Berwick to confront the treasurer, making no secret of his
purpose or of his anger and frustration. His intent was to present his
case to Cressingham in person and to sue for some kind of reason-
able accommodation, some compromise, that would permit him to
remain active in his business affairs while continuing to generate
taxable revenue in the years ahead.

According to Cressingham and his staff, however, Master
Braidfoot never arrived in Berwick, and an extensive search of the
town and its environs failed to find anyone who had witnessed him
entering the town, though many witnesses elsewhere attested to that
having been his destination, and swore to have heard him say he had
important business with Cressingham. Hugh Braidfoot vanished
without trace on that journey, never to be seen or heard from again,
and all his holdings became forfeit to the English administration for
non-payment of taxes.

Word of this iniquity was brought to us eventually in Glasgow by
a monk from Jedburgh Abbey who had been sent specifically to
inform Bishop Wishart of the merchant's death and the storm of
controversy that it had stirred up in and around Berwick. He arrived
with his tidings in the middle of March, by which time Braidfoot
had been missing for more than a month. The Bishop, not knowing
if word of these events would have penetrated Selkirk Forest,
dispatched me immediately to take the news to Will and Mirren. I
rode my horse hard to get there before either of my friends heard the
tidings from any other source, but by the time I arrived the word had
flown ahead of me.

Will saw at once that I was disappointed at having brought the
news too late and tried to put me at my ease, but I could not be at
ease until I had seen Mirren, to gauge with my own eyes how great
a toll this occurrence had demanded of her, and to offer her any
solace and comfort that I could, as former chaplain to her and her
people. She had loved her father deeply, I knew, and would be in
great need of support and sympathy, for he had earned her love

throughout her life, constantly affording her his encouragement in everything she did.

In the end, it was Mirren who ended up consoling me in my misery over having come so late, offering to pray with me before I ever got around to making the suggestion, and generally making me feel more at ease about her peace of mind.

Already within months of completing her term, she was blithely certain that this time she was carrying a daughter, describing the child to me as a sweet little pippin who would act as a natural braking force upon her ebullient and irrepressible son, whom she was preparing for bed as we spoke. She had even named the child already, she told me, having dreamed of seeing her as a fully grown young woman, beautiful, elegant, and self-possessed. Her daughter would be called Eleanor, in honour of Mirren's own heroine, the long-dead but greatly revered Duchess of Aquitaine, and Mirren's mind was made up on the matter. Eleanor Wallace would be as strong a woman as the one after whom she would be named. I listened to her speaking of the child who would be, and I saw how steadfastly she held her own loss at bay, and my heart swelled up with pride and affection for her. Will truly had chosen a pearl beyond price, as the scriptures described.

In the meantime, she said, she was preparing to go home to visit her mother in Lamington, but several matters involving Will had to be settled first, so they had not yet been able to set a departure date.

I knew that Mirren's mother had never recovered from the wasting illness that had stricken her during the year when Mirren and Will first met. For a long time, everyone had thought she was going to die, but Miriam Braidfoot had surprised everyone with her tenacity. That had been in 1289, and for the ensuing eight years, Mirren's mother had been confined to her home and, much of that time, to her bed. But she had lived happily enough, sustained by the love of her husband and the friends who surrounded her. Now, though, with her husband's disappearance and probable death, no one could tell what would happen to the old lady, and Mirren fretted constantly over not being able to rush to her mother's bedside.

Puzzled by what she had said about Will's having "matters" to settle, I was about to ask her what was going on, but we were interrupted by the arrival of several women who had come to collect Mirren, and within moments I found myself alone in the darkening little hut. I rebuilt the fire and then wandered outside into the chilly March half light to look for Will.

Later that night, sitting beside Will at dinner, I watched as the crowd hummed around him like bees swarming about a displaced queen, affording me no opportunity at all to ask him about any of the matters that were on my mind. Bemused, I watched the press of people suck every vestige of attention and awareness out of him, and the experience left me dazed. Each time I saw him nowadays, I realized that my cousin had changed since the time before, becoming more and more of a public figure all the time, a leader and a commander of men even though, to me at least, he appeared to make no effort to ingratiate himself with anyone.

I went to bed that night comparing my memories of the shy and diffident but quietly confident Will Wallace with whom I had grown up to the William Wallace I had watched that night, a towering, confident figure filled with gravitas and authority, dispensing advice and encouragement to people, some of whom I knew he had never set eyes on before. And of all the things that niggled at my awareness, the most illogical appeared to be the one that should not have surprised me at all: this new dimension of respect and deference that surrounded him had not come into being until Will swore his oath to protect his family and avoid risking his life in pointless fighting against vested interests and insuperable odds. In avoiding violence and pursuing detachment, my cousin had assumed a mantle he had never thought, nor sought, to wear, and in so doing had become a new kind of champion in the eyes of the common folk.

2

Isaw no signs of Will when I went looking for him after breaking my fast the following morning, but I knew he was nearby, and eventually I found him labouring in the saw pit in the woods beyond the encampment's southern edge. He was stripped naked, save for a breechclout about his waist, and dripping from the effort of sawing a long, thick plank from a massive oak timber positioned above him over the pit. The fall of sawdust had coated his body, clinging to his sweat-soaked skin and body hair and giving him the look of a great blond bear, and with the enormous muscles of his back, shoulders, and chest engorged by the heavy work, he appeared to be truly gigantic. He saw me coming and he must have read what I was thinking on my face, for he barked a great, booming laugh and heaved himself up and out, beckoning me to follow him as he jogged away towards the nearby stream the men had aptly named the Sawpit Burn. There was a linn a short distance upstream, a waterfall about ten feet high with a large swimming hole scooped from the gravel bed beneath it, and he threw himself into it from the bank, tucking his legs up and shouting in sheer exhilaration as he went, and as the splash died down the surface of the pool was transformed to a golden turbulence by the sawdust released from his body. He surfaced quickly, shook his head violently, then ducked it beneath the surface again, scrubbing at his scalp with both hands before straightening up and flicking his long hair back out of his eyes.

"Hah!" he roared. "That's better. Give me your hand."

I reached out and helped him pull himself up the side of the bank, and as he towelled himself roughly I settled myself on a mossy patch with my back against a tree. It was a beautiful late-summer morning, and the sun had barely risen above the horizon. When he was dry, he tied the towel around his waist, then slapped his palms against his bare chest.

"Garments," he said. "I left them over by the pit, clear of the sawdust. When I am decently clothed again, you and I will be ready for a drink." He hesitated, head cocked. "At least I will be ready. You have that … devout look about you, Cuz, that *priestly* look."

"Are you cold?"

"No, not at all. But I am almost naked, so I wish to dress."

"And so you may, in a moment, but right now I want to talk to you without being interrupted, and I promise I won't tell anyone you were almost naked when we spoke."

In response he smiled and threw himself down beside me on the bank, then knocked me off balance with a straight-armed push. "Speak, then, but tell me first, will you be speaking as Father James or as my cousin Jamie?"

"Can I not be both at once?"

"I don't know. Can you?" He waited for a moment, as though expecting an answer, then grinned slightly. "Never mind. Go ahead. You have my attention."

I took the time to adjust my robe.

"Your wife tells me you can't take her to comfort her mother until several *matters* are settled. What kind of matters, I wonder, can be more important than the loss of a beloved father? And no matter what they are, how important can they possibly be, Will, that you would permit them to keep you here when it's clear Mirren wants to go home to her grieving mother, to share her own grief for her father?"

He sat staring straight faced at me, no trace of raillery in his eyes now, but he made no attempt to speak.

"What, have you no answer? It's a simple enough question. What is keeping you here when it is so important—to your wife and to her family—for you to travel to Lamington?"

Still he made no move to answer me, and I found myself suddenly impatient.

"Why would you even want to stay here at a time like this, Will? To dispense advice to your followers, the way you did last night at supper? Do you not think your wife deserves an equal or even greater share of your concern than strangers do?"

"It is not that simple."

"No, it *is* that simple, Will. It's *simple*. There's nothing complex about it. You should be taking Mirren home, right now, to be with her mother in her time of bereavement. I fail to see how anything can be more important than that."

"Right!" His voice was hard edged. "I heard you. But just because you fail to see something, Father, doesn't mean it isn't there. Do you think I am doing this lightly, without cause? I *can't* leave here now. Soon, perhaps, I hope so. But not now."

"Why not?" I pushed.

"Because we're in crisis."

"Grave crisis, I assume, though there's never any other kind. Crisis over what?"

He looked at me, his jaw set pugnaciously. "Over the price on my head and the bounty placed on any of my men taken, dead or alive."

I felt as though something had writhed and then flattened in my guts.

"That's new. Not the price on your head, we all know about that, but this bounty is new. We've heard nothing about it."

His eyebrows rose mockingly. "In Glasgow, you mean, at the cathedral? How would you hear of it at all? It's a local matter, locally imposed and locally enforced."

"Who set this bounty?"

"A man called Hazelrig. Edward's new enforcer. His title is Sheriff of Lanark."

"Sir William Hazelrig? That can't be. I've met him. He impressed me as a pleasant fellow. Except, of course, that he told me how quickly he would kill you if you ever crossed his path. Apart from that, though, I think you would have liked him."

My cousin was staring at me, both eyebrows raised sufficiently to wrinkle his brow. "You have *met* this man?"

"Yes. I met him in Glasgow at the Bishop's house. He came up with Cressingham when he came to make himself known to the Scots Bishops soon after his appointment."

"And you liked him. Did you like Cressingham, too?"

"I disliked him intensely. The man reminds me of a carrion eater. But I enjoyed Hazelrig. I found him amusing and very pleasant."

"It makes me very glad to know that, Cuz, because your pleasant and amusing acquaintance has hanged two of my men without trial, and ten more who were not my men but were accused of being so. No arguments, no opportunity to deny anything or say anything in their defence. Simply accusation and execution, plain and simple, neat and tidy, and unmistakably English. Oh yes, he's a very pleasant fellow." He held up one hand and dipped his head at the same time as though to ask, "What more can I say?" But he remained quiet for long moments before he spoke again.

"Sheriff Hazelrig has made it his overriding objective to bring about my end. He quadrupled the price on my head about a month ago, in the hopes of tempting someone to betray me, and hard on the heels of that, he offered a bounty of a silver mark for each and every Selkirk outlaw brought to justice or into King Edward's Peace. That means dead or alive. It is a death sentence passed upon any man who is accused of being one of us, Jamie, irrespective of whether he is or not. The accusation is sufficient to cause death because there is no need to bring the man in alive. *Any* dead outlaw has clearly been brought to justice, and will surely never disturb the King's Peace in the future." He watched me, and when he saw my eyes narrow, he nodded. "Aye, it is iniquitous, no one will dispute that. But it is an iniquity sponsored and abetted by the King of England's High Sheriff in Lanark, so who is to gainsay it?"

I shook my head, not quite in disbelief, but because I somehow hoped the truth would prove deniable. "But … what did you do to cause him to quadruple the price on your head?"

"And to pass a sentence of death on all my followers at the same time? Well, what would you think I did? I know you believe I did something, because I heard it clearly in your voice when you asked the question. I did nothing, Jamie. Nothing at all."

"You must have attracted his attention somehow, perhaps without realizing it."

"*Nothing*, Jamie. I said and did *nothing*. And be careful what you say next because your disbelief is starting to irk me. Hear me clearly. We have been inactive here for several months, committing no robberies and staging no raids since the English pulled in their horns back in November. I did nothing to attract the sheriff's notice, and none of my men did, either. He simply decided to make a public example of us, probably goaded by that fat slug Cressingham, or possibly by his own superior, de Warenne of Surrey."

"I see. So what is happening now?"

He sniffed deeply and looked away into the trees. "We have patrols out, in strength. They are moving quickly and constantly, keeping careful watch because we don't know where Hazelrig's soldiers will strike next. The local folk are in terror of being taken out and hanged, and so we keep our people spread out and moving, constantly in touch with one another and ready to attack at the first sign of hostility."

"You're ready to fight."

"Of course we're ready to fight. Would you have it otherwise?"

"Will *you* fight? What about your oath?"

"What about it? My oath is unbroken and I have no intention of fighting. But I can't leave my people, Jamie."

"Aye, and besides, it would be folly to go to Lamington with the sheriff of Lanark on the watch for you."

"Pah! Folly nothing. He wouldn't know me if I walked up and spoke to him face to face. That part of it is not an issue. I simply need to stay here for the time being, with my people. I agree with you that Mirren's place is with her mother. No arguments from me on that, and I feel as guilty as sin because of it. But I can't take her there, and until now I have not had anyone who could, at least not without risk of attracting attention. But now I have the right man. You can escort her to her mother's place on your way back to Glasgow. She'll be safe with you, and I'll send an escort with you. A small group. Men I trust. Four or five."

"Four or five men and a woman and child?"

"Aye, and a priest. What's wrong with that?"

"Priests don't travel with heavily armed men, Will, unless they are liveried men-at-arms. And the same applies to pregnant women with small children in tow. Besides, I doubt that Mirren will go without you."

"She has to. She has no choice. She needs to be with her mother, and I need her to be there as well. I need to know she's safely out of the forest until this nonsense with Hazelrig is over. Will you see to that for me, Jamie?"

I slumped against the tree. "I suppose I will. It seems to me there is a deal of needing going on here, one way and another, but aye, I'll see her safely to her mother's, so be it she agrees to go."

"Good man. As for the escort, you can be sure I'll pick them carefully. They'll be discreet. No one will ever know they're with you, unless you fall into danger. But they'll never be far away from you, wherever you are."

He rose to his feet and towered above me, then reached out a hand to me and pulled me effortlessly to my feet before jerking me forward into an enormous hug.

3

We were a small, subdued group as our two wagons set out from Selkirk Forest towards Lanark and Glasgow, our quietness attributable mainly to the strain surrounding the parting between Will and Mirren and, of course, young Willie. It was a parting neither one wanted, but circumstances had combined to make it necessary.

We were soon out of the largely trackless forest and on the high road to Lanark. Perched on the driver's bench of the first and larger of our two wagons was Alan Crawford of Nithsdale, who would serve as senior driver and cook, responsible for the thousand and one daily details of our journey. Beside him sat Ewan Scrymgeour, who had come to regard Mirren as his own daughter. Big Andrew, his crossbow safely stowed out of sight behind him, and looking like a small boy perched on the driver's bench of the second wagon, would serve as Alan's assistant. Also with us was Father Jacobus, the elder of the two over-cloistered priests I had brought with me when first I came to live in the greenwood. He had grown visibly younger, more vibrantly alive, as the result of his life among the forest folk, nourished and greatly strengthened from ministering to their daily needs and thriving on the joy of it. Robertson the archer and five of his best men were ranged outward ahead of us, out of our sight but screening us from interference from the front and both sides.

The initial awkwardness of the post-parting silence passed more quickly and more easily than I had expected, due beyond a doubt to Mirren's determination to make the best of the situation, and so by the end of the first day's travel, the mood among the group was easier and more relaxed. It was a short day, too, for we were pulled off the road in a sheltered spot well before the sun began to sink. The March weather was consistent—inhospitably foul, cold, and damp— and the sun seemed to be setting earlier each day, instead of later.

Our cooking fire was small and almost completely concealed in a wide, deep-dug pit, and Alan prepared a remarkable meal of stewed goat, with vegetables and meat that he had brought with him, serving it with dried broad white beans he had braised in a deliciously salty sauce that set my mouth to tingling. We sat around the fire for no more than an hour after dinner that night, though, for despite knowing that Robertson and his bowmen were out there guarding us, we knew, too, that we were in unknown country and our firelight would be visible for miles. Just as I was about to retire to my evening prayers, one of Robertson's men stepped out of the surrounding shadows, carrying a brace of fine hares, gutted and tied by the hind legs, that he handed to Alan before slipping away into the darkness again. I knew what we would dine on the following night.

We made better distance on the second day, having been up before dawn and on the road by daybreak, well muffled against the steady, cutting wind, and by three of the afternoon we had travelled more than twenty miles at a steady, ground-eating pace, avoiding the small town of Peebles by detouring a few miles to the south of it. Robertson's people had already found our next camping spot, about five miles beyond that, and one of them waited for us by the road-side and then led us off into the woods, where we found the roofless ruins of an otherwise solidly built and surprisingly spacious house. We pitched our tents within its walls and slept soundly that night, sheltered from the wind that howled outside. We were, by my reck-oning, within fifteen miles of Lanark.

On the morning of the third day, we awoke to a torrential down-pour that had already flooded the low-lying areas around us and showed no signs of abating. Ewan and Alan, as the joint commanders of our little group, stepped outside the shelter of the walls into the greyness of the reluctantly breaking day to try to gauge the wisdom of breaking camp. They came back inside moments later to consult with me and Mirren about whether or not we wished to brave the weather and continue immediately towards Lamington, because they themselves were divided in their opinions.

I looked to Mirren, prepared to abide by her decision, but on this occasion Mirren, normally so straightforward and decisive, could not make up her mind about what she wanted to do. Leaving immedi-ately meant in all likelihood that we might reach Lamington and her mother more quickly, but that was far from certain in the face of such outlandish weather, because according to Ewan and Alan the ground was a sodden quagmire and the wagons might be difficult to handle on steep and muddy surfaces. The alternative, to wait and see, would mean we might lose time initially, but when the weather finally broke and the wind and rain abated, the going would be firmer underfoot and conditions would certainly be both drier and warmer beneath the leather canopies of the wagons. Dryness and warmth for both herself and her young son was, I could see, the more appealing prospect in Mirren's eyes, but I could also see that, precisely because it was so personally justifiable, she was loath to make that decision on her own. And so when she shrugged and turned to me, I smiled at her and made the choice to wait out the storm.

I have wondered a thousand times, over the years, if I might have changed anything by choosing differently that morning, but always my faith in God's all-seeing wisdom convinces me—alas, never for long and never completely—that His will was carried out as He wished it to be.

We stayed in the camp for most of the morning, and for the last hour of that time the wind and the rain gradually died down and then stopped. We had already begun to break camp by then, and were having enormous difficulty in dismantling and stowing our leather tents, for their weight had been tripled by the amount of water they had absorbed. By the time we finally had the wagons loaded and were preparing to pull out, back onto the road again, the clouds were breaking up and clearing quickly, and bright sunlight was lancing down through the gaps here and there in spectacular glowing rays.

No one spoke much as we settled into the journey, but as the miles fell slowly behind us and the sun's warmth dried our wet clothes, a semblance of good humour re-emerged and soon there was a steady flow of banter passing between the two wagons. At one point I twisted in my seat on the driver's bench beside Big Andrew, to respond to a jibe from Ewan in the other wagon, and suddenly found myself racked by an intensely painful cramp in my left foot. My entire leg seized up and I writhed so violently against the pain of it that I lost my balance and fell sideways, barely managing to grasp the side of the bench in time to prevent myself pitching head-first to the ground. Ewan, in the other wagon, saw me jerk and fall sideways, and for a few stupefied moments he thought I had been felled by an arrow.

The ensuing alarm was short lived, though, and turned quickly to laughter when it became clear that I had simply suffered a cramp. Alan muttered something about priests spending too much time on their knees and their backsides, and wondered aloud why it should be strange that their muscles complained of inactivity by twisting into cramps. I remember feeling rather shamefaced as I massaged the feeling back into my leg, and then I hopped down and walked beside the wagons, hobbling for the first few minutes but soon striding easily. I felt euphoric for a short time after that, wanting to run in my exuberance, in sheer celebration of being me and of being alive and of being away, for a brief time at least, from the responsibilities of my priestly life.

Striding out in front, I was a good hundred yards ahead of the wagons as I came to the brow of a little hill, no more than a slight rise in the road. As I breasted it, I saw one of Robertson's archers jogging along the road towards me. I was not alarmed, for the archers were seldom far beyond our sight, but there was something about the way he was coming that brought me to a halt, looking around me and then at the road behind him. He was moving quickly but furtively, keeping close to the bushes that lined the road as he approached. He saw me watching him and raised a hand in greeting, but he did not slacken his pace.

When he reached me he stopped and bent over, panting for breath with his hands gripping his knees.

"Englishry, Father Jamie," he gasped. "Robertson sent me back to warn you. He says there's nothin' tae be upset ower, but he thocht ye'd like to ken they're doon there, at the crossroads at the bottom o' this road. Ye canna see it frae here, but that's where they are. There's a knight in charge, on the biggest horse ye've ever seen, but we couldna recognize his crest or colours, an' he has a couple o' mounted men-at-arms wi' him, forbye about ten archers. They're up to somethin', but we couldna tell what. Watchin' for somebody or mayhap just waitin' to see who gaes by. But Robertson jalouses they'll stop ye and ask ye what your business is, just because they're English."

I thanked him, and he turned away and vanished into the dense growth lining the road. This was not unexpected, and we had planned for it and knew our story. I walked back towards the approaching wagons.

"What?" Alan asked as I pulled myself up on to the stirrup step beside him. Mirren was sitting beside him, between him and Ewan, and all three were looking at me expectantly. I smiled at Mirren and waved vaguely in the direction we were heading.

"One of the archers just warned me that there are English ahead of us, at a crossroads at the bottom of the next slope. A knight, he says, with a couple of mounted men-at-arms and half a score of archers."

"Aye, I know the place. What are they doing, did he say?"

"No. He didn't know. But he and Robertson think they're up to something. Nothing to do with us, though, since nobody knew we'd be coming this way. But he thinks they'll challenge us."

"Of course they'll challenge us. Since they decided to take over the ownership of Scotland they challenge everything. A knight, you said?"

"Aye, fully armed and probably English, for nobody recognized his crest or colours." I looked at Mirren. "So remember, stay calm and don't say anything different to what we planned. The tricky part will be to pretend we didn't know they were there, so don't be peering about for them. If they suspect we knew they were there, they'll start suspecting other things as well—like how did we know? Who warned us? And why?"

She nodded at me, her face calm and peaceful, and I smiled back and dropped to the ground, making my way to the other wagon and pulling myself up to sit beside Big Andrew and Father Jacobus.

4

They kept themselves well hidden, for we saw no sign of them at all as we descended the long slope, even though we knew they were watching us. We reached the bottom of the descent, and the road flattened out just at the entrance to an open glade surrounding the junction of the two roads that crossed there. The glade was filled with shoulder-high saplings of birch and alder, new growth after a fire had swept through there a handful of years earlier, and from the height of the driver's bench, overlooking the saplings, I found I could see clearly in all directions across the burned area to the start of the forest proper again, without moving my head obviously. Nothing was stirring, anywhere I looked, but then from the corner of my eye I saw the lower branches of a big evergreen on the forest's edge pushed aside, and three mounted men emerged and rode directly towards us.

There was no debate over which of the three was the leader, for his appearance spoke loudly for itself. He was dressed in plate armour, which established his identity beyond question as being English. No Scots knight could afford such expensive armour, any more than he could afford a horse large enough and strong enough to bear his weight were he dressed in such a manner. Horse and armour here were emphatically and defiantly Norman-English, flaunting the wealth, puissance, and arrogance of their owner. The colours and livery were unknown to me, the knight's shield and surcoat and his horse's skirts all similarly quartered in red and silver, with alternating diagonal bars in the top right and bottom left quarters and three red swans on a silver field in each of the others. The crest on the knight's enormous silvered helm was a red bird, too—I presumed it to be a swan—flanked on each side by curving spirals of red and silver. A very fine and intimidating picture the man made, trotting towards us, and we stopped to await his arrival.

He reined in directly ahead of us, blocking the road as he raised the visor of his helmet to see us as clearly as he could. His face was hard to discern within the shadowed opening, but I saw a red-veined nose above a bushy red moustache, and then his voice came rasping towards us.

"Who are you people and what are you up to? No damned good, I'll wager. State your names and your business and give me one good reason why I shouldn't take the lot of you into custody."

I stood up, and when he turned his glowering gaze on me I forced myself to smile and addressed him in my best English, since I was convinced that, like most of his ilk, he would be barely literate at best, with no knowledge at all of Latin, which he would sneer at as clerkish nonsense.

"I can give you an excellent reason, Sir Knight. We are engaged upon the affairs of Holy Church. I am Father James and I am a member of the secretarial staff of Lord Robert Wishart, Bishop of Glasgow and senior prelate of the realm of Scotland. My associate here, Father Jacobus, has been with me on a mission to the south on behalf of His Lordship and we are now returning to Glasgow to conclude our business." I indicated Ewan on the other wagon. "The bald man there is the Bishop's uncle, Ewan Scrymgeour, brother to His Lordship's mother, and the young woman with him is his daughter Margaret, who is in mourning for her recently dead husband, killed by bandits near the border with England. We are taking her to be with her mother until she has the baby. The others are all employed by Master Scrymgeour. I have letters of safe conduct from the Bishop, should you wish to read them."

That was sheer bravado on my part and I knew the risk I was taking, for the only documents I had in my possession were two brief sets of notes given to me by Bishop Wishart before I left Glasgow. But I could sense both truculence and outright hostility in the choleric-looking Englishman, and so I decided to try to allay his suspicions by gambling heavily on his being illiterate, knowing that if I was wrong, we might all die here.

The fellow glowered at me for a moment from within the cavern of his helmet, his heavy eyebrows drawing into one thick, unbroken line, then grunted and held out a peremptory hand. "Show me."

My stomach contracted in a spasm, but I maintained my outward composure and dug into my scrip for the two folded pieces of parchment. I handed them, unopened, to the knight.

"May I be permitted to ask your name, sir?"

The knight had removed one of his gauntlets and now held it clamped beneath an elbow as he strove to unfold and open the first letter. He grunted an interrogative sound, then growled, "Redvers. Sir Lionel Redvers of Suffolk. Now let's see here …"

Having finally unfolded the parchment, he held it up and peered at it closely, and I felt the tension drain out of me. Had he been able to read, he would already have seen that what he held was no letter of safe conduct, but a list of brief instructions on what I was to do at various stages of my journey from Glasgow. He said nothing, though, and sat staring at the parchment as though memorizing its contents. Finally he sat up straighter—no easy feat, dressed as he was in full armour—refolded the letter, and returned it to me.

"So be it," he growled. "But you can't leave yet. We are awaiting a marching party here, and until they come no one can pass beyond this point. Where are you headed now? You'll never get to Glasgow before dark."

"No, sir. We had intended to stop at the inn in Lanark town."

Someone shouted in the distance behind him, and the Englishman spun his horse to look back. "They're coming," he said to no one in particular, then looked back at me. "Stay here until we are gone, and then you may follow us. Lanark is no more than three miles from here."

He swung away, pulling his visor closed with a sweep of his hand, then set spurs to his horse and charged off, followed by his two companions. I turned back to Ewan and found him watching me, a strange expression on his face.

"Uncle to the Bishop, you said?"

"Aye. It seemed a fitting description at the time, and it worked. No English knight, no matter how much he detests the Scots, is going to risk giving serious offence to a senior churchman—particularly by interfering with his family."

"You took a risk."

I grinned at him, feeling much better now. "Not as big as the risk I took in showing him that letter of safe conduct from the Bishop," and I explained how I'd banked on the man being illiterate and too vain to admit it.

No one spoke, and Ewan stared at me steadily. "I pray you, in future, don't be so quick to gamble with my life." He shrugged very gently. "I have no great fear of losing it, but I take much comfort from the belief, foolish though you might make it appear, that the disposition of it rests in my own hands."

"And yet it worked, and we have been rewarded handsomely. We can now follow the English all the way to Lanark without being bothered further."

"And we would, were we not due to turn left at the crossroads. Lamington is a mile in that direction."

"Ah! I did not know that. I knew it was near Lanark, but I have never been there. So it's over that way?"

"Aye, it is. Listen, did you not say there were supposed to be a half score of archers with those three? Did you see any signs of them?"

I grinned at him. "No more than I did of Robertson or his men. Archers are hard to see, Ewan. Had you forgotten?"

He threw me a look of pure disgust, then paused, his head cocked. "Well, whoever these people are, they're coming now."

We were less than thirty paces from the point where the two roads crossed, and it was plain from what Redvers had said that the column they were waiting for would cross directly in front of us. We moved forward slowly until we were right beside where the column would pass, and as we moved, the noise of the group approaching from our left grew steadily louder until the front ranks came into view. They were all footmen, uniformly dressed in chain-mail shirts, plain steel helmets, and leather jerkins with a small patch over the left breast, showing a red swan on a white field, and they were walking in the semblance of a march. They came towards us four abreast on the narrow road, and we fell silent as they approached.

Throughout my life, I have been troubled from time to time by terrifying dreams that I have never shared with anyone, whether from shame or fear I cannot truly say. In all of them I am being threatened or pursued by someone or something that is determined to kill me. The details of these dreams are never clear when I finally wake up, shivering, but the overwhelming sense of doom and terror they engender remain with me long afterwards. In all of them, my pursuer is always unimpaired and merciless, but I am always hindered by an inability to run fast enough, to shout loudly enough for help, or to hide quickly enough. In the moments following the appearance of the front ranks of that English column, I somehow fell into that dream state while wide awake. It happened with stunning speed; I simply found myself witnessing a situation that seethed up like milk in an overheated pot and boiled over, beyond my control.

I was watching the approaching soldiery idly, hearing the shuffling tread of their feet and the occasional clink or rattle of a piece of weaponry, and then I saw the English knight, Redvers, approaching again, riding at a lumbering trot from the rear of the marching column. As I turned to look at him directly, I noticed that four of the marching men were carrying a litter of some kind, slipping and sliding and generally making heavy going of it at one spot where the roadway was still muddy and puddled from the morning storm. They were no more than thirty paces from me when one of them lost his footing in the thick mud and almost lost his hold on the litter pole, and it was his muffled cry of alarm, a curse, really, that caught my attention. Mine was not the only notice drawn to him, though, and that is when everything around me seemed to speed up rapidly, leaving me too befuddled to do anything other than watch what happened.

I heard Mirren's voice shouting, "Mother!" and from the corner of my eye I saw her fling herself down from the bench of the wagon and run towards the soldiers. Little Willie bounced in his strapped shawl on her back, his normal daytime roost, while she clutched her skirts above her knees in one hand and waved frantically with the other. I was still blinking and wondering what she was doing when I heard the English knight shout, "Take that woman! Hold her!" and then he was spurring his horse directly towards her, closing the distance between them more rapidly than I could adjust to what I was seeing.

Mirren paid him no attention in her dash towards the litter, and she and the huge warhorse collided directly in front of me with a sound that appalled me. The animal struck her with its shoulder and sent her flying, mother and child spinning like an ungainly top until she crashed to the ground, and only then could I collect myself sufficiently to move. I shouted something, too late either to warn or to protest, and began running to where she and the baby lay in a welter of women's clothing, and as I ran I saw blood trickling from her nose and mouth. Little Willie was screaming, eyes screwed shut and mouth wide open, though I could scarcely hear him over the other noises. Men everywhere were shouting now, but I paid none of them any attention. I threw myself to the ground on my knees beside Mirren, and as I bent forward to cover her and the boy, someone kicked me in the head.

I know I was kicked only because I was told about it afterwards, for the blow broke my jawbone and knocked me senseless. I was kicked elsewhere, too, thoroughly and methodically, for when I regained awareness I was bruised all over and had several broken bones. I ought to have been killed, I suppose, but my priestly apparel may have saved my life.

Ewan and Andrew managed to escape. As archers, they both knew they needed distance between them and the enemy, and so as soon as Ewan saw what was happening—and he saw it far sooner than I did—he seized his bow case and quiver, called out to Andrew, then leapt down from the wagon and ran, using the vehicle's bulk to shield him from English arrows.

There were no English arrows, though, because Robertson and his five men had already stalked and killed the ten bowmen Redvers had brought with him, so as soon as the two marksmen had gained sufficient distance to allow them to shoot clearly, they turned back towards the enemy and set about killing Englishmen. Redvers the knight attempted to send his footmen against them, but from less than a hundred paces Ewan's arrows and Andrew's crossbow bolts could punch right through their inferior chain mail, so they retreated, having no stomach for a frontal assault across open ground against marksmen now being reinforced by others as Robertson and his men came running from the woods and joined the fight. Only Redvers himself and his two mounted men-at-arms were strongly enough armoured to face the Scots fire, and in attempting to close with them, they proved that only Redvers was immune to the Scots arrows. Ewan, with his great bow of yew, brought down both men-at-arms with armour-piercing bodkins, and a direct hit on Redvers's breastplate from twenty paces, though the missile glanced off and away, almost unhorsed the knight, who lost his sword while fighting to stay in the saddle and then turned and lumbered away to rejoin his men.

Moments later, the rearguard of Redvers's column came charging to the rescue of their lord and master. They were crossbowmen, a dozen strong, and they had, it appeared, been lounging far behind the rear of the column, bored and distracted by having had nothing to occupy them since the beginning of their sweep. They might have been effective when they finally arrived, Ewan said, had Redvers known how to deploy them, but they were at a disadvantage from the outset, with Ewan and three of Robertson's men armed with yew longbows harassing them with accurate, long-range fire before they could come close enough to organize themselves into any kind of useful formation. Four of the twelve went down in the opening exchange, and the remaining eight were sufficiently rattled by the unexpected accuracy of the Scots' shooting to start falling back immediately. None of them, clearly, had any wish to die beside their first four comrades. They withdrew behind the wagons Ewan and Andrew had abandoned. They then had the advantage over Ewan's group, who could not move forward without risk.

It was now a situation in which neither side could hope to make progress, and in a very short time, the English reorganized themselves, set up defensive formations, and made ready to leave, watched by the eight Scots archers who had bested them at odds of five to one.

Even in defeat, though, the English won, for Ewan saw two of them snatch Mirren up from where she lay beside me and throw her unceremoniously across the back of a horse belonging to one of Redvers's two dead companions. He could have shot them dead from where he stood, but they would simply have been replaced by others, and he was afraid of hitting Mirren, the boy, or me by mischance. Besides, as he told me later, he only had two arrows left in his quiver.

They loaded her and her son hurriedly into the larger of our two wagons, and then they led the wagon to the litter and quickly loaded

Mirren's mother onto it as well. Keeping an eye on the distant Scots, they smashed the smaller wagon's wheels and killed its team of horses. They then moved out and away, taking the road to Lanark and leaving their dead behind them, though no one had any doubt that they would return in strength within the hour to bury their own and hang any Scot foolish enough to be within reach.

Throughout it all, I lay unconscious in the junction of the cross-roads, bleeding from my ears.

CHAPTER NINETEEN

I

In the general discussion surrounding the disappearance of Hugh Braidfoot, we learned later, someone in Lanark had let slip that the missing man was the same Braidfoot whose daughter Mirren had married the outlaw William Wallace. That story had very soon reached the ears of the sheriff, William Hazelrig.

Hazelrig had been singularly unsuccessful in putting down any of the local Scots outlaws or even interfering with their illegal activities, which consisted mainly of poaching venison, and because he had been unable to stop them—they insisted upon some imagined right to refuse to die of starvation—he was afraid people were laughing at him, and so he pounced on this new information as a means of salvaging his name. He anticipated that the dutiful daughter might at this difficult time be tempted to return to visit her ailing mother, and it seemed likely to him that she might even be accompanied on such a visit by her outlawed husband. And so he had dispatched Sir Lionel Redvers to take the mother into custody.

What Hazelrig had hoped to achieve by doing that was unclear to me at the time, and even now, decades afterwards, it still makes me shake my head in disbelief. Had he chosen to keep a discreet watch on the Braidfoot household, he would easily have taken Mirren when she arrived, and even had Will not been with her, he might thus have been able to lure him out of the forest on a mission of rescue. But by instead arresting the blameless Miriam Braidfoot, the sheriff was giving clear warning to Will and his wife to stay well away from Lanark if they valued their freedom. Had Sir Lionel Redvers's little expedition passed by that crossroads even one-quarter of an hour earlier, we might never have encountered them, and much might have been different. We would have turned towards Lamington and discovered that the lady Miriam had been taken, and we would then have returned to Will in the forest, to initiate inquiries through Bishop Wishart. But Fate decided to abet Hazelrig's efforts.

As soon as the English left, Ewan ran over to where I lay, expecting to find me gravely wounded because of the blood he could see on the side of my head, but he found me to be merely unconscious, with a strong pulse and breathing easily. He made me as comfortable as could be and set Andrew and Father Jacobus to watch over me while he and the other six archers hurried after Redvers's departing force, to be within sight of them before the enemy had any chance to do anything further with Mirren and her mother. He had lost custody of Mirren, he would tell me long afterwards, but he was prepared to die before losing track of her altogether.

By the time Ewan arrived back, I had regained consciousness, though I could barely move against the pain of my broken ribs. It hurt even to breathe shallowly. Besides which the pain in my head was like a throbbing drum beat, and my vision had not yet returned to normal, so I still saw two of whatever I happened to be looking at. Despite all of that, though, I was fully *compos mentis* and I was pleased to see Ewan step into the light from our fire that night. It was to be the last pleasure I experienced for months, and it was snuffed the instant I saw the look on his face.

I was flat on my back, lying close to the fire, and for the first few moments he ignored me, speaking quietly to Andrew, and the tone of his voice told me he thought I was still unconscious. When he finally asked if my condition had improved at all, the little man nodded towards me. "See for yourself," he said. "He's been awake for more than an hour. But he can't talk and he can't move. His jaw's broken, along with several other things. Nothing too serious, but he's not going to be running around for a month or two."

A moment later, Ewan was kneeling above me.

"How are you? Can you get up?"

"No." I was as startled as he was to hear my voice emerge in a cracked, feathery whisper, but it was the first sound I had made since being injured and I could not believe how much pain and effort it had caused me to utter that single syllable. I tried to grit my teeth and regretted it immediately. Then, when my heartbeat had slowed down again and I thought I could control myself, I forced myself to speak gently, whispering, almost breathing the words as I asked, "What's wrong?" It emerged, almost inaudibly, as *Oss ong?*

He had been peering at me with concern, but now he scowled. "What's wrong with what? With your face? You've been worked over with heavy boots. I'm surprised you can even open your eyes, let alone whisper."

I closed my eyes and the pain started to dissipate immediately, but I forced myself to look at him again, seeing the agony in him, and mouthed, "Where's Mirren?"

I saw panic grow and blossom in his eyes as he struggled to put into words what should never have needed to be said. Finally, though, he found his voice, and for the next half-hour I lay and listened, appalled, to what he had to say.

"Everything's gone to Hell, Jamie," he began. "In the space o' an hour, it a' went bad … We went after the English, to keep an eye on whatever they might do wi' Mirren, but we hadna been going for a quarter of an hour before one o' Robertson's bowmen found the body of wee Willie lying at the side of the road. It was an accident that he found it—he had moved off the road into the underbrush wi' everybody else when word came back from the man in front that somebody was comin', and he almost knelt on the wee boy before he saw him. There were no wounds on the body. Nothin' to show what had killed him. He was just dead, and somebody had thrown him aside, into the bushes …"

I felt my heart threatening to burst, but I could neither move nor make a sound. But Ewan was far from finished.

"That was the start of it," Ewan continued. "But once it had started, there was no stoppin' it. I couldn't even take time to bury the poor child, for fear I'd lose track o' Mirren, so we set him aside and left him there until we could come back. When we reached Lanark, I left Robertson and his men to wait for me in the woods, and I went into the town to see what I could find out about the women. I went to the archers' company attached to the garrison and spoke to the man in charge there. It was safe enough. None o' the garrison archers would ha'e been out on the road that day.

"He was a Welshman, and I told him who I was, and that I'd served in Edward's campaigns in England and France in the days before Edward became the King. His name was Gareth Owens, and we got along, and I fed him drink in a tavern later that night, then picked his brains on the sheriff and that knight called Redvers. I asked him what had happened to the women prisoners brought in that morning ..."

There was roaring in my ears, and my head was still filled with images of the beautiful, laughing child who had been Will's first-born, but I could still hear Ewan talking, and later, when the pain and emptiness in my soul had receded for a while, I had no difficulty remembering what he had told me.

Owens had looked at him strangely when he asked about the women, and to disarm the fellow Ewan had chuckled lewdly and said he had seen them being brought in. Something in the look of the younger one, he told the man, had made him think she was a tooth-some piece, even heavily pregnant as she was. She had roused his curiosity as well as his lust, and now he wanted to know if she would be held for long, or if he would be wasting his time lingering in town in hopes of seeing her when she was freed.

Owens sat staring at Ewan for long moments, as though trying to decide whether or not to believe what he had said, but then he twisted right around in his seat and called to a man sitting a few tables behind him.

"Sit ye down," he said when the newcomer reached their table. "This man is Ewan Scrymgeour, one of us, though half Scotch, and an archer for years with Edward when he was still prince. Ewan, this is Dyllan. He is from south Wales and has never handled a bow in

his life, and thanks be to God for that. The only thing this one is fit
to handle is a ring of keys, but he handles those very well, don't you,
boyo? Dyllan is head jailer here, so he's the one you need to talk
with." Ewan nodded a greeting at Dyllan, who was tall and cadaver-
ously thin, with deep-set eyes over heavy, dark pouches. "Drink
some beer with us, Dyllan. Ewan has some questions for you and
talking is thirsty work."

He waved an arm to one of the tavern wenches, signalling her to
bring more beer, and when he turned back he found Dyllan staring
at Ewan's face.

"What happened to you?"

Ewan sniffed. "War club. A mace. At Lewes, against de Montfort
and the barons. I was a boy, my bones still soft. Lucky, I was told."

"Jesus," the jailer said in a hushed voice, but then he fell silent as
their fresh beer was brought to the table, and when the serving
woman left he raised his pot in a silent salute and drank deeply, then
belched appreciatively and sat back.

"What is it you want to know?" he asked. "Gareth's not a man to
waste another's time, and if he says you're good, then you're good
to me, so ask away."

Ewan hesitated, seeking the best way to frame his question, but
before he could speak at all, Gareth interjected. "There was two
women taken in today, into your place. One of them was young,
Ewan says, and comely. What can ye tell us about 'er?"

Dyllan was looking at Ewan strangely. "You find that attractive,
her being big and ready to whelp any minute?"

Ewan made himself grin. "No, but when she does whelp she'll be
over it soon and ready to go again. Who is she, d' you know?"

The jailer shook his head. "I don't know. I'm only the jailer. They
don't tell me things like that. My job's to keep 'em penned up. I
don't need to know who they are. But I know the one you're askin'
after's mad. She's crazed and out of 'er mind, she is. The other one
was 'er mother."

"Was?" Ewan told me afterwards how difficult it had been for
him to keep his face from betraying him. "Y' mean she's dead?"

"Aye. She were dead when they brung 'er in. Didn't find out, though, till we tried to lift 'er out o' the wagon she was in. She were gettin' cold by then."

"Then it's no wonder the daughter's mad with grief."

The jailer shrugged. "Aye, mayhap. But that aren't all. I tell you, I was glad to get out o' that place at the end o' my shift t'day. That's the wust day I c'n recall in there, and I've seen some bad uns."

"Ah," said Ewan. "Then let's not talk about it. All I really want to know is, when will she get out?"

"When will she *what*?"

Gareth spoke up again. "'E wants to know whether 'e should stay 'ere for a few days, looking to meet up with 'er when she gets out, or whether he'd best be on his way and forget it."

"Oh …" Dyllan's headshake was slow and ponderous. "No. Best move on, friend. She won't be coming out again, that one. And even if she did, she wouldn't be no use to you. She were screamin' about some snapper, some little 'un what 'ad got lost. I never saw no youngster there, but she was screamin' mad, cryin' is name and howlin', throwin' 'erself around. And then she found out the other woman was dead, and that made her worse. Went proper mad then, she did, and flew at big Simon, tryin' to scratch his eyes out. Wrong thing to do, that was. Big Simon's not too clever, and 'e's got a nasty temper. Smacked her in the head with his ring of keys, he did, and then kicked 'er in the belly when she went down. 'E only kicked her the once, but that was enough. It shut 'er up for a while, but then she started pukin' an' bleedin' all over the place."

Ewan grunted. He told me it took all of his strength not to reach out and choke the jailer, but he knew he had to remain calm. "What happened then?"

"Well, she was 'avin' 'er baby. All we could do was watch till it were done."

He made himself grimace. "She had her baby?"

"Aye, but it was dead when it come out." The jailer shook his head in what might have been regret, then picked up his beer and took another long drink. "Jesus," he said, "I've never seen so much blood."

Ewan ground his teeth together fiercely and asked quietly, "And what about the woman? Did she live?"

"Oh aye. At least, she was alive when I left. I threw 'er the blankets off the old woman's litter, but she wouldn't move off the floor, so I just covered 'er up and left 'er there."

"On the floor. You left her there ..."

"Aye."

"And what happened to the baby?"

"It were dead."

"I know it was dead, Dyllan. I asked what happened to it."

Dyllan looked down into his pot of ale, and then he said, in a very quiet voice, "Simon fed it to the pigs with the rest of the mess."

Ewan drew a great breath and stood up from the table, gripping his left thumb in his right fist to keep himself from lashing out. "Well, then," he said calmly, "no point in waiting around to see her. I doubt she'll look as good again as she did this day." He forced himself to nod to the jailer and then looked at Gareth Owens.

"I'll be on my way, then. Mayhap our paths will cross again someday." He reached into his scrip and laid a silver coin on the table. "The drinks are on me until this runs out. I thank you for your time and kindness."

Gareth stared down at the silver coin and then grinned widely. "We'll drink to your good health, Archer, and you're welcome back here any time."

2

By the time Ewan finished, his face was streaked with tracks where the tears had scoured runnels through the dirt and road dust caked on his sunken cheeks, and I was racked in agony from the sobs that wrenched me and which I was powerless to resist. I could not find a single word to say that would serve any purpose other than to break the silence between us. I have no memory of how long we remained there, immersed in our grief, but it seemed to me afterwards that it must have been a long time. Finally, though, Ewan raised his head and looked at me, scrubbing fiercely at his eyes with the sleeve of his rough tunic.

He bent over me then, bringing his ear close to my mouth and being extremely careful not to touch me in any way.

"Talk to me. Can you do that, if I stay like this?"

"I don't know," I wheezed, unable to move my jaw. "I'll try."

"What do we do now, Jamie?" I said nothing, and he added, "We have to do something. We can't do nothing. But what do we *do*? We have to tell Will, and how will we do that? This will kill him, *kill* him."

"No." I could barely get the small word out, and Ewan stooped quickly again to place his ear close to my lips. I breathed slowly, then tried again, hearing my own words mangled by my inability to move my broken jaw. "No. He won't die ..." That emerged as "Ee owned eye," but Ewan jerked away and looked at me and I knew he had understood. I took several steady breaths before I tried again, articulating each word as slowly and clearly as I could. "You'll have to tell him, Ewan. I can't. I can't talk."

He nodded, and then he asked, "What'll we do with you now? I can't take you back in that shape. You'd die on the road. You might die anyway, if you can't eat anything."

"Yakobus," I whispered. "There are monks in Lanark. Yakobus will ge' me there ... 'morrow ... An' they'll ge' me to G'asgow ..."

Ewan prepared to stand up, but I hissed at him. "No!"

"What?" He bent to my lips again.

"Can't go ... can't go back wi'out knowing ... Back to Lanark, about Mirren ... Can't tell Will he's lost his children and not know how his wife is. You have to go back and make sure she ... she's well."

"Jesus, Jamie, how can she be well? She's lost her bairns and her mother."

"Not her life, though ... Not her life, pray God. Find out, Ewan."

This time his headshake was decisive. "All right. We will. We'll make a bier for you tonight, from bits of the wagon, then we'll leave first thing in the morning and we'll take you with us. There's eight of us, not counting Jacobus, so we can take turns carrying you in teams of four. It's only three miles. We'll leave you with the monks and I'll go back into Lanark. When I know how Mirren is, I'll go and tell Will. You'll get to Glasgow in the meantime, as soon as you can travel, and get your friend Wishart started on setting Mirren free. There must be something he can do, otherwise what's the point of being a bishop?"

And so it was. Under Ewan's guidance, several of Robertson's bowmen spent time that evening making a carrying frame for me out of two floorboards from the wrecked wagon. With cross pieces made from wheel spokes and the whole thing tied together with pieces cut from the harness reins, it was ungainly but light and well suited to its purpose.

I barely slept at all that night, unable to find comfort or relief from the pain of my ribs and head, but the following morning, strapped tightly into immobility in my new bed, I fell asleep on the road before I had been carried for half a mile and slept like a dead man, undisturbed by stops or bearer changes, until they woke me up in the humble monastery outside the walls of Lanark. Ewan was bending over me, looking very serious and telling me something that appeared to be important, but my head was swimming and the pain was unbearable and I must have passed out again. I remember waking up again some time after that, to find an aged monk holding a cup to my lips and forcing me to drink some foul-smelling brew, and then I remember nothing for several days until I awoke to find Father Jacobus sitting close by my side, peering intently into my face.

Startled to see his face so near my own, I blinked myself awake and tried to sit up, but that was an unwise thing to do, since I had forgotten about my injured ribs and I almost passed out again from the pain of trying to move against my restraints.

When I recovered from my near swoon and was able to catch my breath again, I discovered, with a flaring surge of horror, that I was utterly mute, incapable of even opening my mouth.

Jacobus leaned towards me. "You can't speak," he said. "Your jaw is wired shut. I have never seen the like of it. Can you hear me? Blink if you can." I blinked eagerly and he held up a hand. "Are you really here this time?" He interpreted my confusion correctly, for he nodded quickly and held up his hand again.

"I thought you were here yesterday. And the day before, and the day before that. But you weren't, because you couldn't remember me having been here when I came back next time. Yesterday I would have sworn on oath that you were fully here. Do you remember me being here yesterday? If you do, blink once. If you do not, blink twice."

I blinked twice and he frowned, then reached into the depths beneath his scapular and pulled out a folded letter, holding it up so that I could see my own name written on the front of it.

"Do you recognize this?" he asked me.

I blinked twice, with exaggerated slowness, and he sighed and leaned in closer, speaking more to himself than to me. "Yet again then, I must try. You appear to be wide awake, alert and aware of me, but I thought the same thing before, and here you are, with no memory of any of it."

He sighed again. "Father James Wallace. Do you recognize that name?"

I blinked once.

"Is it your name?" *Blink*.

"Do you know where you are?" That stopped me, for I did not know how to respond. I *thought* I knew where I was, in a tiny monastery near Lanark, but suddenly I was unsure. Jacobus was watching me and must have divined what I was thinking, because he went on, "Do you remember speaking of the monks of Lanark?" I blinked, and he nodded. "Well, that is where you are. You have been here for five days, and have been in the care of Brother Dominic of Ormiston. Brother Dominic spent his life as a Knight Hospitaller. He was crippled early in the siege of Acre and is one of the few survivors of that catastrophe. He was shipped back to England, but his family is Scots, and so he came to Lanark and became hospitaller to the brethren here, using his medical and surgical skills for the good of the community. It was he who encased your body in restraints and wired your mouth shut to ensure that the break in your jawbone will heal cleanly, and he has been treating you with medicines from the Holy Land, medicines he calls opiates, to keep you free from pain. Sadly, those same medicines also cause you to forget everything that happens. Dominic believes, though, that it is better to have you slightly confused and free of pain than it would be to have you bright-minded and in constant agony. And so he feeds his opiates to you in the honeyed milk that is the only food you can consume. He says, in fact, that as long you are confined to bed and unable to move, honeyed milk is all the food your body needs. Thanks be to God that your ability to suck is unimpaired, for were it not, you would surely starve to death in the midst of plenty." He broke off, looking perplexed, then asked, "Does none of what I am saying sound familiar? I have told you all of this three times already."

I gazed straight at him and blinked twice. *No, none of this is familiar.* He shook his head in bemused disbelief, then looked away.

"Brother Dominic says it will take months for your injuries to heal, and weeks, at least, before you will be fit to travel to Glasgow. He told me that if all goes well, you should be able to sit up without restraints within the month, but you will be feeble and weak at first and will have to learn to walk again and to eat solid food again, as though you were an infant. And that reminds me of what else I must ask you. Remember, one blink for yes, two for no."

Blink.

"Do you know who I am?" *Blink.*

"Do you know a man called Ewan Scrymgeour?" *Blink.*

"Is he a friend of yours?" *Blink.*

"Do you remember sending Ewan Scrymgeour to gather information?" *Blink.*

"Can you remember where you sent him?" *Blink.*

"Was it Lanark?" *Blink.*

"Do you remember what it was that you instructed him to find out?" *Blink.*

"Aye … Well, that's good. Because Ewan's not here now. He came back, three days ago, but you were too sick to talk with him, drifting in and out of awareness, and he had no time to wait for you to wake up properly. It was more important, he said, for him to reach Will in the forest before anyone else could. And so he dictated a message to me, for you to read when you grew well enough, and left it in my care. Since you cannot move, would you like me to read the letter to you?"

Blink.

"Very well, then. I must tell you that the words are Ewan's own, exactly as he spoke them. He explained to me very clearly that he wanted me to transcribe his words verbatim. That was difficult, for he was speaking in the vulgate, and all my training has been in the formal Latin of the Church. Nevertheless, I have managed, I believe, to capture his words exactly." The elderly priest sat up straighter and carefully unfolded the single sheet of parchment he was holding. Then he moved away, holding it at arm's length and tilted towards the small window that was the room's sole source of light, and when he was satisfied that he could see sufficiently well he coughed to clear his throat. "Can you hear me clearly?"

He paused, as though waiting for an answer, and then he came quickly back to my bed and peered down at me with a contrite look that might have made me laugh under other circumstances. "Forgive me, Father James," he said. "I forgot you cannot speak. Could you hear me clearly?" I blinked once, and he moved away to the window again, clearing his throat nervously for a second time before he began to read.

"*Jamie,*" he began reading, his tone declamatory. "*They tell me you will live and probably come out of this with no permanent damage. I'm glad of that. I am sorry I can't stay here to wait for you, and I know you know that already. My place is in Selkirk, with Will, since you can't be there, and I am sick with the thought of what I have to tell him. I am sick of it all, Jamie; sick to my soul of the*

*pettiness and cruelty of men who should be better than they are; sick
of the greed and the ambition of men who are called noble but who
disgrace the very name of manhood.*

*"I went back to Lanark, as you bade me, knowing you were right
and that I needed to go back. Gareth Owens was not there when I
arrived, but some of his men recognized me from the previous night
and made me welcome enough. I asked them about Mirren, but no
one there could tell me anything. They were archers and none of
them had been there when we met Redvers, so most of them knew
nothing about what had happened. So then I went looking for the
jailer after that, the one called Dyllan, but he was off duty and had
gone into Lanark for the market day.*

*"Soon after that I found myself out by the swine sties, searching
the muck for any signs I could find of a dead baby, though I knew
myself mad for even looking. The pigs were snorting and wallowing
in their filth and I wanted to take my bow and kill every one of them.
But they were just being pigs, doing what God intended pigs to do.
It was the swine who fed such food to them who deserved to die for
what they had done.*

*"Gareth arrived back late in the afternoon, and he had been
drinking, so I plied him with more ale and followed up on the story
of Mirren, telling him I hadn't been able to stop thinking about her
losing the baby. I called it a brat. He was looking at me strangely, I
saw, but there was no anger in him. And then he poured me more ale,
and put an arm around my shoulder. He told me that hours later,
after I had left, he still remembered the way I looked when I asked
Dyllan about leaving her lying on the floor in all that blood, and he
had felt ashamed. He and Dyllan were both very drunk by then, he
said, having used up the entire shilling I had left them, but that only
added to the shame he felt, and so he had convinced Dyllan to go
back to the cell to look in on her, and they had found her dead in a
corner of the cell, in the middle of a big pool of blood.*

*"The animal called Simon, the jailer on duty who had knocked
her down and kicked her, grew angry when Dyllan challenged him
for an explanation. The bitch had gone mad, he said, screaming and*

howling for some brat she'd lost, crying out his name, Willie, and throwing herself at the cell door, trying to break it down. He had finally lost patience with her noise and gone back into the cell, where he had knocked her down again, after which she had obviously learned her lesson, since she hadn't made another sound.

"So there you have it, and that's the message I am going now to deliver to Will. His family is gone, wiped out at the whim of exactly the kind of man he refuses to follow or recognize. His son is dead, at less than a year and a half. His second child is dead, murdered and still-born, its sex unknown, its body fed to pigs. His wife's mother is dead, for the crime of having given her daughter to Will Wallace. And now his wife, too, is dead, murdered by a witless, shambling monster.

"That the monster is dead changes nothing and affords no satisfaction, but I cut off his head myself and fed it to the pigs that night, before I left Lanark castle.

"I have to say that Gareth Owens surprised me. I heard the following day that he took a report of what had happened to the sheriff, the next morning: two women arrested and then abused and murdered in the sheriff's cells with no official supervision between their being admitted and Gareth's own complaint. Redvers was arrested immediately, but nothing will come of it. English law decrees that no English knight may be accused of a crime by anyone of less than knightly blood. Hazelrig could charge him with dereliction and irresponsibility, but he would have nothing to gain by doing so, and the charges, if seen as frivolous, might return to haunt him someday.

"This is the kind of incident that Scotland's people are fighting against, this wanton disregard for the lives, freedom, and rights of anyone not of noble birth. This is the kind of excess that breeds revolt, and Will Wallace will have much to say about it, once his first grief has turned to the need for vengeance. And when that happens, I would not like to be in Hazelrig's shoes.

"I'll say adieu and hope we'll meet again someday, Jamie. Get better soon, and get yourself back to Glasgow and to Wishart,

though I fear the news of this will be familiar to the Bishop before you can reach him. Be well."

3

Iwas an invalid for more than a month and a half, although I was improving visibly after three weeks, despite a drastic loss of weight and muscle tone caused by a liquid diet and a complete lack of exercise. By the end of the fifth week, the bindings around my rib cage were less tight and I no longer had to be restrained while I slept, so I could breathe more deeply, though it still pained me to do so, and the thought of laughing or coughing chilled me. I was permitted to leave my bed in the seventh week, but it took me four full days to build up the strength to walk for fifty paces. After that, though, I grew stronger daily, and Brother Benedict soon removed the iron wiring from my jaw. Two days after that I could eat normally again.

A week later I was back in Glasgow, having made the journey by wagon and accompanied by Father Jacobus. Bishop Wishart made us both welcome and we found the entire cathedral community agog with the news of armed rebellion in the north and in the south.

Only then, after an interval of almost three full months, did I learn what had been taking place during my time recovering.

Wishart had heard the news of Miriam Braidfoot's arrest from her parish priest, who was outraged by the arrest and confinement of one of his most devout and influential parishioners. When he then heard of her subsequent death in custody, he launched an official diocesan inquiry, in the course of which the investigators learned that Mistress Braidfoot's daughter Mirren, or Marian, had somehow contrived to have herself killed by what was officially described as misadventure in precisely the same prison and on the same day as her mother. Sir Lionel Redvers, who had been responsible for the arrests of the women, was arraigned by the cathedral chapter, but he laughed at the summons and refused to attend the hearing. A week later he was ambushed and murdered one evening outside Lanark. He was accompanied by a round dozen mounted troopers, all of whom died with him, their weapons unbloodied and their bodies riddled with hard-shot arrows. Redvers himself had been dragged from his horse and decapitated. His body bore no other wounds. His head was never found.

The arrows, of course, indicated clearly that the outlaws of Selkirk Forest were responsible, and William Hazelrig assembled all his forces for a pre-emptive strike into the greenwood, calling for them to assemble on a given morning near the village of Lamington, and apparently seeing no irony in that choice of rallying points. Among the forces that assembled were a half-score of veteran archers whom none of the others knew. The newcomers were freshly arrived from Wales, they said, dispatched north as part of a new intake of Welsh bowmen recruited for the wars in Scotland.

The sheriff's expedition reached the forest outskirts and searched the woods diligently for three days, finding nothing and no one, but during that last night, in the middle watch, the darkest part of the night, the outlying sentries died in silence, while the newly arrived archers set aside their bows and used daggers and stealth to surprise and kill the guards on duty inside the camp. The man guarding the entrance to the sheriff's tent likely neither saw nor heard the arrow that killed him and threw him backward into the tent, and before Sheriff Hazelrig knew what was happening, he was clubbed sense-less and abducted. Once free of the sleeping encampment, the archers were joined by the others who had approached in the dark-ness and who had spent the previous hour disposing of the outlying guards and preparing pitch-dipped fire arrows. When the word was given, a hailstorm of flaming missiles swept the English camp, setting fire to tents and sleeping men, and the ensuing slaughter was merciless. Very few of the English sheriff's punitive expedition escaped alive.

William Hazelrig, King Edward's sheriff of Lanark, was found dead the following day. His hands had been severed and his throat cut, and a parchment scroll was fastened to his chest with a deep-driven dagger. The scroll said simply:

In Memoriam
Marian Wallace
Requiescat in pace

The news of Wallace's vengeance sent shock waves rippling across the whole south of Scotland, and for two weeks no English force of any description moved anywhere, least of all into Selkirk Forest.

By the end of that second week, Robert Wishart himself was in Selkirk Forest, haranguing Will. Andrew Murray had raised all of Scotland north of the Forth in rebellion, and the English up there were in total disarray. Wishart reminded Will, forcibly, that Murray, too, came of a knightly family but that his opinion of the magnates and their divided, self-centred, and ever-fluctuating loyalties was precisely the same as Will's. Murray's army was an army of the common folk, the Scots people who provided the solid backing underlying the community of the realm. Now was the time, Wishart said, for Will to join Murray, to throw in his lot with the northerner and march with his own people from the south to unite the whole of Scotland under their joint leadership. They knew each other. They admired and respected each other. And they were friends, sharing a detestation of all that kept Scotland from being what it should be, a strong, free land.

Wishart was an eloquent persuader, a fact that I knew well. He was also a bishop and a lord of the Church who ought not to have been fomenting rebellion. But above and beyond all else, Robert Wishart was a patriot who believed in his heart of hearts that Scotland had a destiny that could be fulfilled only if it rid itself of English occupation, certainly, but also of the English loyalties and English obligations evinced by its most powerful lords in their tenacious adherence to feudal allegiances that had lost all relevance. I now believe that Bishop Wishart was a man born before his time in that respect, a man of keen insight who foresaw the inevitable death of the feudal system that once governed all of Christendom but has fallen into ruin these past two hundred years.

My main belief about Robert Wishart, though, is that through his patriotism and his enthusiasm, his manipulative ways and his iron, stubborn, single-minded wilfulness, he brought about the end of the cousin I had known and loved. Perhaps I am being too harsh, too judgmental, but that is what I now believe. When Robert Wishart left to return to Glasgow on that occasion, he left a different man behind him than the William Wallace I had known.

The man who followed him out from the greenwood shortly afterwards, emerging, as some Englishman has written, like a bear from his forest den, was the William Wallace all men know today, Edward Plantagenet's scowling, giant, merciless nemesis, and all England, along with much of Scotland, would regret his awakening. The laughing archer I had known was gone forever, obliterated in the destruction of his beloved Mirren and their children. The implacable avenger who came out of Selkirk Forest finally had set aside his long yew bow forever and taken up the massive sword his friend Shoomy had brought him in earlier, better days. I found it strange, thereafter, that the enormous sword, elaborately beautiful and lethal and taller than an ordinary man, should so completely usurp the place held for so long in Will's life by his great yew bow, but as he himself pointed out afterwards, the bow lacked the close immediacy of a hand-held blade, and the sword he swung with his enormous archer's muscles enabled him to smile more closely, face to face with every enemy he met.

As Will Wallace, he had promised his wife he would not fight against England and would look to his family's safety first and above all. But he had failed her, he believed, losing her through his own carelessness and despite his knowledge of the dangers of being anywhere near the English. Now, he swore, he would not fail her memory, and his revenge would be without precedent and without equal; nor would he rest until all Scotland was scoured clean of the reek of English occupation. And so he marched to meet his destiny, and all the folk of Scotland flocked to follow him, to Stirling Bridge.

He never spoke Mirren's name again.

GLOSSARY

aboon	above; over
aey	always; invariably
bairns	children
braw	fine, pretty, admirable
chiel	child, fellow
cowpin'	falling, tumbling
dae	do
'gin	if
girnin'	grimacing, weeping
jaloused	guessed, deduced
lintie	a linnet (songbird)
skelped	slapped
stirk	bullock, steer
Tearlaigh	Gaelic for Charles; pronounced "Chairly"
tha'e	those
tulzie	scrap, tussle, skirmish
wha	who
wheen	number; a few

ACKNOWLEDGMENTS

There is an astoundingly wonderful seafood restaurant called Keracher's in Perth, Scotland, and whenever I think of my most recent trip there, in September 2008, I do so with reverential awe of the excellent cuisine—there is nothing better than Scottish cooking at its finest—and with gratitude for the hospitality tendered to me by the owners, Peter and Pam Keracher and their family. I spent a number of delightful evenings there in well-fed contentment during the latter weeks of my stay in Perth, just down the road from the Palace of Scone, contemplating the life of Sir William Wallace and the yet-unformed book I was to write, and wondering what I could ever find to say about him that would be as fresh and different as the extraordinary food I was enjoying.

By the time the *Braveheart* epic was released in 1995, serious Scottish historians and academics had been assiduously ignoring William Wallace for almost a hundred years, because, understandably enough, they had come to believe that it was impossible to differentiate between the man and the myth that had grown up around him in almost seven centuries. Emerging nationalism and romantic, wishful thinking had combined, over that time, to turn him into a chimera, an entity that has an existence of its own but was neither human nor supernatural. But with *Braveheart* came a renaissance of scholarly scrutiny of Sir William Wallace.

Professor Edward J. (Ted) Cowan is professor emeritus, formerly professor of Scottish history, at Glasgow University, and a couple of decades ago I had the pleasure of working with him a few times when he was professor of history and chair of Scottish studies at the University of Guelph, Ontario. In those days, we delivered a number of joint presentations (I believe the most accurate description would be *entertainments*) on the history of the Scots influence in Canada—Ted supplied the academic, historical realities, sweeping the gaping crowds up into his grasp in a way I have seldom seen equalled, and I illustrated his invocations with appropriate songs and poems to hammer home his various points. It was great fun and worked remarkably well, so Ted's name was the first that sprang to mind when I began contemplating a research trip to Scotland in the autumn of 2008.

During one short visit that year, when I found him at Glasgow University's Crichton Campus in Dumfries, Ted presented me with a treasure trove of stimuli in the form of an anthology called *The Wallace Book*, edited by him and published in 2007 by John Donald, an imprint of Birlinn Ltd. of Edinburgh. It's a collection of twelve essays by leading historians and critics from Scotland and England, and the work is described on the cover as examining "what is known of [Wallace's] career from contemporary sources, most of which, unusually for a national hero, were created by his enemies."

I got lost in those essays, pragmatic and clinical as they are, because as I read them I found myself swimming in a flood of strik-ingly fresh ideas that swept me away into new realms of speculation and conjecture, which is food and drink to any historical novelist. And so I am greatly indebted to a number of very brilliant people, all of whom had me salivating for months over new possibilities, but none of whom should be held accountable for my perhaps egregious misinterpretation of what they wrote. For all those nudges towards novel interpretations, I am beholden to Fiona Watson, research fellow in history at the University of Dundee, for her incisive piece "Sir William Wallace: What We Do—And Don't—Know"; Michael Prestwich, professor of medieval history at the University of Durham, for his English perspective on the Battle of Stirling Bridge; A.A.M. Duncan, emeritus professor of Scottish history, University of Glasgow, for his biographical insights in "William, Son of Alan Wallace"; Elspeth King, director of the Smith Art Gallery and Museum, Stirling, for her observations on the material culture of William Wallace; Alexander Broadie, professor of logic and rhetoric at the University of Glasgow, for his fascinating thoughts on John Duns Scotus and the idea of independence; Alexander Grant, reader in medieval history at the University of Lancaster, for his essay "Bravehearts and Coronets: Images of William Wallace and the Scottish Nobility"; and, of course, to Professor Cowan himself, for his perspective on Wallace in "The Choice of the Estates."

Those essays, and the imaginative flights they gave rise to, were delightful episodes in preparing the new book, but I should also pay tribute and offer thanks to several other sources of fundamental understanding and general appreciation of the history and the complexities of Scotland at the time I was writing about. Ted Cowan figures there again, with a book called *For Freedom Alone*, which examines the origins of the astonishing 1320 Declaration of Arbroath and the ideas from which it grew. G.W.S. Barrow's book *Robert Bruce and the Community of the Realm of Scotland* has been invaluable to me, too, as has Peter Traquair's panoramic study of the Scottish Wars of Independence, *Freedom's Sword*. As the man said in *1066 and All That*, "History is what you can remember." Tongue in cheek as that is, it is nonetheless true, and I found all of the sources named above to have been both memorable and enjoyable.

There is, however, one more source of a lifetime of enjoyment and inspiration that I must acknowledge. Is there a literate Scot anywhere who has not been touched and influenced at one time or another by the writings of Nigel Tranter? It is one of the great regrets of my life that I never had the chance to meet the man and thank him for the uncountable hours of pleasure I have derived from his writings. I remember that when I first read his novel *The Wallace* many years ago, I was awestruck by the potency of his voice, and I truly think that has been a contributory factor in my decision to call this book *A Tale of William Wallace.*